the
opposite of
hallelujah

ALSO BY ANNA JARZAB

All Unquiet Things

the
opposite of
hallelujah

ANNA JARZAB

DELACORTE PRESS

BJT 10-10-12 16.99

Text copyright © 2012 by Anna Jarzab
Jacket photograph copyright © 2012 by Kelly Miller

Grateful acknowledgment is made to Service Publishing for permission to reprint lyrics from "The Opposite of Hallelujah" by Jens Lekman, copyright © 2005 by Jens Lekman. All rights reserved. Reprinted by permission of Service Publishing.

All rights reserved. Published in the United States by Delacorte Press, an imprint of Random House Children's Books, a division of Random House, Inc., New York.

Delacorte Press is a registered trademark and the colophon is a trademark of Random House, Inc.

Visit us on the Web! randomhouse.com/teens

Educators and librarians, for a variety of teaching tools, visit us at RHTeachersLibrarians.com

Library of Congress Cataloging-in-Publication Data
Jarzab, Anna.
The opposite of hallelujah / Anna Jarzab. — 1st ed.
p. cm.
Summary: For eight of her sixteen years Carolina Mitchell's older sister Hannah has been a nun in a convent, almost completely out of touch with her family—so when she suddenly abandons her vocation and comes home, nobody knows quite how to handle the situation, or guesses what explosive secrets she is hiding.
ISBN 978-0-385-73836-1 (hc) — ISBN 978-0-375-89408-4 (ebook) — ISBN 978-0-385-90724-8 (glb)
1. Sisters—Juvenile fiction. 2. Ex-nuns—Juvenile fiction. 3. Guilt—Juvenile fiction.
4. Children's secrets—Juvenile fiction. [1. Sisters—Fiction. 2. Nuns—Fiction. 3. Guilt—Fiction. 4. Secrets—Fiction.] I. Title.
PZ7.J2968Opp 2012
813.6—dc23
2012010882

The text of this book is set in 13-point Bembo.
Book design by Angela Carlino

Printed in the United States of America
10 9 8 7 6 5 4 3 2 1
First Edition

This one's for Alicia, of course, with love;
and in memory of Helena Bieniewski.

But sister, it's the opposite of Hallelujah.

It's the opposite of being you.

You don't know 'cause it just passes right through you.

You don't know what I'm going through.

—JENS LEKMAN

Provability is a weaker notion than truth.

—DOUGLAS R. HOFSTADTER, *Gödel, Escher, Bach: An Eternal Golden Braid*

1

When I was twelve, I started telling people at school that my older sister, Hannah, was dead. I didn't put a lot of thought into it. I just figured it would be easier than explaining what had actually happened to her. You'd think the phrase "contemplative nun" would mean something to kids who'd been attending Catholic school their entire lives, but it really didn't. To them, nuns were old women who wore nude panty hose to hide the varicose veins in their legs and seemed like they'd slap you with a ruler as soon as look at you. Nuns were practically pre-historic, and it didn't make any sense for my then twenty-three-year-old sister—tall, thin, blond as Barbie—to be working on her fourth year at the Sisters of Grace convent in Middleton, Indiana. But she was.

So I lied. I didn't get what the big deal was. I hadn't seen Hannah for longer than half an hour a year through an iron grille since I was eight, and those visits consisted mostly of my parents nervously babbling about work and how I was doing in school while Hannah sat with her hands folded in her lap, serene, listening but saying virtually nothing. She wasn't dead, but she wasn't part of my life anymore, so I simplified the story.

It wasn't long before my teachers caught wind of the rumor. When Ms. Hopeshed, my music teacher, who was very sensitive, heard, she called our house to express her sincerest condolences over the loss of my sister. Mom and Dad were furious with me.

"How dare you tell people that Hannah is dead!" Mom screamed. I'd never seen her so angry, and she very rarely yelled at me. I was practically an only child, and my parents and I were close, or I thought we were. It didn't occur to me that they might have other loyalties.

Stubborn and defiant as always, I refused to deny the pragmatism of my plan. "Well, it's sort of *like* she's dead," I pointed out. It was, I thought, an unassailable argument. "We never see her. She never calls or comes home. What am I *supposed* to say?"

Mom took a deep breath and steadied herself before answering.

"If you talk like that in school, people are going to think you wish Hannah was dead," she told me. "They'll think you're a liar who hates her sister. Is that what you want? Is that who you are?"

I stared at my shoes. "No, I guess not." I knew a losing fight when I saw one, but I didn't quite see where all this was coming from. It was a lie, yes, and lying was wrong; I'd been told that a million times over the course of my life. I knew it was possible I hadn't done the *right* thing, or the *best* thing. But how was I supposed to explain my sister's absence when nobody had ever given me the words? So I'd improvised. One look at my mother's face and I knew I'd be better off keeping that justification to myself.

"Good." She didn't sound convinced, but I think she knew that was as much as she was going to get out of me. To my mom, this was a problem that couldn't be solved with an apology, and even as we stood there not looking at each other, she was formulating a game plan. "I told Ms. Hopeshed the truth, and I expect you to do the same with everybody you told that horrible lie to. Do you understand me?"

"Yes," I said.

She paused at the door and pointed at me. "You'd better fix this, Caro."

"I will," I promised.

I'd severely underestimated what this would mean for me at school. The next day, deathly afraid my mother would have them make an announcement over the PA system if I disobeyed, I took back my lie and started telling people it *felt* like Hannah was dead, but that she was alive and (presumably) well at the Sisters of Grace convent in Middleton, Indiana. The kids in my class labeled me "Caroliar," which became a popular playground taunt, and the reputation stuck with me until I went to high school and made new friends and everyone except them basically forgot I existed.

Hannah was a touchy subject in our house for years. We almost never talked about her, and after she'd been at the convent for two years, Mom packed up all her things, hid them in the garage, and let me move downstairs into her old room. There were only a few photos of her in the house, none of them taken when she was older than eighteen. "We're going to Indiana" was the euphemism my parents used when we'd been scheduled for one of our annual visits to the convent, and apart from the traditional "she seems happy," nobody ever said anything on the topic on the way there or the way back.

So it wasn't like I was the only liar in the house. We all acted like Hannah was dead; all I did was take it one step further and bury her.

Telling the truth wasn't my only punishment. My parents arranged for me to have three one-hour counseling sessions with Father Bob, the pastor of our church. We weren't what you would call devout Catholics, but we went to Sunday Mass every once in a while and never missed on holidays. I'd had all the appropriate sacraments and so had Hannah, even before she decided to marry Jesus.

Father Bob was very concerned about me, or so he said. My parents had asked him to explain the ins and outs of religious vocation to me, so that I might be a little more prepared the next time someone asked me what had happened to Hannah: why she had gone away, why she was never coming back. Father Bob was nice and patient, but I didn't care to hear anything about Hannah's chosen life.

"Carolina," Father Bob said. "It was God's will that Hannah go to the Sisters of Grace. It was God's will that I become a priest. That's how vocation works."

The word "vocation" made me want to barf. To me it was a synonym for "prison," for a particular kind of abandonment. I hadn't seen much of the world at that point, but I knew it was full of things I wanted. I knew I would want a boyfriend, and eventually a husband, maybe a couple of kids. I knew I would want a house and a yard and a dog—I wanted the dog most of all at that age. I knew Hannah couldn't have those things, and it was bizarre to me that she would give it all up. At one time, I believed that Hannah hadn't chosen to leave, that she'd been taken, but that was only when I was very young.

"Do you mean she *had* to be a nun? That she didn't have the option not to be?" I asked. I knew what it was like to be told where to be, what to do, how to act, and what to say every moment of your life, but I'd always believed that once you were grown up you got away from all that—you got to be your own person. I didn't know what to think about Hannah's "vocation." Did she have the choice to go away, or didn't she?

"No, not exactly. God doesn't force us to do anything, even his will. He only calls us to be our best selves, to serve our natural purpose as his creation. For Hannah, that purpose is sisterhood. For me, it's priesthood. For you, who knows? You're still young. Maybe God will give you a vocation, too."

"No way!" I cried out. "I'm *never* going to be a nun. I don't even like church."

"Okay then," Father Bob agreed. "Maybe not."

In the last week of August before my junior year of high school, something unexpected happened. I was still on summer vacation, slowly finishing up the summer assignments I'd been carefully avoiding since June. I talked to my best friend Erin on the phone for a couple of hours (she was at her grandmother's house outside Minneapolis, dying of boredom), swam in the pool in the backyard of my other best friend, Reb, and put in some quality time in front of the TV. Mom called me in to dinner at seven; when we were all seated, I noticed that they weren't eating, and I asked what was wrong.

Dad explained; Mom didn't seem to have the words. They had gotten a phone call earlier that afternoon from Mother Regina, the superior at Hannah's convent, saying that Hannah had decided to renounce her vows and leave the Sisters of Grace permanently. They were taking the news exactly as I would've expected them to—with shock and disbelief. I asked if they'd spoken to Hannah, but evidently she was too upset to talk to anyone just yet. I wondered whose choice it was for her to leave—hers, or Mother Regina's.

"And she's going to come and live here?" It was a stupid question, really. Where else would she go? She'd entered the convent when she was nineteen and she'd been gone eight years. There was no way she had any friends left after such a long absence; I didn't get the impression that she'd ever had friends to begin with. Hannah had never been on her own before. It seemed impossible that she could make it alone.

"Of course!" Mom snapped. Whenever Hannah came up in conversation, Mom got sharp with me.

Then it occurred to me to ask the question that probably should've been my first. "Why?"

"Why what?" Dad poked at the chicken on his plate. There wasn't an appetite left at the table.

"Why is she leaving the convent? I thought she loved it there." My parents had stopped dragging me to their yearly visitation with Hannah when I was thirteen. I'd never hated anything more in my life than going to that convent; it was too unnervingly quiet, too sterile, too cold, not to mention totally boring. Not long after the whole "my sister's dead" fiasco, I wasn't having any of it. The fit I threw when they tried to cart me down to Indiana to talk to a virtual stranger through iron bars was epic. I screamed and pouted and threw things and made myself sick rather than go.

Mom and Dad made a valiant effort at forcing me; they shouted back, threatening me with unprecedented restriction and even, in a moment of desperation, resorting to bribery. Eventually they gave up.

They always came back from Indiana saying that Hannah looked happy, in a way. Always "in a way," later clarified by the word "serene." She was calm and quiet, neither excited to see them nor bothered by their presence. She never fully engaged, just listened patiently to their stories (mostly about me, Mom admitted) and responded carefully and clearly to their questions. She never revealed too much, she never gossiped or chatted, and she never seemed happier to see them than she did to see anyone else. I once overheard Mom crying to Dad that Hannah didn't care about them or seem to recognize them as her parents. Mom almost never cried, and the sound of it broke my heart. Vocation or no vocation, retreating like that was Hannah's choice alone.

"Apparently she's not happy there anymore," Mom said. She was tense and upset, I could tell, but I didn't understand why. Wasn't this what she had wanted since Hannah went away? They'd desperately wanted her to fail as a nun; maybe they'd even prayed for it, although everybody's faith in God had taken a hit when he stole my sister away. They'd wanted her vocation to be false, for her to despise the convent and come back home, even if it meant she had to be kicked out. I think they'd wanted it so much because they were afraid it wouldn't happen. From the moment she hit puberty, Hannah and the habit seemed destined to collide.

I didn't remember much about Hannah, and I wasn't even sure if the memories I did have were true or just cobbled together from photographs and other people's stories. One of the things I did recall was that Hannah always wore her school uniform, even when she was at home or in public. She wore pajamas to bed, but that was it. Mom bought her tons of clothes that ended up stacked neatly on her shelves and in her drawers with the tags still on; she wouldn't back down, despite Mom's begging.

"She could be just as stubborn as you when she wanted to be," Mom said after I found a photograph of Hannah wearing her uniform at the Saint Louis arch, a vacation I didn't even remember, although I was definitely there for it, age two, sitting atop Dad's shoulders, wearing a pair of plastic yellow sunglasses with lenses shaped like stars. My poor mother. She wanted Hannah to be happy, but she would've settled for normal. Hannah didn't stop wearing that uniform until she graduated from high school, when she started attending Loyola University, but even then she was nothing but the picture of modesty.

"When?" I asked.

"Next week," Mom said, searching my face for something, though I wasn't sure what. "Saturday."

"Fine," I said, shoveling a spoonful of peas, now cold, into my mouth to keep from having to say anything else.

"Fine? That's it?" Dad asked, a little anger creeping into his voice now, too. They were both furious, my parents, but they didn't appear to know why or at whom. They had never understood Hannah's decision to go into the convent, which I guess was why they were never able to explain it to me, and also why I never really tried to talk to them about it. Now that she was coming back, we were all more confused than ever.

"What do you want me to say?"

"Aren't you happy your sister's coming home?" Mom was practically pleading with me to say, yes, I was totally stoked about Hannah's leaving the convent.

I couldn't say it, though. I couldn't think of anything *to* say, which was unusual for me. I just shrugged.

"How can you *not care*?" They stared at me, like I was some kind of unfeeling monster, which was unfair. I didn't care because there was nothing to care *about*. Who was Hannah to me? A few albums full of pictures tucked away in a drawer and a handful of letters and Christmas cards full of distant religious platitudes. There had been a point in my life when I wished there had been more, but that was over now.

"I barely know her!" I reminded them. "She left when I was eight and I haven't seen her in four years—"

"By choice," Mom said.

"Yeah, I remember. But you can't expect me to jump for joy about this—she's practically a stranger to me."

"She's not a stranger, she's your sister," Mom said. Dad shook his head in disappointment.

"May I be excused?" I requested, not waiting for an answer before pushing my chair out and gathering my plate. "I've totally lost my appetite."

☆ ☆ ☆

Back in my room, I wanted to call someone, but every time I reached for the phone I thought about what I would say, and put it back down. "My sister, who ran away to become a nun, is coming home"? My friends would think that sounded like a good thing, and to the untrained ear I guessed it did. I wanted to call Derek, my . . . boyfriend was probably the proper term, although we'd never called each other by those words: "boyfriend," "girlfriend." We'd been going out for close to four months, but two of those had been over summer break and he'd been away at camp in northern Wisconsin for six weeks. He wasn't due back for another week, the same day we were supposed to pick up Hannah from the train station, and he was unreachable by cell phone. No reception. A letter wouldn't get to him in time, either. And anyway, I wondered if maybe Derek wasn't really the sort of guy you told things like that to. I supposed I would find out soon enough, but in the meantime it looked like I was on my own.

I was lying on my bed, staring miserably at the ceiling, when Mom knocked on the door.

"Come in," I said, not getting up or tearing my eyes away from a crack in my ceiling, which, if you squinted, looked vaguely like the coast of California. It had been there for as long as I could remember, probably since Hannah was a kid, which was a strange thought: Hannah as a kid, long before I was even born.

Mom took a seat on the foot of my bed. "I understand why you're feeling unsettled. I wish I could fix it, but I can't."

She put a hand on my shin and sighed. I sat up on my elbows. "She's your sister. She loves you. And I know you don't remember very well, but you love her, too."

"Okay," I said, unconvinced.

"When you were born, Hannah was eleven," Mom

said, the words barreling out in a gush of nostalgia. "She wanted to hold you always, and she'd get angry if anyone else besides Dad or I tried to. You used to stare into each other's eyes and smile. Every day, right before she got home from school, you would cry, and then she would come through the door and you would light up and reach out your arms for her to take you. You adored her, and that's what *she'll* remember. So don't act like a brat when she moves back in. It'll upset her."

"Wouldn't want that," I said under my breath.

"Don't you *miss* her?" Mom asked. I knew my mother well enough to understand what she was really saying: *I miss her.* And it was crazy, but I could feel the jealousy creeping up my throat, putting me in a choke hold. If they missed her so much, did that mean I wasn't enough?

"No!" I cried. "She could be anyone moving into the house. If you told me you were going to take in some distant cousin, I wouldn't be happy about that, either."

"How is that even remotely the same thing?"

"I don't want her here." I kept saying it, but they weren't listening. They didn't want to hear. It was like we were speaking different languages; theirs was the language of the past, mine the language of the present. Why couldn't they just understand?

"For God's sake, why?"

"Because I like our family the way it is! I don't want things to change." I couldn't even bring myself to imagine what having Hannah in the house might be like. What it might be like to have her sitting across from me at the dinner table in what for years had been just an empty chair. What it might be like to shop with her, watch TV with her, argue with her, laugh with her. How bizarre to have a sister and still be an only child. How was I supposed to know how to live with someone with whom the only thing I shared was DNA?

"Don't think of it as change," Mom advised. "Think of it as everything going back to the way it was."

I let out a laugh, harder and harsher than I had intended. "Do you really think that's what's going to happen?"

"I don't know," she admitted. "But I really hope so."

2

It probably would've been simpler for the Sisters of Grace to put Hannah on a plane to Chicago, but they were nothing if not old-fashioned. Hannah was coming home by train.

Technically, Hannah could've switched lines in the city and taken another train straight into town, but Mom was adamant that we meet her.

"She's been in that convent for years, and we hardly ever went into the city back then," she fretted, when I brought it up. It was a week later, Friday, and Hannah was scheduled to arrive the next day. My parents were noticeably on edge, especially Mom. She'd scrubbed every surface in the house until it gleamed, gone on a grocery-shopping tear, and even weeded in between the bricks in the front walkway, her most despised chore. I helped her, but she was still running around like a maniac, finding every random thing that *had* to get done before the weekend, trying to make everything perfect. "What if she gets lost, or hit by a car or something?"

"Mom, she's twenty-seven," I pointed out. "She knows how to cross a street."

"She's not used to all the people! And the noise and the confusion—it'll be hard for her. Can't you sympathize with that at all?"

I couldn't, really, but I let it go. "Okay, fine, chill out."

"You're coming with us," Dad said without bothering to look at me.

"No way. Absolutely not. I won't."

"You will," he said calmly—too calmly, like he was forcing it. Like he wanted to reach across the table and smack me, and he probably did. For a second I wondered why I was doing this, torturing my parents with stubbornness, insisting on being mean about Hannah just to be mean. But then he said, "It's no use arguing," and I did what I always did in that situation—I argued.

"I have homework to do," I said.

"It's summer," Mom said.

"Yeah, but I have to prepare for the first week," I reminded her. "That's what happens when you're forced to enroll in four AP classes—they give you tons of crap to do over the summer. I need to finish."

"We're not picking Hannah up until tomorrow afternoon," Dad said. "Finish tonight."

"I can't tonight! It's Erin's first day back from her grandmother's. We're going to hang out." I didn't tell them that Erin's parents weren't home and she was inviting more than just me over, of course.

"Yeah right," Dad said. "You're not going anywhere. You're going to stay home and finish your summer work so that you'll be free as a bird to pick Hannah up with us tomorrow. And that's *final*."

I glanced at my mother, but all she did was nod to emphasize Dad's decree.

I wasn't going to stay in all night doing homework. I was much further along than I'd told my parents, and anyway, I had plenty of time. I couldn't admit that to them and ask permission to go to Erin's, but luckily for me I had a lot of experience sneaking out of the house undetected. I said good night to my parents, who were already in bed, propped up on pillows watching television, then went downstairs, closed the door to my room, and shut off the light. Ten minutes later I left the room silently, pulling the door closed with the handle still turned, so there was nothing but the slightest click when I let go. I left through the garage, exiting the side door and unlatching the gate. Then I walked quickly to the corner and flagged down Reb, who'd come to drive me to Erin's.

The party was already in full swing by the time we got there. Reb dragged me into the kitchen and poured me a very strong vodka and Red Bull, which I chugged to catch up to the others. Erin walked into the kitchen draped all over Peter Armand, who played baseball for our high school. She looked drunk and happy; his cheeks were lightly smeared with pale pink lip gloss. She threw her arms around me and squeezed tight.

"I missed you!" she cried. "I'm so glad to be out of my grandmother's house, I can't even tell you. There's only so much *Wheel of Fortune* a girl can watch, y'know?" She grinned, but at Peter, not at me. He smiled back.

"Isn't he cute?" she whispered. "I didn't think he'd come, but I texted him anyway and he *showed up*! Can you believe it?"

"Sure," I said, glad for her. She'd been goofy over Peter for months, since midway through the past semester, but Erin was goofy over a lot of guys; her affections ebbed and flowed like the tides, so you never knew who she liked at the moment until she told you.

"Yes, we're all *thrilled*," Reb said, rolling her eyes. "Lucky you, Erin. He's a real hunk of meat."

"Oh shut up," Erin said, swatting at her with a dish towel. "Just because you haven't gotten any since—"

"Conversation over!" Reb cried, grabbing my hand and dragging me out of the kitchen. "Have fun with your boy toy!" she called back to Erin.

"Ugh," Reb said, tossing herself onto a vacant sofa. "I love her, but seriously, Peter Armand? Just the thought of him bores the crap out of me—boys should be wild and mysterious, not dumb and beefy. Erin has some taste issues."

"More for us," I said, finishing off my drink and trying not to grimace as the vodka stung my throat. I had a chronic beer-face condition; no matter what I was drinking, I ended up looking like I'd just eaten a live tarantula. It was very sophisticated.

"Seriously," Reb said. "So what's up, buttercup? You've been pretty quiet since we got here."

"Nothing," I said. "Just drinking it all in."

She smiled and shook her head at me. "It is pretty exciting. I mean, *a house party*? In the *suburbs*? Who would've thought such a magical thing could exist?"

I laughed.

Reb folded her legs underneath her and tipped her cup at me. "So you excited for school to start, brainiac? I hear some of the whiteboards got replaced over the summer," she said in a singsong.

"Is anyone ever excited for school to start?" I asked. "Are *you*?"

"Oh, God, no." She scoffed. "But that's because

they're making me retake geometry—did you know that a D-minus isn't a passing grade?"

"Really? I thought Ds got degrees," I said, acting puzzled. Reb wasn't a great student, which wasn't to say she wasn't smart; she just hated doing what she was told, which included completing homework and studying for tests. Her parents were always on her case about it, but when I asked her why she didn't just put a little more effort into getting her grades up so that they would back off, she narrowed her eyes at me and said, "And give them the satisfaction?" There was no convincing her. Reb was who she was, and she knew what she knew, and she wasn't apologizing for it to anyone.

"Urban legend." She yawned. "School sucks, but what can you do? It's been a pretty good summer."

"Sure," I said. Actually, it'd been a nerve-wracking summer—for me, at least. I'd spent way more time than I would've liked to admit worrying about what Derek was doing at camp hundreds of miles away, anxious about every missed phone date or unanswered email, even at times doubting that we had ever been together in the first place. I hadn't expected Derek to like me, or to want to date me, and when it happened, I had been so taken by surprise that when he left for camp soon after, I started to wonder if I'd imagined the whole thing.

"When does Derek get back?" Reb asked, sensing, as was her gift, what I was thinking about.

"Tomorrow. I was going to go over to his house after he got home but—" I stopped midsentence, wondering if I should tell anyone about Hannah. Reb and I met in high school, and by that time Hannah was long gone. It was possible Reb didn't even remember that I had a sister. It felt like a lot of explaining to do.

"I have this family thing," I finished lamely. "Can't get out of it."

"That sucks," Reb said. "When's it over?"

"Never," I sighed. She cocked her head and looked at me questioningly. "I don't know. It could be a long day."

"Bums," she said. I didn't know if she was shortening "bummer" or talking about my parents. Either way, it was a little incongruous and funny. Reb was funny-*looking*, too. She had this weird hair that was straight in some parts and curly in others, mixed up all over her head. She didn't own a brush, so it always looked wild and ridiculous, but in a cool way. She had long thin legs and long thin arms, freckles, and a little bit of a belly, and guys were always telling her how sexy and gorgeous she was. Not that Reb needed their approval. She said and did whatever she wanted and didn't care what anybody thought, or never let on if she did.

Erin was different. Girls like her were the reason the word "cute" was invented. She personified it, with her big blue eyes, pert nose, and diminutive height. She was the only girl I knew who owned real pearls and actually wore them, regularly and unironically. And contrary to Reb, Erin was as boy-crazy as they came, to the point of casually dating several boys at once.

I was . . . well, it was hard to say. If I had to make a judgment about my looks, I would say I was inconspicuously nice-looking. I was tall, with blue eyes and thick, wavy blond hair that I wore down and long. I could've stood to lose a few pounds, but I was too lazy and not vain enough to do anything about it. I wasn't as confident as Reb, or decent at faking confidence, like Erin, so I sort of faded into the background of most social situations, including school.

During my awkward phase I spent more than a little time staring at Hannah's graduation picture over the fireplace and wondering if someday I might look like her. Hannah was gorgeous, at least before she entered the convent, because that's how unfair the world is. What a waste. If she was going to be a nun, couldn't she at least have been ugly? Who knew what she was going to come back looking like, but in her graduation photo, which still had its prized place on our mantel, she was radiant. Long blond hair and blue eyes—like mine, but way prettier—great skin, tall and effortlessly thin. She got all the good genes and at the first possible second covered everything up with a habit.

"Did Derek like camp?" Reb asked, clearly trying to draw me out. "Have you heard from him?"

"Got a letter a couple of days ago," I told her. "He's

having a lot of fun up there. Ever since we got together he's been talking about that camp and finally going back as a counselor—or junior counselor, I guess. You don't get to be a full counselor until you're eighteen. He's sad to be leaving." Derek got shipped off to the same summer camp six years earlier when his parents were finalizing their messy divorce, and he said that rather than making him feel abandoned and lonely, the camp saved him. If they had it year-round, that was where he'd choose to be, he said.

I was excited about Derek's return, but I was nervous, too. We'd known each other pretty well for about a year before he asked me out, and when he came home at the end of the previous summer, he bragged about all the girls he'd made out with under the dock, which I guess was an amorous place at summer camp. I hadn't had the guts to ask him before he left if our relationship status applied while he was in Wisconsin, and it seemed ridiculous to put the question in a letter and wait in agony for a response, so I decided to have a little faith. It was a hard thing for me to do, and very soon I was going to see whether it was justified. The thought of it made my stomach drop.

"Reb?" I asked tentatively.

"Yeah?"

"Do you think it's possible that Derek cheated on me at camp?"

Reb thought about the answer before giving it, as

was her way. "I don't know," she replied finally, saying the words slowly. "I mean, I think he really likes you. But I don't like to predict people's behavior because it puts funny ideas in your head and then half the time you're wrong. So."

I was silent.

"I know that's not the answer you wanted to hear," she said after giving me a quiet minute. "But I don't want to make you any promises just to soothe your ego or whatever."

"I know," I said, secretly wishing she'd just said she didn't think he'd ever look at another girl now that he was with me. "Thanks."

"You're welcome." She smiled broadly and yanked me off the couch. "I think you need a refill."

We wandered into the kitchen. Erin had the contents of her father's liquor cabinet displayed on the counter, and Reb set to preparing me a drink; when she was the designated driver, she liked to play bartender, and since she was the only one of us with her own car, she'd gotten pretty good at it. I was more than a little buzzed by then, but I didn't want to let on and look like a loser. Reb handed me a Solo cup full of something that smelled like nail polish remover and fruit snacks.

"Reb," I said. "Do you believe in God?" The second I said it, I realized I had no idea why I was asking, and from the look on her face, neither did Reb.

But that was what I loved about Reb—she was always game. She took a while to consider the question, then said, "Oh, I don't know. Probably."

"Probably?" Reb was usually so sure about everything, one way or the other. It was odd to hear her expressing anything like doubt or uncertainty.

"I mean, I'm Jewish, right?"

"Right," I said, not exactly sure where she was going with this.

"So it's really tough to say no," she continued. "It's not like my family is very observant or anything—I don't think I've been to temple since my bat mitzvah, which was, like, a zillion years ago—"

"Three," I reminded her. I didn't meet Reb until freshman year, so I didn't go to her bat mitzvah, but knowing Reb, I was sorry to have missed that party.

"—but God always had a place at the table, I guess," she finished. "He was always around, somewhere, like a—a crazy uncle? 'Crazy' is the wrong word....You know what I mean."

"Sort of," I said.

"Why do you ask?" Reb took a leisurely sip of whatever mocktail she'd whipped up for herself, peering at me with interest over the rim of her cup.

I shrugged. This would've been the moment to talk about Hannah—she was the reason I'd brought the subject up in the first place—but I didn't like to start conversations without having some idea where they were going. I let it drop. "Just curious. I don't think we've ever talked about it."

"Well, yeah," she said, as if it was obvious. "Nobody talks about that stuff, really."

"True," I said. Now that I thought about it, I realized I had no idea if Erin believed in God, or Derek, either.

"Do you believe in God?" she asked, as I knew she would.

I sighed. "Jury's out," I said. "Empirically, there's no evidence. You can't prove it—scientifically, I mean."

Reb laughed. "Oh, Caro," she said, putting a hand on my shoulder. "You're such a nerd."

"Thanks."

"What I mean is you're so up here all the time," she said, jabbing a finger at her temple. "I'm pretty sure most people who believe in God don't think about him *scientifically*."

"Yeah, well, maybe they should," I said.

"Maybe," Reb allowed.

The truth was that I had never given God much consideration, and I guess when I had, I'd mostly thought about him as some kind of robber bridegroom straight out of *Grimm's Fairy Tales* who stole young women away from their homes. My religious upbringing, for all its bells and whistles—the Catholic school education of my childhood, the floofy white dress I'd worn to my

First Communion, the five rosaries I'd gotten from my grandmother over the years, all hidden away in the bottom of my jewelry box—wasn't very deep or particularly insightful. My parents (well, my mother—my father was always curiously evasive of the subject) mostly spoke of God when they were angry with me. "God can hear you," when my mouth was especially sharp or filthy, or "God says, 'Honor thy father and thy mother,'" when I was being disobedient. And of course there was Christmas, with the blown-glass nativity scene my mother treasured, despite Joseph's having long since lost one of his hands and our often misplacing the baby Jesus. But other than that, after Hannah left, God stayed up in the attic, like the toys and old clothes I'd outgrown that my mother couldn't bring herself to part with.

I crept quietly into the house the same way I'd gone out. It was around four o'clock, and I was sure I'd gotten away with it, but when I turned on the light in my room, my dad was sitting in my tufted armchair, dozing lightly. I yelped when I noticed him. He opened his eyes and lifted his head slowly, a deep frown on his face.

"Where were you?" he asked. He was weirdly calm, and he looked tired. Was he up because he was waiting for me, or because he couldn't sleep?

"Erin's," I said. "Like I told you."

"Did you forget the part where your mother and I said you couldn't go? I thought you said you had home-work to do."

"I worked on it for a while," I said. It wasn't untrue; between dinner and saying good night, I'd gotten fifty pages of *Beloved* read for AP English. "I'm almost done."

"I see." He narrowed his eyes at me. "Are you drunk?"

I'd sobered up a little on the way home, so I wasn't totally hammered or anything, but even when I was tipsy, it was hard to stop myself from swaying. "No."

"You're lying."

There wasn't much I could say to that. "I'm sorry," I told him.

"No, you're not," he said with a sigh.

I stared at the floor. "Are you going to tell Mom?"

"Not this time." He got up and walked over to me. "Look at me, Carolina."

I met his eyes and saw the disappointment in them. It never failed to make me feel small. I bet he never looked at Hannah that way. Hannah was perfect. It was a lot to live up to, and I didn't even want to *be* perfect; I *wanted* to be *me*. But somehow, with St. Hannah always hanging over my head, that didn't seem like enough.

"Your mom's very stressed out about Hannah," he said. "The last thing I'm going to do is give her an ul-cer by telling her about this. But I'm watching you, kid. No more sneaking out, no more talking back to us, no more being mean about Hannah. You're going to treat everybody in this house with the love and respect they deserve, or so help me, you will regret it."

"Fine," I said, turning away. "Threatening your daughter. Super-great parenting, Dad." I gave him a very sarcastic thumbs-up.

"It's not a threat, Caro," Dad said. "It's a promise."

3

Dad knocked on my door early the next morning.

"Get up," he commanded, poking his head in.

I hid under the covers and groaned. It was only eight, on a weekend, *in the summer.* I refused on principle to rise before ten.

Dad yanked the covers all the way off. "Get up," he repeated. "Your mom's making breakfast."

"Hannah's not even here yet," I whined, burying my face in a pillow.

"This is a special day. Mom feels like making breakfast. Remember what I said last night—or were you too drunk?"

"Fine!" I shouted. "I'll be out in a second."

He came back fifteen minutes later to find me curled up, clutching one of my pillows and snoring lightly.

"Caro, I swear, if you're not up and out of that bed in two seconds flat—"

"Okay!"

"I'm not leaving until I see you walk out this door," Dad said, standing aside so that I could pass. I rolled out of bed and got to my feet, glaring at him as I stepped into the hallway and trudged to the kitchen.

"Good morning, sunshine," Mom said, abnormally chipper.

"Morning," I grumbled. "Pancakes?"

"Or French toast—what would you like?"

"Um . . ." I weighed my options carefully. "French toast."

Mom slid two slices onto a plate and put it down in front of me. "When does Derek come home?" she asked, like she had any interest in the answer to that question. Sweet of her to try, though.

"Today," I said glumly. I didn't know what I was more apprehensive about—Hannah's arrival, or Derek's. I just had this feeling that something was about to go horribly awry, but I couldn't decide which was the doomed homecoming. The uncertainty sat in my stomach like a brick and refused to move, no matter how much French toast I consumed.

"Oh, bad timing," she said. "But you can see him tomorrow."

"Thanks for the permission," I snapped. I could feel my parents' glares at my back, but I didn't care. They were used to this. It was how we interacted. They built the walls; I pushed against them; they pushed back. It was our family dynamic. We loved each other, the three of us, and I never said anything that was too bad to be instantaneously forgiven (aside from that one time). But now that Hannah was coming home, they were suddenly sensitive.

"Don't talk to your mother like that," Dad said from the other side of the *Trib.*

"Like what?" I slammed my fork down on the table and pushed my plate away. "Like she's *ruining* my *life*?" I knew how melodramatic it sounded, what a ridiculous thing it was to say, but that ugly, gnawing fear was working away at my insides. All this sudden change was giving me emotional whiplash.

"Are you crazy?" Dad tossed the paper to the side and leaned in at me on his elbows. "Do you hear yourself?"

I took in a deep, agitated breath. My parents were both staring at me, probably wondering what mouth of hell this demon they called their daughter had risen from. I knew I was being selfish, but I was *feeling* selfish. I didn't want to go pick Hannah up in Chicago that afternoon; I wanted to see my boyfriend, who I'd talked to only through pen and paper and a few rushed pay phone calls for three months. At least Derek wrote me. I hadn't gotten a personal letter from Hannah, like, ever. She wrote one to all three of us every Christmas, and they weren't very interesting, anyway, just a few paragraphs about how she was full of the Spirit and happy in the Lord. Barf. I wrote her every month for two years, told her about my mean fourth-grade teacher and my first crush and getting my ears pierced, before I stopped bothering.

"Have it your way. But just because you're forcing me to go with you doesn't mean I'm going to be happy to see her, so you can take your complete, perfect family fantasy and shove it." I got up from the table so fast my chair screeched across the tile, and ran off to my room.

I flopped onto my bed and began to sob. Hot tears spilled down my cheeks and my head began to throb. It wasn't fair; it wasn't right. Why couldn't she do this two years from now, when I would be in college and wouldn't have to take orders from anybody?

Eventually I stopped crying and went to the bathroom to attend to the aftermath. I rinsed my red, splotchy face off with cold water and patted it dry with one of my mother's soft cotton towels. I took a couple of aspirin for my headache, massaged my temples, brushed my hair. I got dressed and took a few deep, cleansing breaths. Reb was really into yoga, and she was always babbling about how breathing long and slow, focusing on nothing but emptiness and clarity, released tension and quieted the mind. It didn't totally work, but it did calm me down a little bit, enough to make me feel that I could go back into the kitchen, face my parents, and submit to my punishment.

"Are you done?" Mom asked as I wobbled into the room. Dad just lifted his eyebrows expectantly.

"Yeah," I said.

"Tantrum's over?" Dad confirmed.

"Pretty much," I told him, slumping back in my seat. The kitchen table sat four—six with the extension, which Dad had put in the night before. "Who's coming to dinner?"

"Nobody," Mom said. "I just thought it'd be nice, now that Hannah's going to be home, if we had a little bit of elbow room."

"We're leaving at one," Dad said. "Be ready by then. Are you finished with your summer work?" He gazed at me meaningfully.

"No," I said, avoiding his eyes.

"Well, you'd better keep going," Mom warned, as if I didn't always complete my schoolwork, in full and on time. As if it wasn't the only way in which I was perfect. "I thought you were going to have it done last night."

"I didn't get to all of it," I said, avoiding Dad's stern gaze.

"Get cracking," she said, motioning vaguely in the direction of my room.

"Can I at least finish my breakfast?"

Dad reached into the pantry and tossed me a granola bar. "Here. I'll let you know when it's time to leave."

☆ ☆ ☆

Three hours later, I was buckled into the backseat of my parents' Acura. My stomach was wriggling; I was nervous. I'd texted Derek a little while before to see how far away from home he was, and finally got an answer—"Just got reception. Two hours away. Talk to you tonight?" I answered, "Yes! Can't wait," and put the phone away after Dad caught me looking at it.

"No texts today, kiddo," he said. "No calls. Today is about family." My parents hated cell phones. They shared one between the two of them, "for emergencies," and I had to really fight to get my own. My cell phone was the centerpiece of Dad's Kids Today rant, something he liked to pull out at parties after a beer or two; he had this theory that the more we were connected, the more we separated ourselves from each other. He called it false closeness. Dad was something of an armchair philosopher.

"I can't even go out later tonight to see Derek?" I asked. "It's his first night home from camp!"

"Tomorrow," Mom said. "That's what I told you."

"Promise?"

"No," she told me. "I'm not promising you that. But probably, *if you behave.*"

I buried my back into the seat. "All right. I'll be good."

"Don't just be good," Dad said. "Be *happy*."

"Don't get your hopes up."

"Then don't even think about leaving the house to-morrow," Mom said.

"Fine. I'll be happy." I pasted a fake smile on my face. "See? Happy."

"Better be," Dad muttered, pulling out of the drive and heading toward the expressway.

☆ ☆ ☆

As much as my parents thought they knew what to expect, I don't think any of us did. There wasn't a whole lot of parking at the train station, so Dad waited in the pickup lane and Mom dragged me inside to look for Hannah. I wasn't sure I would recognize her; after all, so many years can change a person. But when we ascended the escalator, there she was, the tiniest of suitcases in hand, looking for all the world like a normal twenty-seven-year-old woman. Well, a normal twenty-seven-year-old woman with severe agoraphobia. In the whirling dervish of noise and people that was the Northwestern train station, Hannah appeared to be totally freaking out.

It took me a few minutes to realize that she was wearing the same clothes she'd gone into the convent with. They were simple: long black pants, a pressed white shirt, sensible black flats. Nothing flashy, nothing . . . worldly.

She wasn't wearing any jewelry, not even a cross. Not that I had expected her to wear a cross. After all, she'd left the convent—I assumed she'd left God behind, as well.

But Hannah's clothes weren't the first thing I noticed about her.

"She's so *thin*," I whispered to Mom, who shushed me. But I couldn't stop staring at her. I hadn't seen Hannah in a long time, but I didn't remember her looking that bony and drawn. And weirdly, her hair seemed to be a different color. In all the pictures, it was so light it was almost platinum; now it was way darker, even darker blond than mine. I'd had no idea that could happen to a person.

"Don't say a word," Mom warned me.

Hannah relaxed slightly when she saw us. Her expression, terrified in the presence of so many people, changed as we walked toward her. For a minute I thought she'd drop her suitcase and run to us, arms open, but she didn't. She let us get right up to her, smiled finally, and then said, "It's so good to see you."

If I had been a cat, my back would've gone up. She sounded like a TV news anchor greeting her audience. Mom reached out and put her arms around Hannah, but I stopped short. Hannah stepped easily into the hug, and she closed her eyes, still smiling.

When they finally let go, Hannah stood there, waiting for me to embrace her. I didn't even try, so she stepped forward and I felt Mom's hand on the small of my back. I leaned into her hug; it was gentle but not particularly familiar. She smelled foreign, like soap and train. Her shoulder blades were sharp beneath my fingers, and for a second I felt like I was falling. How had this happened? I pulled back and gave her my biggest smile, because I knew I should.

"You're so tall," Hannah said.

"I know," I said. "I . . . grew."

"It's been a long time." Hannah brushed a thick strand of hair out of my eyes and looked into them. She seemed to be searching for something, but I couldn't guess at what. I stared back, struck by this sudden thought: *Our eyes are the same color.* I knew that already, of course. I'd seen pictures. But it was different in the flesh.

"Okay," Mom said, a little too loudly. "Let's get going, Dad's waiting with the car." She picked up Hannah's bag and charged into the crowd. I shrugged at Hannah, who looked a little lost without her sole possession, and marched after Mom, Hannah trailing behind me.

Back in the car, Dad wore a toothy grin. "Hey there, Goosie," he said, reaching past his headrest to grasp Hannah's hand. She let him, grinning back. They had the same smile. I'd never noticed that before. I'd also never known Dad to call Hannah "Goosie"; I guessed it was a nickname from a long time ago, maybe even a time before me.

"Hello, Dad," she said. She was sitting upright and stiff; when Dad let go of her hand, she let it drop softly to her lap. "How long have you been waiting?"

"Oh, not very," he told her. "Everybody buckled up?" We nodded. "Then let's get out of here."

I looked out the window as we sped through the city. The expressway flung us out into the suburbs, where brick buildings gave way to identical houses, and trees as green as jewels lined the quiet streets. I kept checking my phone for a text or a missed call from Derek, but there was never anything. Maybe he hadn't gotten home yet, I reasoned. Maybe he was tired and took a nap. At least I wasn't going to have to make excuses or tell him about Hannah. The thought of explaining the situation to anyone was exhausting, and I planned to put it off as long as possible.

"Are you waiting for a call?" Hannah asked, gesturing at my cell phone, which I was gripping so tightly my knuckles were whitening.

Dad glanced at me in the rearview mirror. "What did I tell you about that phone, Caro?"

I shrugged, letting go of it; it fell into my lap. "My boyfriend gets home from camp today. He said he'd call."

"Oh. I didn't know you had a boyfriend." She sounded surprised, although I couldn't tell if it was because I had a boyfriend or because nobody had told her. For the first time it occurred to me that I didn't know exactly how much, or what, my parents chose to share about me in letters, or during their annual visits with Hannah. Maybe I wasn't the only one going in blind. Maybe I was just as big a mystery to Hannah as she was to me.

"Yeah, I do," I said.

"What's his name?"

"Derek," I told her. "We've been going out for about four months."

"How long has he been at camp?"

"About two of those," I answered. "It's been a long time since I've seen him, and now I probably won't get a chance until tomorrow."

I didn't even mean it like she was the reason, though of course she was, but Hannah stared down at her hands and I felt guilty, then silly for feeling guilty. Mom turned around in her seat and eyeballed me dangerously, which didn't help.

"You'll live," she said, a note of warning in her voice.

"That reminds me. Mom, can I borrow the car tomorrow? Reb invited me over to use the pool." I didn't really have any plans with Reb, but I was laying the groundwork for a quick escape in case I needed one.

"I was going to take Hannah shopping," Mom said, shaking her head. Hannah looked up shyly at her name. "I'll drop you off, though."

"That's *almost* the same thing," I grumbled.

"Caro," Dad said.

"That's fine," I told Mom. She raised her eyebrows but nodded and turned back around, so that was the end of it.

"When does school start?" Hannah asked.

"Monday," I told her, staring at the back of my dad's headrest and flipping my cell phone over and over in my hands, willing it to ring but knowing it wouldn't.

"Are you excited?"

"For junior year? Not really," I said. "It's the hardest year. It counts the most for getting into college. At least, that's what my teachers keep saying. And the academic Nazis up there." I jerked a thumb at the front seat.

Hannah laughed, a soft, staccato sound, like a stone skipping across the surface of a pond. Erin once told me my laugh sounded like a flock of geese honking, but I was pretty sure she was just trying to be funny. "Yes, I remember junior year," Hannah said. "Vaguely."

"It must feel like a long time ago," I said. Eleven years. That was how long it had been since Hannah had been where I was. I glanced at Hannah; she was sitting behind our mother, facing the same direction, and I was surprised to notice that they had the same profile, the same perfect, straight nose. Absently, I touched my own nose, wondering if I had it, too.

Hannah stared out the window. "It really does."

4

Mom and Dad had changed Hannah's room (or, I guess, my old room) into an office–slash–sewing room a couple of years earlier. Mom had run around the entire week since we'd found out Hannah was coming home, trying to approximately re-create Hannah's old space, but it didn't really work. Her aversion to clutter won out over her desire to make the room look like it had eight years before, so most of Hannah's possessions—stuffed animals, school notebooks, journals, her eraser collection—stayed in the garage. Her books had migrated to my shelves about a year after she'd left, when our parents finally had to admit she was gone, and the walls were bare. They had bought her a new set of furniture from Ikea, new bedding and curtains, had the carpet shampooed, and scrubbed the room from top to bottom. It was less like Hannah's old room than ever.

The new Hannah appreciated the ascetic cleanliness, though. "It sort of reminds me of my cell," she said when Mom asked. Mom looked at her in horror, but Hannah just angled her head and gave a closed-mouthed smile. "I love it, Mom, it's great. Neat and simple."

"Are you sure?" Mom's eyes crinkled at the corners with worry; behind them her brain was whirling like the Tasmanian Devil, trying to process Hannah's comment and recalibrate accordingly. In no way did she want to remind Hannah of the convent, although she probably couldn't have explained why. Was it because Hannah had left the cloister and Mom didn't want to remind her of her former unhappiness, or was it because she didn't want to tempt her back to it? "We can go to Target tomorrow on the way to the mall and pick up some new things. More colors, maybe."

"No, no, it's fine," Hannah insisted. "More than fine. Fantastic. I hope you didn't go to too much trouble."

"It was no trouble at all," Mom said, beaming. "I'm going to go start dinner."

"Do you want help?" Hannah asked. I did *not* ask, trying as always to fade quietly into the background and praying Mom forgot I was there. I hated helping with dinner. In our house, whoever didn't cook dinner had to do the dishes. I much preferred that.

"No, you should rest," Mom told her. "Caro can help me."

I let a quick breath out through my nose.

Hannah glanced at me. "Mom, really. I do that—I used to do that all the time. I like to cook."

"No," Mom said firmly. She put her arm through Hannah's. "You can come sit in the kitchen and talk to me, though."

"Okay," Hannah agreed, walking with her into the hallway and down the stairs. I followed, my eyes trained on their retreating backs.

They say idle hands are the devil's workshop, and Hannah must have subscribed to that philosophy, because she refused to do nothing while Mom and I prepared beef Stroganoff—her favorite, or it had been eight years earlier. She begged for something to do, so I passed her an onion and commanded, "Chop." She took the knife up and began turning out thin, perfect slices of onion without shedding a tear.

"Caro," Mom said, grabbing my arm.

"What?"

Mom cocked her head at Hannah and gave me a

stern look. *Talk to her.* I shook my head, but she persisted. I sighed.

"You must be a really good cook, Hannah," I said.

"No," Hannah said. "I'm not at all. But everyone had to cook, and I had plenty of turns, so I can do the basic things." She gestured with the knife toward her pile of onions. "Ta-da."

I nodded. "That's pretty impressive. What kind of stuff did you guys eat, um, in there?"

"Normal stuff," Hannah said. "We raised our own vegetables, so everything was really fresh. Lots of meat and potatoes. Lots of stew. I don't know." She shrugged. It was hard to gauge how much to push her to talk about the convent, but it was the only point of reference I had. I foresaw a whole lot of awkward silences in the near future.

I shot Mom an *I gave it the old college try* look and went to the pantry to grab a bag of egg noodles.

"What do you think you might want to do after high school, Caro?" Hannah asked.

I hesitated. "I . . . don't know. Don't worry, I don't want to become a nun or anything."

"Caro!" Mom looked like she wanted to lock me in my room until I learned some manners. I didn't have the heart to tell her that was probably never going to happen.

"I wasn't suggesting that," Hannah said, looking down at the cutting board, where her onions sat gleaming.

"Either way. If you wanted to, I certainly wouldn't try to talk you out of it."

"You wouldn't?" I asked. Mom glared at me, but I was genuinely curious now. "Didn't you hate it?"

"I didn't hate it," Hannah said, her voice barely above a whisper.

"Then why did you leave?"

Hannah looked up from the counter at me and smiled a smile that was like the shutting of a door. "It's complicated."

"I bet," I said, returning to my task, which was starting to seem impossible. "Mom, I think we're out of egg noodles. Do you want to use penne instead?"

"No, we have some," Mom said. "Look harder, Caro."

"I've looked, there's none here."

Mom narrowed her eyes at me. "What do I get if I find them?"

"Um . . . the credit?"

"Look harder."

I did another halfhearted search through the pantry before calling it quits on the egg noodles. "Okay, a week of dishes."

"With no complaining?"

"With *minimal* complaining."

"Even if you make dinner?"

"Even if."

"Deal." Mom walked to the pantry, and within a

minute she'd found a bag of egg noodles shoved behind a giant Costco pack of Stove Top stuffing. She handed them to me with a self-satisfied smirk. "Be sure to put the rubber gloves on before you wash. A week of that will give you dishwater hands."

"Thanks for that helpful tip, Martha Stewart, I'm going to write that down," I said good-naturedly.

"Next time let me look first," Hannah suggested, in an attempt to get in on the joke. I jumped; I'd forgotten she was even there.

☆ ☆ ☆

I didn't hear from Derek at all that day, or the following morning. I spent the entire night tossing and turning, and I wasn't the only one. Hannah's bedroom was right above mine, and even though she'd supposedly gone to bed right after dinner, insisting she was tired, I could hear her treading the carpet restlessly above my head into the wee hours of the morning.

It was a strange sound, louder and more anxious than the lazy creaks and settling noises the house usually made. The things we think about at night, in the dark, are much more phantasmagorical than the things we think about when the sun is up; as I was kept awake by Hannah's footsteps looming over me, my mind wandered, not to what she was doing at that moment, but what it had been like for her in the convent. I'd never been in her room there, and it had never been described to me, so I imagined it—dark and cold and empty, Hannah in the center of it, alone and lonely, dreaming of escape.

I slept through Sunday breakfast. Mom had taken Hannah shopping, and by early afternoon, they still weren't back. We were less than twenty-four hours away from the start of junior year, and Derek still hadn't found the time to let me know he was alive. Well, I knew he was alive. He'd updated his Facebook around midnight, and again at noon on Sunday. I left a comment on his wall but got no response. A couple of hours went by and I called him. No answer.

"Hey, Derek, it's me—Caro—you know—your girl-friend," I said, pressing the heel of my palm into my fore-head. That was the first time either of us had used that word to describe me. I shouldn't have been the one to do it. "Anyway, I was just calling to talk, see how you're doing, maybe see if you're free tonight to get together or whatever. So, um, call me back. Okay . . . bye!" I shut my phone and flopped backward onto my bed, burying my head under a pillow. I hated myself so much in that moment.

"Do you think he's avoiding me?" I asked Erin over the phone minutes later. I didn't really want to talk to her about this, but I thought maybe if I was on the phone with somebody else, he would call. Staying off the line and staring at it, waiting for it to light up, hadn't worked.

Maybe directing my focus elsewhere, making myself a little bit less available, would. I don't know where I get this stuff, honestly.

"Um . . . no, probably not," Erin said. It was obvious to me that she was barely listening.

"What are you doing?"

"I'm on IM," she told me.

"With Peter?"

"No, Joe."

"Joe *Price*?" Joe was another guy from our high school. I didn't know him very well, but he had dated our friend Jessica the previous year, with more or less disastrous results. They'd broken up in March, but it still seemed wrong for Erin to be hitting on him—if that was what she was doing. I'd give most people the benefit of the doubt, at least at first, but Erin used IM as a tool of seduction. She was much wittier and braver over the Internet than in real life, and she used that to her advantage, to reel them in.

"Yeah, we've been chatting all summer, pretty much," Erin said. "I didn't want to tell you because I knew you'd think I was betraying Jess, but really, they broke up a long time ago, and it's high school."

I drew a deep breath. "Okay, whatever. You didn't sound too sure when you said Derek wasn't avoiding me. Do you think he's avoiding me? Tell the truth."

Erin sighed. "I don't know. It's hard to say. You two

have been apart for months, so while I wouldn't normally tell you to worry, if everything's fine between you, then he should be dying to see you, if only to get some action. Summer camp can be a lonely place for a guy with a girlfriend back home, if you catch my drift."

"I catch it, thanks for that." I shook my head. "So you're saying he got with some other girl at camp?"

"That's not what I said."

"Okay, so you're saying he wants to break up?"

"Again, *not what I said.*"

"Then what? What was your point?"

"I didn't have one! You asked a question and I answered it: yes, it is weird that he hasn't called." Erin paused. "So, what are you going to do about it?"

"I don't know. What would you do?"

"Break up with him first," Erin was quick to say. "Never get dumped. That's my motto. Never, ever, ever get dumped. It's totally humiliating. If you think someone's going to break up with you, you should launch a preemptive strike."

"You should really cut back on the military history documentaries," I advised.

"My grandma had the TV set permanently on the Hitler Channel this summer," she told me. "I didn't have a choice." Erin called the History Channel the Hitler Channel, because every time she switched it on, they were showing a program about World War II. Erin swore that at least a third of the time, the first word she caught was "Luftwaffe."

"Try reading a book next time."

"Whatever."

"You really think I should break up with him first?" I asked, twisting a chunk of hair around my pointer finger. It was a nervous habit I'd had since childhood.

"I think you should do whatever you feel like doing," Erin said. "But yes, I think you should break it off first. Even if he doesn't *think* he wants to break up, if he's not breaking down the front door to see you, his head's obviously not in the game."

"Don't you mean his heart?"

"Uh . . . no." I heard the IM ping in the background. "Caro, I've got to go, Joe wants me to meet him for coffee in ten. Are you okay to be on your own?"

"Yeah," I said. What did she think I was going to do, stick my head in the oven because I hadn't heard from Derek in forty-eight hours? Not likely. "I'll live."

"Great. See you at school tomorrow."

I hung up the phone and paced my room for a while, thinking about what Erin had said. It was typical Erin advice—get out clean. She'd dated a lot of guys and considered herself an expert at playing the game. But I wasn't so sure. I wasn't Erin; I was me. What would I do? I had no idea.

A few minutes later, there was a knock on my door.

"Come in," I called. Hannah poked her head through the door, as if she was trying as hard as possible not to disturb my privacy or pry. She glanced around the room with interest, and I felt a geyser of protectiveness surge up inside me until I realized that she was just trying to remember what the room had looked like when it had belonged to her. "What's up? I didn't hear the garage door."

"I was tired, so Mom dropped me off and went back out, to the grocery store, I think."

I nodded, waiting for her to elaborate, but she just stood there, running her eyes over every inch of the place. "So . . . how can I help you?"

"Oh, right. I wanted to see if you were interested in taking a walk," she said.

"I thought you were tired," I said.

"Of shopping," Hannah told me with a sheepish smile.

"Thanks," I said. "But I'm kind of busy."

"Busy doing laps around your bed?"

"Busy trying to decide whether or not to break up with my boyfriend before he breaks up with me," I said, chewing on my thumbnail. I shouldn't have told her that. It was too personal, and it wasn't like she was going to have any useful advice for me on the subject.

"Oh." She looked embarrassed, like she'd trespassed on me in some way. "I'm sorry. I'll leave you alone."

"Thanks," I said. She closed the door, and as I heard

the click of the latch, I thought maybe I should call her back. But then what? I wasn't going to get her involved just because I felt guilty about not needing her around.

But I couldn't keep my thoughts to myself, so I called Reb. The first thing I did was sell Erin out.

"Erin's out on a date with Joe Price," I told her.

"That's kind of skanky, don't you think?" Reb asked.

"Totally," I agreed. "What does she think she's doing? Jessica's going to run her up the flagpole if she starts dating him. And what was all that crap with Peter on Friday night, if she's going to hook up with Joe?"

"Maybe she's keeping her options open. It's not unheard of," Reb pointed out.

"How can she like two guys at the same time? I can barely keep my head on straight with one."

"Derek issues?"

"Yes. How did you know?"

"The tone of your voice. You sound a little bothered." She paused. "Also, common sense."

"Derek hasn't called since he got home from camp. He texted me yesterday when I was getting—when I was with my family, saying he'd call me later that night, but he didn't. I called him today, but no answer. Do you think he's trying to avoid me or something?"

Reb hesitated. I reminded myself that it didn't necessarily mean anything, that she always took her time before answering the hard ones.

"Reb?"

"I'm thinking. Did you talk to Erin about this?"

"Yes."

"And what did she say?"

"To break up with him before he breaks up with me."

"Flawless." I couldn't tell if she was being sarcastic. She and Erin didn't always see eye to eye on things like this. And by "didn't always see eye to eye," I meant *never* did.

"So you think that's what I should do? You think he's going to end our relationship?" *Say no,* I thought, but only because I believed she would say yes.

"I have no idea," Reb said. "It's hard to say. But not calling after you guys have been separated for most of the summer isn't a *good* sign."

"Ugh, why won't anyone just say what they think?" I cried, knocking my head softly against the wall.

"Okay, you want to hear what I think?"

"Yes!"

"He's probably going to dump you."

"What? Seriously?" I wanted to throw up.

"Yes. Derek is a cool guy, but he's not the relationship type. He likes girls in general, but I don't think he wants to be with one girl specifically. Even if that one girl is as awesome as you are, Caro," she added, because she's a good friend like that.

Even though I hated what Reb was saying, I couldn't disagree with it. Derek had always seemed out of my league, not because he was smarter or better-looking or more popular than I was, but just because he never seemed to need anyone. He held everybody at arm's length; he was friends with a lot of people, but best friends with nobody; he liked a lot of girls, but he didn't love any of them. When he started to pay special attention to me, at first I couldn't trust or believe it, but when he finally won me over, I thought I'd changed him, or his feelings for me had. Maybe he'd thought that, too, for a hot second, but it was becoming very clear to me that we were both wrong.

I sank onto my desk chair and put a hand to my forehead. "So how do I do this?"

"Break up with him?"

"Yeah. I've never done it before. Obviously."

"You sure you want to do that? I mean, without talking to him first?"

"If I talk to him first, he'll beat me to the punch," I said. "Erin's right, getting dumped is completely humiliating. I won't be able to show my face at school tomorrow if that happens. I have to do it, and I have to do it tonight."

"Okay," Reb said. "Let's come up with a plan."

5

Hannah was upstairs, Mom was still out, and sneaking out of the house when Dad was watching sports was almost criminally easy. I felt a little pang of guilt for boosting his car, but I wasn't going to be gone for very long; I just hoped Mom wouldn't get back before I did.

Ten minutes later, I was standing at the end of Derek's driveway, sending him a text: "I'm outside, we need to talk." Within a minute, I got one back: "Okay, be right there."

I felt like I was going to be sick right there in his mother's hydrangeas. This was where it was all going to end. Maybe I should've known that from the start; maybe

I had. I never thought I'd be in this situation, though, treading through a conversational minefield to break up with him before he could break up with me.

A few minutes later, Derek came out his front door and strolled toward me. He smiled when he caught my eye and held out his arms for a hug. I let him hold me, because I loved the feeling of being touched by a boy, especially this particular boy. I loved the way he always squeezed me a little too tightly, the way he ran his finger-tips lightly down my back as he released me. He didn't try to kiss me, though, I noticed.

"How was camp?" I asked when the embrace ended.

"Pretty good," he said. "How was everything here?"

"Pretty lame," I said. He laughed softly.

"Want to take a walk?" I suggested.

"Sure. Park?"

"Yeah." There was a park two blocks from Derek's house where he and I had hung out most afternoons and weekends before he left for camp. It was large and full of trees. We used to take a blanket from the trunk of his car and lie out in the shade as far away from the noisy play-ground as possible. He would run his fingers through my hair and I would close my eyes and just enjoy the feel-ing, the murmur of his voice as he talked about nothing in particular. We'd spent an afternoon together just like that right before he left for camp. I'd thought I might want to say "I love you," but I'd held back, and now I was glad.

We walked to the park in near silence. I didn't try to take his hand and he didn't try to take mine. I spent the time psyching myself up, reading his body language for any evidence that he might not be plotting exactly what I was, that he might want to stay together, that he might still like me enough to want to keep being my boyfriend, but there wasn't any. It was pretty clear what he wanted, and now I was in a race with him to say it first. I hated this game, but my dignity was important to me, and I'd be damned if I was going to lose it to a boy I should've known better than to date in the first place.

It was sunset, so the park was deserted. I steered him toward the swings and sat down in one, pushing off the ground with the toes of my Converse and drifting back and forth lazily.

"Caro—" he began.

"Hold on a minute," I said, my mind spinning.

"I think we should break up."

"No!" I shouted.

He arranged his face in his most sympathetic expression, which for Derek was pretty much just a douchey smirk. "I'm so sorry. I really like you, but I don't think I'm ready to have a girlfriend. Being at camp made me realize that."

"This isn't fair," I groused, shoveling wood chips with my feet.

"I know," Derek said.

"No, goddammit, *I* was going to break up with *you,*" I told him.

"Oh. Well, that's convenient." He didn't believe me at all. In fact, just the opposite. He was really smirking at me now, probably thinking, *Poor Caro, trying to save face by saying she wants to break up.* What a dick.

"No, seriously," I said. "I want to break up."

"That's what I just said."

I groaned. "Derek, stop being such an asshole. I came here to end our relationship. You just beat me to it."

"Sure," Derek said. "That's fine. If that's what you want to tell people, you should. I won't say anything."

"It's not a story!" I yelled. "It's the truth. And you will definitely say something, I know you."

"There's no need to get hostile," he said.

"I'm not being— Ugh, just forget it." I launched myself off the swing, stumbling a bit on the landing. Derek reached out a hand to steady me, but I shrugged him off. "Don't touch me."

"I want us to still be friends," he said halfheartedly.

"Don't hold your breath," I snapped, walking away, tears of frustration pricking at the backs of my eyes. Fortunately, I didn't actually cry; that would've been even more embarrassing. Derek didn't follow or call out after me. When I reached my car, I looked back, but he wasn't there. I wished I hadn't looked back.

☆ ☆ ☆

"Crap," I said out loud as I pulled into the driveway. Mom's car was parked in the garage; she was back, and there was no way I was getting away with sneaking out when I was supposed to be confined to the house.

"What are you doing?" Mom asked as I went in through the garage. I trudged down the hallway to face her; she and Hannah were sitting on the couch in the family room. Hannah was pretending to be engrossed in a back issue of *Smithsonian;* she looked up with mild curiosity when I stormed in.

"Going to my room," I said glumly.

"Where have you been? I didn't give you permission to go out." She knew where I'd been; my mother knew everything, always. It was her freakish gift.

"Dad did," I lied. I didn't even care if she believed me; I just wanted this conversation to be over so I could call my friends and rail against Derek in private.

Mom called me out. "He did not. Do you think I'm an idiot?"

"Can we just drop it? I have homework to finish." I didn't want to cry. I knew if I escaped to my room right that second, I could avoid it, but if Mom kept pressing, I might burst like a water balloon. The only thing I hated more than crying was having people see me cry.

But my mother, bulldog that she was, would not be

deterred. "No, we can't 'just drop it.' When have you ever known me to 'just drop it'? You're my *child,* and when I tell you to do something—or not to do something—I expect you to listen."

"Okay, Mom, I get it, I'm a terrible daughter. Can I go now?" A part of me knew that the reason most of my schoolmates were such entitled twits was that their parents didn't expect anything out of them or discipline them when they misbehaved, and I knew I was likely not to turn out like that because my parents were old school and demanded obedience and I probably should be grateful they weren't disinterested zombies who spoiled me so I would go away, but at that moment I wished my mother would disappear in a puff of smoke.

"Go where?" Mom demanded, not getting the hint. Hannah looked uncomfortable, her eyes darting from Mom to me and back to Mom, her shoulders tense and the corners of her mouth pointing straight down like little arrows. I thought she might intervene, and maybe she was thinking about it, but she kept quiet in the end— which was fine. Mom and I had these little squabbles all the time; we didn't need her help progressing through the stages. Stage 1: Confrontation. Stage 2: Teenage back talk. Stage 3: Real talk. Stage 4: Forgetting all about it.

"To my room. To do my homework. So that I don't start the year off with a zero. Is that okay with you?" Teenage back talk: check. Stage 2 was a go.

"I don't think you're hearing what I'm saying," Mom said.

"I hear you! I didn't ask permission to go to Derek's, or to use the car. I'm sorry. Believe me, it did *not* turn out as I planned." The levees broke and tears poured down my cheeks.

"What happened?" Hannah asked, getting up and putting her arm around me.

I knew she was just trying to help, but I didn't want her comfort, or anyone else's, for that matter. Hugs couldn't cure humiliation. I stepped out of her embrace and wiped furiously at my eyes. "He broke up with me," I told them.

"Oh, Caro," Mom said. Her forehead wrinkled in sympathy. "I told you that you were too young to have a boyfriend."

"Mom! Is that really all you have to say?" That was just typical. Mom thought high school boys were a distraction, and she would've been happier if I didn't date until I had my master's degree. To her credit, she hadn't tried to keep me from going out with Derek, but she did love to make it difficult.

Hannah stood by, rigid after I shook her off, but her eyes were soft with sadness on my behalf. Anger swirled around me like a mist—anger at Hannah, at my parents, at Derek, but most of all at myself for winding up in this situation when I had known better. I felt like the world's biggest loser.

"Okay, calm down," Mom said, lowering her voice. "It's going to be all right. There are plenty of boys out there, boys who will really like and appreciate you. Derek is a doofus—Dad and I have always thought so."

"Really. A doofus." I couldn't believe she thought that was going to make me feel better, but sympathy for sympathy's sake wasn't Mom's style. Real talk: check.

"Did you love him?" Hannah asked.

"What? No!" Ugh. They weren't getting it. "He wasn't returning my calls or my texts, and Erin said that he was probably going to break up with me and to do it first before he got the chance, so I went over there to dump him and before I could get a word out, *he* dumped *me*. And now I have to go to school tomorrow and everybody's going to know about it and I'm going to be totally humiliated. That's why I'm crying!"

"You're really not sad about him at all?" Hannah seemed mystified about the whole thing, but you couldn't really blame her for that; she had been celibate her whole life and locked in a convent for almost a decade. She didn't even have the benefit of having watched years and years of wildly unrealistic relationships on television like I had. But I could see her point, sort of. The situation did sound convoluted coming out of my mouth.

I sighed. "Of course I am. But mostly I'm so pissed off I could scream. *He* asked *me* out! *He* asked *me*! And then he acted like I was just a stranger with some pathetic schoolgirl crush who he was letting down easy."

"You seem really upset," Hannah said. "Maybe you should go lie down. I can make you some tea?"

"I don't want tea," I said. "I just want this whole nightmare to be over."

"What can I do?" Hannah asked, clearly bewildered by my melodrama. Mom was watching the two of us with rapt attention, as if we were exotic animals.

"Turn back time," I said. "Give me a do-over of the last hour so I can dump Derek via email. Do you think *God* would do that for me?"

"Caro," Mom said, using her scariest Voice of Steel. "You're going to go to your room right now and collect yourself. Then you're going to come out and apologize to Hannah."

I turned toward Hannah and started to say I was sorry, but Mom interrupted me.

"Not now. When you're really sorry."

"It's okay, she doesn't have to," Hannah said softly.

"No, it isn't," Mom told her sharply. "She has to learn to control herself and watch her mouth. We're not your friends, Caro. You can't talk to us like that."

I shook my head at her and walked away, bursting into my room a few moments later and throwing myself onto the bed. My inability to hold a thought in my mind that I didn't express got me in trouble a lot at home, but I'd never fought as much with my parents in one short period of time as I had in the past few days. Plus,

I'd said that really shitty thing to Hannah, which even I knew was unfair. The only thing that would have made it worse was having to talk to someone about it, which was why I ignored two of Reb's calls and one of Erin's.

Unfortunately, they would not be put off. I got a text from Reb that said, "Pick up. Heard about you and Derek. How are you feeling?" and one from Erin saying, "I thought you were going to dump him first. What happened?" I texted Erin back with "He's a quicker draw" and called Reb. I knew that at the very least, she would coddle me.

"I'm so sorry about this, Caro," Reb said when she picked up the phone.

"How did you find out so quickly?" I asked.

"Erin. I think Derek might've told some people and it got back to her."

"I just got home from his house—how has he had time to declare his new relationship status to the entire school?"

"Blame the Internet," Reb said.

"Ugh. This is so awful." I put a pillow over my face. Was it possible to intentionally smother yourself?

"It's not that bad. People break up all the time. It's *high school*, remember? It's not like you were married for twenty years and suddenly you're a single mom living on a fixed income." Reb stopped talking abruptly, then said, "And apparently I'm not over my parents' divorce."

"Did you really think you were?" I asked.

"I can barely hear you. Your voice is muffled."

I threw the pillow on the floor. "Better?"

"Much. Anyway, I know you're super upset right now, but I just wanted to give you a little perspective—it's not the end of the world! You will survive. You will love again."

"I wasn't in love with him," I insisted. Of that, at least, I could be sure.

"I was kidding."

"I know."

"You want to get out of your house? I'll take you for ice cream to celebrate your newfound independence," Reb offered.

"Can't," I said. "I think I'm grounded."

"No problem. I'll come over." Reb, whose parents were notoriously lax when it came to rules and punishments, didn't quite understand or respect other people's restrictions.

"Bad idea. Mom's on the warpath."

"What did you do that was so horrible she's locking you in your room right after you've been dumped?"

"Don't ask."

"Okay, I won't. Do you want me to pick you up tomorrow morning? I know Diva's sort of a clunker, but it beats the bus." I could hear the smile in her voice and couldn't help feeling a little better. Reb was good at being upbeat for other people; she would've made a great cheerleader, although I would never say that to her, given her deep-seated hatred for cheerleaders.

"I would be honored to ride in Diva," I said.

"Good. See you tomorrow at seven-forty-five sharp. I'm honking once, then leaving." Rides from Reb came with hard-and-fast rules. I wasn't a very punctual person, and she left me behind a lot.

"I'll try my best. Thanks, Reb."

"No prob, Bob."

I hung up feeling relieved. Sure, Erin would hassle me at school the next day about letting Derek dump me, but Reb knew exactly how I felt and was on my side. And as soon as she was done lecturing me, Erin would be, too. I wasn't alone in the world.

In fact, I was the opposite of alone; my world had just gotten a little more crowded.

☆ ☆ ☆

The entire first floor was empty. Dad was probably upstairs in the spare room, reading or watching television, and Mom was in bed already; I could hear a *Golden Girls* rerun blasting from the other side of the door. Hannah, I figured, was in the guest bedroom—her room now. I couldn't imagine what she might be doing; at least she wasn't pacing the floor like she had been the night before. I knocked tentatively, hoping she'd tell me to go away.

But no. "Come in," she called.

I stepped into the room hesitantly, not knowing quite what to expect. I found her sitting up in bed, reading *The Bell Jar.*

"Hey," I said, without even thinking. "Is that my book?"

"Yes," she responded. "I took it from your room while you were out—I hope you don't mind, it didn't look like you were reading it."

I shrugged. I didn't like the idea of her or anyone in my room, going through my stuff, when I wasn't there, but it wasn't the opportune time to bring it up. "I read it sophomore year in English class." I paused for a second, then ventured another question. "Do you like it?" It bothered me that I couldn't even predict how she would react to anything. Not only did I not know Hannah; I'd never known anyone even remotely like her.

"It's one of my favorites," she told me. "I read it in high school, too, for class, but I'd forgotten most of it."

"It's one of my favorites, too." Hannah smiled at that. "Were you allowed to read at the convent?"

She shook her head. "Just the Bible, of course, and some theology. No fiction."

"That would really suck for me," I said. "I can't imagine not being allowed to read."

"It did suck," she agreed. Hearing her say that was so weird that I sort of laughed.

"So . . . ," I began. "I just wanted to say that I was

sorry for what I said to you earlier. About God. I didn't mean it. I was just mad. Not at you. Just at the situation."

"I understand," she said, nodding in sympathy. "And anyway, if I thought God would turn back time for you if I asked, I absolutely would."

"Ha." I couldn't tell if she was joking or serious. Probably a little bit of both. Then I voiced a question that had been lingering in the back of my mind since I'd found out she was coming home: "Do you even believe in God anymore?"

Maybe it was too personal. Maybe it was a stupid question. Hannah's face became more serious, and she hesitated for so long I wondered if she would even answer. But then she sighed and said, "I don't know. Sometimes I think maybe I still do, but there were stretches—long, painful stretches in the convent—when I just couldn't anymore."

"Is that why you left?"

"I left for a lot of reasons, but that was one of them. It was probably the root of all the problems I had in there." She closed *The Bell Jar* and put it in her lap, folding her hands over it delicately.

I wanted to offer her something, some consolation, in exchange for the comfort she'd tried to show me earlier, but it wasn't exactly my strong suit.

"Father Bob says that faith is nothing without doubt," I said. It sounded so lame coming out of my mouth, especially because I didn't even really believe in or think about God, like, ever. But I had always remembered that, what Father Bob said about faith. He said that doubt provided contour to faith, like shading in a drawing, that it allowed you to see what was really there. At the time we were learning how to sketch in art class, and I felt like it was the one thing he said that I actually understood.

"He did?" she said flatly.

"He says it's normal."

"Who's Father Bob?" Hannah asked.

"Just this priest my parents—Mom and Dad—made me go to a while back," I said.

"For what, an exorcism?" She smiled at her own joke.

"Um, not really. Sort of. Symbolically, I guess."

"Do you want to sit down, Linda Blair?" she asked, patting the comforter.

"Sure. Your pop culture references are a little dated, you know." I sat on the edge of the bed, twisting my hands in my lap. Out of the corner of my eye, I glanced at Hannah. The warm yellow light of the table lamp picked up the gold highlights in her hair and cast shadows that fell softly on her face. When I'd seen her at the train station, I'd thought my memory had been overly kind to Hannah's looks, or maybe it was just that life and age had eroded some of them. She had looked gaunt and drawn, tired and pale and fragile, like a porcelain doll that had been badly propped in its stand. But now I could see that she was just as beautiful as she had always been. I was struck by a sudden envy: why couldn't I look like that? I was plain and unremarkable-looking, loud and unrefined. I was a bull in a china shop, and she was the china.

"Tell me about your symbolic exorcism," she said, giving me a curious look. I felt my face grow hot.

"Okay, well, 'exorcism' is a strong word. Mom and Dad just thought I wasn't adjusting properly to you being gone," I said. "Wasn't adjusting properly" was a pretty vague euphemism for "told everyone you were dead," but it seemed stupid, when we were talking so nicely, to ruin it with details.

Hannah looked away guiltily.

"Don't worry about it, I was fine," I rushed to assure her. "Anyway, they made me talk to Father Bob—you really never met him?"

Hannah shook her head. "We don't all know each other."

"Yeah, I guess that makes sense. Well, he's the pastor of St. Robert's now."

"So what did you and Father Bob talk about?" Hannah asked.

"Just, you know, God. And you. He used the word 'vocation' a lot."

"That sounds about right." She gave me a tight smile. Did she resent being talked about like that, like her life choice constituted a tragic event I had to be coached through? If she did, she didn't say it.

I cleared my throat, suddenly uncomfortable and

eager to bring the conversation to a close. "My point was: faith and doubt. One can't exist without the other."

"That's a good observation," Hannah agreed, although she didn't seem particularly impressed by it. She'd probably heard it all before.

"Well, remember, it wasn't mine. It was Father Bob's." I glanced at the clock. It was almost midnight. "I've got to go to bed. School tomorrow, first day."

"That's exciting," Hannah said brightly.

"Not really," I said, getting up from the bed. "Thanks for accepting my apology."

"Thanks for apologizing," she said.

"You're welcome."

6

By the time I made it to the kitchen the next morning, in my pajamas, Hannah was already there, dressed, making breakfast and brewing coffee. She looked tired, but there she was, at seven a.m., puttering around like the day had already begun. I was still holding out hope that I was dreaming, that I would wake up in my bed with three or four hours left to sleep. But no—it was the first day of my junior year, and Reb was going to pick me up in forty-five minutes.

"Good morning," Hannah said.

"Is it?" I grumbled. I didn't know how she could bear

to be up at that hour, especially since I knew she hadn't gone to sleep until late the night before. I had dozed off at almost two a.m. to the sound of her slight weight pressing against my ceiling.

"I don't know," she admitted. "Are you allowed to drink coffee?"

"Yeah. But I don't like it."

"Oh, okay. Do you want some tea?" I shook my head. "What about food? Are you hungry? I can make you some eggs or pancakes or whatever you want. I'm well versed in breakfast foods." I noticed that she wasn't eating, just carefully nursing a glass of water. There was a bowl of grapes on the counter, but she didn't touch them. I wondered if she was fasting. Father Bob said that was one of the ways nuns prepared themselves spiritually for prayer. But that was silly: she wasn't a nun anymore, after all.

"No, thanks. I don't eat in the morning, usually. Not on school days—no time."

"Then what did you come in here for?"

"Something to drink." I took a carton of orange juice out of the fridge and poured myself a glass. "I'll just bring a granola bar with me," I said. I narrowed my eyes at her. "Aren't you going to eat?"

"Oh," she said cagily. "I already had something."

"How long have you been up?"

"Since five," she said, as if that was completely normal.

"You didn't even go to bed until two! That's craziness."

"It's a force of habit," Hannah said with a sigh. "You should go get ready. Do you want me to pack you a lunch?"

I should've known the previous night's heart-to-heart with Hannah was a bad idea. Now she thought we were buddies—or worse, she thought she was my mom. Lecturing me about eating breakfast? Offering to pack my lunch? Nobody had treated me like that since the fifth grade, and even then I'd resented it. What did she think I was, some kind of baby? When she was my age, she was reading advanced religious tomes and secretly plotting her escape to a nunnery. It doesn't get much more grown up than that.

Just then, Dad trotted in, yawning and running his fingers through his hair. "G'morning, girls," he said.

"Hey, Dad," I said, draining my juice glass and beating a quick exit. He called after me and I slowly retraced my steps—backward—to the kitchen.

"Yes?" I asked.

"How are you getting to school?"

"Reb's picking me up."

"Oh, good. Okay, well, I can drive Mom to work and leave you her car, Hannie, just in case you want to go somewhere today," he said.

"That's okay, Dad, really," Hannah said, squirming a little.

"No, it's not any trouble. I'm sure we'll be doing

it a lot for this one"—he jerked his thumb at me and smiled—"now that the state of Illinois has deemed her worthy to drive."

"Fools," I said, and he laughed. Dad joked, but you could tell he was proud of me for getting my license, especially after the countless hours he'd spent at his own risk trying to teach me to drive. At the time, Mom said he was more excited than when I took my first steps as a baby.

"No, I don't need the car."

"Are you sure? Because it's fine with me—" he pressed.

"Dad!" she shouted, throwing the dish towel she'd been holding down onto the counter. I started like a skittish kitten. It was the first time I'd seen Hannah even raise her voice. "I said I don't need the car, okay?"

"Okay," he said, chastised. Hannah stalked out of the room, still steaming. Dad turned to me with sad eyes and asked, "What did I do?"

"She can't drive," I pointed out. I couldn't believe I'd figured out what was bothering Hannah and he hadn't.

"Sure she can, I taught her myself," Dad said.

"Her license is definitely expired, and when do you think she last drove a car?" I said. "Eight years ago?"

"Oh." Then, in typical Dad fashion, he rallied. "Well, she'll just have to relearn. That won't be hard—when she was your age, Hannah caught on really quickly, and this time it should be even easier for her."

That didn't seem like the only problem, judging from Hannah's reaction. "Maybe she's afraid," I said.

"Maybe," Dad said, but he didn't look convinced. "And if she is, we'll cross that bridge when we come to it. But you need to get ready for school. When's Reb coming?"

I glanced at the clock on the microwave. *Shit.* I had no idea it was that late already. "In fifteen minutes," I said, switching into panic mode.

"You'd better change, then," Dad said, settling down at the kitchen table with a cup of Hannah's coffee and the paper. "Unless you want to go to school in pants with sheep on them."

☆ ☆ ☆

All my friends, especially Reb, really bought into the first-day-of-school-outfit ritual. They shopped all summer for the perfect clothes, as if there was something about the first day of a new year that made you more visible than usual. I, however, didn't care that much, which was good, because that morning I didn't have time to care. I took my patented five-minute superfast shower, blow-dried the roots of my hair and left the rest to air-dry, wriggled into a pair of old jeans, and pulled on a T-shirt I'd ordered off the Internet that said FIJI IS FOR MERMAIDS.

Aside from the first-day-of-school thing, a lot of girls

in my position would've dressed up to the nines in the hopes that their ex-boyfriends might see them and instantly regret their hasty decisions to break up, but that wasn't my style. First of all, I was so angry with Derek I didn't want to get back together with him; I just wanted him to drop off the face of the earth so that I could forget he ever existed. Second of all, I wasn't going to give him the satisfaction of thinking I tried to make myself look extra beautiful just for his benefit. Third of all, I'd briefly considered it, but I knew it wouldn't work.

I did put on some makeup, though. There wasn't any reason to show up looking like I'd just emerged from a coffin. I did have a little bit of vanity.

Just as I was leaving my bedroom, I heard Reb honk from the end of the driveway. As I bounded out the front door and down the driveway, she started to pull away.

"Hey!" I cried out. "I'm on time!"

She stopped and I got in on the passenger side. Reb looked at me and grinned. "Just checking to see if you were paying attention."

"What *happened*?" Erin asked, pouncing on me at my locker.

"It's over, can we please not talk about the 'why' part and focus instead on the 'what now' part?" I pleaded. "Like, what do I do *now* to ensure that people aren't laughing at me behind my back for all eternity?"

"Hell if I know. This all could've been avoided if you'd just broken up with him first, like I told you to." Erin shook her head. "Why didn't you call me back last night?"

"To avoid this exact conversation," I said.

"Ease up, Erin," Reb said. "I know this is hard to understand, but this situation isn't actually about you."

"Oh shut up," Erin said, but lightly. The three of us were constantly sniping at each other, but always out of love. Well, almost always out of love.

"Let's get to class, the bell's going to ring in about five seconds," I said. We had our first class, Advanced French IV, together. It was the only high-level course Reb was enrolled in, but Erin and I were both AP-track students, so we had most of our classes together. Reb kicked our asses in French, though.

We had the same French teacher as the past year, so we generally knew what to expect, but Madame Hubert was in an especially foul mood that morning. None of us was really *thrilled* about having to sit in a stuffy classroom speaking another language at eight in the morning, but she was pretty fired up about something. She snapped at Reb, Erin, and me for being late, even though the bell didn't ring until after we'd dropped into our seats, and almost broke the projector screen by pulling on it too hard. I heard someone whispering in the back that Madame and her husband were getting a divorce, but I had no idea how they could have known that. Whatever it was, Madame was totally losing it, and I texted as much to Reb, who looked at me from the other side of the room and nodded.

About halfway through class, as Madame was lecturing us in rapid French about the Impressionist movement (Advanced French IV had a serious French culture component) and clicking through slides so quickly it was hard to know which one she was talking about, the door swung open and a new boy strode in.

New Boy was average height, well muscled but not too thick, with dark blond hair that he wore longish, but not rock-star long—more like teen-heartthrob long. The room was dark, so I couldn't make out much more than that. He paused at the door and glanced around for a second, finally locating Madame at the back of the class, still clicking furiously through slides. I rubbed my eyes and yawned.

New Boy walked up to Madame and handed her his tardy slip, which she took with a tortured sigh. "Pah-well Sob—"

"*Pavel,*" he said. "The 'w' makes a 'v' sound."

"Sorry," Madame said in French. If there was anything she understood, it was the importance of proper pronunciation. "And how do you say your last name?"

"*Sob*-chak," he said. "S-o-b-c-z-a-k."

"*Sob*-chak," she repeated. "Okay, Pawel. Take an empty seat."

He gave her a small two-finger salute and dropped into the chair right behind me. I turned back to the slides as Madame prattled on about Monet. A minute later, I felt a tap on my shoulder. I turned and saw Pawel twirling a pencil between his fingers.

"Yes?" I asked.

"What the hell is going on right now?" he asked, gesturing with his pencil toward the screen.

"Madame is lecturing about Impressionism," I said. This didn't spark any recognition in his eyes, so I explained further. "For our cultural component."

"Uh, what?"

"Don't you speak French?" He at least knew enough to understand what Madame had been saying to him earlier.

"Well, yeah, but what's a cultural component?" he asked.

I shook my head at his ignorance. "In Advanced French IV, we're not just supposed to learn the French language anymore. Madame is going to teach us other things, but in French. And we're going to have to write papers."

"About what?" He looked perturbed by this information.

"French literature, French art, French history," I said. "Didn't they tell you that when you signed up to take the class?"

"No," he said. "They didn't tell me anything, they just plugged all the classes I've already taken into the computer and it spat out this schedule." He handed me a folded piece of paper.

I looked over his schedule. "You're on the AP track," I pointed out.

"Yeah," he said, leaning back in his chair. "Super."

I gave the paper back. "Well, why don't you just go get it changed?"

"I probably will," he said, his eyes drifting toward the screen at the front of the room, where Madame had just put up a picture of Monet's *The Cliffs at Etrétat*.

I nodded, then directed my attention once again to Madame's lecture. A couple of minutes later, I felt another tap on my shoulder.

"What?" I asked with a little glare.

"My name is Pawel," he said, extending a hand for me to shake.

I took it and smiled, feeling a little guilty for snapping at him. "Caro," I said.

"Cool." He dropped my hand. "Nice to meet you."

"You know, flirting with New Boy only works if your ex is actually there to witness it," Erin said as we walked toward physics class, post-lunch.

"Erin, keep your voice down," I hissed. "I wasn't flirting with him. He just asked me why Madame was spitting about Impressionism, and I told him."

"He shook your hand," Erin pointed out.

"Yeah, and it was totally hot," I said sarcastically.

"You don't have to get defensive," Erin said. "It's a good strategy. I'm just pointing out that in order for it to be effective, Derek's going to have to see you flirting with New Boy."

"Okay, again, I wasn't flirting, and also, his name is not New Boy," I said.

"Yeah, but it's weird and foreign and instead of saying it wrong, I think I'll just call him New Boy," Erin said. "He *is* new, right?" Even Erin, who was highly social, didn't know everyone at our school, which was huge, the size of a small university.

"I think so," I said. "He's on the AP track."

"Hmm, interesting."

"For now. I think he might try to have some of his classes changed. He didn't seem thrilled about French IV's culture component."

"Wuss," Erin said. "Well, whatever. And you were flirting—I saw that smile."

"He's cute," I said. "And I think his eyes are green, which is rare." I knew they were green; I noticed it right away. How could I not, with his face inches from mine?

"He *is* cute," Erin agreed. "Funny name, though."

"I think it's Polish," I said.

"Maybe I'll just call him Polish Boy instead," Erin said. "So where were you this weekend? I didn't see you at all."

"You saw me Friday," I pointed out.

"Well, yeah, but not after that."

"I told you, I had a family thing."

"Oh, yeah. How'd that go?"

"Fine, I guess."

"What was the nature of this 'thing'?" Erin was such a busybody, always in everybody's lives, sniffing out rumors and gossip like a truffle pig.

"No big deal. We just went into the city for a while."

Erin narrowed her eyes in suspicion. "Why?"

"I'd rather not talk about it right now, all right?" I rubbed my forehead. "I've got a headache."

"Want some aspirin?" Erin asked, riffling through her purse. She always carried a bottle of aspirin, because she got headaches a lot. Reb said it was all that gossip putting pressure on her brain.

"No, thanks, it'll go away on its own," I said.

"Caffeine," Erin prescribed. "You need caffeine."

"It's too late to go to the vending machine now," I said.

"Suit yourself," Erin said.

"Hey, French Girl!" Erin and I both turned, not really because we thought *we* were being called, but because it was a bizarre way to address someone. Plus, the person said it pretty loud, startling us.

As Pawel approached, it was clear he'd been talking to me. "Hey, wait up," he said.

"Did you just call me French Girl?" I asked.

"Yeah," he admitted, looking sheepish. "I forgot your name. I have a terrible memory."

"That's okay, we've been calling you New Boy," Erin told him, smiling flirtatiously. The girl was incorrigible.

"She's been calling you that," I said. "My name is Caro."

"That's right!" He snapped his fingers. "I knew it was something weird."

"Says the guy named Paulo," Erin said, rolling her eyes.

"Pawel," Pawel and I said. We looked at each other and he laughed. "Jinx," he said.

"Whatever. You two go ahead and talk amongst yourselves. *I* refuse to be late to physics." Erin patted my shoulder and took off.

"Erin," I said, gesturing at my retreating friend.

"I'll probably forget that," Pawel told me.

"Okay, so what's up? I have to get to physics, too," I said, gazing after Erin forlornly.

"Building 2, room 307?" Pawel asked.

"Um, yeah?" I briefly considered the possibility that Pawel might be a crazy stalker.

"Me too." He breathed a sigh of relief. "I have no idea how to get there, and I thought maybe you'd be going in the same direction. Well, I hoped you were. Can I walk with you?"

"Well, it would be awkward for you to just follow me there," I said, smiling. "So yeah."

"Thanks. So what's your real name?"

"Carolina," I told him, picking up the pace. We would probably be late enough as it was, and I knew our physics class would be organized in lab groups of four per table. I expected Erin to save me a seat, but it might not be possible. She was quite popular in science classes and well known in the geek world for being a great partner, because she understood everything and would take the lion's share of the work.

"I have a cousin named Carolina," he told me. "We call her Karolcia." He pronounced it *Ka-ROL-cha*.

"That's way prettier than Caro," I said.

"Oh, I don't know," he said. "They both have their charms."

"Karolcia," I repeated. "So you're, like, really Polish, huh?"

He laughed loudly. "As opposed to fake Polish?"

"As opposed to kind of Polish, the way I'm kind of Irish," I said.

"My parents are from Poland," he said. "If that's what you mean."

"Yeah, that's what I would call 'really' Polish. Do you speak Polish?"

"Yeah. I had to do years and years of Polish school as a kid."

"You speak Polish *and* French?"

"Well, I mean, once you know one language, it's easier to pick up another one," Pawel said. "And French is a breeze compared to Polish."

"Easy A, then, I guess."

"Yeah, pretty much." He ran his fingers through his hair and rubbed the back of his neck.

"Stairs," I said, opening a door to my right that led to a staircase. It was almost empty now, which meant the bell would ring any second, which it did. "Damn."

"You care about being late?" Pawel asked, sounding surprised. He had this lazy, casual way about him that suggested he didn't take boundaries like schedules and school bells all that seriously.

"A little." I cared a lot, actually, but I knew he'd probably think I was a huge tool if I said so. "The likelihood of getting to be in Erin's lab group is slim to none now."

"So you're one of those girls who has to be with her friends, like, every second, huh?" He gave me a curious expression, like he was trying to figure me out.

"No," I insisted. "Erin's just really good at science. Everybody wants to be in her lab group." I was also good at science, so it wasn't like I was going to fail without Erin, but I didn't want to get stuck with a bunch of slackers who would heap all the work on my shoulders.

"Sorry," he said, grinning. "I guess you'll just have to struggle through on your own."

"Thanks for that." I stopped in front of room 307. "This is us."

Pawel opened the door for me. "After you," he said gallantly. I shook my head at him and walked into the classroom, where Mr. Tripp was already going over the syllabus.

"Glad you could join us," Mr. Tripp said sarcastically. "What are your names?"

We told him and Mr. Tripp pointed right in front of him to lab tables one and two, each with one empty seat. Erin was at table number three, on the other side of the room. She gave me a sad face as I trudged to table one and dropped my bag onto the floor. Unfazed, Pawel did the same at table two. He was sitting right behind me again, but this time his back was to me.

Mr. Tripp handed us each a syllabus and then resumed going over it line by line, pacing the room as he read. When he had passed us by, Pawel leaned back and whispered, "This is going to be the best! Class! Ever!"

I laughed softly. "You know it."

"That is the most humorless man I have ever met," Pawel said.

"Just wait until precalculus," I said. "You do have that, right?"

"Yup. Pure unadulterated fun."

7

Pawel was hard not to like, and it didn't escape my notice that I wasn't the only person paying attention to him. We didn't have all our classes together. He wasn't on the AP track for English—"Reading is for readers," he said, only half kidding—and even though he'd tried to get into the film appreciation class when he'd enrolled, it was a popular elective with a waiting list.

"I can't believe you're taking that class," he said miserably as we gathered up our books after physics. "Lucky. This is the part of being a transfer that sucks."

"Is there a part of being a transfer that doesn't suck?"

I asked. We left the classroom and descended the stairs, emerging into a long hallway that connected the two main buildings.

"New friends," he said after a long pause, catching my eye before turning his head toward a large student painting that had been hung on the wall. "Damn, that's ugly."

We stopped and stared at it. It was pretty hideous. At first, it looked like the artist had just painted the whole canvas navy, then dumped globs of different paint on it. The globs were horrible colors, like puke green and salmon and urine yellow. After looking at it for a few seconds, I could see that there was a three-dimensional aspect to it; the artist had taken what looked like pieces of trash (candy wrappers, bottle tops, packs of cigarettes) and glued them onto the canvas, then covered them with the paint. I looked at the little plaque near the bottom right-hand corner of the canvas. It said the name of the artist, and then the name of the piece: *Waste*.

"Wow," Pawel said in mock awe. He shook his head and scoffed: "Art."

I laughed. I didn't have much of an eye for art, either. The creator of *Waste* could've been the next Picasso and I wouldn't have known it. The only art I'd ever really responded to was the work of M. C. Escher, a Dutch graphic artist from the early twentieth century who was famous for his woodcuts and lithographs. Dad loved Escher, and we'd had several prints of his hanging in our house for as long as I could remember. I think I responded to them because they were inspired by mathematics and featured geometrical paradoxes, exploring and showcasing the beauty of the impossible world. Art I didn't get, but math—math I got.

He pulled me backward to look at it from a greater distance. "Does it have wings?"

I squinted. There was a darker part of the canvas that had the vague outline of a person, and the trash seemed to fan out from it to form large wings, like those of an eagle. "Yeah," I said. "I think it does."

"What are you looking at?" The voice belonged to Derek, and it was coming from behind me. I turned slowly, appreciating the paralyzing irony that he would show up when I was less interested in seeing him than I had ever been—and talking to another guy, to boot.

Pawel jerked his thumb toward *Waste.* "This monstrosity," he said, offering his hand for Derek to shake. "Pawel."

"Derek," my ex said. "You new?"

"Yeah."

"Cool." Derek turned to me. Pawel shifted awkwardly; he seemed to sense that he had been dismissed, but wasn't quite willing to leave. "How're you doing, Caro?"

"Fine," I said coolly. It was just like Derek to think that we could be buddies so soon. I could feel my cheeks growing hot from embarrassment. I didn't particularly want to see him at the moment. I wished he would just go away.

"Hey, Pawel, do you mind if Caro and I have a sec?" Derek asked.

I opened my mouth to protest but before I could get a word out, Pawel shrugged and said, "Sure. See you . . . later, Caro."

I gave him a little wave. "See you." When he was out of earshot, I demanded, "What's up, Derek?" The annoyance in my tone was unmistakable, but he didn't seem to get the hint. Typical. It was amazing how differently you saw some people once the fog of flattery and attention had burned away.

"I just wanted to see how you were," he said. "You were pretty upset yesterday."

"I'm fine."

"Really? You seemed pissed."

"I was pissed."

"That was what was confusing," Derek said. "I thought you might be sad or something, but you were just really angry. Not that I wouldn't be angry if the situation was reversed, but still, it seemed like a weird reaction. Seriously. I was worried."

I drew in a deep breath. Derek didn't know when to quit sometimes. I highly doubted he had spent even a millisecond of his precious time worrying about me, but he needed an excuse to bring it all up again. Just because he didn't want to reel me in didn't mean he didn't want me on the hook.

"Forget it," I told him. "Things didn't go as I planned and I've been under a lot of stress and I just . . . lost it. I'll be fine. I am fine."

"Yeah, I noticed." Derek nodded in the direction Pawel took off in.

"Pawel's a cool guy," I said, hoping that my saying so didn't make me sound too defensive. I mean, what did I care what Derek thought?

"Where's he from?" Derek asked.

"Don't know. I only met him this morning," I said. "If you're so curious, why don't you ask him?"

"Maybe I will," he said.

"You do that," I told him. Why did he care so much about Pawel, anyway? Unless he was jealous. Served him right. "Okay, must get to class."

"Yeah, me too. Later."

"Bye."

He walked off. I stared after him. I felt weirdly out of step. Things were changing fast. Derek had been my boyfriend, and now he wasn't. Hannah had been a nun, and now *she* wasn't. I didn't know how to act normally around either of them. I liked things clearly defined; it was how I made sense of the world. People were either this thing or that thing. Gray areas made me nervous; ambiguity was to be avoided at all costs. That was why I liked science and math. Two plus two always equals four, *always,* and you don't have to explain why; that's just the way it is. There are rules, constants. The speed of light is 186,282 miles per second, no matter what. Rules and constants comforted me; even variables had a feeling of stability to them, because they were always part of an equation that you could solve. But what if it was all variables? What if you never knew what was coming next? What if you couldn't predict which things would change and which things would stay the same? What if there was nothing you could really count on, not even yourself?

As soon as I got home that afternoon, I went straight to my room. My phone rang immediately. "Hey, Reb," I said, propping the phone against my ear with my shoulder and rummaging through my bag for my physics book. "What's up?"

"I heard two interesting pieces of gossip," Reb began. "First, you and Derek are friends again. That was quick."

"Who'd you hear that from?" I asked.

"Eesha saw you guys talking in the corridor between periods," Reb said. "But she insisted that it didn't look romantic."

"It wasn't," I told her. "And we're not friends again."

"Good. You need a break from him. I cannot take any pining."

What happened to all the sympathy I'd gotten the day before? As this situation had reminded me, things changed awful quickly in high school. "Um, okay. What's the second piece of gossip?"

"New Boy. Erin told me you're in love."

I sighed. "I'm not in love with Pawel."

"So he has a name," Reb said. Clearly she hadn't been paying attention in French class. "What else?"

"That's it. His name is Pawel Sobczak and he's a transfer."

"From where?"

"No idea."

"Well, whatever, you'll find out tomorrow. What's he like?"

"Very cute," I said, brightening. "Funny. Nice. Smart, but not too smart. Not one of those guys who thinks he's smarter than you and lets you know it."

"*Is* he smarter than you?"

"Probably not."

"Boy, do you have a type," Reb said.

There was a knock at my door. I practically jumped out of my seat; I wasn't used to having someone else home on weekday afternoons and had forgotten that Hannah was probably around somewhere. "Who is it?" I called, just to be sure.

"Hannah."

"Reb, I gotta go," I said. "I'll talk to you tomorrow."

"Pick you up in the morning?" she asked.

"You bet. Seven-forty-five sharp."

"Or I leave without you."

I hung up. "Come in."

Hannah walked into the room and stood at the foot of my bed. She looked gaunt and tired, and her eyes were red, as if she'd been crying. It struck me again how skinny she was. There were circles, dark as bruises, under her eyes, and her clothes, baggy and wrinkled, hung on her body like curtains. Whatever perkiness she'd had that morning had vanished, like she was too tired to fake it anymore that day. The spell had certainly worn off.

"Did you just wake up?" I asked, and she nodded. "What do you need?"

"I don't know," she said. She pulled her hands, with their long, thin pianist's fingers and pale skin stretched over knobby knuckles, up into the sleeves of her T-shirt, rubbing her fists together through the fabric.

"I have homework," I told her.

"Yeah. Okay." She paused in the doorway on her way out. "Do you want to watch a movie or something later?"

"A lot of homework," I non-answered.

"Okay." Hannah ventured a smile. "How was school?"

"Fine." I was already bent over my physics book, running my eyes over the same sentence again and again. I wasn't really planning to start my homework for at least another hour, but I hoped that my looking busy would discourage her from sticking around.

"Anything interesting happen?" she asked.

"Nope."

"I was walking to the laundry room and I overheard you say something about a boy?" she pressed. "Something about being in love?"

"You were eavesdropping?" I snapped. All I needed was for her to go tell my parents I was in love, especially since it wasn't even true.

She closed her eyes and took a deep breath. "I'm sorry. I just thought . . . we had a nice talk yesterday."

"I really have to get started on this science homework," I said. I knew it was mean, but she made me feel uncomfortable, standing there expectantly but not really communicating what she wanted. One friendly conversation didn't make a relationship, and I still didn't know how to navigate ours, whatever it was.

"All right. I guess I'll see you later."

"Later," I said, turning back to the text and my empty notebook. "Can you close the door behind you?"

As soon as I heard it shut, I rolled away from my desk, propped my feet up on the bed, and opened my laptop.

Let's face it: everybody cyberstalks. It's a fact of teenage life in this century, and I'm okay with that. It was like a tacit agreement among us: everybody liked to know other people's business, so we put up profiles and we took the opportunity to spy on each other from the comfort of our own bedrooms.

Pawel Sobczak didn't appear to have gotten that memo.

After diligent searching on several social networking sites, not to mention Google, all I was able to pull up was a water polo record from his old high school, which turned out not to be very far away. No profiles, no website, not even an old email address. Was he from the Dark Ages? I called Reb.

"No profile, huh?" she said, crunching on something. "Interesting."

"Creepy," I said.

"Oh, I don't know about that. Maybe he's just a private person."

"Nobody is private these days," I pointed out.

Reb laughed. "Says the Facebook addict."

I could think of one other person who didn't have a profile—my sister. If that was privacy, well, then I wanted nothing to do with it.

"Who cares if he has a profile?" Reb asked. "I thought you weren't in love with him."

"It's not love," I insisted. "It's just a little harmless curiosity. Besides, you were the one asking all the questions about him," I reminded her defensively.

"Oh, Caro." Reb chuckled. I could see her shaking her head on the other end of the line. "You're never more transparent than when you like a boy."

"Um . . . thanks?" I glanced at the clock on my nightstand. "I've got to go. I have tons of homework."

"See you tomorrow, loser."

8

The first two weeks of school passed largely without incident, at least as far as school was concerned. My favorite parts of every day were the classes I had with Pawel. My friends teased me mercilessly about liking him, but as long as they kept their mouths shut about it when he was in earshot, I didn't care. I liked how he didn't take things too seriously; I liked his well-timed jokes and generous smiles, his seemingly boundless energy, like that of a golden retriever puppy. He sort of looked like one, too, with his shaggy blond hair. The best part was that he seemed to like me back, at least a little. Every time I saw

Derek in the hallway or the lunch line, I thought of Pawel and it didn't matter as much.

When it came to my family, though, it was a whole different story. Hannah was sleeping all day most days, and she practically had to be pried out of her room with a crowbar at dinnertime. That was my mother's job. Every night as I set the table and Dad scooped out portions of whatever we were eating onto four plates (I had to be reminded more than once to grab an extra setting), Mom went upstairs and knocked softly on Hannah's door. Dad and I busied ourselves with our respective tasks, but we were as silent as possible, each straining to hear what came next.

"Hannie?" she would call out when Hannah inevitably didn't answer. "It's time for dinner, sweetheart. Please come down and eat with us."

Then Hannah would say something, probably a version of "I'm not hungry" or "Eat without me," but Mom wasn't having it. Hannah was thin as it was; Mom was not letting her get away with not eating at least one square meal a day. It already killed her that she couldn't be home all the time to make sure that her twenty-seven-year-old daughter fed herself properly. Of course, nobody actually said these things out loud; I had to glean them for myself.

"I know you're not hungry, Hannah, but you've got to eat something or you'll starve," Mom would say next. "We have dinner as a family, that's always been the rule and you know it." This, Hannah would ignore. Finally, Mom would open the door, or if Hannah had locked it, she would threaten to have my dad take it off its hinges, which usually got Hannah's attention.

Once we were all good and settled around the kitchen table, we'd eat as my parents grilled me about my day. Nobody asked what Hannah had done, and she only occasionally ventured a question herself, preferring instead just to sit there, sullen and withdrawn. After Mom and Dad were out of stuff to ask me about school, they would trade work stories while Hannah and I tuned them out. I would eat, and she would push her food around until Mom or Dad looked her way; then she would lift a measly bite to her mouth and chew on it absently, as if deep in thought. All in all, it was weird, and it kept happening, day after day after day.

Sometimes I would try to get a good look at Hannah out of the corner of my eye, to guess what she was thinking as she rearranged her peas, but most of the time I avoided thinking about it. Every once in a while, I would attempt to imagine her the way she was at the convent. I'd done a little research on the Sisters of Grace; I knew her order still wore the habit, long and black, with a headpiece that covered all their hair, but other than mentally dressing her up like a paper doll, I could never quite picture it. I wondered how much she had changed since coming home. I figured they'd probably let her get away with not eating very much—she hadn't gotten that thin by accident—but I highly doubted they had let her sleep till three in the afternoon and sulk around aimlessly, doing nothing and going nowhere.

Every so often, I would get a good look at her and think, *What happened to you?* But I never would've asked. I wasn't even sure I wanted to know the answer.

As soon as I saw the unfamiliar car in the driveway, I knew something was up. My parents both should've been at work. I opened the front door tentatively, as if I might be triggering an explosive.

"Hello?" I called out, cautiously stepping over the threshold. "Anybody home?"

"In here, Caro," my dad shouted, a little too eagerly, from the family room. I dropped my bag onto the bottom stair and went looking for him.

Dad was perched awkwardly on the leather recliner, right across from my old nemesis, Father Bob. The embarrassment of having to go talk to him after lying about Hannah to my classmates flared up like a rash. Was it possible that he was here about that? I wanted to run from the room, and from the looks of it, so did Dad.

"Um . . ." I didn't know what to say. You couldn't just look a priest in the eye and demand to know why he was in your house, sipping tea from the Grumpy mug your mom brought back for you from a conference in Orlando. You also couldn't laugh, even though the image of a priest holding a mug with the crankiest of the Seven Dwarfs on it seemed pretty funny to you.

"You remember Father Bob?" Dad gestured to our guest, as if, by chance, I hadn't noticed him sitting there.

"Uh-huh," I said. I struggled to find my manners. "How are you, Father?"

"Very well, thank you, Caro," he told me. "And how about yourself?"

"Can't complain," I said. I took a stab at it. "Are you here for Hannah?"

"I was," he said. "Your mother asked me to drop by. But I don't think Hannah wants to see me."

"Mom's upstairs with her," Dad informed me. "I should probably go check to make sure everything is all right. Why don't you keep Father Bob company while I go find out what's taking them so long?"

"I don't—" I started to protest, but Dad was already out of his chair and flying past me.

"I'll be back in a minute," he said. "Please, Father, make yourself comfortable."

A veteran of sixteen years of Catholic education, my father found the clergy sort of unnerving up close. He said it was for the same reason he froze up that one time he and his friends snuck backstage after a Stones concert and happened to come face to face with Keith Richards.

Some people, he said, you're only meant to see from a distance; otherwise you start questioning the natural order of things. Really, I think he got into a lot of trouble as a kid and had bad memories of pre–Vatican II corporal punishment.

With pretty much no other option, I reluctantly sank into the chair Dad had vacated. Tongue-tied and anxious, I kneaded my hands in my lap. An irrational part of me was afraid I'd just start blurting inappropriate things. I might not have been the most religious girl around, but even I didn't want to offend a priest.

"So you came to see Hannah?" I asked after a long pause. I knew the answer, of course—I'd asked that question five seconds ago—but we needed to talk about *something*. Or I did. Father Bob looked content to sit there in silence. Hannah was like that, too. Did it come with the job?

"I did," he said. "I know the transition from the religious life can be difficult, and I wanted to see if there was anything she needed."

"Oh," I said. "That's nice of you."

He smiled. I squinted at Father Bob. He wasn't a young man, but he wasn't old, either. He wasn't handsome, but he wasn't ugly. He was just . . . a priest, I guess. He looked normal. I don't know what I was expecting, and it wasn't like I'd never been in a room with Father Bob before. I was starting to understand what my dad meant about people you're not supposed to see up close. I hadn't been to church in a while, but in my head a priest was a guy in a fancy robe pacing the floor in front of the altar, giving a sermon—performing, basically. Sitting this close, in my own family room, was like, I don't know, pulling back the curtain and discovering that the Wizard of Oz was just a man like all other men. It felt like cheating. It felt like finding out how the trick was done.

"Leaving a convent like the Sisters of Grace isn't easy," Father Bob told me. "And Hannah is very young."

"Not that young," I pointed out. "She's almost thirty."

He laughed. "You'll feel differently when you're her age, I think."

"Probably," I said, although I couldn't imagine ever being that old.

"How do you think Hannah's adjusting?" he asked. He gave me a pointed look, and I could tell he was curious about what I thought. I wondered how much my parents had told him about Hannah, whether they'd told him how thin she was and how she slept in twelve-hour stretches. Did he know about all that? And even if he did, was there anything he could do about it?

"It's only been a couple of weeks," I reminded him, sidestepping the question like I had something to hide.

"I know," he said. "Still, I'd like to hear what you think."

"She seems quiet," I said cagily, not sure how much was too much to reveal. "Kind of nervous and sad."

He nodded. "That's to be expected. Permanently separating from a religious order is not unlike getting divorced, or having a close friend or family member pass away. There is grief involved, sometimes profound grief."

I'd never thought of it that way before. Maybe it was naive of me, or plain inconsiderate, but I had kind of thought it would be like dropping out of college—which Hannah had also done.

"Believe me," he said. "It can be very trying, and not only for the ex-religious, but for the people who love them, as well. How are you finding it?"

I shrugged. "Okay. It's weird."

"I can imagine," he said with genuine sympathy. "You and Hannah are far apart in age, I remember."

"Eleven years," I said.

"And she's been away a long time," he said. "Almost a decade. She must seem like something of a stranger to you."

"Totally," I said. "I feel bad about that, but it's like, what are my options? We didn't grow up together. Before she came home, I hadn't seen her at all in three years." Wow, three years. When I said it out loud, it sounded like eons, but the time had gone so fast, years popping like soap bubbles, there one minute and gone the next, that I'd never stopped to consider how strange it was that it hadn't felt long to me, that I hadn't been keeping count.

"There was visitation at the convent, though," he said.

"That place gives me the creeps," I said with a dramatic shudder.

"I'm not such a big fan of it myself," he told me. "It's very . . . austere. I imagine it must be hard to live there, if you're not the sort of person who's suited for that life."

"Are all convents like hers?" I asked.

"Oh, no," he said. "And don't get me wrong, I'm not speaking ill of the Sisters of Grace. They're wonderful women, very spiritual and devout. But the active orders are more in line with my own personal vocation."

"What do you mean, 'active orders'?"

"Active orders are more about community outreach and charitable work," Father Bob explained. "They teach in schools and run shelters and food banks, a whole variety of things, depending on the order. But the Sisters of Grace are a contemplative order. Do you know what that is? Did anyone ever explain that to you?"

"I think maybe you did," I told him. "But I probably wasn't listening." He laughed again. I seemed to amuse him. I didn't know whether to be relieved or offended.

"You were young," he said. "And I was boring, I'm sure."

"I'm not biting," I warned him.

"Fair enough. A contemplative order of nuns is one

that's devoted mostly to constant prayer and adoration," Father Bob said.

"Adoration of what?"

"God," he said, spreading his hands in what I took to be the polite, priestly gesture for *duh*.

"Right," I said. Duh.

"The enclosure—and by that I mean the retreat from worldly life—is meant to preserve the peace necessary for such rigorous contemplation," Father Bob said. "It isn't easy to pray without ceasing when you're constantly being distracted by the outside world."

"So what you're saying is that some nuns go out and help people and try to make the world a better place, and other nuns just lock the door and shut it out so that they can talk to God all day?" I grimaced. "Seems a little unfair to me."

"You have to understand," Father Bob said, "the Sisters of Grace—all contemplative religious, in fact—believe that by making prayer the focus of their entire lives, they *are* making the world a better place. The power of prayer is a documented phenomenon; it can cure the sick. They're not just talking to God, either. They're focusing their entire force of being on improving the lives of people around the globe. It's a pretty tall order."

"I guess," I said, though I wasn't convinced. You couldn't prove prayer had anything to do with making the world a better place, and the idea that it could cure illness seemed like a bunch of voodoo magic to me, something that probably had more to do with the power of suggestion than it did with God.

"It's not easy," Father Bob insisted. "That life is very demanding. It requires an extremely strong and dedicated will, and an almost complete obliteration of the ego. Can you imagine how hard it is to never think of yourself above others ever again?"

"Are you saying Hannah wasn't strong enough?" I asked. I was peeved on Hannah's behalf. She'd wanted to be a Sister of Grace so badly that she'd sacrificed her youth and her family to do it.

"It appears that the contemplative life didn't bring out Hannah's best self," Father Bob said. "It didn't fulfill her in the way it should have if it was her true, lifelong vocation. That's nothing to be ashamed of."

I looked up sharply at Father Bob. This, I realized, was why he had come. He wanted her to know she wasn't a failure for leaving the Sisters of Grace. I started to wish Hannah had been willing to talk to him. She probably needed to hear that.

Dad came back into the room then, looking sheepish. "I'm sorry, Father," he said. Father Bob rose from his seat, and so did I. "She just won't come down."

"I understand," he said. "I can see that Hannah is going through a difficult time. Maybe she needs to sort some things out on her own first. I'm looking forward to meeting her, though, when she's ready."

Dad nodded, although, really, none of us knew what Hannah needed. If leaving the Sisters of Grace was Hannah's great shame, then this was theirs: they didn't know how to fix her.

"My wife would come down, but . . ." Dad spread his palms the way Father Bob had, but it didn't mean the same thing; it meant *Here are all the things I wish I had the words to explain.*

"I understand," Father Bob said sympathetically, offering Dad his hand. Dad shook it gratefully, and Father Bob turned to me.

"It was nice to see you again, Caro," he said. "If you ever need to talk, you know how to find my office, right?"

I nodded. He smiled.

"Good. Thank you for your hospitality, Mr. Mitchell," he said.

"Evan," Dad said. "Please."

"Evan," Father Bob repeated.

When the door closed behind the priest, Dad asked, "What did you two talk about?"

I shrugged. "Nothing important," I said.

I had to fend for myself for dinner, because my parents spent the whole evening after Father Bob left trying to reason with Hannah in hushed tones behind the closed bedroom door. I stood at the bottom of the staircase for a while, until it became obvious I wasn't going to hear anything. I ended up eating a cold turkey sandwich in front of the television, waiting for someone to come downstairs, but no one did. Eventually I put the dishes in the sink and went to my room.

Around midnight, there was a knock at my bedroom door.

"Come in," I called, shutting my textbook and putting down my pen.

Hannah stepped into the room uncertainly. She looked like she'd been through hell. Her face was all red and splotchy, and her hair was pulled up into the severest ponytail I'd ever seen. It stretched her skin tight against her bones. She seemed so exhausted, emotionally and physically, that I was surprised to see her standing. "Mom and Dad are asleep. I thought you might be in bed, but the light was on and I figured . . ."

I rubbed my forehead. "What's up?" I wanted to ask her why she wouldn't see Father Bob; she had to be more used to priests prying into her business than we were. Or maybe that was it. Maybe she didn't want to be reminded of the reasons she had left. I could see her side of it, but I was frustrated, too. She'd hidden away in her room like a child, but she wasn't a child. How long were my parents going to indulge her? Not to mention I felt sort of bad for Father Bob. He'd clearly wanted to do a good thing, to help Hannah in whatever way he could, and she'd refused even to acknowledge it.

"I was wondering if you'd do me a favor," Hannah said. There was a pause, during which I was probably supposed to say, "Sure, anything," but I didn't. Hannah waited, and when I stayed silent, she continued. "If it's not too much trouble, I was wondering if you would take me to get my driver's license."

I raised my eyebrows slowly; I don't know what kind of favor I expected her to ask of me, but that wasn't it. "You don't need me to do that," I said. "Dad can take you, or if he can't, Mom will."

Hannah chewed her lip. "Okay," she said finally, turning to leave.

"Wait." She looked at me expectantly. "Why do you want me to do it?"

Hannah shrugged. "You don't have to."

"Why?"

"Because."

"That's not a reason," I said.

"I don't know. I just think I'd like you to drive me to the DMV."

"The DMV is a hell mouth," I told her.

"I know."

"I spent four hours at the DMV on two separate days just a couple months ago when I got *my* license. It was awful." I'd failed my test the first time. I wasn't proud of it, especially since the Illinois State driver's test was supposedly one of the easiest in the country, but it was the truth. "I don't want to do that again."

"Okay. I just thought I'd ask." Hannah gave me another one of her patented weak, sad smiles and left, closing the door firmly but quietly behind her.

9

"You're taking your sister to the DMV," my mother said, setting a plate with a bagel on it down in front of me.

"No way!" I cried, pushing the bagel away. It smelled like bribery.

"You're going to do it, and you're going to do it with a smile," Mom said, looking at Dad for support. He looked at me and pulled his mouth into a Cheshire-cat grin with his pointer fingers.

"Ugh, you two are the worst," I groaned. "I was just *at* the DMV!"

"I remember," Dad said. "I drove you there. Both

times. To get the license we paid for to drive the car we generously loan to you. Not doing this for Hannah will disqualify you from using the car yourself. Got it?"

He and Mom stared at me. I relented.

"Fine," I said, taking a bite out of my bagel. It might've smelled like bribery, but it tasted like coercion.

☆ ☆ ☆

Pawel surprised me at my locker that morning. "Hey," he said, leaning against the wall. "Did you get all that physics homework done?"

I nodded. "It took me forever, though. Didn't you do it?"

He shrugged. "I considered doing it. I finished a couple of problems. It was really boring."

I laughed and stood up, slinging my bag over my shoulder. "It's homework. It's supposed to be boring. Come on, we're going to be late for class."

"Do you always do your homework?" Pawel asked, matching my speed as we walked through the hallways.

"Usually," I said.

"You're a straight-A student, aren't you?" His voice had a note of amusement in it.

"Pretty much," I said. There were lots of things I didn't like about myself, but the one thing I was never ashamed of was my dedication to school. Both of my parents believed in the value of a good education, and they had passed that belief on to me. On to us, I mean to say. In the flickering nickelodeon of my early-childhood memories was a short clip of me standing in front of the refrigerator while my mom cooked dinner. I was staring at the various tests and papers sixteen-year-old Hannah had brought home with big red As on them.

Your sister is such a good student, Mom said in my memory. *Are you going to be a good student, too?*

Yes, I told her firmly. At five I was already determined to be just as good as Hannah was. *I'm going to get straight As.*

At least, that was how I remembered it.

"Your parents must be proud of you," Pawel teased.

"Sometimes," I told him. "Mostly they're just annoyed with me."

"Why's that?" he asked.

"They think I have a bad attitude," I said. "But I maintain that it's the other way around."

"And you're the youngest?" he guessed.

"How did you know?" Almost everybody who knew I had an older sister had forgotten years earlier, yet he picked up on it immediately, without knowing a thing about me. "Does my bad attitude scream 'spoiled baby' to you?"

"No," he said, smiling. "First of all, I don't think you have a bad attitude. Second of all, you don't act like a youngest child at all. You work hard, you don't coast. You don't have a car of your own."

"Reb has a car, and she's the oldest," I said.

"Who?"

"Reb. My best friend. She's in our French class."

"Oh, right. I'm not saying that all youngest children have their own cars, or that no oldest children have their own cars, but in my experience a younger child is more likely to have one than an older child."

"I could be one of the exceptions," I said.

"You could."

"Or I could be an only child."

"You're not."

"How could you tell?"

"You're just not. Only children might as well be wearing Christmas lights made out of fluorescent bulbs for how easily they stand out at school. You're the youngest. But you're not spoiled. Curious."

"What are you, some sort of aspiring anthropologist?"

"Not really. This is just a game I like to play."

"Okay, so what made you think I was the youngest?"

He scrunched up his face, as if debating whether to say what he was thinking, or trying to think of a better way. "You don't seem desperate for attention, I guess."

"Thanks?" I wasn't sure how to take that, although it sounded like a compliment, or at least a non-insult.

"There's more," he said. He searched my face as if to see if I was interested in hearing it. I gave him an expectant smile and he continued. "You're friendly and outgoing, but you're also really secure in your friendships, so you don't seem to care very much if strangers like you. I could tell when I first talked to you that you weren't putting on a show. You were just being yourself. But it's weird, you know."

"What's weird?" I asked.

"You're, like ..." He searched for the right words. "You're really into school and obviously a total over-achiever, which fits better with oldest children. But you don't seem to be as neurotic about school as an oldest child would be. My oldest sister, Magda, is a bossy know-it-all but you're not like that."

I nodded, smiling.

"You think it's bullshit," Pawel said.

"No, no." I rushed to assure him.

He held up his hands in a gesture of surrender. "Hey, it's okay. It's just a goofy thing I do for fun sometimes, when I meet new people. It makes it easier, you know. It gives me something else to focus on besides how nervous I am."

"I understand," I said. The notion of Pawel's being nervous around anyone was odd. He seemed so sure of himself, so easy to be around. Had he really been nervous around *me*? If he had been, I couldn't tell.

"So how many Mitchells are there?" he asked.

I considered carefully how much to tell him about Hannah. "Two," I finally said. This was the first time in a long time I'd mentioned Hannah to anybody, even obliquely. Part of me felt like it wanted to tell Pawel everything, every single thing I was thinking and feeling about Hannah, even the things I hadn't quite figured out how to express in words; I thought once I started talking about her, it might all just pour out of me like a dam had burst. But there was another part that was afraid I had already said too much. I was used to pretending Hannah didn't exist, and if I told Pawel, I might have to tell everyone else, too, and I wasn't sure I was ready for that. That part of me wanted to lock it all away where nobody could get at it, where I was free to figure out how I felt and what I wanted at my own pace.

"Older sister?" Pawel said, pulling me back.

"How do you *do* that?" Although it was mostly guesswork, I had to admit that Pawel was skilled at this strange little game of his. "You should take this show on the road, maybe get a job at Six Flags guessing people's ages or something."

He laughed. "It's just if you had an older brother, I'm sure I would've heard about him by now. Baby sisters tend to be proud of their older brothers. They mention them more than they think they do, especially to guys."

"Is that so?"

"Yup."

I could feel myself beaming at Pawel. I was getting a kick out of his confidence in his weird talent, how proud he was of what he could figure out about me just by paying attention. It wasn't something I was used to, having someone really take an interest in me. I loved my friends—there was no doubt in my mind that I'd be lost without them and they tried their best—but they had their own lives and their own troubles and they were mostly focused on those. And Derek—forget it. Derek hardly noticed anything I ever did unless it was directly related to him.

"Maybe I have a reason for keeping my hypothetical older brother a secret."

"Like what?"

"Like maybe he's a CIA agent on assignment in Saudi Arabia and any information I might have about his mission or his whereabouts is top secret and likely to get us both killed," I proposed.

"I like the way you think, Caro," he said. "What's your sister like?"

I hesitated. "Older than me," I said. "Much older."

"Oh, that explains some things," he said, rubbing the base of his neck thoughtfully. "How much?"

"Eleven years," I said, determined that it would be the last thing I said about her. "What about you?"

"You tell me."

But I wasn't nearly as good at this game as he was. I feared I hadn't paid attention to the right things about him to make an educated assessment. So I guessed. "You're the middle. And you're the only boy."

"Right and wrong," Pawel said. "I'm the middle, but I have a younger brother and *two* older sisters."

"Lucky you."

"Honestly, it's not that bad," he admitted.

"We're here," I said, stopping in front of the door.

"Where?" he asked, still looking at me.

"French." I opened the door to Madame's classroom and slipped inside. Reb looked up at me, then to Pawel, who had followed me in, then back at me. When she caught my eye, she winked.

☆ ☆ ☆

"What happened this morning with Pawel?" Reb asked. Erin, who had been picking at her tuna salad sandwich, perked up.

"Walk-and-talk," I said. I was glad Pawel and I had different lunch periods. It ensured that I had fifty uninterrupted minutes to talk to my friends about him, which I'd been doing with increasing and alarming frequency since I'd met him.

"How was it?" Erin asked.

"Good." I couldn't believe how much I liked talking to Pawel. I'd loved *being* with Derek, but I couldn't say that our conversations were the most thrilling I'd ever had. But it was my mission to play it cool. You couldn't be too obvious about liking a guy. You didn't want to be one of *those* girls, as Reb and I called them. Erin was one of *those* girls. We loved her, but she was.

"Do you think he likes you back?" Erin pressed.

"Who says I like him?" I don't know whom I thought I was fooling, but my friends weren't going along for the ride. They knew me too well.

"Uh, you did." It was nice of her not to point out how glaringly obvious it was, how I glowed like a lightbulb every time I was near him.

"Lies! I did not."

"You cyberstalked him," Reb reminded me. "Unsuccessfully, of course, but you did try."

"We cyberstalk everybody."

"Yeah, but you got upset when you *couldn't* cyberstalk him," Reb pointed out.

"I wouldn't say I was upset," I said, correcting her. "I was curious. Interested. Intrigued, if you will."

"I won't. You're smitten," Erin insisted. I opened my mouth to protest, but she held up her hand to silence me. "No, I won't hear it. You love him."

"Will you two give it a rest?" I cried. "I don't even *know* him."

"Well, due to his lack of Internet presence, that would require talking to him," Reb observed.

"I do talk to him."

"I meant talking to him about *him*. Not you."

☆ ☆ ☆

I took Reb's advice to heart and decided to find out more about Pawel.

"So," I said to Pawel as we left precalc together late that afternoon. "Where did you go to school before this?"

"Fairview," he said as if it was the least interesting fact in the world. Pawel didn't seem to like talking about himself. I found it sort of strange. You couldn't get most people to shut up about themselves usually.

"Did you like it there?" Fairview was another big high school, just a few towns over. The Sobczak family hadn't moved very far.

He shrugged. "It was okay. Nothing special. Not like this place," he said sarcastically. He gestured widely, looking a little like Maria whirling around on the mountains of Austria in *The Sound of Music*. I laughed.

"This is a great school," I mock-scolded him. "Look at how shiny the lockers are."

"Good point, counselor," he said, shifting his backpack onto one shoulder. "Locker aesthetics are very important."

"So you transferred because your family moved?"

"Mmm-hmm," he murmured absently. I could've asked, "Is my head on fire?" and I probably would've received the same response. I didn't get the feeling he was ignoring me, really. He just seemed bored by his own story.

"Tell me about your family."

"Why?" he asked, looking genuinely baffled.

I could see that home life wasn't a sufficiently

interesting subject, but I was committed to it. "Because you mentioned them earlier and I want to know more."

"Well, okay. I have two sisters and a brother."

"I got that much."

"So you were taking notes," he said.

I tapped my right temple. "Like a sponge."

"That explains the grades. My parents are from Poland, and they immigrated in the late eighties, when my sisters were really young," Pawel told me. "Jake and I were born here."

"So you still have a shot at the presidency," I said.

"Only when Americans find room in their heart for a Catholic candidate that isn't as devastatingly handsome as JFK," Pawel joked.

"You're Catholic?" I asked, surprised.

"Mass every Sunday," he said, rolling his eyes. "My mom's pretty devout."

"Hmm."

"Did I lose your vote?" he asked, more serious for that moment than I'd ever seen him—not that I had very much experience.

"No." I laughed softly. "You were saying about your sisters . . ."

"I was?"

"No, but I'm asking."

"So there's Magda, who's twenty-two, and Monika, who's twenty. They're both at Loyola, but they come home every weekend to do their laundry, so it's like they never left." He sighed. "And then Jake—Jakub, actually, but he's gone by Jake since he started school. He's thirteen."

"Nice big family."

"Really? I don't know. My parents are both one of ten."

"Wow."

"Yeah. We're good breeders." He smiled. "And it's just you and your sister." I didn't miss the shift back to me, although I had to give him credit for subtlety.

"Well . . . I guess."

"You guess?"

"Hannah's eleven years older than me, and she went away for a while when I was eight, so it's not like we were raised together," I told him. There was a sudden buzzing in my head, a sound like white noise, like the flutter of insect wings, and I could feel the fact of Hannah's absence from my life slipping out of my hands as I scrambled to figure out how much I trusted Pawel, and how much I really wanted him to know.

"Where did she go?"

"Oh, college, and then . . . other places," I said. Maybe if I was vague about it, he would back down.

"That's a great story," he teased, waiting for more.

I shrugged. "So anyway. I was basically raised like an only child."

"But you saw her at holidays and stuff, right?" Pawel asked. "I mean, she wasn't totally gone."

"No, not totally . . ." I knew I was bullshitting him, but I still didn't want to talk to anybody about Hannah. It wasn't that I was embarrassed, necessarily, but that I didn't know how to explain her in such a way that I didn't come off as an asshole and she didn't come off as a total freak. And it wasn't the nun thing; there was nothing wrong with being a nun. It was her age when she went in, and the secretiveness with which she made such a life-altering decision, and now the mystery surrounding her return.

"Where does she live now?"

Here we go, I thought. "At home, actually."

"Really? She must be"—he did the calculations in his head—"twenty-seven now, right?"

"Yeah."

"Kind of old to still live at home." I stiffened, but he barreled right on forward, prying me open with an expectant look. I took a second to consider what he must be like with his family. They were close; they must be for him to assume that I would have no problem talking about my sister, that I wouldn't be secretive or closed off about such a straightforward subject.

"Sure. No, of course you're right, but Hannah just got back from—" I thought quickly. "The Peace Corps. She was with the Peace Corps in Africa and now her term of service is over and she's not quite sure what she wants to do next. So she came home for a little while."

And there she was, Caroliar, back again with a vengeance out of some deep dark pit. My old nemesis, after all that time, come to sweep me away on a wave of misdirection and falsehood. Except I wasn't twelve years old anymore, and I should've known better. I should've told the truth.

"The Peace Corps. That's no joke," Pawel said. "Where in Africa was she?"

Goddammit. Why did I have to lie? I knew precisely zero about Africa. "Chad."

"Cool," he said. "Your sister has kind of a kick-ass life, you know that?"

I smiled uncertainly. "She sure does."

"Hi," Hannah called, hearing me come in through the garage. "How was your day?"

"Fine," I said, taking immediate refuge in my room. She was the absolute last person I wanted to see at the moment, after the way I'd completely lied about her earlier to Pawel. I kept hoping the sick, guilty feeling I had in the pit of my stomach would go away, but it stayed put to remind me how once again I'd denied my sister. Worse still, I couldn't even pretend that I was trying to protect her. It was none of Pawel's business where she'd been and why she was back, and really, who was he to pass judgment on how old she was and the fact that she was still living at home? But that wasn't why I'd done it and I couldn't trick myself into thinking that it was.

I shut the door, threw my bag onto the bed, and sat down in front of my computer. Almost instantaneously, an IM from Reb popped up.

> **Rebelieuse:** I saw you went active. How was precalc?

Reb knew precalc was the last class I had with Pawel. It was her subtle way of getting me to spill any juicy details. Unfortunately for her, there really weren't any.

> **SweetCarolina:** Same old. Equations, parabolas, blah blah blah.
> **Rebelieuse:** That's too bad. I thought maybe things might've progressed on the Pavel front.
> **SweetCarolina:** Pawel. With a W.
> **Rebelieuse:** Really? How . . . ethnic.
> **SweetCarolina:** LOL I like it.
> **Rebelieuse:** I'm sure you do.

I was about to send back a cheeky response when there was a knock on my door.

"Come in!" I called before realizing that since neither of my parents was home from work yet, it had to be Hannah.

"Hey," she said, leaning against the doorjamb. She was wearing a pair of dark sweatpants and a thin T-shirt I recognized as my own. I thought about protesting, but I figured it wasn't worth it; I hadn't worn that shirt in ages. Her hair was back in a ponytail again. She seemed never to wear it down.

When I was little, I was jealous of her hair. I used to beg to brush it and braid it. The memory came out of nowhere, and I must've looked strange, because Hannah asked, "Are you okay?"

"Yeah," I said. "What do you want?"

"I was just wondering if we could firm up a date for you to take me to the DMV," she said hesitantly.

"Whenever," I said, turning back to the computer.

"How about tomorrow?"

"I don't know, I think I'm busy."

"Busy doing what?"

"Um, homework?" At least that was something that was, in one way or another, always true.

"Are you sure you can't squeeze me in?" Hannah looked at me blankly. I could tell she was going to press until I broke.

"Fine. Tomorrow."

"Okay." She paused in the doorway, then said, "Thanks," and was gone.

Reb's latest IM flashed on the screen.

Rebelieuse: Mall tomorrow?

I sighed.

SweetCarolina: Can't. Busy.
Rebelieuse: Pawel?
SweetCarolina: No. ☹ Family stuff.
Rebelieuse: Bums.

10

By the time I got home the next afternoon, I'd forgotten about taking Hannah to the DMV. I remembered as I was walking up the driveway and saw the car Mom and Dad had left behind that day specifically so that Hannah could use it for her test.

Hannah was in the living room, a cold, impeccably decorated room we never used, waiting for me in an overstuffed armchair that dwarfed her. She had Dad's keys in hand, and her purse, a new one Mom had bought her when she'd taken her shopping, was sitting on the glass coffee table. It looked light, as if it didn't contain much. She probably wasn't used to carrying one around and didn't have a lot to put in it. It was just a prop to make her look normal.

"Are we going?" she asked when she saw me.

"You sure you want to do this so soon?" I asked.

"What do you mean?" She sighed. "If I don't drive, I can't get a job or go back to school."

"Is that the plan?" It shouldn't have surprised me that nobody was cluing me in on the Hannah Reacclimation Strategy, since I'd shown less than zero interest, but I felt weirdly out of the loop. It made sense for Hannah to go back to school, but I couldn't imagine her with a job that didn't require a four a.m. Mass. Then again, I couldn't really imagine her as a nun, either. I couldn't imagine her as anything other than what she was, which, at the moment, was a nonentity hovering on the outskirts of actual life.

"Yes," she said shortly.

"Are you going to go back to Loyola?" I asked. She'd only gone there a year. Maybe she wanted to try something new.

"Mom wants me to." It was strange to hear Hannah call my mother Mom. Even I knew how stupid that was, but it didn't stop me from feeling it. "In the spring, I think."

"Is that really what you want to do?" She obviously wasn't over the moon about it. The way she was talking made it sound like a death sentence, not a life plan.

Hannah shrugged. "What choice do I have? What can I possibly do without a college education?"

I shook my head. "I don't know."

"Besides," she said, taking in a deep breath, "I was always good at school."

"So what are you going to do until then?" I asked.

She rubbed the knuckles of her left hand with the palm of her right. "I don't know. Get a job?" She sounded incredibly unsure. It was strange: *I* was the teenager. *I* was the one who Mom and Dad should've been pressuring to go to college, get a job, get a driver's license, pick a plan, pick a path, pick a life. And yet here Hannah was, more than a decade older than me and she was the one without any direction or vision for her future.

"Are you qualified for any jobs?"

"Are you ready to go?" Hannah asked abruptly.

"Sure," I said, holding my hand out for the keys.

We rode to the DMV in silence, got out in silence, entered the building in silence. There was a line, of course, an eternal line full of weary-looking women and bland, depressing, aging, balding men. The DMV was always like that. Even Hannah remembered.

"I hate the DMV," she groaned. She fidgeted with her paperwork, folding the forms in half and then doing it again in the other direction, over and over again until the crease became a hinge and the top half wouldn't even stay upright. We sat next to each other on the blue plastic chairs surrounding the fortress of bored, listless employees, whose tendency never to look up for any reason—not even to greet a customer, or in surprised reaction to the overturning of a couple of chairs by a swarthy eight-year-old throwing a tantrum—made them seem identical, rows of cogs in a limping machine.

"Everyone hates the DMV," I said, examining my cuticles.

Hannah stared ahead, rigid and quiet. Something was simmering in there, and it had to be more than nerves. But whatever it was—fear, anger, depression, uncertainty— she kept it close and said nothing, like she'd trained herself not to let it show. Maybe she had. I doubted Mother Regina smiled on emotional displays. I'd met her once, Mother Regina, when I was ten. I remembered it because *she* was what I thought a nun should look like, but perhaps that was just because she was older and more self-possessed. I was on my best behavior beneath her gaze; it felt as though she could see everything, even what was hiding deep down inside me.

I glanced at Hannah quickly, then averted my eyes before she noticed.

After forty-five seemingly interminable minutes, they called Hannah's name and she went up to the counter, handing her forms to a woman who looked as though she hadn't slept in weeks. The woman stamped the forms and directed her to an evaluator waiting with a clipboard, and they disappeared outside with the keys to the car.

I slumped down in the chair, wishing I'd brought a book with me, or at least my cell phone. Hannah had been in such a rush that all I had was my wallet. I went through it absently, crumpling up receipts and tossing them into a pile in Hannah's vacant chair.

"Hey, Caro!"

I froze. I recognized the voice as Pawel's, and he was the last person I wanted to see with Hannah lurking around. I felt a deep flush crawl up my face when I thought of the lies I'd told him about my sister, how quickly they could be discovered, and how helpless I was to stop it if Hannah came back from her test soon. I hoped he couldn't see it on my face.

"Caro?" He was standing next to me now.

I looked up at him. He was smiling. "Hi," I said. "What are you doing here?"

"Getting my driver's license," he said.

"You don't drive?" I asked.

"I do now," he said, waving his newly minted license in my direction. "All I need is a car."

I laughed. "You and me both."

"What are you here for?" he asked, sitting down and turning so that he was facing me.

"Getting my license." *Said the liar,* I thought. Why was I doing this? I had my driver's license, and anyway he was going to figure out very quickly that I wasn't telling the truth. Why couldn't I just be honest about Hannah, even in the smallest of ways?

"You don't *drive*?" he teased.

"Well . . ."

"What are you waiting for? Your test?"

"Sort of," I mumbled. Eventually Hannah was going to walk through the door and ruin the weak story I'd managed to cobble together. I had no choice but to tell him the truth.

"Actually," I said, "it's my sister who's getting her license."

He looked momentarily taken aback, possibly calculating the complex psychological mathematics that would compel me to tell him *I* was getting my license even though it was my sister who was. "Oh, yeah. What's her name again?" he asked, his face rearranging itself into an expression of mild interest.

"Hannah," I said. "And I don't think I ever told you her name."

"Well," he said, grinning. "My mistake. Wait, I thought she was your much older sister. She's just now getting her license?"

"She had one a long time ago, but it expired," I said. "The Peace Corps." It was the social equivalent of a faceplant; there was no way I was getting out of this now.

"Oh, yeah." He was trying to figure me out. It didn't

entirely make sense, what I was saying, but I banked on his being too polite to contradict me.

He settled back in his chair. "Well, I'll wait with you. I don't really have anywhere to be, and to be honest you look bored to death."

"That's okay. You really don't have to," I said, glancing at the door.

"It's no problem," he said, putting his hands behind his head. "Why are you being so weird?"

I shrugged and sat back in my chair in an attempt at nonchalance, although I don't think he bought it. "I'm not."

"Do I make you nervous?" he asked, lifting his eyebrows suggestively.

"No." I laughed. Of course he did.

"Good," he said, sitting up. "So . . ."

I waited for him to follow up on that, and when he didn't, I gave him a suspicious look. "Was there something you wanted to say?" I asked sweetly.

"That guy a while back . . . ," he said, looking away.

"What guy?" I asked, genuinely perplexed.

"The guy—the guy in the hallway," Pawel said. He wouldn't quite look me in the eye, and I caught a slight blush in his cheeks.

I shook my head. "I don't know who . . ."

"You know, we were talking about how ugly the painting was, and then that guy came up and wanted to talk to you . . . *alone* . . . ," Pawel said expectantly, waiting for me to catch on and fill in the blanks.

"Right! Yeah, Derek. I forgot about that." I really had forgotten; I was too busy worrying about what I had told Pawel about Hannah.

He chuckled. "I thought he might have been your boyfriend."

"Oh, no," I said. He smiled at me in . . . was that *relief*? My skin tingled. "Not anymore, anyway."

His smile faded a little. "He's your ex-boyfriend?"

"As of the end of the summer," I said.

"And you're . . . over him?"

I didn't want to take too long to answer the question; I knew how he would interpret a pregnant pause. So I blurted out, "Yes. I mean, no. I mean, I don't know, maybe. Probably."

"So . . . no?" Pawel's face was hard to read. I couldn't tell if he was put out by the idea that I might still want Derek, or if he was just gathering information.

"It's hard to say," I told him. "I haven't really talked to Derek since we broke up, except that one time. And it hasn't been that long, so I'm, you know, working on it."

"Working on getting over him?"

"Yeah. Working on getting over whatever it is I need to get over."

"Which is what?"

I sighed. This conversation was the definition of

awkward. It was a relief, though, to talk to him about something I didn't have to lie about. "Not really Derek himself, necessarily, but, like, Derek and me," I said. "You know, *us*."

"Ah." Pawel nodded. "Gotcha." The answer didn't appear to have made him very happy. I should've just said, "Yes, I'm over him." It was close enough to the truth.

"Do you?" I asked, scrutinizing his expression and coming up with nothing.

"Sure. Girls like the couple thing," Pawel said. "It's easier to get over a person than to get over being in a couple with that person for you guys."

"Okay." I scoffed. "*First* of all, 'girls,' plural, don't 'like' anything. Some *people* like being in a couple. Boys and girls. Not all girls are the same, and not all boys are the opposite of what you assume all girls are."

Pawel held up his hands in surrender. "Hey! I'm not trying to be sexist. I like being in a couple."

"You do?" I asked tentatively, trying not to seem too invested in the answer.

"Sometimes," Pawel said thoughtfully. "If it's the right girl."

"When was the last time you *were* in a couple?"

"Four months ago," Pawel said. "Tori. *Not* the right girl, by the way." But he was still smiling, so it couldn't have been that bad.

"Why did you guys break up?"

"Well, I found out I was moving," Pawel told me. "She didn't want to do the long-distance thing."

"Long-distance?" I repeated, scrutinizing him through squinted eyes. "You moved, what? Twenty minutes away by car?"

He nodded. "She thought it would be too hard to stay together if we were at different schools. Her exact words were 'I might meet someone new, you might meet someone new . . . why put ourselves through all that?'"

"Sounds like an excuse," I said gently.

"It was. But I get it. It wasn't like we were soul mates or whatever." He gave a dismissive wave of the hand.

I looked straight ahead, afraid of meeting his eyes. "You believe in soul mates?"

He seemed grateful for the slight topic shift, giving me a wry smile and saying, "I haven't entirely ruled it out. What about you?"

"I object."

"To what?"

"The idea of soul mates."

"You don't believe in soul mates?" He seemed surprised.

"I don't just not believe, I *object*," I said forcefully.

"Why?" He shook his head in disbelief. "You sound so offended."

"I am offended! The very idea of soul mates is offensive."

He settled back in his chair and folded his arms across his chest. "This should be good."

"The concept of one true soul mate is tied up in the idea of predestination," I said. It was like he'd pressed a trigger; I wanted to just shut my mouth already, but I couldn't. "The idea that basically your life is completely mapped out, from birth to death, and there is no possibility for deviation. Choice doesn't matter. I know some people find the idea of soul mates romantic, or comforting, but to me believing in soul mates means absolving yourself of any responsibility for your own happiness. If a relationship doesn't work out—whoops! It wasn't meant to be. *Fuck* meant to be." It was a speech I'd given before.

"Wow." He lifted his eyebrows.

"Yeah." I was so embarrassed. That wasn't a speech I usually gave to guys I liked because it made me sound sort of crazy, but with everything I had on my mind lately, it was hard not to get worked up about questions of fate.

"Okay then. There's no such thing as soul mates. Roger that." He gave me a little salute, but it didn't look like my outburst had bothered him, which was a relief.

"I'm not saying there's no such thing. I'm saying that if there is such a thing, I'll be really pissed off." My moral outrage could erupt like a solar flare, but I always found myself trying to backpedal, to downplay my own position so that I wouldn't seem hysterical. I often wished

I could be more confident in my opinions if they were going to pour out of me like that.

"I'll let the big guy upstairs know that the next time I go to confession," he joked.

I smiled. "You really think God is listening?"

Pawel shrugged. "I don't know. I like to think so."

"Do you think he ever talks back?" I was genuinely interested in his answer. I'd never really thought much about God, but ever since Hannah's return and Father Bob's visit, the idea of him—or her, or whatever—had burrowed into my brain, leaving a little groove of interest behind.

Pawel shook his head. "No. But maybe that's because *I'm* the one who's not listening."

"Pawel?" I asked suddenly. "Do you know what a vocation is?"

"A vacation? What, like a cruise?"

"No," I said, laughing. "*Vo*cation."

He laughed along with me. He'd heard me right the first time. "Yes, I do. It's a calling from God to do his work. Like, become a priest or a nun." I tried not to flinch at the word "nun." "Why?"

The door at the back of the DMV swung open and I thought I glimpsed Hannah right outside, talking to her evaluator. I stood abruptly and shook my head. "No reason," I said. "My sister's done, I'll see you at school."

He stood, too, shifting awkwardly in my path like he didn't know what to do with his body. I dodged past him, turned around, and gave him a little wave. He waved back and smiled. I thought for a second that maybe I should've introduced them, Hannah and Pawel, that it was rude that I hadn't, but it just seemed like asking for trouble.

"You done?" I asked Hannah, strolling up to her. She didn't look happy.

"Yes," she said, stiff as always. "Let's go."

We walked quickly to the door and out into the bright sunlight. I shielded my eyes and went for the passenger-side door, until I realized that Hannah was doing the same thing.

"You can drive," I said. "Take that fancy new license for a spin."

"I didn't get a license," Hannah said, opening the passenger door with the keys and then dropping them into my hand.

"Wait, what?" She slid into the seat and shut the door without responding. I groaned. If she'd failed the test, it meant we had to come back in two weeks. Just my luck.

"Didn't you pass the test?" I asked once we were both buckled in.

"No." She wouldn't meet my eyes. "Can we go home, please?"

"Yeah." I started the car and pulled out of the parking spot. "I wouldn't worry too much. You can retake the test."

"I know."

"I failed the first time, and look at me now!" She looked so miserable I couldn't help making a little attempt to cheer her up.

"I'm going to retake the test."

"So what's the problem?"

"Nothing." She stared into her lap.

"Seriously, what is your deal? People fail that test all the time."

"I know that," she said sharply. But being Hannah, she was immediately contrite. "I'm sorry. I guess I'm just a little upset."

"Hannah, it's not the end of the world," I said.

"I didn't fail it the first time I took it," she said quietly.

"That was a long time ago, and you'd probably just finished driver's ed," I said. "Maybe you should've practiced more before coming here."

"I've never failed a test before," Hannah said, gazing out the window. It was almost as if she wasn't talking to me when she said it.

"Yeah, well, first time for everything." I turned onto our street.

"Who was that boy you were talking to?" Hannah asked, abruptly shifting topics. I swerved a little on the road. "Was that Derek?"

"No, it wasn't," I said. "He's just a friend from school."

"A good friend?"

"A new friend," I said.

"I thought all your friends were girls," she said, squinting at the windshield.

"We're not all nuns," I snapped.

Hannah sighed. "I know you're angry at me, but I'm having a hard time figuring out why."

"Oh yeah?"

"We're sisters," Hannah said. "You can't stay mad at me forever."

"Is that a challenge?"

"No!" Hannah put her hands over her face. I thought she might cry, but when she removed them a few seconds later, there were no tears. Instead, there was a look of determination I'd never seen before. "I would appreciate it if we could talk about this like adults."

"I don't have anything to say." I pulled into the driveway and put the car in park.

"It seems like you have plenty to say, Caro," Hannah said, unbuckling her seat belt. "You just prefer to be passive-aggressive. Do you really think being rude to me will make me go away?"

"No," I said, getting out of the car. She did the same, staring at me over the white-hot roof. After a moment of silence she shook her head at me and walked off toward the house.

11

"I have a project for you," my mother announced over breakfast that Saturday.

"What is it?" I demanded, putting my fork down and staring at her. My father shook his head but made no attempt to jump in, and Hannah wasn't even at the table; she was upstairs, apparently suffering from a nasty cold. She'd been up there since the morning before, and I hadn't seen her at all.

Mom raised her eyebrows at me. "Excuse me? What is *your* problem?"

"You always have a 'project' for me, Mom," I said. "All

week long it's school, homework, bed, repeat. The weekends are for *relaxing*. I want to sleep in and watch TV and hang out with my friends. Is that too much to ask?"

"I'm sorry that the everyday tasks of taking care of the house have fallen on your overburdened shoulders, Caro," Mom said, sarcasm dripping off her tongue. "But we all have to chip in."

"I don't understand why you don't just hire a cleaning lady," I said.

"I don't need a cleaning lady," she said, turning back to her eggs on toast. "I have children."

"Exactly," I said. "There's more than one of us now. Shouldn't Hannah have to do stuff, too? She's home all day, every day. She doesn't even have a part-time job or take classes."

"She's working on it," Dad chimed in. "Now that she has her license, she can find a place to work until she can reenroll at Loyola." He said it like it was a done deal, but from the way Hannah had been talking about it the other day, I could tell it was their plan, not hers. Had they even asked her what *she* wanted? If I was her, I would've resented the interference, but Hannah didn't put up a fight about much. Maybe she just didn't have it in her.

"When did Hannah get her license?" I asked, surprised.

"Didn't you take her on Thursday?" Dad asked.

"Yes, and she failed the test," I told him. Mom and

Dad were both staring at me now, looking completely baffled. "Didn't she tell you that?"

"No," Dad said slowly.

"You mean she *lied*?" A wicked smile crept over my face; I couldn't help it. It was so out of character for sweet, saintly Hannah to lie to my parents. I was torn between being impressed and finding it a little pathetic.

"I'm sure she didn't *lie*." Mom jumped in, always quick to defend her baby. "She just neglected to give Dad the details."

"I asked to see the license," Dad said. He sounded like someone had just let the air out of him. They wanted badly to believe in Hannah, and she made it pretty easy for them. It must've been a real disappointment to find out she was human. "She told me it was upstairs and she'd show it to me later."

"Why didn't *you* tell us she failed the test?" Mom asked me.

"Oh, no, you are not pinning this one on me." I shook my head. "I'm not Hannah's accomplice. I did what you told me to, I took her to the DMV. I'm not responsible for anything else."

"God forbid," Mom muttered.

"If it makes you feel any better, she probably only lied because she didn't want to disappoint you," I said. "You know how she puts so much pressure on herself to be perfect." Mom and Dad nodded, and we dropped the subject.

Well, not entirely.

"Hannah did say that she saw you talking to a boy from school at the DMV," Dad said slyly, not looking up at me, like it was no big deal, like he was barely interested. My parents were so nosy, and so bad at espionage it was kind of sad.

"Are you going to tell us who it was?" Mom gazed at me in interest.

"Who are you, the conversation police? It was just a new boy from school." I was being pouty, which even I found unpleasant, but I couldn't help it. Their curiosity was annoying, their insistence that I bond with Hannah infuriating. I just wasn't in the mood for Happy Family Time.

"What's the boy's name?" Dad asked, cutting to the center of the issue, the way he always did when arguing with me became boring.

"Pawel," I said. "We have a bunch of classes together, and he was getting his license, too. Only he passed the test," I added meanly.

"That's an interesting name," Mom commented.

"It's Polish," I said.

"So he's Catholic." My mom smiled to herself. She loved to do that, act as though I was going to marry every boy I ever spoke to. I think mostly she did it to annoy me, but there was a bit of girlish hope in it. "That's good news."

"Odds are I'm not going to marry a Catholic, Mom,"

I warned her. I didn't get what her hang-up was. We barely even attended Mass now that I didn't go to St. Robert's anymore. What did it matter if I married a Catholic? "You should just come to terms with that now."

"Whatever," she said, dismissing the comment with a wave of her hand. Mom had a streak of if-we-don't-talk-about-it-then-it-doesn't-exist in her. "Is he cute?"

"Hannah said he was," Dad said. He had a goofy, *let's get Caro* smile on his face. They just loved this game. "She said he was boy-next-door handsome. Not very tall, but tall enough for Caro."

"Dad, she spent the last eight years living exclusively with women, most of whom were around before ancient man invented *language,*" I said. "She probably thinks the mailman is hot."

"He does have a certain je ne sais quoi," Dad said, turning to Mom with a conspiratorial wink. "What? You don't think so?"

"You think you're so funny," I said, wrinkling my nose at him.

"If you're honest with yourself, so do you."

Leave it to Mom to get us back on track. "Do you think he's cute?" she asked.

"Who? The mailman? Not my type."

"You know what I meant," she said, laughing. In that moment it felt totally normal—nice, even—to be sharing something with my parents. It wouldn't last—it never did for long—but it made me remember how much I actually liked Happy Family Time.

My mother's "project" for me was to clean out my bedroom closet. I complained about it for a while, which got me nowhere, then avoided the chore for a bit longer, until Mom threatened to stand in the doorway and watch until I was completely finished. My closet was a total disaster, and I didn't relish having to sort through several years' worth of old clothes, school notebooks, and the other flotsam and jetsam that had built up over the years.

The job was dismal until I found where Mom had put Hannah's things after the great purge. Lots of that stuff got packed up and shoved into various nooks and crannies in the garage, and I unexpectedly unearthed it when I was looking for a place to put my own boxes.

Hannah's possessions were way more interesting to me than anything I'd ever owned. It was like looking at relics from somebody's past life. First of all, Hannah was spot-on when she said she'd never failed a test; there was an entire Rubbermaid container full of old homework assignments, pop quizzes, exams, and essays, all with bright red As and sometimes happy faces. There was a whole other box filled with swimming awards, medals and trophies, won in the club team she'd competed on in junior high and her first year of high school.

It was funny to imagine Hannah as part of a team. It made sense that she'd chosen an individual sport, but I knew swimmers: those girls were tight. Reb was one. Maybe she'd never had any friends on the team; maybe that was why she'd quit. Most of the hardware had been awarded for participation or personal bests; she was good, but not a star, especially after she got to high school, which was another possible reason. From the looks of it, Hannah never wanted to be less than perfect at anything. My English teacher would call that her tragic flaw.

Without really understanding why, I felt compelled to go through Hannah's boxes. I was sure she wouldn't want me to; maybe that was part of the allure: the idea that if she found out, she would be angry. But I was curious, even if I would never tell anyone that I wanted to know my sister better.

All we had ever wanted was an explanation. When Hannah left, she said that God was calling to her, that she felt it deep in the recesses of her heart, but it never seemed like enough. My mother sobbed on Hannah's last day at home. I'd never seen my mother cry, never in my whole life. But she cried that day. It was as if Hannah was going to her execution.

There were other things in the cabinet where Hannah's boxes were stored, including a few old photo albums. I opened the nearest one and started flipping through it, looking for pictures of myself. There was a whole series of photos I didn't remember having seen before, images of my parents and me at the Grand Canyon. I couldn't have been older than three, but I knew it was me, because I was wearing the same outfit as I was in one of the framed pictures Mom had on the mantel in the family room, so Hannah must've taken it. I didn't think we'd ever gone to the Grand Canyon, though.

Mom burst through the door and grabbed a bottle of sparkling water out of the mini-fridge we kept in the garage.

"How's it going with your closet, Caro?" she asked, narrowing her eyes at me as if she already knew the answer.

"Hey, Mom, when did we go to the Grand Canyon?" I asked her.

She looked confused for a second. "I don't think we've ever taken you there. Dad and I and Hannah went once, when she was little."

"But look at this picture," I said, handing it to her. I pointed to myself. "That's me. That's my dress."

She shook her head, handing the picture back. The bottle made a soft *psst* noise as she cracked it open. "That's Hannah, sweetheart," she said. "It was her dress first; we kept all her clothes in case we had another girl, and wouldn't you know it?"

"Mom, that's me," I insisted. "I've seen pictures of myself at this age before, it looks exactly like me."

"I know," she said, patting my head gently. "Keep working; I expect you to be finished by dinner." She walked into the house, and I replaced the photo album in the cabinet, unsettled by it. I'd never liked being reminded that my family had once existed quite happily without me in it.

I was about to put Hannah's boxes where I'd found them—after all, it wasn't *my* responsibility to organize *Hannah's* things—when I spied a large square shoe box shoved into the back of the cabinet on its side. It was old and battered, not like the labeled Rubbermaid containers the rest of the stuff was stored in, and my interest was piqued. I tugged on it hard and fell back a little on my heels as it came free and landed in my lap.

The box was soft and worn, as if it had been used over and over again for years, and fastened shut with two oversized rubber bands, which broke when I tried to remove them. The top of the box had been elaborately doodled on with Magic Markers; it was mostly just swirls and curlicues, but in one corner there was a beach flanked by two palm trees, with a sun shining brightly above, and in another, in Hannah's perfect but still somehow childlike penmanship, this quotation: *You don't have a soul. You are a soul. You have a body. —C. S. Lewis.*

I lifted the top of the box and set it down gingerly on an old coffee table that had escaped being sent off to Goodwill during Mom's last flurry of redecorating. It was like some kind of time capsule, what Mom called a keepsake box. I had one, too, a plastic container filled with pictures of me and my friends at various points in my life, old assignments from elementary school that Mom deemed "too cute" to throw out, bad kindergarten art projects, and some random postcards I'd accumulated over the years.

For a long time—it seemed like eons—I just sat there, staring but not touching. I'd poked around through Hannah's other stuff, but there was something about this box, a weird feeling I got while holding it, that told me looking through it would be a violation, like walking through her dreams. But eventually my curiosity won out; I had to see what Hannah thought was worth keeping.

The box was mostly a jumble of old Christmas and birthday cards, most of them from our grandparents or other relatives, aside from one jarring handmade card from me. It was on a piece of white printer paper, folded in half, with a red-and-blue scribble on the front and a green-and-yellow scribble on the inside, underneath which my mother had neatly printed *Happy thirteenth birthday, Hannah. Love, Caro.* There were also a headband with fake pink roses and ribbons glued onto it from when Hannah was a flower girl in someone's wedding; three rosaries, two plastic ones in blue and pink and a nicer one with wooden beads; a handful of small buttons with smiley faces on them; a Christmas ornament shaped like a teapot; a Russian nesting doll the size of my thumb; a well-loved pink elephant eraser; three blue ribbons, all with the word *EXCELLENT!* printed on them, which were either too special to go in the box with the rest of the awards or not special enough; a tiny blue origami wishing star; a key chain from Miami, Florida; and a jumble of small notebooks, postcards, and loose sheets of paper taken from what looked like several different notepads and stationery sets.

Okay. That was far enough. I'd seen what sort of things Hannah wanted to keep forever, and as such things normally were, they were entirely sentimental. It was time to put them all back in the box nicely and start working on my closet before Mom caught me avoiding the task and had some kind of stress-induced aneurism.

Except: the papers. More specifically, the notebooks. Like, for example, the top one with the pink plastic cover on which someone had written *HANNAH* with a gold paint pen, embellishing the tips of each letter with little dots. Otherwise it looked like a regular academic notebook, but then why wasn't it in the box with all Hannah's old school papers? Was it a diary? A dream journal? Or was it where Hannah kept all her old games of M-A-S-H (not that she seemed the type to play M-A-S-H)? I flipped it open before I could stop myself; the first few pages were blank, but then I found something. A letter. The strangest letter I had ever seen. It was written in a loopy, girlish script.

Dear St. Catherine,

This morning I went to Mass by myself. Mom and Dad slept in, and Caro's too young to go without them. So I got a ride with the Dyers from next door. I was afraid they would expect me to sit with them in church, so I pointed to a couple of girls from school sitting in a pew by themselves—they're sisters, and their parents were in the vestibule talking to Father Greg, who had stuck around from the Mass before, which he had celebrated (I memorized the schedule)— and told Mrs. Dyer that they were my friends and I was going to sit with them. When I was sure the Dyers were settled in one of the front pews, I went to the back corner of the church, the last row, where the stained glass makes a puddle of multicolored light on the floor. I like to be alone at Mass. It helps me drown out everything else and remain attentive to the voice of God.

I closed the book and scrunched up my face. The book confused me. *Was* it a diary? It read like one, except all she wrote about was Mass. And it was addressed to St. Catherine. When had she even written it? From the handwriting I would have said maybe middle school. Hannah and I had both attended St. Robert's School, and we as a family belonged to St. Robert's parish—not St. Catherine's.

The first entry ended on the observation about Mass.

I turned the page to the next one, hoping to find something a little juicier. It began the same way.

Dear St. Catherine,

Amanda Brenner told another lie about me today. She told everyone in homeroom that I'm retarded, because I spend so much time with Sister Ruth in the special-needs classroom. She asked me in front of everyone if I was born stupid, or if I had knocked my brains out when I fainted in assembly last year. I tried to explain that I like to help Sister Ruth prepare for her classes, because she's old and her arthritis hurts her, but everyone just laughed at me. Just because I'm quiet doesn't mean I'm not smart. But even Ms. Turner treated me like I was dumb until I got a 100 on our first history test, and to make up for it she always says nice things about me to the class when I do well. It sounds like she's babying me. Amanda Brenner makes fun of me for that, too.

I could just picture Hannah at twelve, all prepubescent gangly limbs and yellow hair pulled back tightly in a ponytail, sitting alone and silent in a classroom while the mean girls took swings at her. My heart swelled with tenderness and empathy for that young version of my sister as I remembered my own uncomfortable middle school years.

I went through the whole notebook, looking for more letters, but there weren't any; the rest of it was full of math problems, what looked like scrap paper where she'd worked out her answers, meticulous nonetheless. But I had a strong feeling that wasn't the last letter, although I couldn't imagine why she would've written them. Keeping a diary was one thing, but correspondence with a saint? That was considerably weirder, though it did seem like something Hannah might do.

I sifted slowly through some of the other papers. There were several of those little Valentine's Day cards your parents made you write out to everybody, a bookmark with sleeping cats on it and a bead shaped like a ball of yarn fastened to the end of a tassel, old Metra tickets from trips into the city, American Red Cross first aid and CPR certification cards, assorted movie tickets, and two pages torn from a "Psalm a Day" desk calendar. On the back of May 17, 1997, Psalm 4, there was another letter:

Dear St. Catherine,

Today I told Sister Ruth that I was thinking about becoming a nun. I thought she would be happy, but she got very quiet and said, "Why?" What I wanted to say was, "Why not?" but you don't talk to a nun like that. Instead, I said, "Because I think it would be nice to live in a place where God was always present, and also I think I would probably make some friends." Sister Ruth was quiet again for a few seconds, then she said, "That's a very nice thought, Hannah, but you're too young yet to make a decision like that. Maybe when you're older, you'll find that you have a vocation. Right now, though, you should concentrate on being a little girl."

I didn't want her to think I was talking back, so I just nodded and finished arranging the books on the shelf before going to homeroom. If I could have said something, though, I would have said, "I don't want to be a little girl anymore."

"Caro?" Mom poked her head in. "How's it going out here?"

"Fine," I said, stuffing everything back into the shoe box and shoving it under the coffee table. I gestured to the rest of the containers. "These are Hannah's, what do you want me to do with them?"

"They can stay in the garage," Mom said. "Hannah will go through them later." Somehow, I doubted that.

"Okay." She smiled at me, and I smiled back.

"Only two more hours till dinner," she warned, shutting the door behind her.

As soon as she was gone, I tucked the shoe box under my arm and rushed to my room, where I hid it under the bed and went back to the task at hand. I wanted to read more, but there would be time later. Reb was sure to have something fun planned for that night, and I didn't want to miss out because I was still stuck cleaning my closet.

☆ ☆ ☆

Reb did indeed call me after dinner and invite me over to her house. She had asked Erin, too, as well as some other people. Her mom was out of town until Sunday night, visiting a sick relative over the border in Indiana, so she had the place to herself and wanted to take advantage of it. I got permission to go to Reb's, but not to take the car, so Erin picked me up.

"Did Reb tell you she invited Polish Boy?" Erin asked as I buckled my seat belt.

"She did?"

"Reb doesn't . . . like him, does she?" Erin asked carefully.

"No, I don't think so," I said, although I wasn't entirely sure. It wasn't like Reb to creep all over someone else's guy, though—but it *was* like Erin to stir drama up for no reason. "She knows—"

"That *you* like him?" Erin waggled her eyebrows.

I smiled. "Something like that, yeah."

"You've never hung out outside school, though," Erin said. "This could be weird."

"Actually, we hung out after school on Thursday." Okay, so it wasn't the *truth* truth. But it was true enough. I seemed to be making that distinction a lot lately.

"Really? Where?" Erin sounded incredulous.

"The DMV," I admitted. "He was getting his license. He's official to drive in the state of Illinois."

"What were you doing at the DMV? You already have your license," she pointed out.

"Yeah, but the picture was lousy," I said. "I went in there to retake it and there he was. We talked for about twenty minutes."

"Can you do that? Just retake your picture?"

"Definitely," I lied. You couldn't do that. I think you'd be laughed out of the DMV if you even tried.

"Hmm." Erin shrugged, but she seemed to take me at my word. "I didn't think your picture was that bad."

"That bad"? I thought it was great. I got dressed up and did my hair especially for the occasion; preparing for the DMV that day took hours. I wished Pawel could've seen me *then*. But I couldn't say that, so I just grimaced. "It was awful."

"Anyway, so you guys hung out at the DMV. Romantic," Erin teased.

I stared out the window. "Indeed."

"What did you talk about?"

"Nothing. Some family stuff. His ex-girlfriend."

"Okay, now that is interesting," Erin said, taking the next turn too sharply in her excitement. "Did he talk about her like he's so in love with her he can't shut up about it, or was he like, 'Yeah, I used to date this one girl but she means nothing to me now'?"

"More like option B. His exact words were, I think, 'It wasn't like we were soul mates or whatever.'"

"Aw," Erin cooed. "He believes in soul mates!"

"He hasn't entirely ruled it out," I said, smiling. I still objected to the idea of soul mates, but I liked the way Pawel said things. He had a good sense of humor, and he seemed to take everything in stride. I couldn't imagine him getting all caught up in some meaningless drama, like some people I knew. He was just *fun*. He liked to laugh and smile and joke around, and I thought maybe I needed a little lightening up. I certainly felt better about things when he was around.

"How sweet," Erin said.

"You know how I feel about soul mates," I reminded her.

"Yes, yes, *I know*," Erin groaned. "You object."

"That's right," I said. "Still. It's cute."

Erin said nothing more, just grinned knowingly as we pulled into Reb's already crowded driveway.

12

The party was already loud and crowded by the time Erin and I walked through the front door. Reb was flirting with a guy I'd never met before near the door to the downstairs powder room. She saw me as I walked toward her, and shouted, "Caro! Your boy is in the kitchen getting hit on by a *very* pretty cheerleader. Go assert your authori-*tay*."

"She's drunk," I whispered to Erin, who nodded. Reb only pulled out the Cartman voice when she was drunk.

"Let's go catch up," Erin suggested, pulling me by the hand toward the kitchen.

"I really wish she wouldn't talk about Pawel that way,"

I complained. "People could hear her and it could get back to him. I don't want him thinking that I think he's my boyfriend or whatever. We hardly know each other."

"Hopefully by the end of the night you'll know him a little better," Erin said, winking. I shook my head at her, but I couldn't help laughing. It was as if she and Reb had joined forces to find me a new boyfriend. It was sweet, and strangely comforting. Usually, there was an uneasy tension between the two of them, a sort of competition. They were each closer to me than they were to each other, and sometimes they resented each other for it, but in this they were a team.

"Caro!" Pawel called when we stepped into the kitchen. He was standing next to a cheerleader, just like Reb had said, but I didn't know her name.

"Hey," I said, smiling. I nodded at his red Solo cup. "What are you drinking?"

"Some shitty beer," he said, slinging his arm over my shoulder. I stared at his arm like I'd never seen one before. It was a casual, intimate gesture, one that filled me with warmth from head to toe. I had to remind myself that he was a little drunk, so it probably meant nothing. "Come on, I'll show you where the keg is."

"Do you remember Erin?" I asked.

Erin stuck out her hand and he shook it. "Hi again."

"Nice to meet you," he said.

"We've met before," Erin pointed out, but he just shrugged and grinned.

"Sorry. I'm bad with names. And faces. Too much pot," he joked, although that was probably true. Then he sobered, like a cloud had passed over his face. "Just kidding, I don't smoke pot." Just as quickly, the cloud cleared. "You guys want some beer?"

"Yeah," I said.

"I think the cups are under the sink," the cheerleader said, butting in. She put her hand on Pawel's arm, but he didn't seem to notice. Instead, he leaned down and extracted two red cups from a lower cabinet.

Pawel took my hand and dragged me out through the sliding glass doors into the backyard, where an unmarked keg was standing in the center of the deck. He let go of my hand, and I was surprised by how empty it felt without his. I looked back at Erin and she made a sad face for my benefit but turned that frown upside down when Pawel handed her a full cup of beer with almost no head.

"You're a pro," she said, taking a sip.

"Lots of practice," he said, handing me the second cup and going to fill his own. When he was finished, he turned to me and knocked my cup with his. *"Na zdrowie!"*

"Na—what?" I asked.

"Na zdrowie," Pawel repeated, pronouncing it *nas-drov-yeh.* "It's kind of like Polish for 'cheers.'"

"Cheers," I said, raising my cup a little and taking a long gulp. Pawel laughed.

Erin lifted her cup and started chugging. When it came to consuming liquids, Erin was a first-class talent. I couldn't drink too fast or I'd vomit, but Erin drank everything like she was a character in a Greek myth, cursed with an unquenchable thirst.

"This is nasty," Erin said, wiping her mouth with the back of her hand.

"Nectar of the gods," Pawel joked, kicking the keg softly with the toe of his sneaker.

"If I didn't know better, I'd think Reb was trying to poison us all," Erin said. I laughed. "I'm going to go see if Joe is here."

"He's in the living room, DJing on the computer," Pawel told her. "Or he was the last time I saw him."

"I thought you weren't good with names," Erin said, narrowing her eyes.

"I'm not. I've known Joe forever—we were in the same traveling baseball league when we were kids," Pawel said.

"Oh! Well, that's nice. I'm going to go find him," she said, shooting me a meaningful look and then sauntering back into the house.

"Godspeed," Pawel said, lifting his cup at her retreating back. He put a hand on my shoulder. I played it cool, like there was nothing special at all about him touching me, but inside I was shaking. "I'm glad you're here, Caro."

"Me too," I said. "Reb's parties are always fun."

"Yeah, she's a good hostess," Pawel said. "Plenty of booze, plenty of tunes, plenty of room."

"That was a beautiful poem," I said.

"I was hoping you'd like it. I composed it just for you." We were looking into each other's eyes, and as his voice trailed off into nothing, I was sure he was going to lean forward and kiss me, but someone called my name and we both looked to find Derek headed in our direction. I glanced back at Pawel and he rolled his eyes at me good-naturedly.

"Hey, guys," Derek said. "What's going on? I just got here. Is that keg tapped yet?"

"Nope," I said. "Go for it."

"Cups?"

"In the kitchen, under the sink," Pawel told him.

"Perfect." I thought he would leave, but he lingered for a couple of moments. "So how are you guys? Did you come here together?"

I shook my head. "I just got here, too. Dinner with the folks."

Derek mussed his hair up absently, and I had a brief flash of running my fingers through it, tugging at it a little as we were making out. That had been months earlier. I blinked to make the image go away.

"Me too," he said. "Well, it's great to see you. Let's talk later, okay?" I knew that he was probably directing that last question to both Pawel and me, but something about the way he looked directly at me gave me a different impression. He gave me a hasty one-armed hug and trotted off in search of a beer vessel.

"He'll be back in a second," Pawel said quietly. "Let's fill up and get out of here."

"Okay," I agreed. Pawel topped off our beers at the keg, then took my hand again and led me around the side of the house.

For a few minutes we just stood there, sipping our beers and trying to make each other out in the darkness. Then Pawel put his cup down on the brick walkway, took mine from my hand and did the same with it, and reached out to touch my face. I closed my eyes.

"I really, really like you, Caro," Pawel said. "I'm sorry if that's weird."

"It's not weird," I whispered. He took a step forward and pressed himself lightly up against me. His breath smelled faintly of beer, but I didn't care. Mine probably—definitely—did, too.

"I mean, I'm sorry if it's weird that I said that," he clarified. "Not that it's weird that I like you."

"I understand," I assured him.

"I'm sort of drunk," he said.

"I noticed," I said.

"But it doesn't matter. Because I would still do this if I wasn't," he said.

"Do what?" I asked.

He touched his lips to mine tentatively. I returned the kiss with enthusiasm, putting a hand against the back of his head and draping my other arm over his shoulder. He reached around and placed both of his hands on the small of my back. We held tight to each other, pulling at each other's lips, tongues gently touching. I felt dizzy and feather-light, like I was about to float away. It felt like there was an acrobat in my chest, jumping and sinking. I held him closer, gripping his T-shirt and pressing my chest against his.

We might have stayed that way forever if we hadn't heard footsteps coming down the walkway. We jumped apart and looked toward the backyard, where Joe and Erin were standing in the honey-gold light of one of the deck lamps.

"Yo, Pav," Joe cried out. "Flip cup tournament starts now. You in or you in?"

"Caro, you're on my team!" Erin called out.

Pawel cleared his throat and glanced at me. I shrugged. "I'm in," he said.

"Me too," I said. My voice was as wobbly as my knees. I must've sounded like I was going to cry, because when I reached Erin, she asked, "Are you okay?"

"I'm perfect," I told her. "Really, really great."

Flip cup is a dangerous game. I don't mean that in a health class PSA sort of way. I mean it in a "been there, drank that, threw up on my shoes" sort of way. I didn't get as drunk as I possibly could have, but by the end of the tournament we were all too wasted to do much of anything. It was close to two in the morning when we finally collapsed; nearly everybody else had gone home, and Joe was already asleep on the floor in the kitchen with a mixing bowl near his head in case of emergency.

I was sitting upright on the couch, with Pawel slumped over in my lap, the back of his neck resting on my thigh, eyes closed. Erin was snoring on the other end, and Reb was sitting near my feet, her head against Pawel's hip.

"I'm drunk," she moaned.

"We're all drunk," I told her.

Pawel's eyes flew open. "I have to go home," he said abruptly, struggling to sit up. I helped him, and he smiled at me, repeating, "I have to go home."

"No, no," Reb slurred. "Stay here. Plenty of beds. You and Caro can have my parents' room." I kicked her. "Ow!"

"Tempting," Pawel said with a yawn. "But I *have* to go home."

"Why?" I said.

"Mass at nine a.m.," he said.

"Oh. Okay, well then, how? You can't drive, none of us can drive," I pointed out. "Do you want me to call your parents?"

"No way!" Pawel protested. "I'll walk."

"You can't *walk*." Reb scoffed. "It's miles! What about a cab?"

A cab! Why hadn't I thought of that? I'd never called a cab in the suburbs before, but it couldn't be that hard. "Do you have any cash?" I asked Pawel.

"No cash," Pawel moaned.

"Crap," I said. "Neither do I."

I looked over at Reb, who dug around in the pockets of her jeans before pulling out a couple of crumpled one-dollar bills. She handed them to me with an exaggerated frown. "You can have these."

I smiled at her. "Thanks, Reb. But I don't think it's going to be enough."

"No cab?" Pawel asked. I shook my head.

"Is anyone here sober?" I called out, hoping that someone we didn't know was still there would emerge, keys in hand, ready to pass a Breathalyzer. No such luck, though. Anyone with common sense had left hours before. "Shit."

Erin snorted and woke up, grimacing. "Ugh. What happened?"

"Flip cup," Reb answered. Erin nodded and rubbed her eyes.

Pawel grabbed my shoulders in a moment of sudden inspiration. "Your sister!"

My eyes went wide. "Absolutely not. Shut up. I'll call my dad, he'll come."

"You want the first time your dad meets me to be *this*?" Pawel asked. My heart leapt at the idea that he wanted to impress my parents, that he planned on meeting them in the future. *The kiss in the backyard wasn't just a fluke,* I assured myself. He really, really liked me. He'd said so himself. "Please, Caro, call your sister."

"What sister?" Reb asked. "You have a sister?"

"She just got out of the Peace Corps," Pawel bragged for me. *Oh, God.* This night was dissolving into a total cringe-inducing nightmare.

"Really?" Erin said, her voice tinged with suspicion.

"Yeah," I muttered, regretting the lie for the billionth time. "She just moved home."

"When?" Erin demanded.

"End of the summer," I admitted.

"You didn't tell them?" Pawel looked totally baffled. He watched as his brilliant idea fell apart and condemned him to a long walk home.

"It's not a big deal," I said. "Who cares? It's just my sister. It's not like I have a secret love child I didn't tell you about."

"Thank God," Pawel said.

"Wait a minute, how come Polish dude knows about this and we don't?" Erin looked furious, way angrier than I thought the situation deserved. But then again, beer did bend the edges of common sense, and Erin had very little of *that* to begin with.

"He ran into us at the DMV," I said. "Come on, Pawel, help me find my cell phone, I'm going to call my parents." I stood up and tugged at him, but he remained prostrate.

"Why can't your sister come get us? She has her license now!" he argued, the words pouring out sloppily.

"Oh my God, Pawel, I'm going to kill you. Will you please stop talking about my sister?" I hissed.

"Is that why you were at the DMV? You told me you were having your picture retaken!"

"Erin, who cares why she was at the DMV?" Reb yawned, leaned her head back against the couch, and closed her eyes.

"Fine! I'll look for the damn thing myself." I thought I remembered leaving my purse in the kitchen, so I went in there to look. I eventually found it under a mound of garbage on the floor, which was awesome. My phone was almost out of battery, but it had enough to call home. I *really* didn't want my dad to have to come pick up me and my new boyfriend (was he my boyfriend? I still wasn't entirely clear on that point) because we were drunk at a party, but it didn't look like I had another option.

"Call your sister!" Pawel was not getting it at all. I wondered if he was always this obtuse.

I dialed the house and waited, my stomach in knots. It stopped after one ring, and rather than my dad's sleepy, irritated voice on the other end of the line, I heard Hannah. "Hello?"

"Hannah?"

"Caro? Where are you? Why are you calling the house so late?"

"I need someone to come pick me up from Reb's house," I told her. She wouldn't do it. She didn't have a license, or permission to take the car, and there was no way she would leave the house at that hour without telling my parents. I was so screwed.

"Can't you just stay there until the morning?" Hannah's voice was hushed.

"No," I said. "My friend . . . he has to get home before dawn. Can you come and get us?"

There was a pause on the other end of the line. "I can't drive," Hannah said finally.

"You *can* drive," I reminded her. "You just don't have a license. Look, it's not that far. I can give you directions, it'll take twenty minutes to get here and get us home, I promise."

"If you want me to wake Dad up, I will," Hannah said. "But I'm not coming to get you. It's illegal."

"Illegal schmillegal," I said dismissively. "Who cares? It's half an hour, tops. There aren't any cops out at this hour, and as long as you don't run a red light, you're golden. Come on, Hannah. Can't you just do me a favor?"

"Caro, are you drunk?" Hannah asked, horrified.

"A little," I admitted. "Please? You're my sister, for Christ's sake."

Hannah hesitated and, finally, relented. "Okay. But just there and home, I'm not taking you through any drive-throughs or anything."

"Hannah, you're a saint! We'll wait for you on the porch." I gave her directions to Reb's house and hung up my cell, which was beeping at me incessantly about its low battery.

"Okay, Pawel, we have a ride," I said, walking into the living room. Naturally, he was asleep. Perfect.

I needed Erin's help to get Pawel out to the car and stuff him into the backseat. (Reb had fallen asleep again.) I pushed him and he went down like a log, breathing softly. He looked peaceful and calm, the complete opposite of the way I felt getting into the passenger seat and meeting Hannah's eyes.

"Who is that?" she asked. She was fully dressed, her hair in a ponytail, and sat stiff and upright in the driver's seat.

"Pawel," I told her. "You remember the guy I was talking to at the DMV?"

"Is he your boyfriend?" she asked.

"I don't know," I said. "But he *is* really drunk, so let's just get him home, okay?"

"Fine." She put the car in reverse and pulled out of the driveway. "I'm going to need directions."

"I'll tell you where to turn." Before Hannah had gotten there, I'd woken Pawel up and made him program his address into the GPS on my phone. How people lived before mobile Internet, I'll never know. I was just praying we could outrun the phone's imminent death.

We sat there in silence. I could tell she was fuming, stewing, and steaming mad at me, but I didn't know what to say to her. She was overreacting, but if I told her that, she'd just overreact to it. She had an overdeveloped sense of morality; she saw this as my asking her to break a law just to cover my own ass, and she was as angry with herself for doing it as she was at me for asking.

I couldn't take it, that quietly bubbling anger. I had to say something.

"I'm sorry," I told her, staring out the windshield at the dark streets coming at us. "I know you didn't want—"

"Don't."

"Hannah, I get that you're angry, but I just don't think this is such a big deal."

"Of course you don't," she snapped, not looking at me. "You're a spoiled brat. You think everything you want is your God-given right, and that everyone else in the world is just here to provide it for you."

"That's not true," I protested. "I just asked you for a ride!"

"You called up the house at two in the morning and begged me to pick you and your drunk whatever-he-is up and drive you home on an expired license after just failing a driver's test so that you both can hide from your parents that you were ever drunk or together or out until two in the morning," Hannah said. "Wouldn't it have been better just not to get drunk in the first place, or maybe not even go to this party? But you wanted to, so you did, and now here we are."

"Fine! You're pissed. I understand."

"No, Caro, you don't understand. You don't even *try* to understand. You live in a world that revolves completely around you, and you never once, not even for a second, try to see what other people might be experiencing or feeling. You just never think about anyone else, and it's beneath you." Hannah shook her head.

"If I'm so awful, if this is such a terrible inconvenience for you, then why did you agree to do it? I called the house for Dad, anyway." I bit the inside of my lip hard to prevent the tears pressing at the backs of my eyes from spilling all over my cheeks. It was late, Hannah was yelling at me, and I was so, so tired.

"Oh, you know why I did it," Hannah said.

"Actually, no, I don't. Tell me why."

"Because," croaked Pawel from the backseat. "She wants you to like her."

Hannah's eyes met mine for a brief second, then she turned her head away.

"Next left," I mumbled, reaching back to brush a piece of hair that had fallen into Pawel's eyes. "First house on the right."

13

When I woke up on Sunday morning, my parents were gone, and Hannah, I assumed, was still asleep. As usual, there was a note from my mother: *By the time we get home: water the plants, wash the kitchen floor, take out the recycling.* Chores were the price I paid for never wanting to run errands with them anymore.

I would normally have waited until the last possible moment to do everything, but since I didn't know when they would return, I just did a quick, half-assed job on everything and went back to bed. My head felt like it was going to explode, and my entire body was shaky, like the muscles under my skin were vibrating. I was uncomfortable and miserable and I just wanted to lie around all day, but I couldn't fall back asleep. I reached under my bed and grabbed Hannah's keepsake box. I riffled through it for another letter and finally found one on a folded piece of yellowed stationery that said FROM THE DESK OF EVAN MITCHELL on it.

Dear St. Catherine,

Sister Therese called me into her office today. I was afraid that I was in trouble for something, but she just wanted to talk about Sabra. They're going to create a memorial for her in the main entrance of the school, right next to the statue of Our Lady. They're also going to put a special page into the yearbook for her. There will be a picture, and a space for notes from her friends. Sister Therese wanted to know if I would contribute a letter. I told her I didn't know, but I would think about it. I don't know what I'm going to do.

It was starting to dawn on me how clueless I was about Hannah's entire life. I could guess that maybe Sister Therese had been the St. Robert's principal back in the day (by the time I got there, the principal was a dude and his name was Mr. Fredrickson; he was universally loathed), but I couldn't know for sure. And as for Sabra, I had no idea. A memorial would mean that she had died, but how? And were she and Hannah friends? I couldn't remember her having any particular friends, but I was pretty young when she left, and would have been only about a year old when Hannah started the diary—or whatever I was reading. And I didn't remember any memorial at the front entrance to the school, nor were there any statues there. The first thing you saw when you entered St. Robert's School was a giant cross.

I was so engrossed in my thoughts that I jumped when I heard the garage door open. A few moments later, there was a knock at my bedroom door.

"Come in," I called, tucking the letter into the notebook with the pink cover and shoving the whole box back underneath my bed.

Hannah stepped inside and closed the door. "I saw your boyfriend at church today," she said, avoiding my eyes.

"You went to church?" I asked, taken aback.

"I had to go sooner or later." She sighed. There was clearly more to the story, but I didn't feel like it was my place to ask. "He looked pretty sick."

"I'm sure he was." It was my turn to sigh. "And he's not my boyfriend."

"Really?" Hannah looked straight at me now. "It seemed like he was."

"Well, maybe. We haven't talked about it."

"Oh. Okay."

"It's complicated."

"Is it?"

"Yes." I stared at her. There was so little in her face for me to see. I'd never found someone as inaccessible as Hannah. Did she want Pawel to be my boyfriend? Did she care one way or the other? I couldn't tell. "Is that it?"

Hannah nodded. "I just wanted to let you know."

"That Pawel was hungover this morning?"

"That he was well enough to go to Mass." Hannah smiled her enigmatic smile and left the room.

☆ ☆ ☆

Pawel called me after church. It was wonderful to hear his voice; I'd started to convince myself that the previous night had been just a drunken hallucination, brought on by too much beer and too much wanting.

"So how are you feeling?" I asked after the usual pleasantries.

"Like death," Pawel groaned. "And your family saw me in church! Insult to injury."

"Did they talk to you?" I asked, horrified.

"Your sister did," Pawel told me. "In the vestibule, while your parents were talking to the priest." I wondered if it was Father Bob. There were a couple more priests at St. Robert's, including one I called Father Boring; he always seemed to do the holiday Masses, and as soon as the homily started I could feel my eyes begin to droop. I couldn't help it; it was a Pavlov's dog–style reaction.

"God, I'm sorry about that."

"It's fine. She's nice. It was weird, because all I know about her is that she was cool enough to drive us home at two in the morning and not tell your parents about it," Pawel said. "And that she was in the Peace Corps."

My chest tightened up. "Did she . . . talk about that at all?"

"Nope, didn't come up. Would it be okay if I asked her about it sometime? You know, once the gut-wrenching humiliation of last night wears off."

"So in, like, two or three years?" I asked, sidestepping the question.

"I was pretty wasted, huh?"

"Yeah," I admitted. "But I wouldn't worry about it so much. Everybody was pretty wasted."

"I'm glad I kissed you before we played flip cup," Pawel said.

"Oh, did that happen?" I teased.

"Ha-ha, very funny."

"It's kind of hard to hear you," I said.

"Because I've buried my head into the pillow and I'm not moving until it stops pounding, which could be never," Pawel moaned.

"So what did you and Hannah talk about?" I asked, trying to sound nonchalant.

"She just asked how I was doing," Pawel said. "It was mostly 'hi, how are yous.' She seemed kind of . . ." He didn't finish the thought.

"Kind of what?" I asked.

"Awkward. I figured that was just because what do you say to your little sister's boyfriend after carting his ass home piss drunk at dawn?"

Boyfriend. "Yeah, that makes sense," I said. Maybe I should've reassured him that Hannah was always a little awkward, regardless of the situation, but that just would've invited more questions.

"That was a test, by the way," Pawel told me.

"What was?"

"I called myself your boyfriend and you didn't flinch."

"How do you know I didn't?" I said. "You can't see me."

"I can tell," he said.

"Was I supposed to flinch?" I asked.

"I was hoping you wouldn't," he said.

"Then I passed?"

"You did. A-plus, Carolina Mitchell. Top of the class."

"You want to be my boyfriend?" I confirmed.

Pawel's voice got quiet. "I do. Do you want to be my girlfriend?"

"Yes," I said. "Definitely."

☆ ☆ ☆

Dear St. Catherine,

When I went to confession this week, I told the priest everything about Sabra. It isn't like he doesn't know, because everybody knows. It was in the paper and everybody at school was talking about it, the teachers and the parents and the students. God knows. He was there with us—at least, I hope he was. Everybody knows. But it took me six months to go to confession, which I know makes me a coward. I've been carrying this sin around on my shoulders and I was afraid to tell the truth. Why is it so hard to admit to something you've done if there's nobody left to tell?

It was Father Dawson in the confessional on Saturday. I hadn't taken confession since my first confession in fourth grade, so I didn't remember how to do it. I asked Mom to drive me to church specially, and at first it made her worried, I think. She asked me to please talk to her first, so I told her it had to do with Sabra, and she didn't ask any more questions. The therapist in the church office, Mrs. Lang, says that no matter what, I should always be encouraged to talk about Sabra, although this is the first time I've really wanted to. Mom drove me to church and waited in the car, like I asked. She wanted to come inside with me, but I asked her not to.

Father Dawson isn't a priest I know personally. He's very old and usually just stays at the rectory, but

I guess he decided to hear confession. It doesn't take
very much work, maybe it's good for him because he
gets to be helpful but all he has to do is sit and listen.
So I confessed to him and he said the strangest thing.
He said, "Child, you don't need any absolution. Go
home and thank God for your health and pray for the
soul of your friend."

I told him that I needed a penance and he refused
to give me one. "You've done nothing wrong," he said.
I didn't want to correct him, because you don't correct a
priest. So I just thanked him and left the confessional.
Mom was sitting in the pew right outside, not close
enough to listen in. When she saw me, she smiled and
told me that she had her own confessing to do, could I
please wait for her in the vestibule? So I did. Then we
drove home together, and I didn't ask her what she had
confessed, and she didn't ask me. I wonder if she got
a penance.

Sabra. That name again. This letter had been more
illuminating than all the ones that had come before it.
Clearly, Sabra had been a friend of Hannah's, and she
had died. It seemed like Hannah held herself responsible,
but the priest had told her it wasn't her fault. So which
was it?

I went looking for my parents and found them in
the kitchen, working on dinner; Mom was wrist-deep

in hamburger meat and Dad was at the sink, peeling potatoes.

"Meat loaf for dinner," Mom said, patting and molding the pile of hamburger. "Can you preheat the oven to three-fifty, please?"

"Sure." I set the temperature on the oven and then went to the fridge for a soda. "Can I ask you guys a question?"

"Of course," she said, placing the meat loaf into the pan she also used to make banana bread, and going over to the sink to wash her hands, bumping Dad aside with her hip.

"What's up?" Dad asked, stacking the peeled potatoes into a pyramid.

"Who's Sabra?"

I saw Mom's shoulders tighten up. She didn't turn to look at me right away, just shut the water off, shook her hands free of droplets, and wiped them dry on a kitchen towel. I saw Dad dart a quick glance at her face, then focus all his concentration on the potato pyramid, as if he hadn't heard me at all.

Finally, Mom faced me. "How do you know about that?" she asked.

"I don't," I said. "I want to know."

"You should really ask Hannah," she said, going to the fridge and getting out a bag of fresh green beans. She dumped them onto the large glass cutting board and started snapping off the ends, ferociously, as if they'd committed some heinous crime. Dad went back to his peeling, pretending not to listen. "That's her story to tell."

"I want you to tell me."

"I really can't, sweetie," she said, her voice wavering. "Hannah would be upset if she found out you heard it from me first."

"Why?" I couldn't ask Hannah without telling her how I knew to ask in the first place, and I was sure that the breach of privacy wouldn't sit well with her. Better to learn from Mom and Dad and never have to discuss it with Hannah at all.

"It's a very sensitive topic," Mom said. "We haven't talked about it since before Hannah was in high school."

"Do you think it has something to do with . . . you know." I waved my hand euphemistically, and it was a testament to how much we all had to tiptoe around the subject of Hannah's vocation that my mother got what I was saying immediately.

"I don't know about that. It was a long time ago," Mom reminded me. "Hannah has always been a very pious young woman. I hardly think . . ." She let the words die on her lips and hesitated, as if she was really thinking about it for the first time. "I don't know," she said finally. "You could ask her that, too."

"Dad?" I asked in my sweetest voice. My father had always been the soft touch of the family. For the first time since I entered the room, he turned to me and opened his mouth, as if he wanted to say something but did not yet know what.

"Evan!" Mom's tone was sharp and unyielding.

Dad shook his head. "I'm sorry, sweetie. Your mom's right."

"Okay. Fine." I had to drop it now. Mom looked so sad and adrift I knew I couldn't press harder without hurting her. "Do you need help with something?"

Mom shook her head. "No, honey. We're all set in here. I'm just going to sit in the family room and watch some TV while the meat loaf cooks."

"I'll watch with you," I said, walking over and putting my arm around her shoulders. "Is there anything good on?"

☆ ☆ ☆

Later, in my bedroom, I cracked open my laptop and pulled up Google, then typed the only things I knew about the situation into the search box.

SABRA MEMORIAL DEAD MAPLE GROVE ILLINOIS ST. ROBERT'S

To my complete and total frustration, nothing came up that was in any way illuminating. There was a Wikipedia article about a massacre in Beirut (not it), an alumni directory for the comparative studies department at Ohio State (not it), and a list of scholarship recipients for a society devoted to radio personalities (definitely *not* it). Sabra wasn't a common name, but nothing I typed in to try to clarify the situation (even my own sister's name) helped bring up anything even remotely related to whatever had happened to inspire my sister to write those letters back in 1997.

I shut my laptop in annoyance after accepting that nothing on the Internet could help me. It wasn't a total surprise; most of the local newspapers didn't even have online article archives that went back further than the year 2000, ditto with obituaries and memorial notices. But I couldn't believe there wasn't *anything*.

I was too nervous to ask Hannah about it; I didn't want her to know that I had been going through her things, secretly investigating a part of her life that she obviously wanted kept private. So I did the only thing I could think of: I looked for another letter, and found one, this time scribbled on half a piece of loose-leaf binder paper that was torn at the bottom.

Dear St. Catherine,

   Today was my first day of eighth grade. I was hoping things would be different, but they weren't really. I walked by this group of girls from my homeroom on the way to my locker, and they whispered things at me as I passed. I don't think they even care about Sabra anymore—nobody talks about her, and it's almost like she only mattered right after what happened, and last year on the anniversary. But the things they say about me are the same.

Every time this happens, I think of Evie Klein. The girls are mean to her, too, and the boys. They call her Skeevie Evie, because nothing in her name rhymes with "fat," which is another thing they call her. I try to feel sorry for her, but what I really feel is jealous. I wish they would call me fat. Or ugly or bitchy. Anything but what they say about me would be better, even though it's still mean, even though I know it makes Evie feel terrible. She sits alone all the time in homeroom while we eat lunch, and at recess. She never seems to have anyone to talk to.

Evie tried to talk to me once, maybe because she thought since I always sit alone, too, we could be friends. I was polite, but in a way that let her know we weren't going to be friends. I can't have friends anymore. Poor Evie.

Who didn't want friends? I'd always had friends, not a lot of them, not a whole obnoxious group, but a few really good friends that I trusted and liked. I didn't know what I would do without Reb and Erin, even if Erin did get on my nerves. Who would I talk to about stuff that was important to me? Was this why Hannah had written these letters in the first place? Because she had nobody to say the words to out loud?

The thought made me too sad. I jumped on the computer to see if anyone was online, hoping that talking to one of my friends would help me shake the gloomy feeling that had settled over me. Reb was active, so I double-clicked on her username and IM'd her.

SweetCarolina: You should know that Pawel considers me his girlfriend.

Rebelieuse: How do you know that? Are you psychic now?

SweetCarolina: He said so!

Rebelieuse: GASP! With his very own lips?

SweetCarolina: No, he borrowed someone else's. YES OF COURSE.

Rebelieuse: That boy wasted no time locking you down. It's kinda quick, don't you think?

SweetCarolina: I like him. A LOT.

Rebelieuse: Derek who?

SweetCarolina: Seriously.

I almost told Reb about Hannah. I don't know what came over me, but I typed "You know how my sister's back? I said she was in the Peace Corps, but that was a lie. She used to be a nun and now she's not." Then I deleted it. It was a stupid thing to say over IM, just out of the blue like that. Reb wouldn't know how to respond and I wouldn't know how to explain and eventually one of us would get tired of writing "um" or "okay" and would make some excuse to sign off so that we could pretend the conversation had never happened.

Why was I making such a huge deal out of Hannah in my head? Nobody was going to care that she had been a nun! It wasn't interesting or awful or tragic or even gossipy. And if I told people the straightforward truth, they probably wouldn't even mind very much that I had lied about it. But there was this feeling, like a rope tied around my throat, and every time I thought *Just tell them already,* the rope tightened and I wound up saying nothing.

After a couple of minutes, I made an excuse to Reb and signed off.

14

"So when are you bringing your young man around for dinner?" Dad asked in a very dad way, not looking up from the paper.

It was the following Sunday. I hadn't even looked for another St. Catherine letter since the weekend before; I still wasn't quite sure I wanted to go any further, if in fact there were more of them. Things with Pawel were great; he and I were trying out the whole dating thing with the usual activities—holding hands in the hallway, glancing meaningfully at each other and smiling during class, making out furiously in an empty classroom before last period. I didn't have the energy for anyone else's darkness and had pushed the Sabra mystery to the back of my mind as far as it would go.

"Um, never," I told him. Hannah laughed softly as she stirred a couple of drops of honey into her tea. I'd forgotten she was even there. She was even thinner than before, her hip bones jutting out from underneath her T-shirt. Nobody said anything; nobody even seemed to look at Hannah too closely. The air was practically vibrating with everything that remained unsaid. And yet it was clear that my parents were unnerved by her appearance. Mom always tried to force her to take extra food at meals, and I'd overheard them arguing (or more accurately, my parents were arguing; Hannah was being calmly, but firmly, resistant) about her going to see a nutritionist. She had been home only about a month and a half and she was already overwhelmed with all the talk about getting a job and going back to school. But at least she sat still and pretended to listen when it came to those topics; when her health came up, she would invent an excuse to leave the room or just refuse to discuss it. So for now the plan was wait and see, but they couldn't wait forever. Hannah was erasing herself before our very eyes.

Because we couldn't have an honest conversation about what was really going on at the breakfast table, my parents went straight to the default: unnecessarily involving themselves in *my* life.

"Tonight's good for us," Mom said. "Why don't you call him right now and invite him over?"

"Mom!" I cried. Part of me knew it wasn't a good idea for Pawel to come over and meet my parents—my *family*—after we'd dated for only a week, but another part of me understood that it was a relationship rite of passage and if it happened, it meant that Pawel was really my boyfriend.

"Oh, I'm sorry, did I imply that this was an option?" Mom opened her eyes wide. "You can't argue your way out of it, Caro, so don't even try. Go call him."

"Mom, no," I begged. "Please, not right now. It's too soon. It's too weird." I glanced at Hannah, but she gave me a smile, which meant I was on my own. I couldn't really tell what she thought about Pawel, if she thought anything about him at all.

I wondered if she had liked a boy once—or more than once—and never acted on it. I wondered if she wanted me to have the experience she never got the chance to have.

In this case I'd be happy to indulge her. After all, I really liked Pawel. I couldn't believe that he liked me back and wanted to be my boyfriend, but he did; he'd said it himself. Introducing him formally to my family was a completely different thing, though, especially because of the lies I had told him about Hannah.

But my parents would not back down. "If you're

dating a boy, we want to meet him," Mom said firmly. This kind of madness was not unprecedented. A week after Derek and I had made it official, she made me drag him over for brunch. I should've known it was going to happen with Pawel, too.

"Ugh, *fine*," I said, getting up from the kitchen table and walking down the hall to my room. I was going to have to prevent Pawel from asking questions about Hannah, and her from revealing anything that would tip him off that I had lied. As long as I could do that, I was in the clear.

"Does he eat meat?" Mom called.

"As far as I know," I told her, picking up the phone.

"Karolcia," Pawel answered.

"Is that what you're calling me now?" I asked.

"I'm trying it out," he said. "What's up?"

"My parents want me to invite you over for dinner tonight," I said, dialing up the grudging tone in my voice so he knew that I knew that it was a drag. "You don't have to come if you don't want to. I'll make something up about you having to go to your grandmother's or whatever, just say the word."

"Dinner with your family, huh?" He paused for a few moments to consider the offer. "What's on the menu?"

"No idea," I said. "My mom's a good cook, though."

"And it won't be weird, you don't think?" he asked.

"Oh, it'll definitely be weird," I said, pressing the heel of my hand hard against the bridge of my nose and squeezing my eyes shut. That was it. I'd just convinced him not to come, and now that I knew that, it was apparent how much I'd wanted him to say yes and how disappointed I was that he probably wouldn't.

"Sold. What time should I be there?"

"Seriously?" I asked, trying to keep the surprise and excitement to a minimum. I knew the boy liked me, but going full dork on him over dinner with my parents was inadvisable.

"Yeah, sure, what the hell? Your sister probably already thinks I'm a drunken fool, but maybe your parents will like me," Pawel said with a groan.

"She doesn't think you're a drunken fool," I said. "Well, okay, she might. But she hasn't said anything to them about it."

"That's troubling, don't you think?"

"Hmm. Maybe." I decided not to think about it too hard. "Speaking of my sister, can I ask you a favor?"

"Anything," he said. I could hear the smile in his voice.

"Things with Hannah are a little . . . sensitive right now," I said carefully. "It'd probably be best if you didn't, um, mention anything about what I told you. About the Peace Corps or anything."

"Why not? It's nothing to be ashamed of," he said.

"I know, I know," I said. "But just, could you not? It'll just make everyone uncomfortable."

"Is something wrong, Caro?" he asked, his tone switching from playful to serious. "You sound upset."

"I'm not upset, I'm just nervous," I told him. "I want to make this as not-weird as it could possibly be."

"Got it," he said.

I let out a small sigh of relief. Thank God for Pawel. Derek would've gone out of his way to make the whole thing awkward just to watch me squirm, thinking it was funny. "Okay, well, seven should be good. The menu is a work in progress, so it'll have to be a surprise. Get excited." I caught my reflection in the mirror. I was grinning like an idiot. I was glad he couldn't see me.

"I'll try. But no promises."

"This is going to be a nightmare, isn't it?" I asked Pawel when he arrived. We were standing close to each other in the foyer, and all I wanted was to reach out and touch him. He was wearing a freshly laundered T-shirt (I could smell the fabric softener when I leaned in for a hug) and jeans with Converse, and he looked great. I didn't look that bad myself. I'd flat-ironed my already straight hair into a sleek, shiny curtain, done my makeup, and put on a new light cotton sweater with dark jeans. He smiled at me and I smiled at him.

"Nah, it'll be fun," he said, putting his arm around my shoulders.

I glanced up and saw Hannah coming down the stairs. "Oh, hi," I said. Pawel shifted awkwardly and let go of me. "Hannah, you remember Pawel."

She nodded and gave the tiniest of smiles. "I do. It's good to see you."

"Ditto," he said. "I'm sorry about—"

She shook her head and held up her right hand. "Forget it."

"Okay," he said, stuffing his hands into his pockets and giving me a look of extreme discomfort.

"I think dinner's ready," she said. "Do you want to come into the kitchen?"

I shrugged. "I guess. Time to face the firing squad."

Pawel laughed. "It's not going to be that bad." But he was anxious, too. He kept opening and closing his fists and there was a thin layer of sweat on his brow. He wiped it away with the back of his hand under the guise of brushing some hair out of his eyes, but I could tell. It was the first time I'd ever seen him like that. Usually he was so calm and laid back, like nothing could touch him. It was cute, but it also worried me. He could promise me all he wanted that he wasn't going to mention what I'd told him about Hannah, but you could never tell what people were going to say when they were nervous.

My dad was sitting at the kitchen table and my mother was puttering around near the stove, scooping things out of pots and into dishes.

"Well, hello," Dad said, taking his glasses off and setting down the book he was reading. He stood and shook Pawel's hand.

"Hi, Mr. Mitchell, it's good to meet you," Pawel said politely.

"Same here," Dad said.

Mom came over and beamed at Pawel. "It's so nice to have you here, Pawel. I hope you like chicken cacciatore."

"I do, it's one of my favorites," he said. "Thank you for inviting me."

"You're very welcome. Have you met Hannah?" Mom glanced at Hannah, who was setting the table. She looked up and gave another tiny smile.

"Oh yes," Hannah said. I held my breath, completely incapable of predicting what she would say next. "Just now."

At Mom's urging, we sat down at the table and unfolded our napkins in our laps. Pawel was seated next to me. I couldn't get a good look at him without turning my head and being obvious, so I just sat there, examining my plate as if I was afraid it might have the atom-sized remnants of a former meal on its tooth-white surface. Time rolled by like a car in neutral, slow and steady, and full of something—not tension, not really, but an awkwardness so thick you could choke on it.

The first half of dinner was mild and pleasant and as good as you could possibly expect for that sort of thing, the sixteen-year-old daughter bringing home a new boyfriend while her well-meaning but anxious parents and virginal older sister looked on. Hannah was even eating somewhat normally, if glacially. And then Pawel asked something, and the house of cards I'd built with unnecessary, idiotic lies collapsed in on itself.

There had been a period of soft silence, and Pawel was trying to break it. He started out with nice, innocuous statements about the warm weather we were having for the season, which my parents followed up with questions about his family. He told them about his parents' immigration and his siblings.

"Have you ever been to Poland, Pawel?" Mom asked.

"Oh, yeah," he said. "My mom and dad like to take us back every few years to visit family."

"That's exciting," she said.

"Sometimes, but it's mostly, like, hanging out at my grandfather's farm and stuff," Pawel told her. "And eating until I burst. My *babcia* is an amazing cook and she pretty much feeds us constantly the whole time we're there."

"Have you ever gone anywhere else in Europe?" Dad asked.

"Yeah, we've gone to Italy a few times, and France and Germany," Pawel said. "And my mom has a sister who lives outside London, so we've visited them a few times."

"How wonderful," Mom said. "We keep hoping we'll be able to take the girls to Europe one day. We want them to see the world; Evan and I both traveled a lot when we were younger, and it drives us crazy that they haven't gotten to have the same experience."

Pawel's face contorted in confusion. The moment expanded and contracted quickly, and in that second I knew what he was going to say; I felt it coming at me like a freight train. I gripped my silverware hard; there was nothing I could do to stop him.

"But, Hannah, you've traveled around a lot, right? Caro told me you were in Africa."

All the air in the room congealed, and it was like we were in suspended animation. Thoughts bounced around in my mind like balls in a bingo cage. I had asked him not to say anything! Was he doing it on purpose? He couldn't be, he was Pawel, he cared about me, he promised me he wouldn't. I couldn't believe I had told him that stupid lie! My parents were going to kill me. What would Hannah say? What would *I* say? Why had I invited him to dinner? Why had I lied? Why oh why oh why had I *lied*?

Hannah's eyes narrowed, then widened in disbelief. My parents both glanced in her direction and then glared at me in fury. Nobody knew who should say something first as Pawel spooned a piece of chicken into his mouth and chewed, blissfully unaware that he had said anything wrong. I dug the tips of my fingers into his leg; when he caught the look of alarm on my face, it dawned on him that he had done exactly what he'd promised not to do, and he mouthed, *Sorry!* But it was too late. He didn't even understand the gravity of what he had done. What *I* had done.

"Caro told you I was in Africa?" Hannah asked.

"Yeah." Pawel squirmed. "In the, uh . . . Peace Corps." He turned to me, my parents, sweeping an apologetic gaze across the whole table. "I'm sorry, I shouldn't have . . ."

"Actually—" I began, hoping that if I could do some damage control, he might not think I was a total psycho, but Hannah interrupted.

"I wasn't in the Peace Corps," she said carefully, setting her fork down next to her plate and avoiding my eyes. "Until recently, I was living in a convent as a Sister of Grace."

Pawel turned his head to look at me. I gave him a pained shrug, the only thing I could muster.

"You mean you were a . . ." He searched for the word.

"Nun," she said with purpose. "Caro lied to you."

"Why do you have to put it like that?" I demanded.

"Because that's what you did," Hannah snapped, her saintly facade breaking. Her eyes filled up with tears, and she looked like she might slap me.

"Why?" The bewilderment in Pawel's voice made me want to cry, too. He had never considered the possibility that I would lie to him.

"Caro, I cannot believe you would do this again," Mom said, raging.

"Again?" Pawel and Hannah said in unison. At that, I

did start to cry. Not loud, ugly sobs that shook the room, but my eyes began to leak and I felt very close to losing it right there at the dinner table.

"I didn't mean to . . . ," I said weakly, gripping the edge of the table with the tips of my fingers.

"I'm not hungry anymore, may I please be excused?" Hannah's voice was so tight you could strum it. Mom nodded; Hannah got up from the table and disappeared into the hallway. We listened to her footsteps as she went up the staircase, and then there was silence.

"I'm sorry," Pawel said after a while. "I didn't know."

"Of course not," Mom rushed to assure him. "Please don't feel bad. This is Caro's fault."

Pawel finished his dinner quickly, apparently sensing that it was not a good night to linger. I couldn't wait for him to go, but I knew his presence was the only thing holding back the avalanche of my parents' wrath, and that once he was gone, I'd get the lecture of a lifetime, full of the screaming and grounding Mom and Dad were so good at.

I was allowed to walk Pawel to the door, and once we reached it, he asked me if I would go with him to his car. I could hear the clatter of dishes being collected and loaded into the sink, so I nodded and followed him to the driveway.

"What happened back there?" he demanded as soon as we were out of my parents' earshot.

"I warned you not to say anything," I snapped.

"Wait, *you're* mad at *me*? You lied to me, Caro!" He was trying not to sound hurt, but of course he was. And irritated, too, maybe even straight-up angry. "You made me look like a total ass in front of everyone."

"I'm so sorry. Of course I'm not mad at you."

He turned and stared at me. "You need to talk to your family."

"No, I need to talk to you," I insisted, taking his hand. He let me, but it was limp in mine. "I can explain the Hannah stuff."

Pawel ran his fingers through his hair and sighed. "You know what? It's not even that big of a deal, and I know it's not, but it's still so weird that you've been lying to me all this time about something I don't even give a shit about!" He shook his head. "No, it's not that I don't give a shit about it, but it wouldn't have changed the way I felt about you if I knew Hannah was a nun or a sister or whatever. What exactly was the point of lying to me about that?"

"Because I always have," I told him. It was a stupid thing to say, but it was the truth. He rolled his eyes.

"You don't understand," I continued. "I just didn't want to have to explain what was going on with her, and I know it doesn't matter but, like, sometimes things that don't matter actually matter a lot, so I lied."

"You didn't want to explain what was going on with

her, or you didn't want to find out what was going on with her?" Pawel asked, and I felt my stomach go into free fall. Of course he was right. I knew that. Lying about Hannah was the way I avoided having to figure out what to say about it, or what I felt about it besides anger and resentment.

"Both," I admitted. "But if it doesn't matter, then why are you mad at me?"

"Because. Look, I'm a pretty honest person, I think. I tell the truth. I don't make shit up. And it's important to me that the people I trust and care about are the same way. And if you lie about something small like this, then how can I believe you'd tell the truth when it's something big?" Pawel looked at the ground and took his hand from mine.

"You don't understand," I said again.

"Yeah," he said sharply. "I don't."

"She's so hard to deal with, Pawel, you have no idea."

"There's something wrong!" he cried. "Can't you see that?"

"What?"

"I can tell, and I don't even know your sister. She looks miserable, and she looks—" He paused to choose his words carefully. "She looks too thin. Have you ever even asked her what's going on with her, or do you just ignore it altogether? There's something wrong, and you're too scared to face it, so you lie and lie. I'm sorry, but that's just—it's just fucked up, is what it is."

"Pawel . . ." I couldn't think of anything else to say, so I just let his name hang there like a white flag. *Please don't be mad,* I thought, but I didn't say it.

"I'm going to go. I'll see you later."

"When?" I pleaded, hating the desperation in my voice.

"I don't know, just . . . later," he said, getting into his car and turning the key in the ignition. "At school."

I could feel the tears pressing against the backs of my eyes, but I bit down hard on my lip to keep them in. I had some dignity. I wasn't going to cry out here, where people could see me—where Pawel could still see me, in the rearview mirror, if he'd been looking. Which he wasn't, I knew. My vision blurred, but no tears fell, and I was proud of that.

15

When I went back inside, the tribunal was waiting.

"Caro, sit down," Dad commanded, face like a thundercloud.

"You don't have to lecture me, I know exactly what you're going to say." I pouted, taking a seat.

"Oh, I'm sure you do," Mom said. "Because we had this same conversation *four years ago.*"

"This is not the same," I insisted. "I didn't tell Pawel she was *dead,* I said she was in the Peace Corps."

"It's not the *lie,* it's the *lying,* Caro, Jesus!" Dad yelled.

"Yes, let's talk about Jesus for a second," I yelled back. "Isn't it all his fault in the first place? Hannah elopes with

Jesus, they get divorced, and now we're all forced to kill ourselves to accommodate her fragile self-esteem!"

"You'd better lower your voice right now," Dad growled.

"Why? Because the baby might hear me? Come on, Dad, seriously. She's not a child, she's an adult, and I'm sorry if I hurt her precious feelings but how do you think *I* feel?" I asked.

"Oh, we know exactly how you feel," Mom said. "We spoiled you growing up and now you're jealous of Hannah coming back into the family. You can't handle it when everything's not about you."

"That's not true! I just can't *stand* it that you both are so afraid of her. You think she left home because she didn't love us, and now that she's back, you don't want her to hate you enough to leave again," I said. Their expressions were stoic, but I could tell that I'd hit them where it hurt. *There's something wrong!* Pawel had said. And they were just ignoring it. I wasn't the only one who was afraid to face things. "She didn't leave because she didn't love us, she left because she was selfish and she came back because she's selfish and we're all selfish and that's not going to change, so just stop treating her like she's going to break and get a grip already. Can't you see that all you're doing is ignoring what's really going on?"

"Please illuminate us, Caro," Mom said angrily. "What is *really* going on?"

"Hannah is sick," I said. Pawel had been the first one

to say it, but I'd known it was true since the first time I'd laid eyes on her. "She's skinny and she won't eat and she sleeps all day. She's depressed, can't you see?"

"That's enough," Dad said. "You're finished talking. Now is the time to listen."

"What are you going to do, throw me in jail?" I grumbled.

"First, you're going to apologize to Hannah," Mom said. "*Again.* You're losing all your car privileges, and we're grounding you indefinitely."

"Indefinitely?" I shrieked. "For telling one lousy lie?"

"No," Dad said. "For turning your back on Hannah and this family, for being hurtful to her when you should be supporting her. You've been rigid and mean about this from day one, you've never even made the smallest effort with your sister."

"We were giving you time to adjust, but you refused to, and that's over now. You're going to shape up and get on board with the plan of helping Hannah, and you're not going to get your privileges back until you do." Mom folded her arms and set her mouth in a stern line.

"That's what you think," I said. "You can't stop me from doing what I want to do."

"You grossly underestimate our power over you," Mom said. "You can rage and cry and lock yourself in your room, but at the end of the day you're going to do what we say if you want to have any kind of social life whatsoever, so if you're smart, you'll skip the drama and go apologize to Hannah right now."

"Over my dead body," I snapped.

"If it comes to that." Dad got up and stood over me. "Go."

"You have got to be kidding me," I mumbled under my breath as I trudged up the stairs. I waited outside Hannah's door for several minutes, listening to her moving around in there, hoping she'd turn off the light and go to sleep and I wouldn't have to deal with this until the morning. When it seemed as though there was no hope of that, I knocked softly.

"Come in," Hannah said.

I walked in and shut the door behind me. Hannah was sitting in an armchair near her bed, reading. She closed her book, using her finger to mark the page, and dropped it into her lap.

I glanced at the shelves Dad had built into the wall, where the overflow from my own bulging collection of books came to gather dust. It was like she was working her way through my entire sophomore-year reading list, title by title. Was it intentional? I wondered. Was she trying to find me in the books I read? If she was, this wasn't the way to do it. The books I loved—the books that had become a part of me, or had a part of me in them to begin with—were all downstairs in my nightstand, near enough for me to reach over on a sleepless night and crack their well-worn spines. I kept the important things close.

I sat down on the edge of Hannah's bed. "Look, I'm sorry." It came out sharper than I had intended.

"For what?" she asked. There was a hard look in her eye that banished any hope I might've had that she wouldn't be angry. A sudden wave of guilt flooded over me.

"What are you sorry for, Caro?" Hannah prompted me again when I remained silent. I guess I hadn't expected her to be so difficult, but something had changed inside her in the past half hour. There was a toughness in her voice that was new to me, and I considered the possibility that she wasn't as fragile as she let on.

"For lying about where you've been," I said. "I guess I didn't realize how much it would hurt you if you found out."

Hannah sighed. "Is that the best you can do?"

"What?" I asked.

"Because if it is, then you should leave," she said. "I don't have the energy for you anymore."

The condescension in her voice sprang loose all the anger that the guilt had pushed away. "*You* don't have the energy? What about me? I'm so sick of having to tiptoe around you, Hannah!" I cried. No matter what I had done wrong, it didn't erase the facts that Hannah had left and that nothing right was going on in our house.

"You've made that much pretty clear. I'm sorry to have inconvenienced you."

"You chose to leave. You don't just get to come back and have everything be perfect, you know," I told her. "You have to deal with the messes."

"Like what?" she said, challenging me.

"Like Mom and Dad and how devastated they were when you left home like that," I said. I wanted to point out that she'd starved herself into another mess, but I was too scared to bring it up. *Coward,* I thought to myself meanly. "Like the fact that you and I didn't grow up to-gether and you can't manufacture a relationship instantly just because it suits you. You *left.* You don't get to pretend like we're the ones who need to change."

She shook her head. "I really wish I could make you understand."

"What's so difficult to explain, Hannah?" I challenged her. "I'm not a little girl anymore, and neither are you. We should be able to talk about these things."

Hannah paused to think. Finally, she said, "I'm sorry you're so angry with me." Her eyes softened. "I never meant to cause you any pain. You or anyone else. I know you're being protective of Mom and Dad. It was hard on them when I left. They felt like they'd done something wrong. That wasn't lost on me. And I'm sorry. I should have told them. I never, ever wanted to make them feel like they failed me in some way." She said these things with such earnest sincerity that I was struck by a sudden shame, as deep as the melancholy echo of a church bell.

I took a long breath and held it. I did that sometimes, when I felt like I didn't have a good grasp on things, and it was strange but the seconds without air would stretch and loop like taffy in a puller in a candy shop window, and it seemed like I could go forever, because there was no panicky scrambling feeling in my chest, just a sense of calm that spread through me like warm water.

"You see . . . ," Hannah continued, watching me closely. I let the breath out. "I thought I was doing what God wanted me to do. I thought I was being called to a higher purpose. When you believe something like that, you have to be willing to make the sacrifices necessary to fulfill that purpose. Does that make any sense?"

"I guess." I shrugged. It didn't, really, to me, but I could see how it might to her. Maybe it was just that I didn't believe in a higher power, Judeo-Christian God or otherwise, but I suppose that if I had, it wouldn't have been such a big leap.

"Do you remember me from before I went to the convent?" she asked. "I mean, in a real way? I know you were really young."

"Not as much as I should," I admitted.

"I had a rough adolescence," she told me. "I didn't

have any friends in junior high and high school. I was lonely, and I spent a lot of time in my head. And in church. I thought . . . I thought I was being punished for something. I chose a religious life because it asks so much of you, and I wanted to give everything up. Maybe I just wanted to prove that I could. I thought it would wash away my sins and bring me closer to God."

"What sins? What did you think you were being punished for?" This was what I most wanted to know, but even though I said the words, they came out tasting like dirt. It felt crude and gossipy to ask this question of my sister. And why should she want to tell me? How had I earned that sort of honesty?

Hannah didn't answer the question, and I felt a strange sense of relief. "Maybe it was because I was lonely that I wanted it so badly, but I really believed that I had no friends for a reason—that it would distract me from my true contemplative purpose. I thought the quicker I could get into a cloister, the better. I didn't know then how hard it would be, and how unprepared I was. How young." She stared down at the book in her lap, stroking the edges of the pages with her thumb. "You never know how young you are."

"So you became a nun because you were unpopular in high school? That seems a little extreme," I said.

"Caro, you're not listening." Hannah pressed her lips into a thin line. "I'm trying to explain to you why I left."

"Okay," I whispered.

"I went because I thought God wanted me to go," Hannah said. "And to me, at that time of my life, that was the most important reason to do anything. Maybe it was selfish, and maybe I should have given more thought to how it would impact the people that loved me, but I believed so completely in my vocation that I couldn't imagine delaying a second longer than I absolutely had to."

"And it was harder than you expected?"

"No," she said. "It was exactly as hard as I expected, but not in the same way. What I finally had to come to terms with was that even though I went into the cloister, I was still the same person. I was convinced that if I sacrificed everything, I would be changed. That I would be better, more whole and less afraid. But I was no different in there than I was outside, and I wasn't prepared for how difficult that would be. I was too naive. I didn't know anything about God."

"Like what? What didn't you know?"

She smiled. "Let's just say maybe I should've joined the Peace Corps instead. At least then I would've spent eight years doing something useful."

"What do you mean?" I asked, genuinely interested. I thought of what Father Bob had said about active orders versus contemplative orders. Maybe Hannah had simply chosen the wrong order. But something told me that the vein I had struck ran deeper than that.

"It's okay, Caro," she said, a tone of finality in her voice. "It's not easy to explain the choices I made—I'm finding it hard to do so myself. I understand why you lied. I'll talk to Mom and Dad for you, try to get you a stay of execution."

I waved her off. "No, that's okay. They're right. I shouldn't have lied about you. It's not like you were in jail or something. Nobody has to be ashamed, least of all me."

"Jail," she said, turning the idea over in her head. "Now, that's the story you should've told."

Something shifted inside me during my conversation with Hannah that night, and I went to sleep feeling better than I had in months, but I woke up early with a heavy feeling in my stomach. The yelling match with my parents and the talk with my sister had taken so much out of me I'd forgotten all about Pawel and how freaked out he was by my craziness—personal and familial. In the bright light of the early morning, though, I remembered, and I was afraid of what would come next.

When Reb showed up in my driveway, I was sitting on the porch with my bag in my lap, picking at a piece of plastic that was coming loose from my sneakers. As I trudged to the car, she rolled down the passenger-side window, leaned over, and called out, "Morning, sunshine!"

I didn't respond, just grimaced as I opened the door and slid in. She frowned and said, "You don't look good. What's up?"

I rubbed my eyes. "I'm fine."

"I don't believe you, Caroliar," she joked. I jerked up, surprised by the nickname. I hadn't heard it in a long time, and I felt a brief twinge of paranoia—had someone *told* her?—but then I reminded myself that even Reb, she of a thousand friends, didn't really know anyone I went to grade school with, and that it was just a coincidence. It wasn't even that clever of a pun. "Spill."

I glared at her. "*Don't* call me that."

"What?"

"'Caroliar,'" I said. "I don't like that."

"Okay, crazy," she said, rolling her eyes. She pulled out of the driveway without even turning around and set off down the street like we were in *The Fast and the Furious.* It was amazing to me that Reb had managed to get her license when Hannah could not. "What's your problem, Caro?"

"Ugh," I groaned. "I just did a really stupid thing and now I'm grounded and I think Pawel hates me and I just want to crawl under the covers and die."

"That's a bit much for a Monday morning, even for you," Reb said. "What exactly happened?"

I sniffled. "I told Pawel that my sister was in the Peace Corps. Which he blurted out at your party. And which I confirmed."

"So? Is it a big secret?" She looked at me, and I realized that Pawel wasn't the only person I'd lied to.

"No, it's not true," I told her. I stared at myself in the side mirror in an attempt to avoid her gaze. "She was a nun."

"Like . . . a nun?" Reb asked. "Like, a crucifix-and-penguin-suit-wearing, Mother Teresa kind of nun?"

"Isn't a penguin suit a tuxedo?" I asked, laughing a bit.

"I don't know, maybe. Why did you lie?" she wondered. In her typical Reb way, she was asking out of interest, not anger.

"Personal reasons," I said vaguely, hoping she would just drop it.

"And what does this have to do with Pawel?" she asked.

I told her about what had happened at dinner the night before. Reb let out a low whistle.

"Sounds like you really freaked him out," Reb said carefully.

"I think I did," I said. "And he doesn't know me well enough to know that I'm not crazy."

"Well, in all fairness, I know you pretty well and I still think you're crazy," Reb said. When I didn't laugh, she punched me softly in the shoulder and smiled so wide it was like she thought she could grin me into a better mood.

"Don't joke," I whined. "Can't you see I'm in pain?"

"Yes, I know."

"I might be a little nutty, but I'm not a compulsive liar or something," I insisted. "It's just that things with Hannah are complicated and I didn't have the energy to explain something to him that I didn't even understand. I didn't know how much I'd end up liking him, or that he'd end up liking me, and now I've ruined everything just as it was getting good."

"I'm sorry, friend," she said. "It does sound pretty crappy. Let me know if I can do anything to make it easier."

"Well," I said. "You can take us through the McDonald's drive-through so I can get a Diet Coke as big as my head. That might help."

"You got it," she said, taking the next right.

☆ ☆ ☆

Reb and I were almost late to French, and I didn't have time to catch Pawel before class. He was sitting in the back of the class next to Erin; I waved, but only Erin waved back. Reb and I were relegated to being four seats apart in the front. I got called on three times, which was great, because I hadn't done the reading. *Madame n'était pas contente.*

"Pawel!" I called as soon as the bell rang. Pawel disappeared out the door, and I raced to catch up. "Pawel!" I said again, taking his elbow. He stopped and looked at me blankly. "Didn't you hear me calling your name?"

"Oh, no, I guess not," he said, moving to the side and leaning against the lockers. "What's up?"

"What's up?" I stared at him in disbelief. "I wanted to talk to you about yesterday."

"What about it?" he asked, his eyes trained on a poster on the opposite wall.

"You're still mad at me for lying, aren't you?" I asked, my heart sinking. He wouldn't even look at me, and it was obvious he wanted nothing more than for this conversation to be over.

"No," he sighed. "I mean, maybe. I don't know. Look, Caro—"

"You know what?" I said, waving it off. "You're right. I lied and I was wrong and I don't deserve your forgiveness. Forget I ever existed." It took all my strength to turn around and walk away from him. I sucked my lip to stop the tears that were welling in my eyes from spilling out all over my cheeks.

"Caro!" Pawel shouted, but I didn't stop. I couldn't; I would've ended up a puddle in the middle of the hallway if I had, no matter how badly I wanted to.

☆ ☆ ☆

The day passed slowly. I watched the clock with the vigilance of a bird-watcher waiting for a yellow-bellied sapsucker to emerge from behind a canopy of leaves. All I wanted was for school to be over so I could rush home

223

and bury myself beneath the covers and never emerge. I couldn't believe that I'd been dumped for the second time in a semester; that had to be some kind of record. I was such a loser. Breaking up with Derek was one thing; after it happened, I realized how little I'd really liked him. But losing Pawel was different.

I *missed* him, already, so much that it hurt. It was amazing the way you could feel the absence of someone you cared about. As we walked to lunch, Reb reminded me that I hadn't known Pawel for very long, and there was no telling how I would've felt about him in a few days, much less months, but I couldn't be convinced. I liked him—*really* liked him—and I couldn't bear the idea that he was walking around thinking I was a crazy person.

But that wasn't the only thing. It was *my* fault, and I hated myself for that. I wanted time travel to be possible, so that I could go back to when I told Pawel that lie about Hannah, and not do it. I couldn't believe how one small choice could affect something so big, but if there was anything we were learning in physics, it was that the universe was causal. If the flutter of a butterfly's wings could cause a hurricane halfway around the world, my one stupid lie could take down my fledgling relationship like a sumo wrestler, no questions asked.

When we got to the cafeteria, Reb headed off to the lunch line and I slumped down into a chair next to Erin at our usual table.

"What's going on?" she asked, popping a baby carrot into her mouth. "You look glum."

"Glummer than glum," I muttered, laying my head down on the table.

"Why? Trouble in paradise with Polish Boy?"

"You might say that." I groaned. "I totally screwed up. He hates me."

"Caro, what did you do?" Erin asked, gripping my arm and pulling until I looked up. "Did you . . . *cheat*?"

"God, no," I cried. Leave it to Erin to jump to the most dramatic scenario possible.

"Then what?"

"I lied," I said, biting the inside of my mouth nervously.

"About what?" she asked, taking a bite of her sandwich.

"My sister."

"He's mad at you because of your sister?" She looked disappointed. Nothing juicy about that.

"I think he's madder about the lie."

"Well, what did you say? Does it have something to do with the party?" Erin guessed.

"No."

"Okay, the twenty questions thing is getting old. Spill."

"I told him that my sister just got back from the Peace Corps," I said, bracing myself.

"Wait—you told *us* that. At Reb's."

"I know," I said. I was hoping she'd been too drunk to remember, but apparently not.

"You *lied* to me?" I nodded. "What was she really doing before she came home?"

I took a deep breath. "She was a nun."

"She was a *nun*?" Erin repeated. "Why would you lie about that?"

"I don't know!" I said. "I just did."

"But—but I'm your best friend," Erin said slowly, a look of betrayal falling across her face like a shadow. "Why would you lie to *me* about that? I know you probably better than anybody else. Right?"

"Please don't be mad," I begged. "I can't take it if you hate me over this, too."

Erin shook her head. "I can't believe you lied to me."

"It's not that big of a deal," I said.

"Well, to *you* it isn't. Obviously you have no problem lying to people about stupid shit, so to you of course it wouldn't be a big deal. Does Reb know?"

I knew this was dangerous ground. I could feel her eyes on me, accusing and hurt, and I did something really, really stupid.

"No," I lied. "I haven't told her yet."

Erin nodded. "You should."

"I will," I said.

Erin put her hand on my shoulder. "I'm really sorry about Pawel. I know how much you like him."

226

"Thanks," I said, trying to smile.

"Maybe it's not the end," Erin said. "You never know with boys."

"Yeah," I said. "You never know."

Reb came up to us then and put her tray down next to Erin's. "Hey, mopey," she said. "What did Pawel say when you talked to him?"

I shook my head at her, but she didn't catch on.

"Whuh?" she asked, mouth half full of pizza.

"You know about Pawel?" Erin asked sharply.

"Uh, yeah. Was I not supposed to mention it or something?" Reb asked, looking sheepish and confused.

"You're unbelievable, Caro," Erin said, throwing the rest of her lunch into her bag and grabbing her books. "No wonder Pawel broke up with you. Nobody likes a liar." She stormed off without a backward glance while Reb stared after her, completely mute.

"What's her problem?" Reb asked.

I just sighed and put my head back down on the table.

16

It seemed unfair that I should have to endure yet another class period with Pawel and Erin after alienating them both so thoroughly in less than twenty-four hours, but as my parents are so fond of pointing out, life isn't fair—and neither is high school. I trudged toward physics with half a mind to bolt, spend the period in the bathroom, and take my punishment for skipping like a woman. But pre-programmed as I am never to ditch class or cheat on tests, I went anyway. The door felt as if it weighed a literal ton.

I was happy to see that Pawel wasn't in class yet. If I was lucky, maybe he had gotten sick from the tuna fish casserole at lunch and had to go home. It was awful to be wishing food poisoning on my ex-boyfriend—the "ex" part of that stung more and more by the minute—I knew that, but I couldn't help it. I simultaneously wanted to see him and couldn't stand the thought of it. I was all twisted into knots, and my brain was fuzzy and unfocused. My lab table was going to hate me that day, because there was no way I was getting any work done, but they'd have to take a number and get in line.

Erin walked in a few moments before the bell rang and sat down at her table. I tried to catch her eye, but she had her back turned to me. When class started and Mr. Tripp began handing out pieces of paper, I decided it was okay to breathe a sigh of relief: Pawel wasn't coming.

I looked at the paper. *SCIENCE FAIR,* it said in huge block letters. And it wasn't an application; it was an assignment.

"The science fair is coming up in three months, people," Mr. Tripp said, his face as blank as the dry-erase board behind him. I remembered what Pawel had said about him—*That is the most humorless man I have ever met*—and felt a sad twinge. "For the past few years, I assume your teachers have given you the information, which you promptly ignored, and maybe promised a little extra credit if you entered. Unfortunately for you, this is AP physics, and I am not one of *those* teachers. I'm requiring you to enter the science fair, and I'll be grading you on your projects. If one of you happens to win the whole thing, maybe I can be convinced to add a point or two to your final grade at the end of the semester."

Everyone groaned. This hadn't been part of the deal when we'd signed up to take advanced placement at the end of the previous year.

"I'm going to do you one favor with regards to the science fair, and it's this—you'll be working in pairs, and you don't necessarily have to work with the people in your lab groups. Your partner, your project, your choice. You'll also have sporadic time to work on your projects in class, in accordance with the schedule on your assignment sheet." He waved one in the air, as if we didn't know what assignment sheets he was talking about. "I'll need your partner's name by the end of the period, and a proposed project two weeks from today." He stared at all of us, and we stared back. "Go."

I glanced around the room. People were already pairing off; it was like a feeding frenzy, because nobody wanted to get stuck with the lazy people who never did any work. I regretted my fight with Erin in the cafeteria even more. She wasn't going to ask me to be her partner while she was this riled up.

It took me a couple of minutes, but I quickly realized that with Pawel gone the head count was uneven and one person would end up without a partner. And it was starting to look like that person was *me*.

"Christy," I said, tugging at the sleeve of one of the girls at my lab table. I didn't know her that well, but she was nice enough and pretty smart. "Do you want to work together?"

"Sorry, Caro," Christy said, giving me a look of sympathy. "Julia and I are pairing up." She gestured across the room to where her friend was waving her over.

"Yeah, no problem," I said. I ran my eyes over the faces in the classroom until I noticed Josh Greenblatt scribbling furiously in his notebook. "Josh!" I called. He looked up. I pointed back and forth between the two of us. He frowned and shook his head, jerking his thumb at David Prince, who was sitting next to him.

"Damn it," I muttered.

"Is there a problem, Caro?" Mr. Tripp asked. I hadn't noticed, but he was standing right next to me.

"Actually," I said, trying not to look like my life was caving in on top of me, "I don't have a partner."

"Well I'm sure we can—" he started, but as he was looking down at his clipboard, the classroom door opened and Pawel walked through it. I didn't know whether to laugh at the absurdity of what I knew was going to happen, or cry at the cruelty of the universe in sending in Pawel to be my science fair partner on the same day he'd broken up with me.

"It looks like you're saved, Caro," Mr. Tripp said. "Mr. Sobczak can be your partner."

Pawel looked up at him, startled. "Partner? For what?"

"The science fair." Mr. Tripp handed him the assignment. "Caro can fill you in on the details."

Everyone else had rearranged themselves so that they were sitting with their partners, so there was an extra seat at my table. I pointed to it and Pawel sat down, still looking stunned.

"What's this?" he asked, holding the paper up and frowning.

"Mr. Tripp is forcing us all to do the science fair in pairs," I said. "Before you came in, I was the only one without a partner. I thought you were going to be absent."

"No, just late," he said quietly. "Are we being graded on this?"

"Yeah."

"Okay." He read the assignment to himself. "He's not making this easy on us, is he?"

"Certainly not," I grumbled.

"Well, what are you going to do?" He shrugged. "I guess we're partners."

"I didn't mean for this to happen," I insisted.

"I know," he said, but he wasn't stoked about us working together, I could tell. We spent the rest of the period in awkward silence, flipping through our textbooks independently to come up with ideas for experiments. When we came across any, we jotted them down in our notebooks, and with five minutes left in the period, we switched papers. Mr. Tripp came around and glanced at our lists of potential projects.

"Not enough," he announced. "Think bigger."

"Bigger?" Pawel muttered. "What does he want us to do, build a particle accelerator?"

"I've got an at-home atom-splitting kit we could use," I said. Pawel smiled but didn't laugh.

It was going to be a long three months.

As soon as physics ended, I swept my books into my bag and rushed to the bathroom at the end of the hall, going as quick as I could without running. I must've looked like I was about to burst, but it wasn't my bladder—it was my heart. I didn't even check to see that all the stalls were empty; I just went into the last one, sat down on the toilet, and sobbed. The tears spilled out between my fingers, dripping down the backs of my hands and creating small dark spots on my jeans. I hitched in breath after breath, desperate to shut myself up, but I couldn't. I felt as if I was standing across a large empty room, staring at the stupid girl who couldn't stop crying. I didn't feel sorry for that girl. I hated her. I hated her weakness and her insecurities and her selfishness. The stall was like a cell, the walls pressing in and choking me. I rubbed my face with a wad of toilet paper, flushed it, and raced out of the bathroom.

I wasn't sure where I was going. The bell had rung for

the next period, but I knew I couldn't show up to class looking like such a mess, so I walked out of the building and started for home. I'd never skipped a class before, never faked an illness to get out of a test, but I knew I couldn't stand being in school for one more second. I felt as though I was going to explode, just burst apart into a million jagged pieces. It was two and a half miles to my house, not a short walk, but I needed the fresh air and the sunshine and I had the time. I put on my headphones and turned on the playlist of sad songs I'd created on my iPod especially for occasions such as this.

I barely noticed St. Robert's until I had almost passed it, which was sort of ridiculous, because it was a church with a school attached, not a stealth jet, but I guess I wasn't paying very much attention to my surroundings. Once I saw where I was, I couldn't go any farther. I thought about Father Bob, and how he'd told me that if I needed something, I knew where to find him. "Where to find him" was right there, in the two-story brick rectory that housed the church offices.

I stood on the rectory steps for what felt like hours but was, in fact, only one and a half Hall and Oates songs. (There was nothing quite like listening to "Sara Smile" or "She's Gone" when you were feeling lower than low; Dad had taught me that.) Finally, I took the plunge, pushing open the rectory doors and entering the office.

A middle-aged woman with wiry gray hair and glasses

with thick plastic frames looked up from her computer as the bells above the door jingled.

"Can I help you?" she asked.

"I'm here to see Father Bob," I told her. "I don't have an appointment."

She nodded. "Let me go back and see if he's free," she said, pushing her chair back and rising. "One second. What's your name?"

"Carolina Mitchell," I told her. She nodded again and disappeared into the back of the office.

I'd done eight years of school at St. Robert's, but I'd never been in the church office. We barely ever even saw the priests back when I was in school; every once in a while, they'd take a tour of the classrooms, the teachers stopping what they were doing to let Father Louis (in those days) sit down and chat to us. I'd certainly never visited a priest of my own free will before, and I didn't entirely know whether I was doing it of my own free will now. I reminded myself that I didn't believe in fate, or God. Nothing had drawn me to St. Robert's. I was just there.

The receptionist came out of the back and beckoned to me with one crooked finger. "Father Bob can see you," she said. "This way."

She deposited me in front of Father Bob's office, gave me a small pinch-faced smile, and scurried back out to the main reception area to answer the phone, which had just started to ring.

"Caro?" Father Bob was sitting behind his desk. He tilted his head so that he could see me through the open door. "Why don't you come in?"

I hesitated, then figured I might as well. I'd come that far.

"Sit," he offered, closing a book he was reading. I glanced at its spine as I sank into the chair opposite him, dropping my bag to the floor with a muffled thud. It said *Philosophiæ Naturalis Principia Mathematica.*

"The *Principia*?" I said. "You're reading Isaac Newton?"

"Have you read it?" he asked, setting the giant cloth-bound tome aside.

A short bark of laughter escaped me. "No," I said. "I'm not exactly fluent in Latin."

He smiled. "There are English translations."

"I'm in *high school,*" I reminded him.

"Forgive me. How can I help you, Caro?" To his credit, he didn't ask if it had anything to do with Hannah, although that would be the logical conclusion for my seeking out a priest.

I didn't know what to say, but I knew I had to give him a reason, any reason at all. "I wanted to confess something," I said finally.

"Pardon me?" Father Bob looked slightly confused.

"You know, confession," I said. "I tell you something I did wrong, you give me a punishment."

Father Bob rubbed the bridge of his nose. "Yes, I

know what confession is. And I think you know that this is not generally how it's done?"

"I couldn't wait until Saturday," I said. "It's urgent."

"I see," he said. "Well, what would you like to confess?"

"Seriously?" I asked. He nodded. "Well, okay. I guess I need to explain a little bit. You know Hannah's home."

"I do," he said. Father Bob wasn't thrown at all by my unannounced presence in his office. It was like he had been waiting for me.

"Do you remember the first time I came to see you?" I asked.

"As I recall, your parents were concerned because you told your classmates that your sister was dead," he said.

"Right," I said. "Well, I did it again. Sort of."

"You told people Hannah was dead?" I could see why this might perplex him, since Hannah was demonstrably alive, insofar as you could call what she was doing—sleeping twelve hours at a stretch, hardly eating anything, and moping around without telling anyone what was wrong—living.

"Not exactly," I said. "I told my—I told this boy, a friend of mine, that she had been in the Peace Corps this whole time, when obviously she hasn't been. And he mentioned it in front of my parents, and Hannah, and now everybody's pissed at me, even my best girlfriends, because I lied to them, too. It's a huge mess."

"I see," he said thoughtfully.

"My parents are livid," I told him. "Pawel—"

"The boy," he said. "Your friend?"

I nodded. "He thinks I'm some kind of pathological liar. And Hannah . . . she says she understands, but I can tell she's really hurt. I want to fix it, but I don't know how. I thought that maybe, if you gave me a penance, I could make it right. Somehow."

"Caro, I don't think you came here for confession," he said after a short pause. "I think you came here because you wanted to talk to someone."

"What's the difference?"

"Confession is about making things right with God," Father Bob explained. "Penance is a way of realigning yourself with the universe by meditating on your sin. But as far as I can tell, you have no interest in God. You want to make things right with the people you upset."

"What's wrong with that?" I demanded.

"Absolutely nothing," he said.

"So what do I do?"

"I don't know that there's anything *to* do," Father Bob said. "You've told your lie, been caught at it, and now you're experiencing the emotional recoil of your choices. Nothing in this world can be undone."

"Well, that's helpful," I grumbled.

"Have you apologized to Hannah?" Father Bob asked.

"Yes! And I tried to explain things to Pawel, but he still doesn't want anything to do with me. . . ." I trailed off. I could feel my face flush at the mere memory of the smackdown Pawel had put on me earlier in the day. He didn't want to be with me anymore; that much was clear: message received. And Hannah had accepted my apology, but she didn't seem to forgive me.

"It's not always that simple. Trust takes a lifetime to build and an instant to break. Creation is always more complicated than destruction."

"Destruction seems to be the only thing I'm good at these days," I told him. "All I do is screw things up. What if I'm just not a good person, Father Bob?"

He looked at me squarely, meaning business. "Don't believe for one second that you can't be a certain sort of person only because you were not such a person in the past. Being good is a daily choice; just because you were honorable before doesn't mean you can't betray the people you love, but also, just because you betrayed the people you love today doesn't mean you can't redeem yourself tomorrow. The past doesn't disappear, but it doesn't have to define your future. That's up to you."

"So how do I do that?" I asked.

He shrugged. "If I knew, the world would be a different place. There's no formula. You just have to figure it out for yourself, one step at a time."

Perfect. I'd come to Father Bob for advice, but he was just Yoda in a Roman collar. "How is this supposed to help me?"

"You know, there are some people—religious

people—who believe that the infinite consciousness that created the universe—"

"You're talking about God," I interjected.

He nodded. "Let me put it this way: some people believe that the reason the world appears to us imperfect is that it's not finished being created, that in fact it's in a constant state of growth and evolution aided in large part by the beings who exist within it."

"Meaning us."

"Us, and every other living thing, but of course we're the beings with the most potential for creation that we know of, because of our intelligence and high level of consciousness."

"I'm not sure I understand where you're going with this," I told him.

"What I'm trying to tell you is that with every choice we make, with every act, we help to shape our world and manifest the infinite potential of the universe as reality," Father Bob said.

I wasn't getting it at all, which was more than a little embarrassing. But I wanted to understand. "So I should . . . ," I prompted him.

"I think you should try to do something productive with all that potential. Have you ever made something, Caro? Like with your two bare hands?"

"I made a ceramic ashtray shaped like a heart for my parents at some kid's birthday party once," I told him. "Of course, they don't smoke. . . ."

"You should take up a craft," he proposed, reaching for the *Principia* and replacing his reading glasses on the end of his nose. That was my signal that this conversation was O-V-E-R.

"A craft? That's it? You don't have any other advice?" I couldn't believe it. The one person who was contractually obligated to help me sort out my life was giving me nothing.

"Try knitting," he said. "I hear it soothes the nerves."

"You want me to help shape the universe by knitting?" I asked. He smiled. Of course he was joking. *Knitting.* I mean, really.

"When you're just starting out, it's best to think locally," he said. "Do what you can. Any project you care about will do."

"Fabulous. Thank you," I said sarcastically, getting up and heaving my bag back onto my shoulder. "I'll let you know how that goes."

"Please do," he said. "And shut the door behind you, if you wouldn't mind."

☆ ☆ ☆

"Caro?" Hannah called out as soon as I let the door slam behind me. "Is that you?"

"Yeah," I said, trying to sound normal and failing. I went into my room and closed the door, hoping that Hannah would stay far away. I didn't want to talk about anything; I just wanted to crawl into my unmade bed and sleep. *Knitting.* Honestly. And all that vague stuff about choosing your choices. How about some advice I could actually use?

Hannah was at my door in moments. She knocked. "Can I come in?"

"Not right now," I said, my voice wobbling. "I want to be alone."

There was a silent pause. Then Hannah said, "I understand." But I didn't hear her leave. I waited a few minutes, then opened the door. She was gone.

I flopped down onto my bed and covered my face with a pillow. I sucked in a breath and let the fabric of the pillowcase suffocate me for a second before I released it and pushed the pillow away.

"Hannah!" I shouted. "Can you come in here?"

She did as I asked, standing at the foot of my bed. "Are you okay?"

"No," I said. Tears welled up in my eyes at the sight of her hovering over me, grim and concerned.

She sat down next to me, her back stiff and straight, hands folded in her lap. God, how she could've been a saint, if only she'd been looking up toward the heavens instead of down at me.

"Why are you crying?" she asked.

"Your hair," I wailed.

She touched the ends of it. "You're crying because of my hair? I thought this had something to do with Pawel."

"It used to be that pretty color and now it's dark and weird," I said.

"You're upset because my hair is different?" It sounded like a question, but she didn't look confused. She looked for a second as if she might cry, too. "You know, I had no idea it had changed color until I saw my reflection in the window on the train. We didn't have any mirrors. One of the other sisters would cut it for me, and I never saw any of the pieces. I always used to shut my eyes while it was happening. That first night I was home, I went into the bathroom, caught sight of myself, and threw up."

"Really?" I asked. "Why?"

She shook her head and let out a short, angry laugh. "I have no idea. Vanity, I guess."

"No. You're not vain. I mean, look at that haircut." I reached out and tugged at the very end of a piece that had fallen into her eyes.

"Convent chic," she said. "Very now."

I giggled. "I didn't know nuns could make jokes."

"We can't," she said, mock-seriously. "I've been saving that one for eight years."

"Another joke. Incredible." Then I had an idea, although I wasn't positive Hannah would go along with it. "Why don't we fix it?"

"Fix what?"

"Your hair," I said. "I bet we could get a walk-in

appointment at the salon. You could get a cut, and maybe some highlights."

Hannah looked uncertain. "I don't know, Caro."

"Come on, it'll be fun. And it might make you feel a little better. I've got Mom and Dad's credit card," I told her in a singsong. I was liking this idea better and better every second. Nothing made me feel good like a haircut. There was something freeing about trimming off all the old split ends, and if there was anything Hannah needed, it was to cut loose from the dourness of the convent and step into the light of modern womanhood. Or something.

Hannah glanced at the clock on my nightstand. "How are we going to get to the salon? Mom and Dad didn't leave us a car."

"I have an idea," I said, picking up my cell and dialing Reb's number.

☆ ☆ ☆

Twenty minutes later, Reb dropped us off in front of Hair Quarters, the salon Mom and I went to. I'd called ahead and Erica, our normal hairdresser, had agreed to squeeze us in.

"Thanks, Reb," I said, unbuckling my seat belt. "I owe you one."

"No problemo," Reb said, flashing me an encouraging smile. "Just call me when you need me to fetch you, okay?"

I nodded. Hannah thanked Reb, as well, and we both climbed out of the car and walked into the salon. Erica was waiting for us in the reception area; she greeted us warmly, shook Hannah's hand when I introduced my sister, and guided us to an empty chair, where she commanded Hannah to take her hair out of the ponytail it'd been tied up in and let it fall down to just above her shoulders.

"Yikes," Erica said, lifting it in places and fingering the edges. "Who cut this last, Edward Scissorhands?"

"Sister Augustine," Hannah said. Erica gave me a puzzled look.

"A friend," I said, by way of explanation.

Hannah glanced at the hairdresser with concern. Erica had been cutting my hair for years, and every time I saw her she looked different; at the moment she was sporting a short, angled cut and her entire head was dyed pitch black. But I wasn't worried. Erica would know just what Hannah needed. It was her gift.

"An enemy is more like it," Erica told her. "A blunt cut like this does your face no favors, sweetie. But don't worry, we'll fix it up—add some layers, maybe a little color. When I'm through with you, you're going to look gorgeous."

"Thank you," Hannah said softly, blushing. Even a foul haircut wasn't able to cover up Hannah's beauty; once Erica was done pruning her a little, she was going to be a knockout. I wondered what Hannah's general feelings were about dating; as soon as she stopped skulking around the house all day, she was going to get all kinds of male attention. But knowing Hannah, it would probably just freak her out.

I was sitting in the chair right next to Hannah's. When Erica hurried into the back room to mix the hair dye, Hannah turned to look at me. I must've had a miserable expression on my face, because she put her hand on my leg and asked, "What's going on, Caro?"

I sighed. "I just had a bad day at school, that's all."

"Pawel?" Hannah asked.

"And Erin," I said. "Erin is one of my best friends."

"Okay." She gave me a *tell me more* look, so I just opened my mouth and let it spill out. She nodded throughout my story, making the appropriate sympathetic noises as I related the awkwardness and humiliation of physics.

"He must think I'm a stalker as well as a liar," I said.

"I doubt it. How could you know how things would go?" Hannah said. "It was coincidence."

"Then why do I feel like I manipulated him into being my science fair partner even though I tried to prevent it?"

"Because you're glad it worked out that way and you're afraid he isn't," Hannah told me.

"I'm not 'glad it worked out that way,' God, Hannah." I scoffed. "Oh, sorry."

"You can say 'God' to me," she said, smiling. "Even in vain. It's okay. I'm not the Jesus police."

"Having Pawel as my partner is actually worse for me," I pointed out. "Now we're going to have to spend all of this time together, and he's going to think I'm angling to get him back. Plus, I want to get a good grade, and Pawel's smart, but he's not what you would call a hard worker."

"So you'll have to teach him," Hannah said.

"Ha. That's a good one." I leaned back in my chair and spun it about forty-five degrees. "This stupid high school stuff must be so boring to you."

"No," she said firmly. "It's a nice distraction."

"From what?" I asked. Maybe we were finally going to talk about it—her reason for leaving the convent, her reason for going in the first place, her disordered eating. The idea made me a little nervous; a hair salon didn't seem like the right place for that kind of serious talk.

Hannah frowned. "I have to start working on my college applications. Mom and Dad are really on my case about it—they're afraid I'll never go back if I don't start right away. But it feels like it's too soon. I don't know if I'm ready."

"Yeah, but aren't you sick of sitting around the house all day? Wouldn't it make you feel better to have something to do?" That was certainly the advice Father Bob would've given her.

Hannah sighed. "It sounds like such a silly obstacle, but I don't know what I'd study."

"Well, what did you study before?"

"Theology. I doubt that would be prudent now."

"Because you don't believe in God anymore."

Hannah looked away from me. "It's not that simple."

"I know," I said.

Hannah and I sat in silence for what felt like eons. I was starting to see, from the look on her face, just how complicated her life had really become. The past eight years had changed her. It must have been like being born again, except not in the life-affirming way—in the terrifying way, in which you emerge from blackness into a bright, cold, unfamiliar place, aching with fear.

"It's not losing my faith that upsets me," Hannah said finally. "It's the fact that I'm starting to wonder if I ever had any in the first place."

"You don't think you ever believed in God?"

"I wanted to believe. I really thought I had a vocation, but maybe I imagined it."

"That doesn't seem possible," I said. "You were so sure."

"Was I? Or did I just convince myself that I didn't belong out here, that God would only come to me through contemplation and determined prayer? I tried harder at that than I ever had at anything else in my life! For years I tried to open my heart and hear God speak to me. I kept hoping that one day I would experience some sort of epiphany, but it never came, and the more discouraged I felt, the less able I was to pray, until . . . I had to go."

"Did you talk to anybody about it?" The convent

she'd lived in had been full of other nuns just like her, but older; surely at least one of them had had a similar experience.

"I did," Hannah said. "Mother Regina said that I was too young when I went in, that I wasn't ready to give it all up."

"Give what up?" I asked. Hannah didn't seem to care very much about *stuff*. She owned almost nothing, even now that she was back. Her life was completely unsullied by the material world, insofar as that was even possible, so what was it that Mother Regina thought she was struggling to let go of?

"None of us goes into the convent clean," she said, not looking at me.

"And you left," I prompted. I could see why.

"I didn't," Hannah said. "I stayed. I sat in the chapel and forced myself to pray, but I was doing something wrong. I felt nothing. When I couldn't pray anymore, I would sit in my cell and *beg* for a sign, just something that could tell me he was out there, somewhere, watching over me, but there was only silence."

"What made you decide not to listen anymore?" I wondered.

"I didn't have a choice," Hannah told me. "I was coming to the point where I was supposed to take my permanent vows, and Mother Regina didn't believe the religious life was right for me anymore."

"She kicked you out?" I cried. No wonder Hannah felt ashamed.

"She didn't kick me out. She just told me that she could tell I was having difficulty coping with the strain of the contemplative life and suggested I might consider withdrawing from the Sisters of Grace," Hannah said. "She told me that if I really wanted to come back after I had sorted things out, I should investigate some of the more active orders. She thought the solitude was crushing me."

"Was it?" Hannah certainly looked crushed. It was hard to believe that my quiet, unassuming sister was incapable of living a contemplative life, though. If anyone was made for it, she was.

Hannah nodded. "I still don't know why. So many women came and went while I was at the convent, but *I stayed*. I tried harder than any other novitiate I knew—I worked until my bones ached and I prayed until I had no more words, and . . . nothing. No reward. No grace. Just emptiness."

"Do Mom and Dad know all this?"

"Bits and pieces. I don't think they really understand. I'm not even sure they want to."

I put my hand on her shoulder. "I'm so sorry," I said. "I had no idea."

She gave me a smile, but it was weak and sad and it sent a tremor through me. She looked like a little bird, small and slender and utterly breakable. If there was a

God, how could he abandon someone who was so sincere about following him? I could see why she would lose faith. If it had been me, I would've lost it a long time ago.

"I wouldn't worry about me too much," Hannah said, patting my hand. "It sounds like you have plenty of your own problems."

I wanted to talk more about it, but Hannah had a way of saying things with such finality. Erica came back with a small bowl full of purple goo and started applying it to Hannah's roots. It took almost two hours, but Erica worked her magic and Hannah left looking refreshed, gorgeous, and even a little confident, which I considered to be the greatest triumph of the day.

☆ ☆ ☆

Our parents went gaga over Hannah's new look. That is, after they took the time to grill me about where we'd been, why I hadn't answered my phone, and didn't I know I was still grounded, young lady? They didn't even notice Hannah at first; I suppose it was years of practice yelling at only one child, and the stealth with which she managed to blend right into the background.

"We went to Hair Quarters," I told them huffily, presenting my sister with a dramatic flourish.

"Oh, sweetheart," my mother said. "You look beautiful."

"Thanks, Mom," Hannah said, blushing. She was

happy that they were happy, but even now I watched as she wilted under the beams of our parents' adoration. She hated attention; a haircut was unlikely to change that.

"Really lovely, Hannie," Dad said, giving her a pat on the head.

"Hey, hey!" I cried, waving him away. "Don't mess it up! It took two hours to get that right."

"I didn't know you wanted to get a haircut," Mom said, fingering the ends of Hannah's newly blond, newly layered hair almost in disbelief. "You should've told me, I would've taken you."

"It was Caro's idea," Hannah said, nodding at me. I nodded back. I hadn't felt this good about myself in a long time, and they were right: she did look beautiful.

Mom turned her eyes on me now, gooey with sentiment.

"Don't," I warned.

"I'm going to go upstairs," Hannah said, picking her purse up off the couch cushion. She stopped at the stairs and smiled at me. "Thanks, Caro. I had a really good afternoon."

"Me too," I told her. She meant it, and so did I, but it would take more than a haircut to get us where we were supposed to be, if we ever got there at all.

As soon as Hannah had disappeared, Mom wrapped her arms around me and pulled me in for a nice long hug.

"You're smothering me, Mom!" I cried, struggling halfheartedly against her.

"You did a very nice thing for Hannah today," she said softly. "I'm so proud of you."

"Yeah, well . . ." I wriggled out of her embrace and set about straightening my rumpled hoodie.

Mom put a hand to my cheek. "You have a very good heart, Caro. I just wish it didn't embarrass you so much."

"What does that mean?" I asked.

Mom didn't answer. She just gave me an enigmatic smile (Hannah had learned from the best) and then walked back into the kitchen to check on dinner.

17

"So," Erin said two days later, setting her lunch tray down on the table. I looked up at her. "I've decided to forgive you."

"And what brought on this sudden burst of generosity?" I asked, taking a bite out of my turkey sandwich.

Erin shrugged. "I'm not mad anymore. Can't explain it."

That was how Erin was. When she was mad, she was furious, but she could never sustain it for long, and when she was done fuming, she was more than happy to let things return to normal immediately. Sometimes, when

I thought she was completely out of line, I'd fight her on it, confront her and force her to admit that she was wrong, but this time I couldn't have been gladder that she'd absolved me.

"I'm really sorry," I said. "I don't know why I did it."

"It's okay, Caro," she said. "It's not like I haven't lied to you before."

"You have? When?"

Erin waved me off. "It's not important. We're friends again, that's all that matters."

I gave her a dubious look but decided to let it go. The quicker we dropped it, the better I would feel. "It's too bad you couldn't have forgiven me two days ago."

"What do I look like, Jesus?" Erin scoffed.

"Now I'm partnered with Pawel for the science fair!" I whined.

"Yeah, well, so it goes," Erin muttered, popping a french fry into her mouth.

☆ ☆ ☆

Pawel had taken to sitting on the opposite side of the room from me in French and precalculus. I guess he had to counterbalance the hour a day he spent with his back five inches from mine in physics, because there was no way Mr. Tripp was letting him change lab groups. It wasn't complete radio silence. The day Erin forgave me, he knocked twice on my desk as he passed it in French, and when I looked up, he nodded at me. The day after that, he bumped into me in the hallway and said, "Excuse me, Caro." Each time, my heart fluttered like a ribbon in the wind, twisting and gyrating and making me slightly nauseous, but there was no more flirting, no more joking, and definitely no more kissing. It was as if I'd completely imagined our brief relationship, if that was even what it had been.

"You're being ridiculous," Reb said. She was driving me home, and we'd stopped at the Dunkin' Donuts drive-through for crullers. "High school relationships generally have the life span of a fruit fly, and they end for stupider reasons than lying about your family. Did you screw it up? Yes. Are you alone in having screwed up a probably-going-nowhere junior-year crush-plus? Absolutely not."

"Crush-plus?" I asked.

"Yeah, it's a term I invented. It means one of those flings that's basically a prolonged make-out session and nothing more," Reb said, taking a bite out of her cruller and edging her way into traffic.

"Pawel and I were *not* a crush-plus," I insisted. "We really liked each other."

"I know," Reb said. "I'm just trying to get you to see that you're not the only one who's ruined a fledgling relationship. We've all done it. Remember me and Sam Hansen?" I did remember it. Sam had been infatuated with Reb, but even though she'd liked him back, she had played it way too cool and ended up making him feel like an idiot by laughing when he asked her out. They hadn't spoken since, and Reb seemed to be over it, but every once in a while she'd mention it and I could tell how much she still regretted it. Even now, as she wiped sugar from her mouth, I could see it on her face.

"Good point." I was picking my doughnut to pieces. I didn't really want it, anyway. "I just don't want him thinking I'm some sort of crazy person. That's not who I am."

"I know that," Reb said. "And Pawel will figure it out eventually, if he's not a total moron."

"What if he just doesn't care anymore?" I asked.

"Trust me, he still cares. When you talk in class, he listens. He looks up when you walk through the door. I've noticed. He's just being stubborn."

"How can you be sure?"

Reb shrugged. "I can't. But my intuition tells me it's true."

"I'm supposed to trust the future of my romantic life to your intuition? Oh, God, I'm doomed," I moaned, only half serious.

"Caro!" Reb laughed. "Rein it in, drama queen. In all likelihood, Pawel is not the future of your romantic life. He's just a boy you like. You'll like other boys, I promise."

She put a hand on my shoulder and gave me a hard look. "It's a long life."

"Not if you don't keep your eyes on the road!" I cried as we nearly sideswiped a Hummer. Reb drifted back into her lane and stepped on the gas.

"Don't drop your crumbs everywhere," she warned me. "Those crevices are a bitch to vacuum out."

I glanced into the backseat, which was littered with to-go cups and Taco Bell wrappers. "Yeah, I'd hate for people to think you were a slob."

"Everybody's a critic," she muttered.

☆ ☆ ☆

On Friday, Mr. Tripp gave us the class period to discuss our science fair projects. Pawel didn't look thrilled to be sitting next to me, but he didn't look upset about it, either. It was the indifference that was killing me.

I sat on my stool, stiff and silent, with a thousand possible opening lines whipping through my mind. It was impossible to settle on something casual but worth saying. He was slouched over the table, drawing meaningless shapes in the margins of his notebook. I tried hard not to be too obvious about watching him. I started going through my textbook, turning the pages as if I was searching for something.

Finally, I spoke. "Single-bubble sonoluminescence," I

said without taking my eyes off the page I'd been staring at for several minutes. Real sexy.

"Huh?" I felt Pawel sit up and glance at me.

"For our project," I explained, turning my head slowly and letting my eyes meet his. He blinked and looked away, but before he could cover it I saw the softness of his expression. I didn't know whether to feel relieved or depressed. For the first time, I could tell that his interest hadn't been completely eradicated by my stupid lie, but it was obvious from the way he was acting that he wouldn't be letting me off that easily.

"What's single-bubble sonoluminescence?" he asked, returning to his drawings. I took a good look at them; he wasn't an artist, not like Carson Gallagher, who could sketch an entire true-to-life portrait in a fifty-minute class period. They were just rough symbols to keep his hands occupied. It was endearing.

"Basically, it's an experiment where you turn sound into light," I explained. *Make something,* Father Bob had said. I wasn't crafty; I wasn't going to take up knitting, even though I was almost 99 percent positive he was joking about that. But I did love science. I'd been thinking long and hard about our project, how I could use it for creation, not destruction. I'd spent several hours scouring the Internet for the perfect experiment, and when I read about single-bubble sonoluminescence, I knew I'd found it. *And God said, "Let there be light," and there was light.* Nothing like taking a cue from the pros. Or rather, The Pro. Father Bob would be proud. Or horrified. It was hard to tell with him.

"How?" Pawel asked.

"By directing a sound wave into an air bubble trapped in liquid."

"Oh, that sounds easy," he said, smirking.

Mr. Tripp loomed large behind him. "What does, Mr. Sobczak? Hopefully not your science fair project?"

"Actually, that's what we were talking about." I scrambled to gather some notes I'd made earlier in the period. "I think I—we—want to do single-bubble sono-luminescence."

Mr. Tripp's eyebrows jumped. "That's a little too advanced for this classroom, Ms. Mitchell, don't you think?"

I shrugged. "It's a challenge."

"It's not really something you can do at home," he told me. "You'd need access to the lab, and it'll be difficult to provide a demonstration at the fair."

"What if we video our results and show them on a laptop?" Pawel chimed in. "Is that allowed?" I looked at him in surprise and he gave me an encouraging smile.

Mr. Tripp looked unconvinced, but he said, "I suppose so." He seemed to have caught on to the fact that this lofty goal was entirely my doing. "Are you confident you two can pull this off?"

I nodded slowly. "Yes." I wasn't really sure; I definitely

didn't think I could count on Pawel for anything, except maybe to watch as I did the entire experiment myself. But I liked the idea of a project that would keep me out of the house and my mind on other things. I was doing very well in physics, which was probably why Mr. Tripp was allowing me to attempt this giant project. It felt good to excel at something, even as my entire personal life was falling to pieces.

"Okay," Mr. Tripp said. "I'll put you down for single-bubble sonoluminescence. You'll have to sign up for extra lab time and provide any materials we don't have here. Once you've worked out how your experiment will proceed, we'll make a schedule." He looked us over one final time and shook his head a little. "Good luck, you two."

As soon as the bell rang, I hopped off my stool and left the classroom as fast as I could without sprinting. Pawel called out behind me, but I didn't turn or stop. I was getting that weightless feeling again, like I wasn't part of my own body anymore. I needed to remain in control, so that I wouldn't say something awful or embarrassing to Pawel. Escape was the best course of action.

But Pawel was faster than me. He caught up to me near the stairs and put a hand on my shoulder.

"Are you . . . running away from me?" he asked, furrowing his brow. He looked cute like that, confused and awkward. I knew the last thing he wanted to do was chase me. We were in such a weird place. I thought I might explode from how rapidly our relationship was changing. New friends one minute, boyfriend and girl-friend the next, then nothing, now science partners. It was too much; I was vibrating at a thousand different frequencies at once.

"No," I said. "I have to meet someone."

"Okay," he said slowly, as if he didn't quite believe me. "I just wanted to ask you about the project."

"What about it?"

"It doesn't seem like a good idea to do something so complicated," he told me. "I mean, extra lab time? Can't we do something a little less . . . involved?"

A sudden fury grabbed hold of me. I didn't know why I was so angry with him—or rather, I did know, but I didn't know why it was this, his reluctance to do a stupid science fair project we were being coerced into teaming up for, that tipped me over the edge, but it did; my face was so hot that I thought the blood underneath my skin might be boiling.

"You know what, Pawel? I don't care what you do. I'm doing this project, and you can help me, or not help me, or whatever. I'll do all the work, I'll even put your name on it and you can get the same grade—which will be an A, by the way, because that's just how smart I am. Don't worry, I'm not going to ask you for any help. Okay?"

"Uh, okay?"

"I have to go," I said. I took the stairs quickly and burst out into the crowded first-floor corridor, where I weaved my way through the pack until even if Pawel was following me, I would have been lost to him.

☆ ☆ ☆

Reb dragged me to go get ice cream after school, even though I didn't want any and she was supposed to be off dairy that week because she thought she might be lactose intolerant. Reb had a touch of hypochondria, which annoyed the crap out of Erin, but I thought it was funny. Not that day, though. I just wanted her to let me mope in peace, but she wouldn't. Hence, ice cream, her treat.

"Your ice cream is melting," she warned me, leaning forward to take a semiliquid scoop from my cup. "What's wrong? More Pawel stuff?"

"Yeah. Whatever, he's a douche bag."

"Totally," Reb said. Then she paused to reconsider. "But is he?"

"No," I sighed. "I'm just mad at him, because if I don't get mad at him, I'll be too pathetic to look him in the eye."

"You're not pathetic, Caro," Reb said with a little sympathetic laugh. "You're just in recoil. It's completely normal for you." Funny, that was the word Father Bob had used: "recoil."

"What do you mean, completely normal for *me*?" I demanded.

"Well, you do this kind of thing a lot. If someone hurts you, instead of being all depressed you get angry," Reb explained. "You get mad so you don't have to be sad."

"That's ridiculous! Name one other time that's happened."

"How about the beginning of the school year, when Derek dumped you? He's been trying to be friends, but you keep freezing him out, even though you *know* that he's not the right guy for you and you don't even want to date him!"

"Derek and I are *fine*," I said. "I've completely forgiven him."

"Yeah, okay. Prove it."

"Should I make him a friendship bracelet?" I asked.

"Are you going to his party next weekend?"

"I don't think I'm invited," I said, stirring the melted remains of my Neapolitan into ice cream soup.

"Everybody's invited," Reb said, rolling her eyes.

"Not me, he didn't even ask me to come," I said.

"Did you expect an engraved note? This is a high school party. You tell one person and then let the word travel on the wind." Reb wiggled her fingers to signify word traveling on the wind, which made me laugh. I appreciated the effort, and even though I hated to admit it, it was sort of working.

"Are you going?" I asked.

"Definitely," Reb said. "My mom is in Indiana again for the weekend. I was going to have my own party, but this is better, because I won't have to clean anything up."

"Okay, I'll go," I said. Reb grinned and patted my hair.

"Who's a good girl?" she cooed. I made a face, but she just laughed.

☆ ☆ ☆

"You're going to Derek's party?" Erin asked in astonishment when I told her over the phone later that night. I was in the middle of painting my toenails a dark metallic blue when she called.

"Reb talked me into it," I said, confused. "Should I not go, do you think?"

"I wouldn't recommend it," Erin told me.

"Why, because of Derek? We're friends," I said. "It won't be weird."

"Oh, God, Derek's not the problem," Erin said. "Did you not hear who *else* is coming to the party?"

"Uh, no," I said. "Is there some kind of secret blog about this stuff that I don't know about?"

"Yeah, it's called EverybodyOnTheCheerleading-SquadHasABigMouth.com," Erin said. "Anyway, Briana Garner is coming."

"Briana Garner from physics class?" I asked, propping

my left foot up on my desk and leaning my chair back a little to get the angle just right. "She's nice. Why would I not go to the party because she's coming?"

"I'm not finished," Erin said. "Briana's bringing a date to the party."

"Who's her date?" I leaned forward and slowly painted my big toe.

"Polish Boy," Erin said.

My foot slipped from the edge of my desk and I bashed my knee against it. "Oh, Jesus Christ!" I cried. I glanced down at my leg, which was bright red and throbbing.

"Caro?" Mom called from the hallway. She knocked. "What's going on in there?"

"Nothing, Mom, I just hurt myself," I said. "Go away."

So of course she did the opposite, opening the door and walking in. "What happened? Are you all right?"

"Yes," I said, wincing. "I'm fine."

"Hello?" I heard Erin ask, her voice tinny and faraway-sounding.

"Is there someone in here?" Mom asked, looking around.

"No, Mom, God," I snapped, picking up the receiver from where it'd landed on the ground. "It's just Erin on the phone."

"Oh." Mom stared at me. "You sure you're okay?"

"Yes. Please go," I begged. I was in so much physical

pain that my head felt crowded. I didn't even want to talk to Erin, and contemplated just hanging up on her.

"Fine, fine," Mom said, backing out of the room. "Sorry for showing concern for my child. It won't happen again." She closed the door behind her.

I lifted the phone to my ear. "Sorry. I think I shattered my kneecap."

"Really?" Erin asked.

"No." I sighed.

"Did you hear what I said?" Erin reverted back to full gossip mode. "Briana and Pawel are *going out*."

"That's impossible," I said, my stomach sinking. "It's been, like, two weeks since he and I broke up."

"Improbable, but *not* impossible. Obviously."

"And this is an announcement she made? That she and Pawel are going to Derek's party together? God, insecure much?" I said, trying to distract Erin.

But Erin was a bloodhound, and unlikely to be led off the trail so easily. "Are you sure you still want to go to the party?"

"I don't know," I said. "I'll think about it. For the record, you're advising that I not go?"

"Totally," Erin said. "I don't think it's worth the humiliation."

That was the magic word—"humiliation." I was more obsessed with it than anybody I knew. Erin didn't seem capable of sensing when she was being humiliated (if she was, she wouldn't hook up with half the guys she did), and Reb was too cool to care one way or the other. But I couldn't stand the thought of people talking about me behind my back, laughing at me. The thought of it made me want to crawl out of my skin.

"Maybe you're right," I said. "I'm not going to go." Reb wasn't going to be happy.

18

I thought I'd been pretty clear with Pawel about what I expected from him in terms of the science fair, so I was confused when he followed me out of French class and tried to talk to me about the project.

"Pawel, I told you, I have it under control," I said, digging around in my locker and praying that he would leave soon, before I had to pretend to find the thing I wasn't even looking for. "You don't have to do anything, it's fine."

"That feels wrong," he said, leaning against the wall and fiddling absently with the zipper on his backpack. "Like I'm slacking off."

"It's not wrong if I give you permission to slack off," I told him. *Please go,* I thought desperately. I was starting to get that panicky, disconnected feeling again, like I was a hot-air balloon that had become untethered. "Seriously, don't worry about it."

"It's my project, too," he said, anger creeping into his voice. "You don't just get to shut me out. Tripp asked me before class why he hasn't seen me in the lab with you. He's questioning my level of participation, and I didn't even *know* you were already spending time in the lab."

"It's a big project. Anyway, I'm sure you have better things to do," I said, abandoning the pretense and shutting my locker.

"Like what?" He scoffed.

"I don't know, like hanging out with your new girlfriend," I snapped. *Oh shit.* The second after I said it, I wanted to take it back. That was why I hated the floaty feeling: I never felt like I had any control over what I said or did, and this just proved it. My words echoed in my head like I'd shouted them, and I could sense every pair of eyes in the hallway on me, but when I looked around, nobody was even paying attention.

Nobody except Pawel. He stared at me, openmouthed, as if he had something to say, but nothing came out.

"I'm sorry," I said. I turned and walked quickly down the hallway, silently willing him not to follow me.

No such luck.

"Look, Caro, I don't know what you're talking about,

and I'm not sure you do, either, but I'm going to help you with this assignment, even if it means I have to do this single-bubble somnambulance thing," Pawel said, coming up from behind.

"Single-bubble sonoluminescence," I said. Was he saying that he and Briana Garner *weren't* going out? The question burned at the back of my brain, desperate to be asked. I wished I didn't care so much. I wished I could be who I pretended I was, someone who didn't care or notice or feel anything, but I wasn't that person. Being around Pawel reminded me just how vulnerable I was, how much I had messed up and how much I regretted it. It wasn't just about him. It was about Hannah, too, and my parents. What I had done, why I had done it, and the swirling maelstrom of doubts about what to do next.

Pawel was deeply annoyed, so much that he wouldn't even look at me, his gaze wandering through the space over my head. "Whatever. What do I need to do?"

"Uh, okay. You could book us some more time with Mr. Tripp in the physics lab," I suggested. "Any day after school is good for me."

"Done. What else?"

"We need a container to house the experiment," I told him. "Mr. Tripp doesn't have anything we can use in the lab, so I was going to go online today when I got home and look for something that could work."

"I'll help you," he offered.

"What are you going to do, click the mouse for me? I can do it myself," I insisted.

"Fine. But when it's time to actually work on the experiment, I want to do my share. I'm not going to let you just carry me on this—I'm smart, too," he said. I'd never seen him so defensive before. He didn't understand that this thing I was doing, pushing him away, wasn't about what I thought of him or how smart he was.

"Have it your way," I said, shrugging. "Can I go now?"

"Yeah," he said. He began to walk away, but after a few steps he turned and looked back at me. "You know, this wouldn't be as awkward if you stopped being so difficult."

I was too stunned to think of anything to say to that.

"See you around, Caro," Pawel said.

"What are you doing?" Hannah asked, hauling a fresh load of laundry into the family room. She began sorting socks as I hovered over my laptop, clicking through a Google search for online glassware catalogs.

"Looking for a container for my science fair project," I told her. "You're doing laundry?"

"You say that like I've never washed clothes before," Hannah said. "I did it all the time at the convent."

"Ugh, sorry. I had a fight—argument—something bad with Pawel today at school," I told her.

"Oh. What about?"

I got up from the kitchen table and sat down on the couch next to her basket. "The project, actually. I told him he didn't have to help me, that I'd just put his name on the assignment and he could take whatever grade I got, but he refused. He acted all offended."

"Well, it's a little bit offensive," Hannah said.

"Thanks."

"What do you want me to do? Tell you that you were right? You know you weren't." Hannah gave me a hard look. It looked well practiced. In the last couple of years in the convent, she had been put in charge of the new recruits—the postulants, she called them—even though most of them were twenty, even thirty years older than she was. She had to teach them the rules and scold these grown women when she had her own doubts. If she ever chose to become a mother, she'd probably make a great one. She was already starting to exhibit signs of being like our own.

"I was just saving him the grief of having to do a really hard assignment," I said. "He should be thanking me. Instead, he accused me of being 'difficult.'"

"You're really hurting, aren't you?" Hannah asked, sympathetically putting a hand on my shoulder.

"Hurting? Me? No," I said. A lie, of course, but what was I going to do, cry about it? I'd done enough of that already. "I just feel bad he got stuck with me and I'm trying not to make it worse. But apparently I'm making it worse."

"For who? Him or you?"

"I'm fine," I insisted. "I've moved on. And so has Pawel. He's got a new girlfriend."

"He does?" Hannah looked as shocked as she could manage.

"Well, that's the rumor. He didn't *exactly* deny it when I . . . accidentally confronted him about it today," I said. "Anyway, back to work."

"Hey, hold on. Are you sure you don't want to talk about it?" Hannah fiddled with an old sock. "I don't mind listening."

"It's nothing," I said, trying to ignore the way my stomach was tugging. I began scrolling through yet another website. Fifteen minutes later, I found what I was looking for: a narrow-necked hundred-milliliter round-bottom distillation flask made out of soda lime glass. I ordered it immediately on my parents' credit card and went back and forth about texting Pawel to let him know, until, finally, I just sent "Bought container for experiment. Let you know when it arrives" and left it at that. I got no response.

I was about to retreat into my room when Hannah stopped me. "Caro?"

"Yeah?" I asked, cradling my laptop in my arms.

"I— Mom is taking me to the doctor next week,"

she said. It was news to me. Nobody had mentioned a doctor's visit—not that anyone in this family told me anything. Father Bob was right when he said trust took a lifetime to build and a second to destroy. "And I was wondering if you would come."

"What kind of doctor? Like a lady doctor?"

Hannah stared at me for a second, then shook her head. "No, like a, um, a nutritionist, sort of. Will you come?"

"Yes," I said. I was surprised but pleased. This was a big step for Hannah—and for my parents. They were finally admitting that Hannah had a problem, even if they weren't admitting it out loud to me. And I had some trust-building to do with my family. I was absolutely going to be there if Hannah wanted me. "I will come."

She smiled. "Thanks."

☆ ☆ ☆

A week later, Pawel and I sat across a table from each other in the physics lab with the flask between us. Mr. Tripp was in his adjoining office with the blinds half closed.

"Okay," Pawel said, staring at the flask. "Now what?"

"I showed Mr. Tripp a list of the equipment we're going to need," I told him. "He promised he'd help us get our hands on it. He says he has a friend at the physics department at Northwestern who might rent some of it out to us."

"So we just wait?" Pawel asked.

"No," I said. "I thought we could go over methodology. I made this for you." I pulled a small stack of papers out of my bag and handed it to him.

He took a minute to look it over. "This seems really complicated. Are you sure we can pull this off?"

I nodded. "I've gone over everything about a thousand times. Although I fully acknowledge it might not go exactly as planned."

"You mean we might fail?"

"What would you rather do?" I asked.

"I don't know," Pawel said. He paused for a moment, as if he had something more to say. Then he said it. "Actually, I was thinking maybe we could create a Rube Goldberg machine."

"What's a Rube Goldberg machine?"

"You know, like a contraption that does something simple in a really convoluted way," Pawel said. "I've been sort of obsessed with them since I was a kid. I used to make them out of K'nex."

"If you wanted to do a different project, you should've said something when we had to turn in a proposal," I said. *Amazing.* I'd done all kinds of research on single-bubble sonoluminescence, purchased the flask, and requested the materials from Mr. Tripp, some of which were going to be difficult and expensive to lay our hands on, and now he was telling me he wanted to submit a useless invention made out of a children's toy. "Unbelievable."

"Jesus, Caro," Pawel said, kneading his forehead. "I know you're not thrilled to be working with me, but you could at least pretend to listen to my ideas."

"I'm listening. I'm just telling you that the deadline for turning in our proposal has passed and we can't change our project now," I said. "I don't know what you want me to do about that."

"You know what? You're totally right. I should've said something earlier." He leaned away from the table and folded his arms across his chest. "Why don't you just tell me what you want my help with? I'll do whatever you tell me to do."

"Well, how about, since I'm already familiar with the procedure, you be in charge of recording our observations?" I proposed. "Then we can do the write-up and presentation together."

"Okay, that sounds good," Pawel said, running his fingers through his hair. I loved it when he did that. It made him look sweet and pensive. I blinked a few times to clear my head and when I looked up, Pawel was staring at me.

"You okay?" he asked.

"Yeah, I just had something in my eye," I lied. "It's gone now."

"So . . . are we done for today?" He didn't wait for me to answer; he just started packing up his books.

"Sure," I said.

He gave me a tight smile as he slid off his stool and onto his feet. "See you later," he said, walking to the door.

"Hey, Pawel?" I called out. He turned, and I bit my lip, unsure now about saying what I'd been planning to say.

"Yeah?" His eyes searched for mine, but I kept them trained on a large crack in the linoleum.

"I don't not want to work with you," I said. "I just thought it was going to be weird and I didn't want you to think—"

"I don't," he said. I couldn't see his face, but I could hear the smile in his voice. "We're friends, right?"

"Right," I said, letting my breath out slowly and trying desperately to fight the floaty feeling. The last thing I needed was to blurt out the truth about the friend thing—that it wasn't what I wanted, that I wanted much more.

"Then it's kosher," he said. "Have a good night."

"You too," I managed to say, hoping he didn't hear the crack in my voice as he left the room.

When he was gone, I knocked on Mr. Tripp's window and waved. He waved back and gave me a thumbs-up, which, dorky as it was for a teacher to give his student a thumbs-up, made me feel a little better.

I decided to walk home. It wasn't dark yet, and though it was November, we hadn't had our first snow, so the air was brisk and sharp and clean-smelling. It felt good in my lungs. I bundled up in my puffy coat and wrapped my scarf around my neck to keep the chill out. I turned on my iPod, blasted my favorite sad, sweet song from a folk pop artist I liked, and trudged home, feeling sorry for myself, but not as much as before. Things were not great, but they definitely could've been worse.

19

I almost forgot about Hannah's doctor's appointment. My science fair project, which had started out as just one more annoying class assignment, was occupying most of my thoughts and nearly all my time. Mr. Tripp and Pawel were right to doubt our ability to successfully complete it. Single-bubble sonoluminescence was *way* above our skill level. But when Mr. Tripp offered us the opportunity to back out, to choose something easier, and once again Pawel suggested the Rube Goldberg machine, I got this sudden feeling that if I didn't go through with it, then that would say something about me. I wanted nothing to do with some high school–level project. I needed to do something bold and risky and inventive. I wanted to prove that I was capable. And I didn't care if I failed.

Mom reminded me of the appointment as I ran out the door to catch the Reb bus to school. "The nutritionist, Caro," she said, waving a piece of toast at me haphazardly. Hannah was upstairs, still asleep probably. She had agreed to this "health assessment," as they called it, but she hadn't given up her strange habits, and she wasn't eating any better.

Clearly, she was unhappy about the appointment. She and Mom picked me up after school and Hannah was silent the whole way to the doctor's office. The nutritionist's office was three towns away, and traffic was making us late. The air in the car was clotted with tension; Mom drummed anxiously on the steering wheel and Hannah bit her fingernails, lost in thought. It was as though we were all being ferried by some intangible force of the universe toward an unknowable doom, and even though I knew this was for Hannah's own good, a part of me wished desperately that we could turn back, go home, and bury our heads in the sand the way we had been doing, because it was safer there, where the shadows of oblivion hid the darker truths well.

The atmosphere in the waiting room was no better. Most of the other patients were normal-looking, all women, and I wondered how many had once been where Hannah was now, and how many had come from the opposite direction, who were there to get skinnier.

There was one girl, though, younger than Hannah but older than me, who stood out. She sat in a corner with one leg pulled up, her chin resting on her knee. She surveyed the rest of us coolly and dispassionately, as if we were specimens in some human zoo and she was an alien observer. Her hair was pulled up in a messy ponytail high on her head, and her clothes, a simple ensemble of rumpled T-shirt and jeans, hung off her body in a grotesque way, improbably thin arms and legs jutting out from nowhere, like she was made of matchsticks.

I couldn't help comparing her to Hannah, who sat as far away from the matchstick girl as possible; next to her my sister looked less fragile and wasted, but there was some strange assonance between them, as if they were vibrating at the same frequency, connected by a thread of understanding. The matchstick girl's eyes landed on Hannah and remained there. She didn't appear to be ashamed by her bold-faced staring, and Hannah squirmed beneath the weight of her gaze, the heaviest part of her, and refused to look in her direction. Even after the matchstick girl was called in, she left an invisible thumbprint on the room. I couldn't quite shake off how she had made me feel.

She hadn't come back by the time Hannah was summoned. I looked up sharply when I heard her name called, following it to its source, a sweet-faced young nurse who was obviously tired from a long day. Hannah hesitated before standing up, and she and Mom followed the nurse while I, according to a preordained plan, stayed behind with my homework. Twenty minutes later the matchstick girl returned. She placed a clipboard on the receptionist's desk with a loud clatter and wordlessly grabbed her coat from the rack near the door. She took one last long glance at all of us before turning and leaving, her eyes passing over me as if I wasn't there. I wondered what she was looking for, but I was glad she was gone; she brought up in me a sort of primal protectiveness of my sister, and even though the thought was absurd, it seemed as though if I could shield Hannah from the matchstick girl, then I could shield her from the disease itself.

When I saw Hannah and Mom emerge from the labyrinth of exam rooms, I jumped up, eager to get out of there. Hannah had some papers to fill out, so Mom offered to go pull up the car while I waited with my sister.

"How was it?" I asked as Hannah bent over the forms, pen in hand, marking boxes with careful checks. She just shrugged.

Hannah had just finished sliding the pen back into the cup on the receptionist's desk when the door opened and a woman bustled in, an infant carrier in one hand and a boy of maybe three clutching the other. The little boy was babbling and the baby was screaming its head off as the woman worked to divest herself of her various accoutrements and navigate her team out of the small hallway and into the waiting room.

I glanced at Hannah. "Ready to go?"

But Hannah's face had blanched, and she turned it away from me, searching for something in her purse.

"Are you okay?" I asked. She mumbled something in reply but I didn't catch it. "What?"

The woman had removed her scarf and coat and hung them precisely on one of the hooks in the hallway, and with the little boy on her hip and the carrier in her hand, she passed us, only at the last moment looking over.

"Hannah?" she said. I was completely surprised, and it occurred to me then that I often thought of Hannah as if she was a ghost only I could see. Hannah's head swiveled slowly toward the woman, and her face was as expressionless as I had ever seen it, but in that way my sister had that I now knew hid a churning ocean of feeling underneath.

"Amanda Brenner," Hannah said, the name coming out in a sudden *whoosh*.

The woman laughed. "Amanda Taylor now." She wiggled her left hand and a diamond the size of a boulder sparkled in the overhead fluorescent lights. "I can't believe you're here! I had no idea you were still in town—it's been so long and nobody's heard a thing about you. Are you on Facebook?"

Hannah squinted at her. I had explained Facebook to her already, but she had probably given it no other consideration, had definitely not thought about it as something she should *be on*. "No," she said flatly.

"Well, that explains it, then," Amanda said. "You should really be on, we've got a nice big group of old St. Robert's people on there, and our fifteen-year reunion is coming up. You don't want to miss that, do you?"

"I'm sorry," Hannah said, nearly shaking. "We need to go. Our—someone's waiting for us outside."

"Is this your sister? Of course she is, you can see it in her face. Amanda," she said, offering her hand for me to shake. I took it because I didn't know what else to do, but something inside me rankled as she said her name again, and when our palms touched, I knew why—*Amanda Brenner*. Hannah's middle school torturer, from the letters to St. Catherine I had read not long before. It was hard to imagine this woman, a bit harried but obviously wealthy and well put together, as a child of twelve, but it was completely believable that she had been a mean one.

"Caro," I said.

"And you're what? Eighteen?" Amanda asked.

"Sixteen," I said.

"Oh, God, sixteen!" Amanda laughed again. There was a manic edge to it, probably the result of being a young mother with two children, one of whom was still squalling intermittently from the carrier while the other was doggedly attempting to put every single block in the little toy chest into his mouth. Not that Amanda seemed to notice either of these things, but maybe it was like ambient noise to her by now. "Is it possible we were ever that young, Hannah? It seems like a lifetime ago."

"Amanda, I'm sorry—"

"I just can't believe I'm running into you here of all places. Are you a patient of Dr. Willett's?" She didn't wait for Hannah to respond before barreling forward with her relentless questioning. "Isn't she the best? I've been working with her to lose some of this baby weight. It's totally true what they say, it just falls off with the first one and after the second one it sticks to you like glue!"

"I'm a patient of Dr. Adrian's," Hannah said. Amanda didn't react to that; I highly doubted she was even listening.

"So *what* have you been *up* to these days?" Amanda asked, tilting her head like a cocker spaniel. "Are you married? Kids?"

"No, I—" Hannah didn't want to explain it, and I wanted to help her, to save her from having to give this woman access to any part of her life at all, but I didn't know what to say to stop it.

"Oh, wait, I think I heard something about . . ." Hannah stiffened as Amanda searched for the most diplomatic way to put it. "A convent? Is that right?" She said the word "convent" in a hushed tone, as if it was a dirty word she was hoping her little ones wouldn't pick up.

Hannah nodded.

"So you were a nun?" Amanda pressed. I started to see the meanness in her. She wasn't stupid; she saw Hannah's reaction to her for what it was. She looked frivolous, but I could tell that she was shrewd and her questions weren't as innocent as they appeared. "Are you out now? What was that like?"

"I—" She was trying her hardest, but Hannah couldn't grab on to the magic words, the ones that would make Amanda disappear.

I dug into my pocket and brought out my cell phone, pressing it hard against my ear. "You're outside, Mom? Okay, *okay*. We're coming! Sorry." I turned to Hannah. "That was Mom, she's been waiting at the curb for ten minutes and she's really annoyed." I flashed a cold smile at Amanda. "God, you'd think it was some big emergency or something."

"I didn't hear a phone ring," Amanda said, reaching down to pat her son's head as he slammed his little fists into her kneecap.

"It was on vibrate. Nice to meet you, Amanda. Good luck with that baby weight," I said spitefully. I took Hannah's hand and dragged her past Amanda to the door. "Oh, and I think your kid just spit something up. Take care!"

Hannah didn't speak until we were in the elevator on the way to the building's main lobby. She released a long breath and smiled at me gratefully.

"Thanks, Caro," she said. "I just—I *hate* that girl."

"Yeah, she's totally awful," I said.

"She was really mean to me when we were kids, and then she acts like— Well, it's fine. It's over. I just wish I'd said something better than 'um' and 'I'm sorry' over and over again," Hannah said, closing her eyes and leaning her head against the wall. "But when I saw her, it was like I was twelve, you know?"

I nodded. "What I find particularly disconcerting is the fact that she's breeding."

Hannah smiled. "I appreciate you getting me out of there. I was practically rooted to the floor."

"It's all right," I said. "I've got your back."

"I know you do."

When we got home, Hannah told Mom that she wasn't going to see Dr. Adrian anymore.

"Why not?" Mom asked. "I thought you liked her."

"She was fine," Hannah said. "But I'm not going back."

"You can't just not go back! You haven't even *done* anything yet," Mom said. "How do you expect to get better if you won't work at it?"

"I'm *fine,*" Hannah insisted. "I only went because you wanted me to. I don't need help and I don't need to work on anything."

"That's just not true," Mom said. She darted her eyes at me, as if she was considering asking me to leave the room, but then she sighed in resignation and said nothing. "You're—you need help, Hannah. You're not well."

"I'm not sick," Hannah shot back.

"I know you saw that girl in the office today," Mom said. "And I know she rattled you, but if you don't stop, you're going to become like her and I—we can't bear to see that happen to you, Hannah, we just can't."

"I am not that girl!" Hannah shouted. It was almost too much to believe, the way nervousness and fear had transformed Hannah. I felt as though I was watching a movie, actors who looked a lot like my family playing out an impossible scene. It was almost Escheresque, with how familiar and yet completely unreal it felt.

"You're right, Hannah," Mom said bitterly. "You're not that girl. Because *that girl* is trying to get some kind of help, and you refuse to even acknowledge that you have a problem. And that's what scares me. I feel as though you're slipping through our fingers, sweetheart." Her voice trembled, and it occurred to me that I might, for the third time in my life, see my mother cry. I considered leaving immediately; that was something I didn't want to see, as if it might break some sort of spell or truce and bring the whole world tumbling down.

"I couldn't bear to lose you," Mom told Hannah, who refused now even to look at her. "Not again."

Hannah stood abruptly. "I'm going for a walk," she said, although I'm not sure who she was telling, since she seemed to be speaking not to either of us but at some phantom in the distance. "I don't want anybody to follow me." She whisked her jacket off the back of her chair and stormed into the hallway, where she startled Dad, who was coming in to see what all the commotion was about.

"Hannah, how was—" he said after her, but I cut him off. Hannah disappeared into the garage and, I assume, out into the neighborhood, though by then dark had already fallen.

"Not now, Dad."

"What's going on?" he asked Mom, who just shook her head and took off in the other direction, toward the stairs and her bedroom. A moment later we heard a door slam upstairs. Dad turned to me with an expression of utter confusion. "What did I say?"

"Nothing," I told him. He sat down at the table across from me and I reached over to pat his hand. He slipped his fingers through mine and squeezed.

"You know, Caro," Dad said, "sometimes I think that loving you and your sister is the only thing I've ever really known how to do. But there's always that question—is it enough? I used to think it was, but I'm not so sure anymore."

I smiled at him and squeezed his hand back. "I'm going to get a glass of lemonade," I told him. "You want one?"

"You bet, kiddo," he said. "Thanks a million."

"You're welcome," I said.

☆ ☆ ☆

Dad went upstairs to try to talk to Mom, and I waited for Hannah in the family room, but she didn't come back for a while and I was starting to worry. When she had been gone over an hour, I crept upstairs to see if my parents thought I should take the car and go looking for her. I was about to knock, but the sound of my mother's sobbing made me freeze.

"This is our fault, Evan," she cried. I could hear my father making soft *shhh* sounds, probably rubbing her back.

"Don't say that," he replied calmly as she hitched in a breath. "We did what we thought was best for Hannah given what we knew at the time. What other choice did we have?"

"We should have gotten her some real help," Mom said.

"We did get her help," he told her.

"No. That grief counselor the church sent us to said she was processing everything well, but she wasn't," Mom insisted. "We saw it, but we didn't want to believe it, so we let her just carry on like that for *years.*"

"She was already religious before," Dad reminded Mom. *Before what?* I thought, then I flashed back to the letters—Sabra. Was that really what all this was about? Mom and Dad seemed to think so. But what had happened to Sabra? And how had my sister been involved? I felt guilty for eavesdropping, especially since I knew without a doubt that if my parents knew I was hearing their conversation, they would not be having it, but I couldn't tear myself away. Here was my chance to get some real, albeit cryptic, information about Hannah and I wasn't just going to give that up because of a little moral ambiguity.

"She might have gone into the convent anyway," Dad said. Mom's crying had abated a little; all I was hearing from her now were sniffles. She seemed to have cried herself out. "You don't know it's because of Sabra."

"I know," she said. "A mother knows. Look what she did to herself in there. Our baby, Evan. Every time I look at her I just want to burst into tears."

"Me too," he said. "Me too."

"And Caro!" I jumped at my name, thinking for a split second that Mom knew, in the way she knew all sorts of things it made no sense for her to know, that I was behind the door. "Caro is so confused. That's why she's acting out. She deserves to know the truth. We shouldn't be keeping secrets from each other."

"But Hannah doesn't want to talk about it," Dad pointed out. "And it's Hannah's decision. You said so yourself. It's her life."

"We're a family," Mom said. "We shouldn't be lying to each other, we should be taking care of each other."

"That's what we're doing," Dad told her gently. "It's just not as easy as it was when they were babies."

It was as if someone had put a hook through my chest. I'd had no idea how hard everything was on my parents. I guessed when you were someone's kid, you liked to believe that they had all the answers to all the problems in the world. To hear them casting about for some sort of absolution, some sort of comfort, in the face of all the obstacles they were dealing with gave me a sense of alarming insecurity.

I heard the mechanical growl of the garage door as it opened and shut, and the sounds of my parents shuffling around in their room, probably preparing to come out of it. I sprinted down the stairs and threw myself onto the couch, spreading the pages of *The Crucible* and pretending to read it as Hannah walked into the family room and so did my parents. Mom had cleaned herself up; she and Dad were wearing identical tight smiles. Hannah's face was all splotchy and red; it was cold at night now, and the wind was blowing madly through the trees.

Mom glanced at the clock. "You've been gone for a long time, Hannah. Weren't you freezing?"

Hannah shrugged. "It's not that bad."

"How about we order pizza for dinner?" Mom suggested. "I don't feel like cooking."

"Sounds good to me," I said. The events of the afternoon had wound me up so much I hadn't realized until Mom said the word "pizza" that I was starving. My stomach growled to second the motion.

"Hannah?" Mom said it like a challenge, but Hannah didn't rise to it. She just shrugged again.

"That's fine," she said, turning to leave. "I'll be up in my room."

"How's the homework coming along, Caro?" Dad asked, putting a hand on Mom's shoulder.

"Good," I told him. "You don't have to worry about me, Dad."

"Happy to hear it, kiddo," he said. "Happy to hear it."

20

The cold war between Mom and Hannah continued un-
abated for days. Hannah wouldn't agree to go back to the
nutritionist, but I casually suggested to Mom that maybe
it wasn't about not wanting to work on her health, but
instead about that particular nutritionist (*or,* I added silently to myself, *her other patients, one mean-girl blast from
the past in particular*), and she agreed to look into other
options.

On Friday right after last period, I heard a familiar
voice shout my name from across the crowded hallway. I
turned and saw Derek striding toward me.

"Oh, hey," I said. We hadn't talked much since school started; he'd sort of faded into the periphery when Pawel and I started hanging out, and since we didn't share any classes, it was easy to lose track of him. "What's up?"

"Nothing," he said, shrugging. "Are you coming to my party tomorrow night?"

To my relief, Derek's party, the one I had agonized about going to and then decided not to attend after I found out Pawel was going with Briana, had been canceled because his parents had decided not to go out of town. I figured it was the universe's way of rewarding me for taking the high road, but apparently it was just the universe's way of playing a nasty practical joke. I was not amused.

"I thought you had to call it off," I said.

"Nah, my parents decided to go to Wisconsin this weekend instead, so I had to postpone it," Derek said. "But it's still on. Saturday, nine o'clock. Will you be there?"

"I don't know," I told him. "I'm sort of . . . grounded." Even though it felt like I was approaching probationary period of my incarceration, I was pretty sure my parents were not going to authorize a party, and I was tired of lying to them.

"Really? What'd you do?" He grinned at me like I was about to confide something hilariously naughty.

I shook my head. "Nothing. It was stupid. Never mind."

"You sure you don't want to tell me?" He stared hard at me, like he was trying to use Jedi mind tricks to get me to confess my sins. It gave him this intense look of concentration that I used to think was proof that he was deep and mysterious. I squinted back at him. I thought about kissing him, just lunging at him, pressing my stomach against his and clutching the tuft of hair at the nape of his neck and kissing him the way I had two weeks into our relationship, when I'd gotten over my fear of scaring him off. Not because I wanted *him*. I just wanted something meaningless and physical to make me feel in control.

Finally, he relented. "I guess not."

"Nope," I said. The urge to kiss him passed, and I knew I had to go, as if on its way out of my head the fantasy would project itself onto the wall and Derek would know I was thinking about it. It meant nothing—I knew that for sure—but it made me sad. "I can't come."

"It's not like you've never snuck out of your house before," Derek said.

"Yeah, but . . . ," I protested, although I didn't feel one way or the other about it. The thought of waiting until everyone went to bed (including Hannah, who never seemed to sleep at night) and then tiptoeing out of the house and waiting in the freezing cold for Reb to pull up at the corner was exhausting. There wasn't anything good waiting for me at that party. But I knew I would probably do it anyway, because I felt as though it would mean something if I didn't go.

"I'll think about it," I told him.

☆ ☆ ☆

"For the record," Reb said as Erin leaned forward with her forehead against the dashboard to let me crawl into the backseat, "I never thought this was going to happen."

"What?" I asked as I settled in, clipping my seat belt and pushing my hair out of my face.

"That you would come to this party," she said. Erin handed me a water bottle full of Gatorade and vodka. I took a big swig and gave it back, wiping my mouth with the back of my hand.

"Yeah, well, I just felt like it, I guess," I told her. The vodka warmed me immediately, creating a crackling heat that skimmed my skin. It was nice; the ever-increasing tension at *casa de* Mitchell was wearing on me, and it was good to be free of it, if only for a couple of hours.

"Aren't you worried about seeing Pawel?" Erin asked, and I couldn't shake the sense that she was rooting for drama to unfold. Erin liked a good soapy incident, sometimes going so far as to court them, but her life, like mine and Reb's, was pretty bland most of the time. She sounded excited. "Or Derek? I saw you talking to him yesterday in the hallway."

"That's impossible, your last class is in the other building," I said. "Who told you Derek and I were talking?"

"I saw," Erin said. "I see all." She was already very drunk.

"What did Derek want?" Reb asked, jabbing Erin in the side with her elbow. Erin shrieked and clutched her side, then laughed.

"Hey! That hurt," she said.

"Leave Caro alone," Reb said, then asked me again, "What did Derek want?"

"To invite me to the party," I said, turning up my hands in confusion. "God knows why."

"Well, I guess we'll find out." Reb turned down his street and parked as close as she could to his driveway, which was already overrun with cars. When we stepped out of ours, we could hear the pounding bass and loud murmur of people on the porch, smoking and drinking beer out of party cups and talking at each other. Just looking at them made me cold, but they didn't seem to care.

We strolled into the party arm in arm, mostly to prop up Erin, who was a little wobbly getting out of the car. We made our way through the throng of people in the living room to the kitchen, where Derek had generously provided a keg of cheap light beer. It could've been Reb's party a month or so earlier; they all seemed the same to me these days. Cup in hand, I gazed around the room. Everyone looked unfamiliar to me, and even though Reb and Erin were right behind me, I felt alone.

Just as I was finishing my beer, I lowered my cup to see Pawel gently shove his way past a crowd of identically dressed bleach-blond girls in almost impossibly high heels. For a second I thought he was alone and my whole body relaxed, but then I noticed Briana behind him and my vision contracted, bending at the edges so that Pawel and Briana were enormous, like I was seeing them through a telescope.

Briana waved at me and I cringed. "Hey, girls!" she called out, causing Reb and Erin to turn. Erin bumped me lightly in the small of my back with her fist and I heard Reb whisper, "Mayday."

"Hey," I said, then gulped. Erin, trying to help but hitting hopelessly far from the mark, started filling my cup back up with beer. "What's up, guys?"

Pawel had a strange look on his face, a melting pot of surprise, confusion, and discomfort. "Caro. Cool, I didn't think you were coming."

"Why wouldn't I?" I said, bristling. This was my school, these were my friends, Derek was *my* ex. If anyone's presence should have come as a surprise, it was his.

He shook his head and feigned innocence. "No reason. Can I get past you?"

I was blocking the keg. "Oh," I said, stepping aside and draining half my cup for something to do. Reb gave me a tight smile and glanced at Erin, who was about to open her mouth.

"I'm going to take drunky here to the den," she said quietly. "You come find us when you're done."

"I'm done," I said, but Briana had grabbed hold of my elbow.

"Caro, Pawel told me about your science fair project, and I have to tell you—you are totally insane!" She laughed. "I mean, you take ass kissing to an entirely new level! Single-bubble sontonomolescing? Are you nuts?"

"Are you drunk?" I asked, catching a whiff of malt liquor on her breath.

"Of course!" she cried.

"Great." I turned to Pawel. He shook his head and tossed me a nervous little grin. I felt like a glass of champagne, all liquid, bubbles rising through my arms and shoulders up to my head. He was wearing a green polo shirt, slightly wrinkled, and without closing my eyes I could picture lying down with him on a couch and burying my face into his chest, breathing in the smell of laundry and cotton fibers.

Get a hold of yourself, I commanded, wrenching my

eyes away from him and focusing on Briana. "Single-bubble sonoluminescence," I said, correcting her.

"Whatever! Dana and I are doing insulation," she said, grabbing Pawel's hand and squeezing it.

"Spicy," I mumbled. "Okay, well, this has been fun, but I've got to go. See you kids later."

My face was fever-hot as I bolted from the kitchen, pissed at myself for not getting another glass of beer for the road. I had to either leave right away or get good and drunk so that nothing could upset me, but due to my extremely good luck, I ended up running into Derek instead.

"Caro," he said, pulling me in for a tight hug. "I didn't think you'd make it."

"Yeah, well . . . I did," I said, attempting to sound upbeat. I tried to wriggle out of the hug, but his grip was inescapable. "Are your arms made of titanium or what?"

He laughed. "You're funny, Caro."

"Funny-looking, right?" Oh, God, I was cracking bad jokes at my own expense. I could feel the night slipping from my control. My brain buzzed. Derek's skin had a warm glow in the lamplight. I surrendered and let him keep his arm around me. He ran his hand over my left shoulder and I closed my eyes. Soon he would get distracted and let me go, and I had a plan for that eventuality: I was going to run like hell.

"It's loud in here," he announced, though nobody but me was listening. "Let's go find a quiet place to talk."

There was a change in him. All the careful distance he and I had created between us had vanished with time and beer, and I knew that once we were alone he would try to kiss me. I followed him to his bedroom anyway, hoping that by the time it happened I would want it, that I wouldn't wish it was Pawel who'd corralled me into a private place and put his lips on mine.

We didn't make it to his bedroom. The upstairs hallway was almost deserted, and Derek pulled me into a dark corner near the stairs and pressed me up against the wall with his entire body. He raked his right hand through my hair, lifted my head, and kissed me, lightly at first, and then with more pressure. He wrapped his left arm around my waist, and I let him. I let him kiss me, too, closed my eyes and remembered a time when all I wanted was to kiss him. It wasn't entirely unpleasant; Derek was a good kisser, something my crush on Pawel had entirely erased from my brain, and the part of me that still liked him lit up like a candle in a dark room, sending a column of warmth shooting up my body from my feet to my forehead.

With my lips and hips thus occupied, my mind wandered into the future. What if this was the moment when my life changed? Maybe Derek and I would rekindle things; maybe I'd even go so far as to fall in love with him; maybe I'd forget about Pawel, and Derek would be the boy I wanted. Maybe we'd make a pledge to each other on graduation night, to stay together through college and emerge four years later with a rock-solid relationship. We could move to the city and live together in an apartment in Lakeview, spend a few years making money and raising hell, and then settle down, get married, and have kids. It was crazy, the thought of it, but I let my mind race on with the fantasy anyway.

Suddenly, and without any reason, Hannah glided over the horizon of my thoughts like a hot-air balloon. I wondered again if she'd ever done this, kissed a boy she liked, or could like, in a dark hallway with a party raging below.

"Oh, God, excuse me, sorry." I opened my eyes to see who had stumbled upon us, and when my gaze met Pawel's, I felt like I was going to throw up.

"Hey, dude, what's up?" Derek said. His words were casual, but his tone wasn't. He had to have heard about Pawel and me. His fingers closed around my arm possessively.

"N-nothing," Pawel stammered, embarrassed. For the first time, I noticed that Derek's hand had found its way up my shirt, and I pushed down on his wrist to dislodge it. "I was just using the bathroom." He gestured at the door behind him with his thumb.

"You having fun?" Derek asked. I stared at Pawel, trying to discern something besides discomfort in his face.

"Uh, yeah, tons," he said. "I'll leave now."

"Wait," I said. "I'll, uh, go downstairs with you."

"What?" Derek asked as I extracted myself from his grip.

"I need more beer," I said, shrugging apologetically. "Be right back."

Pawel took off down the stairs without waiting for me, but I caught up quickly when he was slowed moving through the crowd in the foyer. I put a hand on his shoulder and he turned around.

"What?" he said coldly.

"What you saw up there . . ." I didn't know how to explain, but I wanted to, even as I realized how little I owed him.

"Big deal," Pawel said, his eyes on the banister over my shoulder for no reason other than it wasn't my face. "You're back with your old boyfriend, congratu-frickin'-lations."

"Hey!" I snapped. "You don't get to be mad at me, *you* broke up with *me,* and *you* were the one who brought a date to this party. I came with my friends."

"Correct me if I'm wrong, but Derek also broke up with you, and yet you were upstairs with your tongue down his throat." I could tell that as soon as the words left his mouth, he regretted them. His eyes widened with the knowledge that he'd betrayed a personal secret.

I could've let him off easy, but I didn't. It wasn't in my nature. "And why do you care about that? I thought we were *friends*."

"We are friends!" he cried. "I don't want you to get hurt."

"I'm not going to get hurt. Derek doesn't want anything from me besides what you saw up there, and I don't want anything from him," I said, knowing the words were true as I was saying them. Derek was never going to be more than my ex-boyfriend and a casual acquaintance from now on. I'd let my imagination get away with me, because I'd screwed up with Pawel and I wanted to grab hold of something, so I built it myself. "Oh my God."

"What?"

"I need to go home," I said. I felt a surge of pride, like I was finally starting to get it. Finally starting to figure out why Hannah had gone to the Sisters of Grace: she couldn't find peace with God on her own, so she looked for a way to create it.

"I'm too drunk," he said. "I can't drive you."

"Yeah, whatever, I live ten blocks away, I'm just going to walk," I told him.

"You're leaving?" he asked, incredulous. "In the middle of—"

"In the middle of this super-fun party?" I finished for him, knowing that wasn't what he was going to say. "You bet. See you in class, Pawel."

As I walked away, I imagined I left him befuddled in a cloud of dust.

21

Knowing Hannah would be awake when I got home, even though it was two-thirty in the morning, I marched straight upstairs as soon as I snuck noiselessly through the door.

"I get it!" I announced as I burst into her room. She was sitting in her chair, reading.

"Get what?" she asked, turning her eyes to me in that placid, saintly way she had about her.

"Why you went to the convent," I said.

"Okay, so tell me—why did I go?" She sounded bemused, although she wasn't smiling. She rarely smiled when she talked about her time away from home.

"For the same reason I made out with Derek tonight even though I don't really want to be his girlfriend," I said.

"I don't follow," Hannah said. "Your old boyfriend Derek?"

"Yeah."

Her eyes narrowed. "Where were you tonight? Did Mom and Dad know you were out of the house?"

I waved off the question. "Derek took me upstairs and I knew he was going to try to kiss me and I let him because I was trying to convince myself that if Pawel had moved on and was dating someone else, maybe I should, too, and maybe Derek could be that person," I said. "So I kissed him, and I kept kissing him even though it didn't feel right, and I was thinking about you and why I was doing all of this and I just . . . saw it, I guess."

"So you're saying that kissing Derek even though you didn't want to is like how I went into the convent?" Hannah's face was blank. I couldn't tell if she was upset or laughing at me.

"I mean, they're not the same, but you and I both tried to create something that wasn't there to distract us from what was missing," I said. "Don't you think?"

"No," Hannah said. "I don't." She closed her book. "I'm really tired, Caro. It's almost three in the morning."

"Oh, okay," I said. I was confused—was Hannah angry with *me*? Wasn't Mom the enemy these days? It was hard to tell with her. Usually she wanted to talk to me more than I wanted to talk to her, but suddenly the roles were reversed. I felt like I was being rejected. "I guess I'll go to my room, then."

Hannah nodded and rubbed her temples. "Good night."

"Night," I said, leaving and shutting the door behind me.

☆ ☆ ☆

I stayed after school to do some setup for the experiment I planned to run later that week—with or without Pawel—and missed the late bus. On my way home, I took a slight detour and ended up at St. Robert's. I was pleased to see Father Bob and excited to tell him about my science project, which he seemed interested in.

"I'm something of a scientist myself, you know," he said.

"Seriously?"

"You sound surprised," he said. "Before I went into the seminary, I got my master's degree in astrophysics."

"But . . . you're a priest," I pointed out.

"Well observed." He laughed. "What gave it away? The outfit?"

"Isn't 'scientist priest' kind of an oxymoron?"

"There's a great tradition of scientist priests. Ignazio Danti, Jean-Felix Picard, Gregor Mendel—I'm sure you've heard that name before. Father Georges Lemaître, the originator of the big bang theory: also a priest. Compared to them, I'm just an amateur, but I do like to dabble."

"Okay," I responded, not sure what else there was to say to that.

Father Bob said, "It was Einstein, I think, who wrote, 'Science without religion is lame, religion without science is blind.' They need each other to be complete. Are you going to argue with Einstein?"

"I guess not." I mean, the man discovered relativity; the least I could do was give him the benefit of the doubt. "But you can't prove God exists. And isn't that what all science is ultimately about? Proving theories about the universe?"

Father Bob squinted at me skeptically. "Provability is not truth, Caro. Gödel's incompleteness theorem tells us that, if we didn't already know it intuitively, which we do."

"Gödel's what?"

"It's a mathematical theorem about natural numbers," Father Bob said. "It basically says that within a system, there are always going to be statements that are true but nonetheless can't be proven without reference to the system itself, which is impossible because the statement exists within the system. So, I mean, if you were to make a parallel between math and God, in this case the statement would be 'God created the universe.' There's no way to prove that the statement is true or false, because a creator god is necessarily outside of creation, and we, as scientists or mathematicians or philosophers or people of faith, are limited by what we can observe, and we can't observe anything outside of creation—or the universe, or infinity, or whatever you want to call it. Does that make sense?"

"I don't know," I said. "You talk fast." I wasn't a dummy, but I wasn't exactly a PhD, either, and this was pretty advanced stuff.

"Well, it's not a limerick," Father Bob said. "It's a little more sophisticated, but keep thinking about it. Now, how can I help you today?"

"There's something I don't understand," I said.

"Something about Hannah?"

I told him the story of how Hannah shut me out after I came home from the party. "I thought I was finally getting her, and then she turned all cold and quiet. What's up with that?"

"What do you feel you know now that you didn't before?"

"I don't think she went into the convent because she wanted to be a nun," I said. "I think she went in because she was feeling alienated from God, and she thought being a nun would fix the problem. But when I said that, she completely shut down."

"Well, there's probably more to the story," he said. "I saw her once at church, Caro. Hannah is clearly not well."

"I know." I took a deep breath, fully prepared in that

moment to tell him about Hannah's letters to St. Catherine and the mystery of Sabra, but at the last second I found I didn't have the courage. So I changed the subject. "If you were all set to be an astrophysicist, why did you become a priest?"

Father Bob drummed his fingers lightly on the edge of the desk. "It wasn't so much a decision as it was an answer. I felt like I was being called to the priesthood. I knew that I would never be a great researcher. I was by no means an extraordinary scientist. But over the years, I became convinced that I could be a good priest."

"Have you ever regretted it?" I asked.

"We all have our moments of doubt," he said, smiling. "But no, I don't regret it. I love what I do. And I didn't have to renounce my interest in science when I was ordained. I still try to keep up, and to look back." He gestured to the *Principia,* still laid out on his desk.

I pointed to a black-and-white print that hung on the wall above his head: *Waterfall* by M. C. Escher. I was surprised to see it there, and even more surprised that I hadn't noticed it the first time I came in. "I have that same picture on my binder," I told him, showing him. "It's my favorite Escher."

"It's an exquisite piece of art," he concurred. "I became acquainted with his work during my time at the seminary. There was a priest there, Father Rushing, who was something of a mentor to me. He gave me that print.

He said I should keep it with me always, to remind me that there is beauty in paradox. He told me that grappling with faith is a bit like looking at that image, that logic rejects it but that intuition recognizes it as a sort of truth even in its impossibility."

"I just thought it looked cool," I admitted.

"It certainly does," he said. "But it's unnerving, too. It's a bit like staring into another dimension, one that has a different set of mathematical and physical laws. For me, it also serves as a reminder that the mind of God is unknowable, that things that seem contradictory to us only appear so because we have no context for them, or aren't seeing the full picture."

I thought of Hannah and her dark struggles, how little I knew about her, how little she seemed to know about herself. "So if we can't see the full picture, how do we know that we're making the right choices?"

"*That,* I believe, is the whole point of faith," Father Bob told me. "Science and religious belief are very much alike in that way. You can operate based on what you think you know at any given time, but you must always be cognizant that there are forces at work you can't see, or don't understand. It's not enough to blindly believe in what you have been presented with, what you *think* is true. You must always be open to new information, always be listening and watching and experimenting and seeking. Only then can you really say that you're doing God's will."

I stared at Escher's *Waterfall,* my eyes tracing the impossible objects that created the bizarre architecture of its alternate world. There were only two people in the image; one was a woman doing her laundry, blithely unaware of (or perhaps uninterested in) all the strangeness that surrounded her. But there was another, down at the bottom, an obscure figure that leaned casually against a wall, looking toward the waterfall. I liked to think he saw what I was seeing, the completely unfeasible and yet inarguably existent perpetual-motion machine that towered above him. I wondered what he thought of it.

22

With everything that was going on, the holidays snuck up on me. I left home one morning and noticed, for the first time, that the leaves had changed and were falling, blanketing the lawns and sidewalks like confetti.

The snow came in late November, and it carried on all through December until Christmastime. This was going to be the first Christmas with Hannah in the house in eight years, and not coincidentally, it was going to be the first time we'd gone to Christmas Mass in years. The catch was Hannah wouldn't come. She'd stopped going to Mass a few weeks after she and my parents had seen

Pawel there. I guess after all that struggling, she'd decided that she had lost her faith for good. Of course, she wouldn't talk about it. She wouldn't talk about anything at all.

I argued with my parents about attending the holiday service. I figured if Hannah didn't want to go, why should we? Dad might've backed down, but Mom insisted. Something about it being our job to support Hannah in her faith even when she was unsure of it herself—*especially* then, she said.

I'd hoped Father Bob would be saying the Mass we went to, but as it always seemed to be, it was Father Boring. I let my eyes and mind wander during his interminable homily and caught sight of Pawel sitting a couple of rows away from us with the people I assumed were his family. His mother, a short heavyset blond woman in an apple-red sweater, was sitting at the end of the pew, next to his father, who was also short, and completely gray-haired. Beside them were two taller, dark-haired girls—Pawel's sisters—and a small, lean blond boy. Pawel was next to him, at the end of the pew. I watched them intently; Pawel's parents and sisters were listening to the sermon, but Pawel and his brother appeared to be engaged in a silent punch war. They were watching Father Boring, but every once in a while a fist would strike out like lightning and land on a soft shoulder, and then another would follow it up in retaliation. I could tell they weren't hurting each other, or at least they weren't trying, although a couple of times, during a momentary détente, I noticed Pawel reach up and rub his shoulder lightly. It was just boyish restlessness playing itself out in the least disruptive way possible. I couldn't help finding it completely adorable.

During the sign of peace, Pawel turned around to shake someone's hand and noticed me. He lifted his hand and gave me a little wave; I returned it with one of my own, and a smile. He smiled back.

Dad leaned over and said, "There's your boy, Caro."

I shook my head. "No, Dad. He's just a friend."

"You sure about that?" I made a face at him. Dad was just kidding around, trying to get a bit of a rise out of me, but I felt warm inside all the same.

"Come on, Caro, get in here!" Mom called.

"Just a second." I was putting the finishing touches on my gift for Hannah. I'd figured out what to get her only at the last second, after weeks of surfing the Internet and prowling through the aisles at every store in town. Hannah didn't seem to need or want anything, and every time I tried to get her to give me a hint, she shrugged off the subject. It was clear that the whole concept of gift giving made Hannah a little uneasy. Father Bob told me that in the convent, she wouldn't have gotten any Christmas presents. "They celebrate Christmas in a far less traditional way than most," he'd told me. "Or, I should say, more traditional. It's less about gifts, and more about thanks and celebration."

I really wanted to get her something that she would like and appreciate, but like I said, perfect gifts for Hannah were thin on the ground. But as I was thinking about Father Bob, and what he'd said about Hannah and Christmas, I started to get an idea. I found what I was looking for online and had it overnighted so it would get to our house on time for us to open presents, post-Mass and post-brunch.

"Okay, okay, I'm ready," I said, rushing into the family room, my gift for Hannah tucked underneath my arm. I set it down under the tree and flopped down on the couch next to my mother, who curled her arm around my shoulder.

"First, pictures," Mom said.

I groaned. "I hate taking pictures," I said. I was the least photogenic person on the planet. There was literally only one good picture ever taken of me, and it was my fourth-grade school photo. My parents had it blown up and framed, they loved it so much. As no other picture of me had ever gotten such treatment, I couldn't look at that one, propped on the mantel with Hannah's far-superior high school graduation photo, without feeling insulted.

"Too bad," Mom sang. "Evan, can you set the timer on the camera?"

It took Dad almost fifteen minutes to figure out how to do that, and by then I was getting squirmy and annoyed. I was worried about how Hannah would like my gift, and I wanted her to open it *right then* so I could see her reaction. I wasn't very good about being patient, and I loved giving presents. Something about watching someone's face light up when they opened the absolute best gift they'd ever gotten made me feel all warm and fuzzy inside.

Finally, Dad came and squeezed in between me and the arm of the sofa. Hannah was on Mom's other side, sporting her traditional blank expression. It was going to take the most amazing surprise ever to get that mountain to move, and I began to suspect my present wasn't going to get more than the briefest smile out of her.

Five flashes later, I was sitting under the tree, passing out perfectly wrapped presents. That was my job, every year. When I was nine, the year after Hannah left, my mother made me a little felt cap that said "Santa's Little Helper" on it in gold glitter paint. I wore it every year, way after I was old enough to know how dorky it made me look. It was just me and my family, after all. But when we were unpacking boxes of decorations that year, I left it tucked away under a pile of ornaments. For some reason, wearing it seemed like too much of an inside joke, one that Hannah wasn't going to get.

I left my present for Hannah for last. By the time I handed it to her, we were all surrounded by torn wrapping paper, multicolored tissue, and other holiday flotsam and jetsam, as well as new perfume, books, DVDs, various electronic gadgets, and sweaters with the tags on. She accepted it gratefully, if a bit nervously. She carefully peeled the bright red wrapping paper off a large black-and-white coffee table book with Escher's *Waterfall* printed on the jacket.

Hannah looked at me with slight confusion. "Caro, what . . . ?"

"It's a book of Escher prints," I told her. "You know Escher."

She shook her head.

"Sure you do, Hannie!" Dad exclaimed. "I've got a few of his prints on the wall in the office."

Hannah shrugged. "I guess I never noticed."

"He's this artist Dad and I love," I explained. I pointed to the image on the cover. "I have that one on my binder, and every time I look at it nowadays, I just—I don't know—think of you."

She ran her hand gently over the cover. "It's so . . . strange." But she said it in awe, like she was looking through a window into a whole other world and couldn't believe what was right in front of her eyes. "Thank you. I love it."

"You're very welcome," I said. She smiled at me, and I smiled back. I remembered what Mom had said about how when I was a baby, I would run straight into her arms when someone brought me home. For the first time since Hannah came back, it didn't seem like just a story; it seemed like a *memory,* a deeply ingrained connection between two sisters. The feeling was precarious, though; I was afraid that any second she would say something, or I would, and the soap bubble of our fragile sisterhood would pop under the pressure of everything we *weren't* saying.

"I'm glad you like it," I said. I got up off the couch and started scooping the trash into a black plastic bag, careful not to disturb the peace that had descended on our house.

23

A couple of weeks after Christmas, I decided that I was ready to confess my deepest sin to Father Bob. I brought the shoe box with me to his office, even though I had no real intention of showing it to him. My reading the letters was bad enough; I wasn't going to put them in the hands of someone else. Still, I knew that if they weren't burning a hole in the bottom of my backpack, I might punk out and not bring them up. But I had to talk about them. I'd pretty much given up on getting any answers from Hannah and my parents, and I needed Father Bob to tell me where to go from here.

When I got to Father Bob's office that afternoon, he knew instinctively that there was something on my mind.

"What's bugging you, Caro?" he asked.

"What do you mean?"

"You look tense," he said, leaning back a bit in his chair and fixing me with a penetrating gaze, as though if he looked hard enough, he could see right through me. "Are you all right?"

I shrugged. "Sure. Yeah, I'm fine. I just . . . I have something to confess."

"We've talked about this, Caro," Father Bob said. "This isn't a proper confession. We're just having a conversation."

"Okay, then I have something to *converse* with you about," I said. I took out Hannah's box and placed it on my lap. All the letters I'd found were fastened together with a rubber band and placed on top of the rest of the stuff.

"What's that?" he asked.

"It's Hannah's," I said. "From when she was younger. It's got a bunch of stuff in it, like old birthday cards and movie stubs and stuff, but there are these . . . letters, too. To St. Catherine."

Father Bob nodded.

"You look like that makes sense to you," I said. "Which is weird, because it makes precisely zero sense to me."

"It's an exercise I've seen teachers give in Catholic schools sometimes," he explained. "They have their students choose a saint and then write a letter to them. It's a lesson on intercession. St. Catherine is the patron saint of young girls."

"Um, okay. Fair enough." I'd gone to St. Robert's, too, and I'd never had to write a letter to a saint. But I guessed it wasn't the craziest thing I'd ever heard. "Anyway, in the letters, Hannah mentions someone named Sabra, who I've gathered was a friend of hers." Father Bob leaned forward in his chair. He looked alarmed. His expression was freaking me out.

"I think Sabra died," I continued. "But I don't know how, or why Hannah would feel so guilty about it."

"Is that what she says in the letters? That she blames herself?" Father Bob seemed to know exactly what I was talking about, and what it meant, and there I was just babbling away, totally in the dark as always.

"Basically," I said. "This rings a bell?"

"Caro, I want you to come with me," Father Bob said, getting out of his chair and grabbing a thick sweater off a hook on his door. "Grab your coat."

"Where are we going?" I asked. He waited somewhat impatiently in the hallway while I wrangled my belongings together.

"To the school," he told me as I trailed him out of the rectory office and into the meat freezer we were calling an atmosphere.

"Why?" I asked.

"There's something there that I want to show you," he said. "It might have the answers to a couple of your questions."

Answers to my questions. That sounded promising. But I wasn't relieved. I felt like maybe I was about to find out something I didn't want to know. I wasn't a very brave person, just very curious. I was suddenly unsure that if I finally solved the great mystery of Hannah's unhappiness—if that truly was what was about to happen—I would be able to act on such a discovery.

The halls of St. Robert's were quiet. Father Bob marched me straight down the main corridor, and I was buffeted by the sights and sounds of my past, which wasn't painful or joyful, just strange. I hadn't been inside St. Robert's School since I'd finished the eighth grade. It was as though any memories I'd accrued at St. Robert's belonged to someone else and had just been implanted in my brain. It wasn't sad; it was just . . . weird.

Actually, growing up was just one weird thing after another. Friend weirdness, school weirdness, boy weirdness, family weirdness. Weirdness of the self. An endless cycle of weird, your life curling into a shape you didn't recognize, like an Escher lithograph, full of impossible objects and warped reflections.

We turned left into a small, rarely used hallway

that I'd nearly forgotten was there. It had a couple of classrooms that used to be for first and second grade when the rectory was still attached to the school, but after they built a new rectory across the parking lot and tore the old one down, they remodeled most of the school and moved the little kids closer to the library. This had happened while I was still in third or fourth grade.

A second before we arrived, I realized where Father Bob was taking me: the trophy case. I hadn't laid eyes on it in years and years, since I never played a sport or won a trophy in my life and it was a bit out of the way; there was another, more impressive one near the new gym. We stopped in front of it and stared— or rather, I stared, and Father Bob pointed to a large plaque directly to the right of the trophy case, next to a giant statue of Mary. The plaque held an eight and a half–by–eleven school portrait of a girl with long dark hair with a razor-sharp part straight up the middle and a wide smile that showed off a row of glinting braces.

"Who's that?" I asked, even though I was pretty sure I knew.

"Read it," he said. Father Bob was all about this, discovering things for yourself. He said a priest's job was to lead a horse to water, but only if it was thirsty.

The little plate below the photograph read:

Sarah Marie Griffin
b. August 7, 1983
d. January 9, 1996

This plaque was erected on May 23, 1996, in memoriam of Sarah Griffin, called Sabra by her family and friends. Sabra was a sweet, loving girl who brought joy to everyone who knew her. Though her life was tragically cut short, her memory will carry on in our minds and hearts as long as we live.

The students and staff of St. Robert's School

"What happened?" I asked Father Bob in a whisper. Of course. In her letters to St. Catherine, Hannah had mentioned a memorial near the entrance to the school. When she was attending St. Robert's, this had *been* the entrance to the school; they'd moved it during the renovation. We were standing with our backs to the old main doors.

"I asked about it when I first started here," Father Bob told me. "Evidently, Sabra and a friend were sledding in a field behind her house when she fell into an underground well. For some reason the cover had been removed, and the well was covered with snow, but she went right through it. By the time help was called, she was gone."

After a few moments, I asked, "Who was the friend?"

"I didn't think to ask at the time," Father Bob said carefully.

"I have to go home," I said. I took off without another word and only looked back at Father Bob when I reached the door. He just nodded at me.

24

I was hoping that nobody else would be home when I got there, so that I could talk to Hannah in private, but my parents were sitting in the family room. I'd been at Father Bob's a lot longer than I'd thought. But maybe it was for the best; once Hannah and I had had our talk, we could all hug it out as a family.

Because I really believed that once I told Hannah that I knew about Sabra, it would all get better: Hannah would stop being depressed and start eating, we would bond, and our family would feel whole. And maybe when I told Pawel how I had fixed my sister, he would like me again. And I would ace my—our—science project. And my life would be perfect.

But the more you thought you had things figured out, the more likely it was that everything was about to blow up in your face in a spectacular supernova of suck. So I probably should've been a little more calculated when approaching Hannah about what was, presumably, her deepest, darkest secret. But I wasn't.

I laid my burdens down in my bedroom, extracting Hannah's St. Catherine letters from my schoolbag, then took the stairs two at a time to the deserted second floor. When I'd passed through the family room, my parents hadn't even looked up from the television. If only they'd known what I was about to do, they would've stopped me for sure.

I knocked on Hannah's door and got a soft "It's open" in return. When I stepped into the room, Hannah was sitting on her perfectly made bed, slowly flipping through the Escher book I'd given her for Christmas. I felt a twinge of pride. I knew she would like it.

"Hi," she said, more chipper than usual. "Caro, thank you so much for this book. I can't stop looking at it. They're all so . . . strange, and beautiful."

I sat down next to her on the bed. "I'm glad. Which one is your favorite?"

"It's hard to choose," she said, and I nodded. "But I guess if I had to, it would be this one." She turned immediately to the correct page, and I noticed that she'd bookmarked it.

The lithograph she'd chosen was called *Hand with Reflecting Sphere,* which depicted—in case this isn't totally obvious—a hand holding a reflective sphere, sort of like the Bean downtown in Millennium Park. In the sphere, you could see a slightly distorted self-portrait of M. C. Escher in his study, surrounded by books and furniture. It was a little unsettling, because Escher seemed to be looking straight at you, because of course he was looking straight at himself.

"'If you turn it this way... it will show you your dreams,'" I quoted.

"What?"

"*Labyrinth?*" Hannah shook her head. I shrugged. "Never mind."

She smiled and went back to the book. "Okay."

"Hey, Hannah?" She was fixated on the Escher and didn't even look up at me. I put my hand on the book and slowly closed it. "I have to talk to you about something."

"Okay," she said, putting Escher aside. "Actually, I wanted to talk to you, too. I wanted to apologize for being so short with you lately. I know you're just trying to help, but ..."

I nodded. "That's fine, don't worry about it." Here was my opportunity. I could still turn back, accept the little olive branch she'd handed me and walk away.

But I was sick of being a coward. As hard as my self-protective instincts were kicking at me, I was determined to ignore them.

I brought out the St. Catherine letters and laid them in her lap, in the exact spot Escher had just vacated. "I was cleaning my room a while ago and I found a box in the garage. It was your keepsake box, and it had these . . . letters in it. I was hoping we could talk about them."

She stared at the packet of letters as if it was some kind of alien creature, not with a lack of recognition, exactly, but an expression of utter disbelief. "You found these?"

I nodded.

"You didn't read them, did you?" she asked, her voice rising several panicky octaves.

"A little," I admitted.

"You shouldn't have read them," she said. She was eerily calm but deathly serious. I was a bit frightened by her.

"I know," I said. "I know, but I was curious. . . ."

"You were *curious*?" As what I had done started to really sink in, her face contorted with anger. "You had no right to read them. They don't belong to you!"

"I know," I said again. "I just wanted to understand. . . ."

"Understand what?" she fumed. When I didn't answer immediately, she asked again—shouted, actually, barked in a way that scared me, at least for a second— *"Understand what?"*

I had never seen her so angry. I don't think I'd ever seen anyone so angry, or at least that kind of angry, with nothing behind it but betrayal and fear, radiating like waves.

I didn't think she expected an answer to her question, but she repeated it, her entire body rigid and shaking. She was gripping the packet so hard that her fingertips were turning yellow-white and the pages were crumpling in her grasp. It took me a second to figure out how to use my vocal cords. Finally, I managed to gasp out, "Why you . . ." And then I ran out of air.

"You never should've read them!" she screamed. All I could do was nod. I knew she was right; I'd known it from the very beginning, before I'd read a single word. But surely this was an overreaction?

"You are a horrible, selfish monster," she spat. "You had no right to pry into my life like this, Caro, no right."

After I got over the shock of Hannah's shouting at the top of her lungs directly into my face, I started to get pissed, too. "I'm a monster?" I shouted back. "I'm selfish? What about you? You ran away from this family without any concern for anybody else, and when things got too hard, you ran away again. Now you're sick and damaged and you won't even let us help you."

This stunned her. She looked surprised to be standing there, clutching that book like she was going to break it in half, in full battle with me. But she wasn't finished.

"You don't know anything about me," she said.

"I know enough," I said. "Take a look at yourself, Hannah. If what happened to Sabra has something to do with why you're sick, you need to deal with it, because it's tearing this family apart!"

"You don't have any idea what you're talking about, Caro," she said, the warning tone in her voice zooming its way up the threat-level charts to orange. "Get out."

"Let me finish," I said.

"You're finished," she told me.

"But—"

"*Get out!*" she cried. She pushed me back forcefully by the shoulders. "Get out of my room right now!"

I stumbled but didn't fall. Still, she'd shoved me hard. I looked up at her face and saw a whirling panic in her expression, like she was quickly losing control of her carefully constructed world, and all she had in her arsenal to save it was pure instinct. The only way I can describe it is that she was like an animal protecting her cub, ripping apart everything that stood in the way. Her hair was in a wild tangle, her face bright red and her breathing labored.

"I know about Sabra," I told her finally, my last-ditch effort to turn everything around, but I knew in my bones it was too late. "I saw the memorial at St. Robert's. I know who she is, what happened to her. I know you were there."

"Don't," she said, pushing me again, this time in a direction—toward the door.

"Hannah—"

"Don't!" she screamed. She reached around me and swung the door open. Now I was crying, deep wrenching sobs of anger and frustration, and I could see tears in her eyes.

I toppled into the hallway and she slammed the door so hard that it knocked a picture loose from the wall. It crashed at my feet, the glass shattering. I pounded my fist against the door.

"You can't shut us out forever!" I cried, hitting the door again and again and again. "Someday you're going to have to let someone help you or you're going to die!"

My father appeared and grabbed me from behind. He dragged me a few feet away from the door. "*What* is going *on* up here?" he asked.

"All I wanted was to talk to her," I wailed, burying my face in his shoulder. "I just wanted her to tell me the truth."

My mother reached the top of the stairs, steadying herself with a deep breath. She gave me a stern look, then knocked softly at Hannah's door. "Honey? What's wrong?"

"Go away!" Hannah bleated. "All of you, just *go away.*"

"Come on, let's get you to your room," Dad said, steering me toward the stairs. I let him lead me; the fight with Hannah had drained me of all my energy. I felt like the walking dead. I crawled into my bed and clutched a pillow close to my body while Dad sat on the floor, patting my head like he used to do when I was sick as a kid.

"What happened?" he asked.

"I know what happened to Sabra," I told him. His face sagged. I had never seen my father look so lost.

"Hannah won't talk about it."

"Why?"

"It was the most terrifying day of her life," Dad said. "She's spent all these years trying to forget. Talking about it would mean remembering, and that's the last thing Hannah wants."

"It wasn't her fault," I said.

"I know," Dad told me. "She knows. But knowing doesn't make it hurt any less. You have to understand, Hannah was very young when her friend died. She witnessed it. It damaged her. We didn't know how much until she came back home."

I couldn't say much. I just cried. I'd once thought I hated Hannah. I'd thought all she was was a problem, an interloper who came in and stole my parents' attention and pretended she was my sister when she was really a stranger. But she *was* my sister. We had the same small earlobes, too thin to be pierced; the same blue eyes; and the same straight teeth, perfected by years of orthodontics.

But Hannah wasn't the only one who refused to admit to the past. I'd been pretending I had no memories of her, but that wasn't true. I remembered one afternoon—I couldn't have been more than six—when she played an endless succession of games of Candy Land with me, always letting me win. I remembered the Christmas present she gave me when I was five, a delicate blown-glass ornament with my name engraved on it. It sat nestled in our tree every Christmas. I remembered how she begged my parents for a dog, and how she hassled me because I refused to eat carrots. Just tiny, insignificant things, bits and pieces of a shared childhood, but they were there.

Finally, I asked the question that had been bugging me. "Why didn't you help her?"

"We're trying to help her," Dad said defensively. "But you know as well as anybody how resistant she's being."

"No, I don't mean now, I mean back then," I said. As mad as I was at Hannah for how she had hurt our parents, how she was still hurting them, and, through them, me, I was also growing more and more angry with Mom and Dad. She had been only a kid when Sabra died. What had they done to help her? Couldn't they have prevented this?

"We did," Dad said. "But it's obvious it wasn't enough. We wanted to find her a proper therapist. We knew she needed to talk to someone right away but we were afraid that a psychiatrist would push us to put Hannah on medication, so we took her to see a grief counselor we found through the church. Hannah saw her every week for a year. Sometimes we went with her, sometimes she wanted to go alone, but after a while the counselor told us that she had no reason to believe that Hannah was traumatized by what had happened. She said that, in her professional opinion, Hannah was fine. Completely well adjusted."

"And you believed her?" I asked. "Hannah could've been faking it."

"I don't think that she was trying to fool her," Dad said. "I think she believed that if she just turned to God, everything would be okay. She started going to church every day; she would make me get up early to drive her to six-thirty Mass. And she was always religious, more than any other child I've ever seen, and we just thought . . . we thought that was her way of processing her grief."

"Now what do you think?"

"That it was really her way of denying her grief," Dad said. He looked awful, as if all the misery Hannah had suffered over the death of her friend had somehow flooded into him. Maybe that was why the lives of parents always seemed so difficult: because everything their child felt and experienced was carbon copied inside them. "And by deluding ourselves into thinking she was well, we drove her into the convent even though she wasn't ready." Dad sighed. "It was all our fault."

"No, Dad," I assured him. "It wasn't."

"I don't want to put all this on you, Caro," Dad said. "But I think we're learning that the less you talk about something, the bigger it gets. You can't sweep something under the rug forever, can you?"

"I don't think so," I said.

"How did you find out, anyway?"

"I saw the memorial at St. Robert's," I said. "And I found these letters she wrote to St. Catherine. Father Bob helped me put the pieces together."

"Father Bob?"

I told Dad everything. I'd never before mentioned what I liked to think of as my "afternoon sessions" with Father Bob, like he was my therapist or something, which I guess he was. For a while, it didn't seem worth bringing up, and then it seemed so weird that I hadn't said something earlier that I didn't want to bring it up at all. But my conversations with Father Bob were some of my favorite times in the past few months. He didn't pass judgment on me; all he did was ask me questions and try to get me to think deeper about the universe and my place in it. And he really listened to the answers.

Dad was a little stunned that I'd gone to see a priest. "You're the last person I would've imagined would seek religious counseling, Caro," he admitted.

"I'm not really 'seeking religious counseling,'" I said. "I just wanted to . . . talk to someone."

"About what?"

"About . . . stuff," I said lamely.

"About . . . God?" Dad pressed.

"Not really," I said. "I still don't know if I believe in God, you know, in the traditional way. Mostly we talk about science."

"You talk to Father Bob about *science*?" I'd really twisted Dad's brain with this whole Father Bob thing.

"And math, sometimes," I said. "And Escher."

"Ah. Paradoxes. Impossible objects. Great metaphors."

"Yeah," I said. "It's gotten me thinking about a lot of stuff. About Hannah, about how she could've gone into a convent without really believing in God."

"Hannah believed she believed," Dad said.

"She thought being with the Sisters of Grace would fix everything," I said. "But she never did find the faith she needed."

"Still. Your mother might not agree with this—in fact, I'm sure she wouldn't—but I think Hannah had to go," Dad admitted. "All of us, including Hannah, are acting like she made this big mistake, like she failed something, or something failed her. But I'm not so sure that's the case."

"What do you mean?"

"For the first time in her life, Hannah has nowhere left to run," Dad said. "And for the first time in *our* lives, your mom and I can't protect her. My hope is that now that everything's out in the open, we can really start to move forward, as a family. But it all starts with Hannah, and I think she's almost there. She wouldn't have reacted the way she did upstairs before if she was still capable of denying it to herself."

"Does she know that what happened to Sabra wasn't her fault?" I asked. "Did you tell her that, back when it happened?"

"Of course," he told me. "We told her that a million times. The Griffins told her that; so did her teachers."

"Did you know the kids at school teased her?" I asked. Dad's eyes widened; this was news to him. "It's all there in the letters. We ran into one of the girls who used to bully her at the nutritionist's office. I'm pretty sure that's why she didn't want to go back there."

"Why didn't you say anything?" Dad asked. "We need to know things like that, Caro."

"I just didn't think it was my place," I said. "Like *you* didn't think it was *your* place to tell me about Sabra."

"All right, all right, I get your point," Dad said. "We did know that Sabra's little brother, Byrne, never spoke to her again. He was only one or two grades behind Sabra and Hannah, and they played a lot together, the three of them. We offered to transfer her to public school, but she refused."

"Why?" I asked.

Dad shrugged. "I don't know for sure, but it was

the first time she ever threw a tantrum. She fought so hard to stay at St. Robert's we felt like, after everything that had happened, we couldn't tell her no. Whatever made her happy, whatever helped her—we wanted to do that. And anyway, the Griffins moved a few months after Sabra's funeral, so we didn't think it would be an issue."

"She didn't say why she wanted to stay at the school?"

"She said she needed to be close to God."

"I still think I should've known," I said. "A long time ago."

"Maybe you're right, Caro," Dad said, gently putting a hand on my shoulder. "But Mom didn't want to dredge up the past. She didn't see the point, with Hannah gone, and you being so young."

"What about you?"

Dad gave me a small smile. "You'll understand when you're married."

"So what now?"

"I have no idea," Dad said. "I wish I had the answers. But we all love Hannah—that hasn't changed. What happens next is up to her. We just have to be there when she's ready."

When Dad was gone, I shed my clothes and put on my pajamas, then crawled under the covers. It wasn't even that late—only about seven o'clock—but for some reason I could barely keep my eyes open. The fight with

Hannah had completely worn me out. I was so tired that even the incessant whirring of my constantly active brain—a perpetual-motion machine of thought and worry—wasn't enough to keep me awake longer than five minutes.

25

"Are you ready?" I asked Pawel, raising my eyes to meet his. He nodded, jiggling the video camera we'd checked out of the AV lab. "Turn it on."

It was weeks after my fight with Hannah and things had not gotten better. If anything, they'd gotten worse. Hannah wasn't speaking to me, and she wasn't eating; every night, my mother tried to get her to choke down something, but more often than not, the plate she left outside Hannah's door was completely untouched the next morning. Even though she was trying not to make a big deal out of it, Mom wasn't my biggest fan at the moment, either. Only Dad was on my side, but in a silent sort of way. He was just trying to stay as far away from any possible yelling and screaming as he could. As a result, I'd thrown myself into my science project, remembering Father Bob's advice—create. Do something productive with all that potential. It wasn't knitting, but my science project—mine and Pawel's, I kept having to remind myself—was my version of a craft, and it was beginning to take over my life.

But soon, all that would be at an end. This was D-day for single-bubble sonoluminescence. There was no more research or preparation to be done. The experiment was all set. The transducers were glued to the flask with a quick-drying epoxy, and the flask was affixed to the laboratory stand with a three-finger clamp. I poured in degassed water from an Erlenmeyer flask. I fiddled with the knob on the sine generator until I found the correct frequency, watching the oscilloscope closely as I slowly raised it to the maximum.

I had to admit, I was pretty proud of myself. I did very well in school and always had, but this was the hardest I had ever worked on a single project by far. Even Mr. Tripp was impressed with the progress we had made, and he was almost never impressed. I was starting to understand why Father Bob had suggested I find something to do with my hands; it was a distraction from the problems in my personal life, yes, but even more than that, it was great to feel a sense of accomplishment after all that failure. I knew it wasn't going to change the situation with Hannah, or my relationship with Pawel, but I had a feeling that it was on its way to changing me.

"Now what?" Pawel whispered, as if the mere sound of his voice would ruin the entire experiment.

"We're going to create a bubble," I told him. "Keep the camera steady." I used a syringe to introduce a drop of water into the flask. A bunch of tiny bubbles appeared on the surface of the water; some disappeared, but some of the others drifted to the center of the flask and united. "Hit the lights."

Pawel reached over and switched off the lights. I gradually increased the driving amplitude, and the bubble disappeared.

"It's gone," Pawel said. He sounded pretty bummed about it, which was cute.

"Don't break your heart just yet," I told him, placing another drop of water on the top of the flask. The bubbles came together in the middle just like before, and sure enough, they started to glow, like the tiniest point of light in the night sky.

"Let there be light," I said softly. "Zoom in."

"Oh my God, Caro," Pawel cried. "It worked."

"You had doubts?"

"A few." I could hear the smile in his voice. In the dim light from the hallway, I saw him reach over and felt his hand on my shoulder. "This was really cool. I didn't expect it to go so well."

I straightened up. "I'm glad you had so much faith in me."

"I had faith in you," he protested. "I just thought . . . it seemed so unlikely it would work."

"Well, it did."

What I didn't tell him was that I'd spent several afternoons in the lab in the preceding weeks practicing the experiment—failing, trying again, failing again. It wasn't till the other day that I'd gotten it to work, and even though it had happened only once, I was heartened by the possibility. I should've invited Pawel along, but I didn't want him to be there for the close calls and the near misses. I wanted to prove to him that we could do it. I needed him to believe.

"Hey, Caro?"

"Yeah?"

"Before you turn the lights on, can we talk about Derek's party?" The question came out rushed and mumbled, like he'd rehearsed it but was afraid he wouldn't have the guts to say it if he didn't say it quickly.

"Okay. What about it?" The party was long in the past and I thought we'd reached a mutual silent decision not to discuss it. I'd been drinking; we both had been. It seemed undignified to rehash what obviously had been a mistaken conversation.

"I didn't go with Briana just to make you feel un-comfortable," he said. "I went with her because she asked me to, and because I thought it'd be fun. I'm still pretty new. I wanted to meet people."

"Why are you telling me this?" I asked.

"I was just afraid maybe you thought I was angry with you and that I wanted to find a way to punish you, I guess. But I didn't. I don't."

"I understand," I said. I wished he would let it go. If I couldn't be with Pawel, all I wanted was to avoid any awkwardness between us so that we had a shot of be-coming real friends one day, and he was ruining it with all this forced explanatory chitchat.

"Really?"

I took a deep breath. "Really. And I appreciate you clarifying that for me. Now, what I think we should do is . . . we should transfer the digital file onto a DVD and then bring a portable player into the fair, so that we can show the experiment to the judges."

"Caro."

"And I'm going to go home and start working on the display board with pictures of the setup—I took those before you got here, so I'll have them printed at the drugstore and everything—and a write-up. We can work on that together, or separately, or split the work, or whatever you want to do. The fair is in two weeks, but I'd like to get it done before then, just in case. Okay?"

He turned the lights back on. We both squinted in the glare, and I shielded my eyes with my hand.

"Are you okay?" he asked.

"I'm fine," I said, turning away from him to pack up my bag.

"Are you sure?"

"I'm sure," I said.

"I'll help you with the board," he offered. "I mean, I think we should do it together. You can come over to my house after school tomorrow."

I hesitated. It was probably a bad idea to go over to his house and sit on his floor in proximity to him while we glued photographs to a piece of poster board. I wasn't sure my heart could take it. But I couldn't help feeling warmed by the offer, and excited at the idea of spending more time alone with him. I genuinely liked his company, and I missed it, badly.

"Yeah, that sounds good," I said. "I'll bring the pictures."

"Cool." He looked at me. "Good work, Caro."

"Ditto."

The next afternoon, I pulled my parents' car into Pawel's driveway. I'd gotten special permission to take it, since my punishment was still in full effect. That morning, I'd rapped on Hannah's door, feeling for some reason that I wanted to speak to her. She didn't answer, but I went into the room anyway and found her in bed still sleeping.

"Hannah?" Not a peep. "*Hannah.* Are you awake?"

"No," she mumbled. "Go away."

"Are you okay? You're usually up by now," I said.

"Leave me alone, I don't feel good." Her voice was raw. I looked at the armchair where I often found her reading, and wished she was sitting in it right then, being her quiet, solemn self.

"Please get up," I said. "I want to talk to you."

"I'm tired, Caro. I'm so tired, please go away." I thought I could hear tears, but I couldn't be sure. I felt everything drain out of me, all the bitterness and anger. It ran off my skin like water. She wasn't just tired. She was sad, and though it'd been there since she'd gotten off that train, and for years and years before that, I'd never really seen it. Not like I was seeing it now. And the worst part was I'd just sat idly by and watched her drown.

"Okay," I said. "If you need anything today, you should just call me. I'll be at school, but I'll come home, I promise." I waited for an answer, but none came. I left the room feeling anxious. I wanted to put it aside, but I couldn't. I wanted to talk to Father Bob, but I couldn't. I had to go to Pawel's after school. It was the weirdest thing, feeling as though you'd rather spend your afternoon with a priest than your crush. But Father Bob could give me something Pawel couldn't—answers. Or clarity. Or something. Something more than a pat on the hand. Which wasn't going to happen anyway, since I wasn't planning on telling Pawel anything about what had gone on at home. It'd just be one more piece of evidence that I was an insensitive lunatic who hated her sister.

I walked up to Pawel's house that afternoon with no little trepidation. I rang the doorbell and listened to the rustling inside. A few seconds later, Pawel opened the door.

"I have to warn you," he said. "My sisters are back from school, and Jake's had about three sodas in an hour, so it's mayhem in the Sobczak homestead. Prepare yourself."

I laughed, grateful for the imminent chaos; hopefully it would mask the things that I couldn't. "No problem."

As I crossed the threshold, a loud crash came from somewhere in the back of the house.

"Can you cage the creature, please? We have company," Pawel called into the void. He smiled at me. "Jake. If he's not sleeping, he's breaking something."

"I hope you have a permit for him," I said. "The fines for keeping a wild animal without a license are astronomical."

"I think he came with some kind of paperwork," Pawel said. "Can I take your coat?"

"Such a gentleman," I said, shrugging off the sleeping bag I was wearing and handing it to him.

"Nah, just well trained," he countered. "Do you want something to eat or drink?"

"I'm fine," I said. "Should we get started?"

"Yeah, let me put this away and we can go upstairs," Pawel said. He disappeared down a short hallway for a second, then returned without my coat. "Okay. Do we have everything we need?"

"Did you get the poster board?" I'd asked Pawel to pick up a trifold from the office supply store.

"Yeah, it's upstairs. You have all the pictures and stuff?"

I nodded. "And my notes. I figure we can type up the abstract and the picture captions and print them out on colored paper in the computer lab. That way the board will be more dynamic."

"Dynamic, huh?" he asked, raising his eyebrows in what I hoped was amusement.

"To distract the judges from the fact that we don't actually have a demonstrable experiment," I explained.

"Do you really care how we do in the science fair?" Pawel asked, starting up the stairs. I followed.

"No," I admitted. "I just want a good grade. I don't care about winning or anything."

"Good," he sighed. "Neither do I. I just want this thing to be over with."

Something crumpled inside my chest. Did he mean he was sick of working with me?

"I don't really like physics," Pawel confessed as we approached the end of the upstairs hallway. There was a closed door to my left; I assumed it was his, but we stopped in front of it and he made no move to go in.

"So you don't like French, and you don't like English, and you don't like physics," I said. "What do you like, then?"

"Well, okay. I *do* like physics—I just don't like physics class." He shrugged.

"Is this your room?" I asked, pointing to the door.

"Yeah."

"Are we going to go in, or just stand in the hallway all afternoon?" My shoulder was starting to buckle under the weight of my bag.

"Okay, so here's the thing. There's a lot of, um, *stuff* in my room that normally I wouldn't show anybody because it's embarrassing, but I sort of forgot you were coming over today until like ten minutes ago and I didn't have time to put it all away, so . . ." He sighed. "Just so we're clear, they're not toys."

"Pawel, you're freaking me out," I said. "*What* aren't toys?"

He sighed. "I guess it's easier to just show you." He opened the door and I followed him through it.

When I glanced around the room, what I saw sure *looked* like toys. Every spare surface of Pawel's room— dressers, desktops, windowsills, bookshelves, and even parts of the floor—was covered in motion machines made entirely of K'nex, a plastic building set I remembered playing with at day care a long time ago. As I was backing up to get a better look at the array, I bumped into one sitting on a table behind me and set it running. A small plastic container at the very top tipped over just far enough to release a red Matchbox car, which ran down a ramp and crashed into a little plastic tab, which activated a miniature Ferris wheel, which did one full rotation before dumping a glass marble onto a small set of scales. The weight of the marble pushed the other side of the scale up and released another marble, which traveled down a spiral ramp and fell with a *plink* into a cup filled with them.

I looked up at Pawel. "This is so cool!" I said. "Are these the Rube Goldberg machines you were telling me about?"

"Yeah," he said. "It's a stupid hobby of mine."

"It's not stupid," I assured him. "It's awesome. I love them."

"Me too," he said with a proud grin. "My sisters tease me a lot about them. They call them my inventions, but really they don't do anything. I just like thinking them up and building them."

"That's what you draw in your notebooks," I said, remembering the doodles in the margins of his papers.

"Uh-huh," he confirmed. "I should probably be taking notes, but these are just a lot more interesting to me."

"I can see why."

He blushed. "Well, we should get started. I looked at the assignment sheet and presentation is like sixty percent of the grade or something." He handed me a plastic jewel case with a disk inside. "I made a DVD of the results."

"Great, I'm borrowing Erin's portable DVD player, so we can use that at the fair. Cross your fingers no one steals it when we're not looking—I can*not* afford to replace it," I said.

"Maybe we should hire an armed bodyguard to keep an eye on it," he suggested. "Or we could just get Jake to do it. He's amazingly good at kicking people in the shins."

I laughed.

Two hours later, we'd made significant progress on the written portion of the project. I closed my laptop with a satisfied sigh. "Getting closer."

Pawel hoisted himself up off the floor. "I'm going to go to the bathroom. Do you want anything to drink? Are you hungry at all?"

I shook my head. "I'm fine. Thanks, though."

"No problem. Be right back."

I walked around the room, looking for another Rube Goldberg machine to test. They looked so delicately poised I didn't want to disturb anything, but I was enamored of them and wanted to watch another one do its thing. I was just about to set the one on his dresser in motion when my cell phone rang, startling me. I rooted around in my bag for it and answered just before the last ring. The caller ID said "Mom."

"Hey, Mom, what's up?" I asked, running my fingers lightly over the mechanics of one of the Rube Goldberg machines.

"Caro, I don't want to scare you, but we're at the hospital." My mom rarely panicked, but I could tell that she was genuinely upset.

"What's wrong?" I asked, my mind awhirl with all the frightening possibilities. "Did something happen to Dad?"

"No," she said, her voice cracking under the strain of trying to sound normal. "It's Hannah. I came home from work and found her on the floor in her bedroom. Where are you?"

"Pawel's house," I told her. "We were working on our science project—is Hannah okay? She's not—" I couldn't bring myself to say the word "dead." I thought about how quiet and inert she'd been that morning, how I couldn't even get her to come out from under the covers. What if I'd lost my sister just as I was getting to know her?

I had to get to the hospital immediately.

"No! No, no," my mother repeated, nearly shouting now. "But she's very sick, and you know she hasn't been eating as much as she should. . . . Do you have the car? Can you come here right away?"

"I'll be there as soon as I can," I promised her.

"Okay, please hurry, Caro. I love you."

"I love you, too." I hung up. I sank down onto the bed, and for a few moments I just sat there, unsure of what to do. I knew I should run down to my car and drive to the hospital, but I'd started to shake and my vision was blurred by unshed tears. I didn't know if I could drive. I tried to imagine navigating the dark streets in my condition and froze. I needed help.

When Pawel came back a few minutes later, I hadn't moved. He was carrying two cans of grape soda, but as soon as he saw the look on my face, he put them down on a nearby dresser and rushed toward me.

"Caro, is everything okay?" He knelt down at my feet and looked up at my face, his hands on my knees. "Something's wrong. What is it?"

I explained as much as I knew.

"Hannah's in the hospital?" Pawel said. He was stunned for a second, then rallied into action. "Well, okay, let's go, then."

"Can you drive me?" I asked. "I can't—I don't think I should."

"Of course," he said, exhaling a flood of air, as if he'd been holding his breath. "I'll take you in your car and Magda can come pick me up later or something." He stood and took my elbow. I paused for a second, took a deep breath to stifle the sobs, and got back on my feet.

Pawel led me down the stairs. There was a young

blond boy waiting at the door with my coat. Pawel took it and handed it to me, and I put it on.

"Thanks, Jake," he said, ruffling the boy's hair. "See you later."

"See you," the boy said, gawking at me. I must've looked a mess, but under the circumstances it was hard to care.

26

At the hospital, it took a while to find my parents. Hannah had been admitted and given a room, where she was sedated and sleeping. As soon as I arrived, my mother rushed to me and put her arms around my shoulders. She held me for a long time, and when she finally released me, my father did the same. It was a while before they noticed Pawel.

"Hi, Mr. and Mrs. Mitchell," he said politely, offering his hand to my father, who shook it. "Can I get you something? I could go to the cafeteria and bring back some coffee."

They both nodded.

"I'll be right back," he said, looking at me. *Thank you,* I mouthed.

When he disappeared around the corner, I sat down next to my parents in a plastic chair and listened patiently while they explained what they knew.

"The doctor said that Hannah is dangerously thin," Mom said. "She weighs ninety-seven pounds."

Dangerously thin. When I first saw her in the train station, she looked thin, and she hadn't been eating steadily since she'd gotten home, but I would *never* have suspected she weighed less than one hundred pounds. As I thought back, I considered the things she wore—bulky sweaters and loose-fitting shirts, nothing tight that would've shown her body for what it really was. We saw her every day, so while we noticed the change, it never struck me how dramatic it had been. She had always been thin, but it had never been as scary as it was in that moment. I felt sick.

"The reason she passed out was that she hasn't eaten anything substantial in a couple of days," Dad explained. "She's undernourished and very weak. They've hooked her up to an IV and inserted a feeding tube to start getting her some nutrients."

"Can she talk?" I asked.

"She'll wake up sometime tomorrow morning," Dad said. "We can talk to her then."

"Is she going to—um, is she going to live?" I asked. I hated the question, but I had to know the answer.

"We think so," Mom said. I let out the breath I was holding. "But we don't know for sure."

Every time I closed my eyes, I saw myself snapping at her, freezing her out, saying horrible things to and about her. The memories flooded into my mind, overlapping and intensifying to a horrific crescendo of unwarranted cruelty. The fight we'd had about Sabra, how insensitive I'd been. How could I have been so blind to my own sister's pain? For so long, I'd let myself believe that Hannah was fine, that she could handle whatever she was going through alone. I'd wanted it to be true; I hadn't wanted to have to be kind to her, because I resented her so much, and it was my fault we were sitting here now, talking about how likely it was that Hannah would live. Even when I'd finally decided I wanted to help, I'd been too late. People couldn't be saved on our schedules. And anyway, I doubted that I was capable of very much saving.

I tried to send Pawel home. There was nothing he could do; all *we* could do was wait, and there was no reason he should spend all evening in the hospital, keeping vigil over someone else's sister.

"Are you sure you don't want me to stay?" he asked, concern written all over his face. I felt a pang of guilt; he really meant it when he said we were friends. He did care what happened to me, and this whole time I'd been shoving him off because of what? My pride? My inability to accept something good and real just because I wasn't getting exactly what I thought I wanted? Hannah was right: I was selfish.

"I appreciate everything you've done for me tonight," I told him. "But it's getting late and I think we're just going to stay here. You should go home. You must be tired."

He definitely was; I could see it in his drooping eyelids and glassy expression. We'd been sitting in the hospital waiting room for hours and hours with very few updates on Hannah's condition. I was exhausted from the crying and felt strangely blank inside. It was like I didn't have the energy to be sad anymore.

"I don't have to go," he offered. "Your parents are a wreck. You need somebody to keep you company."

"It's okay," I said. "I think I'm just going to sleep."

"Here?" he asked. "In a chair?"

I nodded.

"Caro," Mom called from across the room. "Can you come here for a second?"

"Sure," I said. I sat down next to her and put my head on her shoulder. She ran her hand over my cheek and kissed my forehead.

"Honey, I think you should let Pawel drive you home," she said. "There's going to be no news until the morning, and you should try to sleep."

"I want to stay here with you," I protested.

"I know, but there's no point. You go home for a couple of hours and get some rest—I'll call you as soon as the doctors tell us anything, or Hannah wakes up. Okay?"

"But—"

"No arguments." Dad broke in. "You need to go home. You can come back in the morning."

"Fine," I said. "But I'm not going to school tomorrow. I'm coming right back here, okay?"

"Okay," they said.

I gathered up my coat and bag and followed Pawel out of the waiting room. We walked through the hospital corridors side by side. We didn't touch or talk, but I was aware of his presence, all my senses sharply attuned to his every movement. A sort of strange calm drifted over me like a light blanket. It was comforting to know he was there, and that he was trying so hard to help. Despite the circumstances that had brought us there, I'd never felt so grateful for anything in my life.

When we reached the car, I went to the driver's side and held my hands out for the keys.

"I thought I was driving you home," he said.

"It's my car," I reminded him. "And if you drive me home, how will *you* get home?"

"I'll have one of my sisters come get me," he said. "I'll stay with you until they come."

"You don't have to stay with me," I said. "I'm just going to go right to bed."

"Caro, can you just let me do this? I'd like to drive you home. Put your practical side in storage for fifteen minutes and just inconvenience me for once," he said.

"What does that mean?" I asked sharply. There was all this anger seething under the surface of my fatigue—anger at myself, of course, so much that I could feel it dissolving me into a froth from the inside, but also anger at Hannah for slowly starving herself with no regard for her own life, anger at my parents for not recognizing it for what it was sooner or doing enough to help, and, sort of inexplicably, anger at Father Bob. Where was his God in all this? I tried to clamp down on it, but I'd already said what I'd said the way I'd said it.

"It means that your default is to try to impose order on everything," he said. "You want it all to be just so—efficient and timely and perfect. You think, 'This is my car and if Pawel drives me home, how will he get back to his house?' So even though you're tired out of your mind, you would drive me instead of letting *me* drive *you* and find my own way. You don't always have to do that. Sometimes it's okay to let someone else take on a little bit of the burden. You don't have to spare me."

"When have I ever done that?" I asked incredulously. I felt naked, like I was being read like a page. Sure, I liked order and efficiency—who likes chaos? It seemed pretty reasonable to me.

"How about when you didn't want my help with the

science fair project because you thought it would make me uncomfortable to work with you?" he reminded me.

"One time," I muttered, but I walked over to the passenger side and got in.

"It's not a bad thing," he said, laughing a little. He got behind the wheel and turned the car on. I cranked the heat up full blast, shivering despite my heavy winter coat. "It's a sign of compassion, you know? That you put other people before yourself."

"I'm not compassionate."

"What are you talking about?"

"If I was *compassionate,* I would've been good to Hannah right from the beginning," I told him. "She came home looking like this sad, starved little puppy and I kicked her—I kicked her over and over again. I never listened. I never stopped to consider how she might be feeling. All I did was think about myself. I wasn't used to having her around, and I tried to push her out. My sister! What kind of a horrible creature does that to a person? To a person, by the way, who loves them anyway, even when they're acting like a heinous bitch?"

Pawel shook his head. We were on the road now. I put my forehead against the window and let the streetlamps blur together into a steady stream of light. "I understand why you feel guilty. But you can't put it all on yourself. You didn't make her sick. It's probably why she came home, don't you think?"

"I don't know," I said in a small voice.

"You're a good person, Caro," he told me. "I've always thought so. We haven't known each other that long, but I can tell that you try really hard to do the right thing. That's rarer than you think, believe me."

We sat in silence for a few minutes before Pawel spoke again.

"Jake was sick," he said.

"What?" I asked.

"He was born premature, and he had lung scarring because of it," Pawel told me. "I was only three at the time, but he was sick forever, and when he was eleven, he came down with a severe respiratory infection that almost killed him. He was in the hospital for weeks, so even though I don't know exactly what you're going through, I can imagine."

"I'm so sorry," I said, knowing just how useless those words really were.

He shook his head. "I'm not telling you this because I want sympathy, I'm telling you because . . . my family means a lot to me. Like, the world. More than anything, probably."

I nodded.

"And I wanted to explain—I feel like I overreacted that day at your house, when I found out you lied about Hannah."

"It's okay," I rushed to tell him. "We don't need to talk about it."

"Hang on," he requested. "I've looked back on that

day a few times and tried to puzzle out just what was bothering me, why I broke up with you, like you'd done something to me even though you hadn't really. People lie, all the time, for dumb reasons, I know that. I should've given you the benefit of the doubt."

"Seriously, it's fine." I couldn't have this conversation. My sister was in a hospital bed, being fed through a tube. I had enough guilt swirling around inside me already. I couldn't stand being reminded of the way I had behaved. "I understand why it bothered you."

"This isn't coming out right." He ran his fingers through his hair, tugging hard at the roots as if to anchor himself somehow. "I'm trying to explain—I guess I got upset because I looked at your sister and how sick she was and I saw Jake and I thought, 'What kind of a person could turn her back on her family like that?'"

"Okay, enough!" I cried. "Please, *don't*."

But he barreled on. "Caro, I'm trying to tell you that I was an ass. I just figured, because we had such a great connection right from the jump, that I knew everything there was to know about you. But of course I didn't. I still don't. But I think you're wonderful, and I should've known better than to assume *anything* about you. I should've listened when you asked me to. I'm sorry."

I let out a deep breath. "Thanks," I said. "Just so you know, I don't normally do that sort of thing. It had nothing to do with you, it was all part of my insecurity about Hannah."

"I get that," he said. "I totally get it."

We arrived at my house a few minutes later. Pawel got out and walked me inside. I was glad he'd come with me. It would've been so depressing to walk into that dark, empty house all alone. He followed me to my room and stood in the doorway as I switched on the light and let my coat drop to the floor.

"Do you want me to stay here with you?" Pawel asked. "I don't mind."

"No, thanks," I said. "Thank you, though. For everything."

"Anytime," he said. He held out his arms and I fell into them, pressing my cheek against his shirt and breathing him in. I didn't want to let go, so I stood there for what seemed like forever, clutching him and burying my face in his neck. Our chests rose and fell in sync. Finally, using all my strength, I pulled away.

"Good night," I said.

"Good night," he said back.

After Pawel left, I lay down on the bed, still in my clothes, and pulled a blanket over me. As tired as I was, I couldn't manage to fall asleep. I stared at the ceiling in the dark, missing the sound of Hannah's footsteps above my head. Slow, steady tears slipped down my cheeks, staining the pillowcase, and when I had exhausted every other option, I stopped struggling against the impulse and did the one thing I never thought I would do: I prayed.

Not knowing how to do it the proper way, or even

if there was a proper way, I inhaled deeply until it felt as though my chest had cracked open; the dark stillness of the night rushed in to fill up the space. I could hear the beating of my heart in my ears, and in my head I spoke the words. *Please don't let her die,* I said. *Please don't let her die. Please help her. Help me. Help us all. Help us help us help us. Please, oh please, don't let her die.*

I didn't stop praying until, without noticing, I fell asleep.

I awoke at noon to the sound of my phone ringing. I couldn't believe I'd slept that long, but I still felt tired. I scrambled to answer the call, knowing instinctively it had something to do with Hannah. "Mom?"

"Hi, honey." She sounded tired. "So Hannah's awake now. She's still a bit groggy from the medication, but if you head over now, she should be ready for visitors by the time you get here. Can you drive?"

"Yes, of course," I said, jumping out of bed and grabbing my coat. "I'll be right there."

I burst into the waiting room twenty minutes later. "Can we go see Hannah now?"

"Hold your horses," Dad said, putting a hand on my shoulder. "She's not feeling very well. She's been throwing up all morning, except there's no food in her stomach, so it's mostly bile. The sedatives didn't sit very well with her."

"Okay," I said.

"And she's very thin," he continued. "It was hard to tell with the clothes she wore, but when you look at her, it might come as a shock." It hadn't been hard to tell. We just hadn't wanted to look.

"We want you to be prepared," Mom said.

I nodded. "I'm prepared. Can we see Hannah now?"

"Sure," Mom said.

I held my mom's hand as we walked down the hallway to Hannah's room. Dad pushed the door open and I caught my first glimpse of my sister. She looked ravaged. Her skin was pale and her hair was all greasy and matted against her head. Her hospital gown was so huge on her she looked like she was drowning in it. I thought of the matchstick girl, how Hannah had become her, or maybe she had been her all along. It was all I could do not to cry again. I didn't know what was wrong with me. I'd never cried as much in my whole life before Hannah came home. But for the first time in the past twelve hours, I bit my cheek and held the tears back. I knew they would just upset Hannah.

"Hi," she said as we filed into the room.

"How are you feeling?" Mom asked, sitting on the edge of her bed and taking her hand.

"Okay," she said. "Tired."

"I bet," Mom said. "Are you thirsty?" Hannah nodded. "Caro, pour Hannah some water, please."

"No, that's all right," Hannah said, but I was already doing it.

"Here you go," I said, handing it to her.

"Thanks." She smiled. "Shouldn't you be in school?"

"Yeah right," I said.

"Did you get any work done on your project?" she asked.

"Pawel and I ran the experiment, and it worked," I said, feigning excitement for her benefit. I was just happy that she didn't seem angry with me anymore. "It was totally cool, Hannah, you should've seen it—we *created* light. For a split second, anyway."

"That sounds great," she said. "I can't wait to see your presentation at the science fair."

"Hannah," Mom said, stroking her arm gently. "You're going to be in here for a while, you know that."

She sighed. "I know. I just don't want to miss it."

"Well, don't worry," I told her. "We have the experiment on DVD, so I can bring it in and show it to you."

"Good," she said.

There was a knock at the door and a nurse with long black curls poked her head in. "Mr. and Mrs. Mitchell? The doctor would like to speak to you outside for a moment."

"Okay," Mom said. She got up off the bed. "Caro, you stay here."

"Sure," I said, flopping down into a chair. Mom and Dad left the room and I smiled at Hannah. "What do you want to do? I brought cards."

"Actually," she began, "can we talk?"

"Yeah, sure. What about?"

"They're going to make me see a psychiatrist," Hannah told me. "The doctor thinks that part of my problem is emotional and they want me to get treatment."

"I'm not surprised," I said.

"Me neither. But I know that when I see the psychiatrist, she's going to ask me if I've experienced any traumatic events in my life."

"Oh," I said.

"And I think that before I tell *her* about it, I should probably tell you." Hannah gave me a small smile, but she wouldn't look at me. She wasn't used to talking to people about her feelings, and now she was going to be expected to pour them out to a stranger. "Even though you already know some of it, I guess."

I nodded. "I'm listening."

"It's really hard to talk about it—I never talk about it—so this is going to be difficult." She stared at her lap. "It's just really hard," she repeated.

I didn't say anything. I just waited for her to get to the place where she could form the words. I listened to her breathe—deep, ragged ins and outs that seemed to shake the room. I watched her closely the whole time, studying her, the little movements she was making in preparation to say something. She'd taken hold of a piece of her hair and was absentmindedly stroking the end of it, like a baby with a security blanket. The things that comfort us.

"I'm sorry," Hannah said. Her eyes were wet and she was struggling hard to keep it together. She twisted the sheets into knots in her hands. I put my hand on her arm.

"It's okay. Take your time."

After a few minutes, she opened her mouth to begin again. "When I was in middle school, I had this friend. This was when you were really little, almost just born. You were only a baby, so you won't remember her, but she was over a lot. We used to play with you on the floor of your bedroom. She used to make your dolls talk. You loved that, she would do these voices . . ." She stopped and swallowed hard. "Her name was Sabra."

I nodded. This I knew. I didn't remember the part about the dolls, but that wasn't really surprising; I had to have been pretty tiny for Sabra to be alive. Still, I felt like I could see it. It was funny the way other people's stories could spring to life in wisps of smoke in your head and slowly congeal into something resembling a memory.

Hannah continued. "Actually, that wasn't really her name. Her name was Sarah, but she had a brother, he was two years younger—Byrne. And when she and Byrne were small, he couldn't say 'Sarah' right, he used to call her Sabra instead of Sarah and the nickname stuck. Her family had been calling her Sabra forever by the time we became friends, so that's what I called her, too. Everyone did. Sabra and I went to school together for years before we became friends. Everyone used to, you know, make fun of me, because I was a little strange. But Sabra and I sat next to each other in homeroom and she was nice to me. She just . . . liked me, for some reason, I guess."

"You're a likable person," I told her.

She looked unconvinced. "Anyway, Sabra and I became best friends. We were together all the time. When we were in sixth grade, she died."

"But how?" I asked, even though Father Bob had given me some of the details. I wanted Hannah to explain it to me.

"She fell into a well," Hannah said. "We were sledding and one of the wells was open, but we couldn't see it because of the snow. The water was freezing, and it was so dark in the well I couldn't see her. I should have gone for help, but she kept begging me not to leave her alone. She was so scared."

I could only imagine. Being alone at the bottom of a black hole would be terrifying for anyone, let alone a twelve-year-old girl.

"She made me promise to stay with her, and I did.

I kept telling her that everything was going to be all right, but it started to snow and I was afraid it wouldn't be all right. Eventually, she stopped answering when I called her name. That's when I went for help." Tears were rolling down Hannah's cheeks, but she wasn't heaving or crumpling—she just had giant stately tears running down her perfect face. She closed her eyes and they poured like rain.

"Oh, Hannah," I said. "I'm so sorry."

She hung her head and wouldn't open her eyes. She just sat there, propped up by her pillows, twisting the blanket in her pale hands. "I let her die, Caro. I let her freeze to death in that well, all alone."

"She wasn't alone," I said. "She knew you were there with her." And if Father Bob was right, so was God. But in the face of what Hannah was feeling and what Sabra had been through, Father Bob's scientific spirituality felt small and insignificant.

"But what good did that do her?" Hannah cried. "It's my fault she died."

"It isn't," I insisted. "Hannah, listen to me. You were just a kid. How could you know? Your friend begged you to stay with her and you *did*. No one can blame you for that."

"I blame me," she said.

"Is that why you went to the convent?" I asked. "To escape? Or to punish yourself?" Both of those explana-

tions seemed reductive. I was starting to see how unbe-
lievably complex Hannah's situation was.

"No, no . . ." She trailed off.

"Hannah, please listen to me," I begged. "It's not your
fault. You didn't do anything wrong. She asked you to
stay. I would've done the same thing."

"As for becoming a nun, you know," she said. "It
wasn't that I wanted to run away from it, although probably I did in some way. But after Sabra . . . I started to feel
so ruined. Like there was this dark spot on my soul, and
it made me feel so worthless, so helpless. I knew nothing but grace could wash it away, so I threw myself into
prayer, I became even more rigorously religious than I
had ever been. I wanted purification, and relief, but it
never came, for years and years. I just wanted to find the
God that I had lost, and I thought I would find him in
the convent."

The cosmic unfairness of losing your life before you'd
gotten the opportunity to make something of it or enjoy
it was enraging. I thought of Father Bob, and the God
he believed was beside us in every moment of our lives.
If he really wanted us to be happy, why all the tragedy
in the world? Father Bob would say something sensible
about duality, about joy not existing without pain to illuminate it.

"Think about light," he had said once. "White light is
pure and beautiful, but a world full of it would make us

all blind—not just blind, but also invisible. It's when you subtract that you see all the colors of the rainbow. Subtraction shows us what's there, and what's there is beautiful, too. Pain is like subtraction. Suffering teaches us how to experience and appreciate joy." It struck me now as total bullshit, and also as the truest thing in the world.

Hannah couldn't speak anymore. I got up out of my chair and crawled into the bed with my devastated sister. I put my arms around her and let her rest her head on my shoulder. We lay there long enough for both of us to fall asleep.

27

I woke up several hours later feeling like I was encased in a mist. My contacts were blurry and my brain was stuffed with cotton. Beside me, Hannah was fast asleep, and the world was dark outside her windows. My mother was sitting in the chair across from the bed, reading. She looked up at me with a sad smile.

"Hi, honey," she whispered. "Are you all right?"

I rubbed my eyes. "I think so."

"You and Hannah talked?" she guessed.

I nodded. "She told me about Sabra."

"I knew she would. I'm sorry I wouldn't tell you before—I just thought it was Hannah's place, not mine."

"I understand," I said. I stretched as much as I could without disturbing Hannah. "I'm really wiped."

"You should go home now, maybe do some homework. I want you to go to school tomorrow."

"What?" I cried.

"Shhh," Mom said. "Don't wake her. You're going to school because there's nothing you can do here, and I'd like you to graduate. No arguments. Just get up, go home, eat something, and get a good night's sleep. You can come back tomorrow afternoon if you want."

I was too tired to protest. "Okay."

I climbed out of the bed carefully and headed for the door. Just as I reached it, Mom grabbed my hand.

"I love you, Caro," she said in the most solemn tone I had ever heard.

"I love you, too," I told her. I kissed her on the cheek.

"I'm so sorry." Her eyes were shining and wet in the light of the one small reading lamp.

"For what?" I asked.

"For letting you both down," she said. "I know it's been hard since Hannah came home. I just didn't know what to do. She was so sad, and you were so angry. I didn't want to get between you, but if I'd just told you the truth, maybe we wouldn't be here right now. If I'd just opened my eyes . . ."

"You don't know that," I insisted. "Hannah's been sick for a very long time."

"I'm her mother," Mom said, choking on the words. "How could I not have done more?"

"We all let it go on longer than it should have," I told her. "It wasn't just you. You're a wonderful mother. You just didn't want to see your kid in any pain. It's understandable."

"It's unforgivable," she said.

"No," I said, as firmly as she had ever told me no. "Nothing is."

☆ ☆ ☆

I slipped out of Hannah's room with my coat over one arm and my bag slung on my shoulder. I walked slowly, shuffling along the linoleum like someone hopped up on cold medication. I wasn't even paying attention to where I was going, and as I rounded the corner near the nurses' station, I collided with someone going the opposite way.

"Damn it!" I cried as my bag fell to the floor and spilled papers and pens all over the place. I bent down to scoop everything up; the man I'd bumped into did the same.

"Here you go," he said, handing me a bunch of flash cards I'd made for French class.

I took them, standing up and lifting my eyes. When I saw who I'd hit, a fuse blew in the back of my brain.

"What are you doing here?" I demanded, my tone as sharp as a machete.

"Your father called me," Father Bob said, not reacting at all to the way I was speaking to him. "He said he knew that you'd been meeting with me, and that I might be able to help you—and Hannah, if she'll see me—during this difficult time."

"I ran my experiment," I told him.

He perked up. If there was one thing I believed about Father Bob, it was that he was, at heart, a science nerd of the highest order.

"I got it to work," I said. "After about five dozen failed attempts."

He shrugged. "Well, that's science."

"Actually," I said, "didn't someone once say that the definition of insanity is doing the same thing over and over again and expecting different results?"

He smiled. Now that I'd gathered all my fallen things back into my bag, I'd started walking down the hall toward the doors, and Father Bob had fallen comfortably into step beside me.

"That was Einstein," Father Bob said. "But that only really counts when you're actually running the same experiment over and over again. Eventually, you did something different—you did something right—and you succeeded. Do you feel insane?"

"All the time," I sighed, glancing back toward my sister's room.

"I'm sorry about Hannah," he said.

"Thanks," I said. "Me too."

"Have you gotten a chance to speak to her?" Father Bob asked.

I nodded. "We had a long talk. She told me all about Sabra."

"That's good," he said. "It appears she's been carrying the weight of that tragedy around for a long time. People who are grieving become like whirlpools, Caro. Everything becomes dissolved into ceaseless orbit around them, sucked in and destroyed by the pain they're experiencing. Do you remember what I told you about how being a contemplative nun requires a complete obliteration of the ego?"

"Yeah," I said.

"Hanging on to that sort of guilt and ceaselessly punishing yourself for it is an act of ego," Father Bob said. "It requires an extreme amount of focus on the self. If it can't be overcome, if a person can't forgive herself, it can stop her from really opening herself up to God. At the end of the day, Hannah was probably too young still to enter the convent when she did. She needed more time to come to terms with her loss."

"She was twelve," I said. I sounded pathetic, whiney, but I felt like a hurricane was raging inside me, ripping up trees and houses and playground equipment and tossing them up into a roaring maelstrom of sorrow. "She watched her friend die. I don't understand how your God could let such a thing happen. How *could* he?"

Father Bob took my arm and steered me into a less

public corner. "It doesn't really work like that," he said softly. "If he reached down and plucked every human from the brink of death, the universe would collapse. It's built this way for a reason."

"Don't you dare try to bulldoze me again with that 'perfect system' crap," I cried. "Fuck duality. Do you know how much it hurts to see her wasting away in this horrible place? It *hurts*. What sort of a loving God would create a world where children fall into wells and freeze to death? What sort of a loving God would create a world where the one person who desperately needs comfort is shut out completely?"

"Listen to me," he said sternly. "God never left Hannah. It was *she* who shut *him* out. She looked for him in a physical place and neglected her spirit because she was so afraid of what she might find if she searched for him there. She was so terrified that he had left her, or that he had never existed at all, that she closed her eyes and hid from the world he created for all of us. That is not a way to seek God."

"She worked so hard for all those years, praying and sacrificing so that he would comfort her and he did *nothing!*" I insisted.

"She prayed, yes. She worked, yes. But she wasn't open. She took all of her pain and stuffed it inside of her as a punishment for Sabra's death. That is not a path to God. Forgiveness must be asked for by someone who believes they deserve it. Hannah didn't believe that—I suspect she still doesn't. No amount of prayer can remove the guilt she burdens herself with," he said. "Your great strength is your openness. You *listen*. You believe. Maybe you didn't believe in God before, and maybe now you're angry with him. But that doesn't change the fact that you can *see*. Hannah can't. You have to be her eyes."

"But I don't want to be her eyes," I protested. "I want him to give her sight."

Father Bob shook his head. "I wish you knew how important it is for you to comfort her, to relieve her pain just by listening to her story and assuring her she's not at fault. You don't understand yet how things that seem so small and insignificant to you can change everything."

"I can't help her," I said. "That's the worst part."

"You *are* helping her. You are, I promise you that. But Hannah needs more help than just you can provide. Her darkness is so strong and so vast. She needs more light."

"What does that mean?" I asked.

Father Bob shrugged. "I don't know. Maybe it's your job to figure it out."

I sighed. "She really never told anyone, I don't think," I said. "And never talked about it with anybody who already knew. I really can't imagine that. I can hardly keep my mouth shut most of the time."

"Well, you don't know how you'd react if this had

happened to you," Father Bob said, holding the door open for me.

"True," I said. "Hannah says that when Sabra died, she lost her connection to God. Why do you think that is?"

"It's impossible to know," Father Bob said. "Hannah's faith and her connection to God are extremely personal."

"Have you ever lost your faith?"

Father Bob took a deep breath and stared down the hallway, linking his hands together behind his back as we continued to walk. "More than once," he admitted after a short pause.

"Really?" I couldn't hide my surprise.

"It's the risk you run when you think about God, or spirituality, or the self, or the universe, in a serious way," Father Bob told me. "No one who is deeply considering every angle and facet of their faith has complete conviction in their beliefs. But doubt can also take over in times of despair or confusion, and that's what happened to me. We call it the dark night of the soul, although, for me, it was many nights."

"What's it like?" I asked, shaken by his serious expression.

"Cold and lonely," Father Bob said. "I can only explain it as the most profound despair, a feeling of separation from the universe, from God, from everything around you—you see everything at a distance, as if through a long tunnel, and you become terrified that all you thought you knew was the grossest lie imaginable. It's a truly difficult experience for a person of faith, although I expect these things happen to everyone, even if they aren't religious."

"You think that happened to Hannah?"

"It happens to us all," he said firmly.

"She told me once that she couldn't pray," I said.

"Prayer can be very difficult," Father Bob said. "And not without reason. As Derrida said, it's not like ordering a pizza."

"Whenever I've tried to pray, I've always just, you know, *talked* to God," I said, thinking of how I had prayed the night before for the first time in I didn't know how long. Had I been comforted by it? I still wasn't sure. I remembered the feeling of my chest expanding, breaking open, and being filled by a strange sort of calm, foreign and familiar at the same time. But was that God, or just my tired brain trying to help me sleep? Maybe it was too early yet to call it.

"That's more of the idea. This is the way I've always explained prayer to people who asked," Father Bob said. "There are two kinds, in my view. One is a sort of collective focusing of spiritual energy on a person or an event. Orders like the Sisters of Grace practice perpetual prayer and adoration in the hope of bringing something to pass."

"What's the other kind?"

"It's the opening up of the soul to God, communing with him," Father Bob said. "It's more of a quest than an act."

"A quest for what?"

"Knowledge. Grace. True union with the divine. I find that sort of prayer so much more difficult than the other, because it requires an extreme emotional and spiritual vulnerability. It's frightening, because we're trained not to expose the weakest parts of ourselves, the things that cause us pain and shame and suffering. It's those same things that often block our access to God—basically, we stand in our own way."

We'd reached the front doors of the hospital.

"I guess I should be going," I said, readjusting my bag, which had grown heavy. I felt in all ways weighed down and was anxious to get home and, at least, lighten my physical load.

Father Bob put a friendly hand on my shoulder. "Everything will be all right, Caro. You'll see."

It seemed a touch cliché for him—the scientist priest, handing out platitudes about everything being for a reason, or whatever, but I guessed that was his job. I was so tired, as if I hadn't slept in days. I tried to think of the last thing I'd eaten and couldn't conjure up the proper memory.

"Are you staying?" I asked Father Bob.

"For a while," he said. "I'll have your parents let Hannah know I'm here, just in case she feels like seeing me."

Father Bob fixed me with a serious look. "I want you to remember this, when everything around you appears to be falling to pieces, when it all seems lost: the world belongs to those who stick around and tough it out. Learn from Hannah's mistakes. Never run away from what scares you. It will always come back in the end."

I reached out for his hand, and when he gave it to me, I squeezed it hard, hoping to express in that gesture all the things I still didn't have the words to tell him. "See you later, Father Bob."

He lifted his hand and gave me a little wave. "Later, Caro."

As I started my car, I kept thinking about what Father Bob had said, about Hannah's needing more light. I understood what he meant, but I couldn't figure out where that light was supposed to come from—or how I was supposed to get it.

28

"I need your help," I said. Reb and Erin looked up from their lunches. I'd thought long and hard for several days about what Father Bob had meant when he'd said Hannah needed more light, and I had finally come up with something I thought might actually help. It was a long shot, but I was tired of sitting around and doing nothing.

"With what?" Reb asked.

"I need to find someone," I told them. "And when I do, I'm going to go see him. But I don't want to go alone."

"Who do you need to find?" Erin asked.

"A boy—well, I guess he's a man now," I said. "Byrne Griffin. I don't know where he lives, but it can't be that hard to find out."

"Who is Byrne Griffin?" Erin raised her eyebrows at me. "I thought you were in love with Pawel again."

"He sounds like a soap opera character," Reb said. "I think there was a character named Byrne Griffin on *Days of Our Lives* once. He was possessed by the devil a couple years ago."

"Okay, first of all, cut it out with the L word. Second of all, can we focus?" I demanded. "He's an old friend of my sister's. She's going through something pretty awful at the moment, and I think seeing him might make her feel better. Either that, or it will blow up in my face and they'll both hate me forever."

"Those are the options?" Reb asked.

"Not all of them," I admitted. "He might refuse to come."

"Why? What'd she do to him?" Erin was tapping away on her cell phone, which got Internet service. "What'd you say? Beau Bridges?"

"Byrne Griffin," I said. "Would you stop making fun? This is serious."

"Okay, fine, we're serious," Erin said. "Byrne Griffin. Not a lot of them in the world. How old is he?"

"He's a couple of years younger than Hannah, so like twenty-five?" I guessed.

"Does he look like this?" Erin held up her phone so I could see the tiny picture she'd pulled from Google. It showed a dark-haired young man with glasses and some intentionally scruffy facial hair.

"I don't know what he looks like," I said, squinting at the picture. "That could be him. He looks about the right age. Please tell me that's not a mug shot."

"It's a staff photo," Erin told me. "He works at Loyola. He's a professor there. Well, a PhD student who teaches."

"What difference does that make?" Reb asked.

Erin shrugged. "Just stating the facts."

"His profile on the Loyola website says that he has office hours from two to three Wednesdays and Thursdays," Reb said.

"That doesn't give us a whole lot of time. Okay, here's the plan," I said. "We leave right after we're done eating and drive out to Rogers Park."

"You're suggesting we skip school to stalk this poor guy at his office?" Erin asked. "That sounds kind of, um, desperate."

"I am desperate," I said. "You've got to understand, guys. My sister is in so much pain, and I've been so hard on her, which makes it partially my fault. Not only that, but now I can't say anything to make it better. I think this guy can. Or maybe he can't, but I have to at least *try*."

"What happened to her?" Reb asked.

"It's complicated," I said. I didn't want to go into the

story. It was too sad, and I was trying my best not to think about it much. I preferred to focus on what I could do for Hannah, and finding Byrne Griffin was it. After that, I was pretty much out of ideas. "You just have to trust that I'm not a crazy person and that getting them in the same room might actually do some real good."

Reb crumpled up her napkin and tossed it away. "I'm in," she said. "Why not? You might be crazy, but it's the good kind of crazy. I think."

"Do we have to skip school for this?" Erin whined.

"Yes," I told her. "Please, Erin. You're my best friend, and this is going to be really hard. I need you to be there."

After a moment's hesitation, Erin sighed and nodded. "Okay. I'm in, too."

"Thank you so much," I said. "Eat up, it's almost time to go."

☆ ☆ ☆

On our way out to the parking lot, we ran into Pawel, heading inside with a few of his buddies.

"Where are you guys going?" he asked as we rushed to Reb's car. He waved his friends on and fell into step with us.

"We're on a mission," Erin said.

"What kind of a mission?" Pawel smiled at me and I felt a tingle race up from my feet to my head at close to the speed of light.

"A mission to fix Hannah," I told him. "I think I might've found someone who can help her come to terms with some stuff."

"Who is this person?" Pawel asked. "A psychiatrist?"

"No, a philosophy professor at Loyola," Reb said. "And time's a-wastin'."

"I'll tell you about it later," I promised him. "This is urgent."

"Can I come?" he asked.

"But you have class," I protested.

"So do you. What am I going to miss? I'd much rather help you help Hannah," Pawel said.

"It's okay, really," I said. "You don't have to come. I don't want you to get in any trouble."

"Look, if you're coming, you have to get in right now," Erin said, yanking open the passenger-side door and sliding in. Reb was already behind the wheel, adjusting her mirrors and starting the car.

"This is your last chance to bail," I warned him.

"Noted," he said, getting in the backseat. "Come on, Caro! I thought you said it was urgent."

☆ ☆ ☆

The drive to Rogers Park didn't take very long, but to me it seemed like an eternity. I was wracked with nerves. I couldn't even imagine how Byrne was going to react when I brought Hannah up. According to her, they hadn't spoken since Sabra's funeral. It had been fifteen years; more time had passed since Sabra had died than she had spent alive. Hannah had said that Byrne and Sabra had been so tight they might as well have been twins. If her death had done to him even close to the amount of damage it had done to Hannah, this impromptu visit was unlikely to go very well. But maybe I was underestimating Byrne. Maybe he was ready to face his demons. I couldn't give up on him until I knew.

"Does anyone know their way around here?" Reb asked, switching on her turn signal.

"You can't go down there, it's a one-way street!" Erin shrieked.

"I knew that," Reb muttered, continuing straight.

"We're going to die, aren't we?" Pawel asked me sotto voce.

"God, I hope not."

After twenty more minutes of driving around in a haze of absolute cluelessness, we finally found a lot we could park in without a permit. The four of us tumbled out into the cold, only vaguely certain which way we were supposed to be headed. Erin had pulled up a campus map on her phone, but it was tiny and not all that helpful.

"Oh! Oh!" Reb cried, pointing a gloved finger. "I think that's it. The Crown Center!"

"Finally," Erin grumbled. "I think my nose is going to fall off."

We tromped with a renewed sense of purpose toward the Crown Center. As we approached the doors, I checked my watch. It was quarter to three. I was seized by a sudden panic. What if Byrne wasn't there? His office hours weren't technically over, but if nobody had come to see him, or he'd canceled them, or there was an emergency, he might not be there. Every second that passed without Byrne and Hannah's being in the same room seemed like an eon. After doing so little to help my sister in the past, and now discovering there wasn't very much I *could* do, I was comforted to think that bringing her and Byrne together might make a positive difference. I couldn't fail at this—I just *couldn't*. It would break my heart.

Byrne's office was on the third floor—number 301. We climbed the stairs in a clump, moving slowly so that I could update Pawel on what we were doing there.

"This professor guy is an old friend of my sister's," I said. I didn't want to talk about Sabra to him. I hadn't told my friends the full story, either. I finally understood how my mother had felt when I'd asked her about Sabra a few months before: it wasn't my secret to tell. Talking about it in any way with people who didn't know Hannah seemed like a betrayal, like gossip. There was no better way to show my reverence for what had happened than with my silence.

"And you think seeing him might help her get better?" Pawel asked. I could tell by the way he was looking at me that he wasn't just curious. There was genuine interest and concern in his voice.

"I hope it will," I said.

"Me too." He smiled at me and put his hand on my shoulder.

We shuffled down the hallway, slowly creeping up on room 301.

"Do you want us to go in with you?" Reb offered. Erin and Pawel nodded in support.

I shook my head. "I think this is something I'm supposed to do alone. Besides, it's weird enough to have one teenager busting in on him during his office hours—four might be overkill."

"Good point," Erin said. "We'll wait over there." She pointed to a long wooden bench that ran along the opposite wall, and headed for it.

"Good luck," Reb said, pulling me in for a hug. "I still have no idea what we're doing here, but I'm rooting for you, Care Bear."

"Me too," Pawel said. Then he added, "Care Bear."

"Yeah," I said. "You're not allowed to call me that."

"Why not? Reb did," he protested.

"I'm special," she told him, flashing him a smug grin.

"You got that right," I said. "Now get out of here. I'm nervous enough as it is."

Pawel reached over and squeezed my arm. "It's going to be fine."

I took a deep breath. "I know."

Pawel smiled at me and walked over to the bench, where Reb and Erin were already sprawled out. I turned to the office door, gathered up all the courage I had at my disposal, and knocked.

"Come in."

I pushed on the door, which was slightly open, and walked into a closet-sized office. Bookshelves took up whatever wall space there was, and another whole stack of shelves was crammed into a corner near the window. There was nothing on the walls but a map of what looked like Italy in a crappy frame, faded and browned with age, and two diplomas, although I couldn't read them. An ancient-looking space heater rattled away on the floor, giving off a faint burnt smell.

"That's got to be a fire hazard," I said, the words coming out of my mouth before I could stop them.

"How can I help you?" The young man sitting at the desk looked up at me in slight distress. In the silent moments that followed, I could almost see him flipping hurriedly through his mental Rolodex, trying to match a face with a name and a class and coming away empty-handed. "I'm sorry, remind me what your name is."

"I'm not one of your students," I told him, and he

relaxed for a second, clearly glad that his memory wasn't disintegrating, until he realized that there was very little reason for a teenage girl who wasn't in one of his classes to be visiting him during office hours. "My name is Caro Mitchell."

"Hello, Ms. Mitchell." His speech was stilted, and I could tell that the whole distinguished-professor thing was an act, from his cultivated stubble to his mussed just-rolled-out-of-bed hair to his horn-rimmed glasses to his worn tweed jacket with leather arm patches. He looked like a little boy pretending to be a professor. It made me like him a lot. "What can I do for you?"

"I came—" I started to feel weak in my legs, and a wave of nervousness washed over me suddenly. I gestured to the chair across from his desk. "I'm sorry, can I sit?"

"Oh, please," he said. "Go ahead. Are you okay? You look kind of pale."

"I'm fine," I said dismissively. The significance of the moment wasn't lost on me, and I was starting to lose my nerve. "I came to ask you for a favor."

He narrowed his eyes at me. "I'm afraid you're going to have to be a bit more specific."

"Right. Okay. So I know there's no way you'd re-member me, because the last time you saw me I was still a baby—if you ever met me at all, which maybe you didn't—but I think you probably remember my sister. Hannah Mitchell."

His face dropped. "You're Hannah's sister?" He

pushed his glasses up the bridge of his nose. "Of course, you'd be all grown up now. You look like her. What are you, about sixteen?"

I nodded.

"I haven't seen Hannah since I was a kid. Is she all right?" he asked. He seemed to be carefully weighing his words, not saying too much, not being specific.

"Not really," I told him. His eyes widened and I knew what he was thinking. "I mean, she's alive, I don't mean to scare you. It's just that she's . . . well, she's sick. Physically and, um, spiritually. I was hoping you could help her."

"Me?" Byrne put his hand over his heart. "How can I help her? What's wrong with her?"

"She's very depressed," I explained, speaking as quickly as possible so I could get all the words out before the tears came. "She's not eating. She's in the hospital now because she collapsed. She's had a really hard time readjusting. You heard that she was a nun, right?"

"No, I didn't hear that. Hannah was a nun?" He repeated it in a dull way, as if the information wasn't quite sinking in. It must have been years since he'd even thought about Hannah, and now here I was, shoving it all at him at once. It was starting to feel like an ambush. "I guess that's not a huge surprise."

"No?"

"I remember her being very religious," he said

flatly. "I'm a little confused. What does this have to do with me?"

"She's been through a lot. I'm not trying to diagnose her or anything, believe me, but I think—there's just a part of me that really believes that so much of what she's going through now, what she's been going through for over ten years, has to do with Sabra's death." I held his gaze with my own, willing him not to look away. I knew if he looked away, I would never convince him to come. There was a faraway expression on his face, like he'd plunged deep into a memory and he was in danger of being carried off by the current. His eyes were filled with profound sorrow, and I ached for him, and Hannah, too. And Sabra, for never having gotten to grow up. The unfairness of it all seemed to take up all the space in the room. It was getting hard to breathe.

I gave him some time to process everything. Just as I opened my mouth to speak again, he said, "Is Hannah in therapy?"

"Yes. Or she will be, soon. But I really think it would help if you visited her," I said. There. I had done it. I'd asked him to do the hard thing, the thing I didn't know that I could ever do if I was in the same position.

"Why would that help?" he demanded. "It would probably just make it worse."

"Well, burying it hasn't done her very much good," I snapped, instantly regretting it. How could you lose your patience with someone in so much pain? And yet it was easy. I'd done it to Hannah over and over again. I'd pretended I hadn't seen how much she was struggling, but of course I had. I could see it now in Byrne—not the same darkness, but the loss. That was painfully real. I couldn't turn away from it anymore.

"I'm sorry," I said. "I know this is hard. Believe me, I wouldn't be asking if I didn't think it would really help Hannah."

Byrne took a deep breath but said nothing. He wasn't even looking at me anymore; he was staring off to the left somewhere, so intently that I turned, expecting someone to be standing there.

"Professor Griffin?" I asked, hoping to shake him from whatever mind trap he'd fallen into.

His gaze drifted slowly back to me. "I'm sorry," he said.

"It's okay. I just—will you please come see Hannah? I think it could help her come to terms with a few things. She's so alone in this. She's been keeping it inside for so long, I think being able to hear you say that it wasn't her fault might start the healing process." My heart was bloated. It felt as though it had swelled up so large it was pressing against my rib cage. I wanted so badly for him to agree to come to the hospital. *Say yes, say yes, say yes,* I repeated in my head, hoping against hope to make it happen through sheer force of will.

"Unless, of course, you *do* blame her," I said in a voice so quiet it was almost a whisper.

He shook his head. "Of course not. But the fact that Sabra might be alive today if Hannah had immediately gone for help is hard to forget. I couldn't be around Hannah, knowing that."

"So you won't do it?" I steeled myself against the tears. I was not going to cry in this stranger's office. I was sick of being a weepy mess. There had to be a stronger me inside who was capable of withstanding all the sadness.

"I'm sorry," he said again. I could tell he meant it. And to my surprise I wasn't angry with him. Hannah, who I wouldn't even claim as my own sister a few short months earlier, was sick in the hospital and I was hardly keeping it together. I didn't even want to imagine what it would be like to lose her entirely, before I'd really gotten to know her. Sabra was gone forever. Even after all these years, the pain had to be nearly insurmountable when faced head-on.

But I couldn't let it go that easily. I'd come to convince him, and I'd never forgive myself if I didn't try as hard as I could to make that happen. "How can you say no?" I pressed. "She's in so much pain. You can't just let her go on shouldering all the blame for something that happened when she was *twelve years old*, something that wasn't even her fault!"

Byrne took a deep breath. "I'm sorry I've upset you," he said. His voice shook slightly, and I felt a flush of shame. If seeing Hannah was going to be torture for Byrne, was it really fair for me to keep pressuring him? It was hard to do what was right for everyone.

I tugged at my ponytail. "You haven't upset me. I just really wanted to help her."

"I'm so sorry Hannah's sick," he said.

"Please stop saying you're sorry," I said. "It just makes me feel like a jerk."

"You're not a jerk," Byrne insisted. "I get it, I really do. There isn't anything I wouldn't do for . . . If someone I loved was sick, I'd go to any lengths to help them. But I don't think Hannah and I seeing each other is the Hail Mary pass you're hoping for, Caro. I can't do it. Maybe that makes me a coward."

I shrugged.

"But it doesn't change the fact that I just *can't,*" he said.

"Thanks for taking the time to see me," I told him, standing up. "I appreciate it. I'm sorry about . . . all this. Bringing it up."

"No," he insisted. "You shouldn't be. If it was the other way around, I'd knock on every door just on the off chance that someone could help. I wish I could do something."

"You can," I said. "But I understand why you won't."

I slipped out the door, too afraid to look at the expression on his face.

For a moment, I was drained of all feeling except that of powerlessness, but the space hope had left behind started filling up quickly with resentment and anger. As much as I understood Byrne's decision, I raged against it. His sister was dead—what more could he do for her? My sister was alive, but in need of something from him. Why couldn't he give that to her? What was the harm in saying, "It's not your fault"? How hard could that possibly be to do?

On top of everything, there was a bitter feeling of failure. I was lost in the enormity of what I'd failed to do.

Desperate to leave, I glanced down the corridor to the bench where my friends were supposed to be sitting, but it was empty except for a piece of paper torn from a notebook. I walked over to it and read the note.

Gone for coffee. Text when you're done.

I folded the note three times and stuck it into my pocket.

☆ ☆ ☆

Erin, Reb, and Pawel were at the Starbucks across the street in the student center. I lingered outside the door for a moment, letting the brisk winter wind chill my hot face and watching my friends talk and laugh. After our breakup, I'd thought my relationship with Pawel was over, but looking at him now through the frosty window, I knew that wasn't the case. He'd ditched school to provide moral support for a mission he didn't even really understand. He was my friend, and he cared about me. And the girls were like sisters to me. How did a person get so lucky? I was momentarily rooted to the spot by the magnitude of it.

Reb caught sight of me outside and waved me in. I smiled at her, opening the door and bringing the cold in with me.

"How'd it go?" Pawel asked, as sincere as I'd ever seen him. I wanted to put my arms around him and hug him so tightly he couldn't breathe. I wanted to bury my face in his neck and have him stroke my hair. Instead, I tried to look like everything was okay. I felt like I owed them that for being so invested in something they didn't understand.

"Okay," I said, and that was that. I could have broken down and cried about how hopeless everything was, how my one chance to help my sister had dissipated like smoke at the very tip of a bonfire, but as much as I still believed that, I refused to accept the truth of it. I might not be able to fix Hannah's heart, or turn back time so that she could go for help and save Sabra, but I could still be her sister. I could still be her friend. My ears still worked and my heart was open.

I had felt closed before, hunkered down with my familiar friendships and rigid schedule, but I felt it now, the widening of a space I hadn't even known was there. I'd been split open like a log. It was uncomfortable and scary, but painless. The best part was that now that I knew the space was there, I realized how very much there was to fill it with, and how much room there was left over for new and beautiful things still to come.

☆ ☆ ☆

I asked Reb to drop me off at the hospital on the way home. All three of them offered to come in with me, but I politely declined.

I found Hannah awake in her room, reading a book my mother had brought her from the hospital gift shop.

"Is it any good?" I asked, setting my bag down by her bed and dropping into the chair.

"Oh, not at all," she sighed. Her eyes were tired but her smile was genuine. I felt a small hope flicker to life. "How was school?"

"Good. Boring. You know, the same. How're you feeling?"

"Better," she said, emphasizing the word, as if saying it with enough confidence could make it true. But I could see a bit of a change. She looked better. Already she was less pale and sallow, the dark circles under her eyes lighter, the bones jutting out beneath her skin a little less pronounced. "They've been feeding me through a tube," she said.

"Yeah, I know."

"It's humiliating. I feel like an invalid," she complained. The hope gobbled the words like oxygen. She was whining instead of languishing in a deep, inexpressible sadness. That had to be a positive development.

"Well, if you'll just agree to eat something, they'll take you off the tubes," I said, although I didn't know if that was true. It sounded right. But maybe I was pressing too hard on a tender spot. I glanced up at her face, but her expression hadn't changed. She didn't respond, and I fished around in my brain for something else to say, something apart from her illness and her darkness.

"I've tried. I can't keep much down. They're going to send me to a rehab clinic when I'm strong enough," Hannah said, doing her best to avoid looking at me. "They don't think I can go home without treatment."

"Oh." I couldn't tell from the tone of her voice how she felt about it, but knowing her, I figured she probably wasn't thrilled. Hannah wanted nothing more than to shove her issues into a dark corner. Just telling me about the clinic had to have been hard for her; she must've thought I'd find out anyway.

"I don't want to go," she said, tears springing to her

eyes. "The doctor was telling me about it. He said it was 'secure,' but what that means is that they lock you in and don't let you talk to anybody except the staff." She glanced down at her hands, which were folded neatly in her lap. "Reminds me of another place I don't want to be."

Knowing that there was nothing I could say to make it better, I fished around in my brain for another subject, something to distract her. "I'm building something for Pawel," I told her finally.

For the first time since she'd entered the hospital, she visibly perked up. "What are you building?" she asked.

"A Rube Goldberg machine," I said. "Out of K'nex."

"What?"

"K'nex. Do you know what an Erector set is?"

"Yes." She said it like, *Duh, of course.* But she knew better than anybody that recognizing such a pop culture reference was not a given for her.

"Like that, but plastic," I said. "Anyway, a Rube Goldberg machine is a complicated motion apparatus that performs a simple task in a convoluted way. Pawel wanted to do one for the science fair, but I made him do single-bubble sonoluminescence, so to thank him I'm making it to serve as a part of our display at the exposition."

"What does a Rube Goldberg machine have to do with single-bubble whatever?" Hannah asked.

"I don't know," I said. "Nothing, I guess. I just want it to be there. And I want to make it for him."

"What does your machine do?"

I shrugged. "No idea yet. I have to go to the toy store after school tomorrow and buy all the pieces. You should see his room, Hannah—it's filled with these things. They're completely amazing, so complex and fascinating. I totally get why he's obsessed with them."

"Intricate causality," Hannah murmured. "Like little worlds unto themselves."

"Yeah, sort of." I put my feet up on the edge of her bed and leaned back in the chair.

"That's really nice of you, Caro," she said.

"You say that like you're shocked," I teased. "Like I never do anything nice."

"You know I don't mean it like that," Hannah scolded gently.

"Can I ask you a serious question?" I looked toward the window. Someone—a nurse; my mother, maybe—had drawn the curtains back and the shades up. I could see a pair of birds tussling on the sill. Not everything left in search of warmth at the onset of a barren winter. For some reason that was a comforting thought.

"I guess."

"Have you ever been to Sabra's grave?" I didn't want to look at her face, but I could see her stiffen on the very periphery of my vision.

"I don't want to talk about that," she said, straightening her bedding, creasing it again and again into meticulous lines.

"Hannah, I really think—"

"I mean it. I'm not ready."

"Okay," I said after a long pause. "But whenever you are—"

"I know."

29

I spent all weekend working on the Rube Goldberg machine. It wasn't nearly as easy as it looked, and I wasn't creative enough to completely invent it end to end like Pawel did. I cheated by looking up some machines online and incorporating bits and pieces of them into my design. That was another thing—the design. I was sure, with my knack for physics—I'd turned sound into light, for heaven's sake!—that I could build one pretty easily on the fly, but it was soon cripplingly obvious that it wasn't going to be that simple. I stood in my room for a long time, surveying the large mass of children's toys scattered on the floor, incapable of piecing even two of

them together without second-guessing myself and ripping them apart again.

Then I remembered Pawel's doodles and realized
that he *always* planned his machines out beforehand.
It was probably the most meticulous side of him: the
side that produced those insane works of art. Because it
was art. They were beautiful. I wanted to go over to his
house again just to see them whir to life. I grabbed some
loose-leaf binder paper from my bag and a pencil and
started sketching out the mechanism, including a list of
objects—marbles, rubber bands, coins—that I wanted to
incorporate.

I was almost done with the drawing when I looked
up to find Dad standing in the doorway.

"How long have you been there?" I asked.

"Just a while," he told me. "It's coming along nicely."

"I haven't even started," I pointed out.

He nodded at my blueprint. "Sure you have."

I let a long stream of air through my lips. "I've been
working on this plan for about three hours now. I was
crazy to think I could build the whole thing in a few
days."

"Not crazy," he said. "Just optimistic."

"I don't even know why I'm doing it," I said. I tucked
a strand of hair behind my ear. "It's going to look so out
of place with the rest of our experiment. The judges are
going to think we're bonkers."

"So? I thought you didn't care about winning the

science fair," Dad said, sitting down on the edge of my bed.

"I don't," I told him. "Do you think Pawel will like it?"

"Well, to be fair, I don't know him very well," Dad reminded me. "But I think he'll feel flattered when he sees all the work you put into it."

"I hope so," I muttered, running my fingers over the plans.

"Do you want some help?"

"Are you sure you have time?" He probably needed to go to the hospital. Mom had been there all day.

"For you, Caro? Always," Dad said with a smile. He grabbed the blueprint from me, and we got to work.

☆ ☆ ☆

The day of the science fair crept up on me. Between school and the machine and finishing the presentation board for our project and visiting Hannah in the hospital, I didn't realize the fair was Thursday until it was Wednesday. Pawel called me that night to make sure everything was ready for the expo the following afternoon.

"I'm sorry for doubting you before," Pawel said after we finished discussing the particulars.

"When did you doubt me?" I asked, mock-appalled.

"When you said you wanted to do single-bubble sonoluminescence and I told you it was too difficult," he said. "I was totally wrong. You really pulled it off."

"*We* did," I insisted. "You helped a lot."

"A lot more than you thought I would, maybe," Pawel grumbled.

"Hey! You told me off and I reined it in," I reminded him.

"Anyway, I just wanted to say that. You were right, I was wrong. It was a kick-ass project. Thanks for letting me be a part of it."

"Can you repeat that?"

"Thanks for—"

"No, before that."

"You were right, I was wrong?"

"Yeah. It's my favorite phrase. To hear, of course. Not to say."

He laughed. "Of course."

"I'm really looking forward to tomorrow," I told him, lying down on my bed and staring at the ceiling. I crossed my eyes to make the minuscule paint bubbles match up, but they wouldn't; they were all too different.

"You are?"

"Not the presentation part—I hate that stuff, talking in public and putting on a show. So much smiling and nodding. But I like seeing what other people have done, and having people look at what we've done and say how cool it is."

"You sound like you've done this before."

"Once or twice. Science is kind of my subject."

"And thank God for that."

I was over-the-moon happy talking to him like this—a calm, casual, friendly conversation—but it was time to hang up before it went on too long and lost its luster. "I'll see you tomorrow, Pawel."

"Good night."

"Good night."

"This is quite the production," Reb said, strolling into the auditorium behind me, carrying my presentation board and chewing a piece of spearmint gum, the tang of which floated over to me and made me think of Christmas. "Who knew people got so worked up over science?"

It was indeed a circus. There were people *everywhere*—students (some of whom I recognized; most of whom could have been space aliens for how unfamiliar they looked to me), teachers, parents, judges, little siblings who'd been snatched out of day care to see their older brothers or sisters in action. The craziest thing of all was that it wasn't a county or regional or state fair—it was just our district, the high school and middle school. I pressed my fingers against my forehead, kneading and rubbing to try to relieve the tension. Crowds and loud noises always gave me a headache.

And the nerves, oh, the nerves. I wasn't even trying to win anything and I was a roiling, sparking mess on the inside. It was really the machine I was worried about. I'd finished it in the wee hours of the morning, but after the foggy stupor of near sleep had been replaced by the stark glare of early morning, I was beginning to think it wasn't the best idea I'd ever had, no matter what Dad had said. It was certainly incongruous with our project, and what if Pawel thought I was making fun of him? Or worse, what if he didn't care at all? It was also possible that Mr. Tripp would think we were just goofing off and fail us right there in front of everyone. I didn't think any of those things would happen, exactly, but the fear was there all the same, lurking around in the dusty corners of my K'nex-addled brain.

"Hey!" Pawel said, running up to us. "I found our table, 34F. What's that?" He pointed at the Rube Goldberg machine I was trying not to drop. I'd slid it onto a second presentation board and covered it with the lightest blanket I had, the one my grandmother had sewn for me when I was a baby.

"A surprise," I said. He reached over to lift the blanket, but Reb slapped his hand away.

"No spoilers, Poland," she scolded, shoving the

417

presentation board into his hands. "Here, take this. I'll help you, Caro."

Pawel rolled his eyes at me as he walked off.

By the time we'd slowly lumbered our way to 34F (the machine wasn't in the sturdiest of conditions), Pawel had everything else set up. There was the presentation board, with its write-ups and captioned photographs and formulas and diagrams all meticulously laid out in an eye-pleasing pattern. I'd thought Pawel was going to kill me when I had insisted on everything being just so, but it did end up looking great, which he then had to admit grudgingly to me.

There was also a large computer monitor that Pawel had borrowed from his dad, which he'd hooked up to the DVD player I'd borrowed from Erin so we could show the video of our experiment to the judges. That was where the Rube Goldberg machine came in. Or at least, where I was hoping it would.

"Now can I see what's under the blanket?" Pawel asked.

"No way," I told him. Reb helped me slide the machine onto the table.

"Seriously?"

"Seriously. I promise, you'll be happy you waited."

We had a little time still, so I slipped off to the bathroom to brush my hair and apply some lip balm. I came back ready for my close-up just before the judges arrived at our table.

Pawel began our presentation by describing the steps we took in preparation for the experiment, and I followed with a description of the experiment itself. For the finale, we were supposed to show the video that Pawel had shot in the lab. But first, my surprise for Pawel.

I lifted the baby blanket off the Rube Goldberg machine and folded it carefully. When I looked over at Pawel, he was grinning.

"Was this part of the experiment?" a confused-looking woman with wiry gray hair and Coke-bottle glasses asked.

"No," I said. I winked at Pawel. "This was just for fun."

I tipped the little platform that held a marble and the machine spooled into motion. The marble swirled around a plastic funnel before dropping into a metal measuring cup Dad and I had borrowed from the kitchen, which disturbed the delicate balance of a seesaw made out of a plastic ruler, which knocked another marble out of its container and sent it soaring down a long track of hamster tubes left over from my brief pet-owning experience. (I don't want to talk about it.) The speed of the marble going down the tubes gave it just enough force to snap against another ruler, vertical this time, causing it to hit another marble sitting on top of what looked like a roller coaster track built entirely of K'nex, and at the end of the track was the pièce de résistance—a small lever, which, when tripped, released one of those goofy birds with the weights in their beaks. It tipped downward, and because I had positioned it in just the right way, it struck the play button of the DVD player and our video started up. I'd layered about thirty seconds of Handel's famous "Hallelujah" chorus over the video, because when all is said and done, I'm a bit of a smart-ass.

The judges were impressed with our experiment and congratulated us for conducting it successfully, but they still seemed confused by the Rube Goldberg machine and chose to ignore its existence.

"Sonoluminescence," a tall, professory-looking type said. "It's not an easy project."

"It was all right," Pawel said. They nodded and shook our hands; we thanked them, and they left. As they walked away, I could hear one of the other judges grumble, "Not sure what *that* was supposed to be, though." Pawel and I laughed. Mr. Tripp, who'd watched us give our presentation from a few feet away, gave us a thumbs-up.

"Caro," Pawel said. He couldn't stop smiling, and I felt overcome by the headiness of pleasing him so unexpectedly. "That was amazing. Did you build this by yourself?"

"Yeah," I told him. "I mean, I stole the idea for parts of it off the Internet, but basically I made it. Do you like it?"

"Like it? I think it's awesome," he said, running his fingers back and forth through his hair. "When did you have time? These things can take forever."

"I made time," I told him.

"Clearly. I'm really impressed. Can I keep it?" he asked shyly.

"Do you want to?"

"Yeah, sort of. I don't even know where I'd find room for it, but I definitely want it," Pawel said. He looked at me. "Nobody's made me a Rube Goldberg machine before."

He ran his fingers gingerly over the machine's delicate moving parts, admiring the design and craftsmanship. It wasn't as sophisticated or creative as his—actually, it looked more like a Frankenstein machine than a Rube Goldberg machine, all cobbled together and awkward—but he didn't seem to notice. "So cool."

I noticed Father Bob a few tables down, completely absorbed in some middle schooler's terrarium project. "Pawel, I'll be right back."

"You came," I said, standing next to Father Bob and leaning over to examine the contents of the terrarium. It actually was sort of elaborate, with many different species of plant life all coexisting robustly in the same environment, and it had obviously been well taken care of. I wondered if this kid would win some sort of prize.

"I did," Father Bob said. "I wanted to see your experiment. Thank you for inviting me." I'd left a message for him at St. Robert's that morning. For some reason, it felt wrong presenting the project without my friend, the scientist priest.

"What did you think?"

"I think it went very well," he said. "Pawel looks happy."

"He's obsessed with those things," I said. "I wouldn't be surprised if he tried to make out with it later behind the bleachers."

Father Bob finally turned to look at me. "How's Hannah?"

"Okay," I said. "I don't know. It's hard to tell."

He put a hand on my shoulder. "People take time to heal. Be patient with Hannah. She needs your strength, you can't rush her." He gestured at the terrarium. "These plants took months of careful nurturing to grow, and look at them now. There's a lesson in that, I think."

"Yeah," I said. "You're probably right."

"I am right. You'll see," he told me. "Congratulations. You did very well today."

"Hey, Father Bob?" I don't know why I thought he would give me a straight answer to this, but I couldn't not ask.

"Yes?"

"Is it possible that God could be both loving and silent?"

He didn't even hesitate. "No," he told me, and with a smile he turned around and walked away.

30

I helped Pawel pack the Rube Goldberg machine (which he'd named Bubba), the monitor, and the presentation board into the backseat of his car and sent him off with a cheerful wave. For the first time since Hannah had ended up in the hospital, I felt like the weight that had settled in my chest had been lifted. I could breathe easily again. The science fair probably had nothing to do with it, other than the fact that it had gone so well that I felt capable of something for the first time in a long time. I dreaded going back to the hospital. I felt useless there, and sad. I wanted Hannah to recover not only so that she would feel better, but so that we would never have to set foot in that dreary place ever again.

My mother picked me up at school and took me home. We were going to get some freshly laundered clothes for Hannah, who was sick of wearing hospital gowns and complained constantly of being cold.

"Can you go get the mail, honey?" Mom asked as I got out of the car.

"Sure," I said. We'd done a pretty crappy job of keeping up the house lately; piled on the porch were newspapers, which Mom gathered up in her arms as she entered the house, and the mailbox was almost too full for the door to close properly. I had to give everything a good strong tug to get it out.

I flipped through it as I slowly made my way to the door. There were tons and tons of catalogs, offering everything from cashmere sweaters to lawn gnomes, but that wasn't unusual. Then there were bills and credit card offers, a postcard from my aunt and her family, who were vacationing in Hawaii, and, finally, one letter for me. To say I was surprised would be an understatement; I never, *ever* got mail, unless you counted the biannual reminders from the dentist that it was time for my cleaning.

The letter was sort of bulky, too, which was weird, and wrapped in a cream-colored envelope with the Loyola University logo and return address in the upper left-hand corner, which was weirder. Byrne was the only person I knew even remotely associated with the school; it had to be from him.

"Did you get something?" Mom asked from the kitchen. I nodded. "From whom?"

"Nobody," I said. "Just an old friend. How long do I have before we leave for the hospital?"

Mom glanced at her watch. "I'd say thirty minutes. You don't have to come if you don't want. I know it was a long day for you."

"No, I'm coming," I said. "I just have to take care of a few things first."

"Okay," she said, smiling. "You know, your father and I really appreciate all the support you're giving Hannah. I'm sure she does, too."

I smiled back at her. "No problem, Mom. I'm sorry I didn't do it sooner."

Mom turned her head away and swallowed hard; I could see she was on the verge of tears. "Don't leave your bag in the hallway."

I went into my room and shut the door, ripping open the letter. I sat down on my bed and unfolded it carefully, my eyes jumping straight to the bottom of the page to get a look at the signature. As I'd expected, it was from Byrne, and the reason it was so fat was that there was a second letter inside—longer, it seemed, from the heft of it—which read *Hannah* in his jerky, boyish script on the otherwise unmarked envelope.

Dear Caro,

I hope it's all right that I'm writing to you. I feel terrible about our conversation, and I wanted to make sure you understand that I do care a lot about Hannah and what she's going through. I've thought about Hannah so many times over the last fifteen years, because she was Sabra's best friend, and there's not a day that goes by that I don't think about my sister. Which is why it's so hard for me to see Hannah. I know it's the right thing to do—after all, it's been so long, and she's in so much pain—but I can't. I still haven't really gotten over Sabra's death myself, and maybe I never will; I'm pretty certain my parents won't. I've written Hannah this letter, though, and I trust you and your parents to decide whether giving it to her is a good idea. For a while I wasn't sure I could actually bring myself to write it, but my dad said something that helped me figure out what I wanted to say to her. He told me that part of his anger is that Sabra missed out on growing up, missed out on so many things that she would've loved—high school, boyfriends, dances, college. And when he said that, I realized that Hannah probably missed out on a lot of that, too, which is the exact opposite of what Sabra would've wanted, for either of them. And that's something I wanted to tell Hannah: not to let her anger, or sadness, or guilt over

*what happened to my sister prevent her from living
the life that she deserves to have. I really hope it
helps.*

   Sincerely,

   Byrne Griffin

I took a deep breath. I tucked Byrne's letter to me
back into its envelope and turned the one addressed to
Hannah over in my hands. I could've opened it, and for
a while wondered if I should.

But poking around in Hannah's personal life had already caused enough problems between her and me. I
folded the letter and put it into the back pocket of my
jeans, figuring I wouldn't make a decision about what to
do about it until I spoke to my parents.

Mom called my name from the front hall. "Caro, it's
time to go!" I found her standing by the door with a
big gym bag full of things for Hannah hanging off her
shoulder.

"Here, let me carry that," I offered, slipping the strap
over my head.

"Thanks," Mom said. "Let's go, okay? Dad's probably
already there."

"Hey, Mom?"

"What's up?" she asked. We both settled into the car

and put on our seat belts while Mom started the ignition and backed out of the driveway.

"I did something, but I don't know if it was the right thing," I told her.

Mom kept her eyes on the road, but the expression on her face was really nervous. And she had a right to be nervous; after all, I'd done some pretty stupid things in the past few months. "What did you do?" she asked slowly.

"I tracked down Byrne Griffin and went to see him," I said. I waited as she tried to place the name.

"Sabra's brother?"

"Yeah," I confirmed. "I wanted him to come visit Hannah in the hospital. I thought it would help if he told her that Sabra's death wasn't her fault."

"Oh, honey," Mom said with a sigh.

"I know," I said. "Anyway, he wouldn't come."

"I'm sure it's difficult for him," Mom said. "After all this time." I couldn't read her expression, which freaked me out. Whenever I was confused, I turned to my mother. She was always so certain about everything. But not anymore.

"He wrote Hannah a letter, though," I told her, taking it out of my pocket and laying it in my lap. "He said he trusts us to figure out whether or not it's a good idea for her to see it. I didn't want to make a decision without you."

"That was a good call," Mom said. "Did you open it?"

"No," I said. "Do you think we should?"

"I don't know, I—We'll have to talk to your father."

"Okay," I agreed.

☆ ☆ ☆

Dad was already in Hannah's room, so Mom went in to fetch him for a family caucus.

"We'll be right back," she assured my sister, closing the door tightly behind her.

"What's going on?" Dad asked, looking slightly suspicious, slightly alarmed. He folded his arms across his chest and leveled a curious look at both Mom and me.

"Caro, why don't you explain?"

I told Dad all about how I'd gone to see Byrne, and about the letter that had arrived for Hannah that day. I gave both of them Byrne's letter to me to read, and when they were finished, I tried to find some certainty in their faces, but there wasn't any. We were silent for a few minutes.

Finally, I said, "We're going to have to figure something out."

"I don't know," Dad said, rubbing his chin thoughtfully. "She's been feeling better since she came here. I don't want her to have some kind of setback, and since what happened to Sabra seems to be at least partially the cause of her problems, I don't want to . . ." He trailed off, unwilling to say what we were all thinking: would this letter from Byrne send her back over the edge, for good this time?

"I think we should show it to her," I said decisively. I felt proprietary over the letter; after all, Byrne had sent it to me, not to my parents. And I didn't think what he had to say would hurt Hannah. I wouldn't have gone to him in the first place if I had thought seeing him would upset her in the long run. I knew it probably would at first, but if he really didn't believe it was her fault, and wanted her to know that, what could possibly be the harm of her hearing it?

I tried to explain this to my parents, but they seemed unmoved.

"Hannah needs to move forward with her life," Mom said. "Not delve back into past tragedies."

"Yeah, that worked out pretty well for her at the convent," I said.

"That was different," Mom said.

"How?" I asked. She couldn't come up with a response to that.

"Caro has a point," Dad said. Mom glared at him, but he stayed strong. "Hannah can't seem to forgive herself, but maybe if someone who was just as close to Sabra tells her she shouldn't blame herself, she might listen to them."

"That's why I wanted him to come in person," I said. The letter was, in all honesty, a disappointment and a really lame substitute.

"I understand why he couldn't," Mom said softly.

"So we're agreed, then?" I asked. "We show Hannah the letter?"

"I'm sorry, when did we agree to that?" Mom asked.

"We can't keep it from her forever," I pointed out. "And the longer we wait, the more pissed off she's going to be when she reads it. It might even really hurt her then. Now is the time, while she's coming to terms with things and she's in the hospital. We might not get another chance as good as this."

"I agree with Caro," Dad said. He put his arm around Mom's shoulders. "You can't protect them from everything."

Mom frowned. "We can't take it back once we've done it. We can't make her unsee it."

"I think it's time we stop keeping secrets in this family," Dad said, giving us both a knowing look. "And that we stop babying Hannah. We let her go on too long doing herself harm so as not to upset her, and look where we are now."

Mom said nothing; she just sighed and nodded.

I'd asked permission to be the one to give Hannah the letter, because I wanted to explain to her just how it had come to be written at all.

"You went to see Byrne?" she asked. The letter was lying in her lap, unopened. She stared at it as if I'd told her it was a piece of the moon, an almost impossible alien artifact laid in the palms of her hands. "Why?"

"I wanted to help you," I said. "I asked him to come see you, but—"

"He didn't want to." She brushed lightly at her eyes.

"No," I admitted. "But there are still things he wants to say—he wrote them down and sent this to me, to give to you."

She pushed it away. "I can't read it," she said.

"Why not?"

"I'm afraid," she told me.

"I know," I said. "I am, too. Mom and Dad and I couldn't decide whether or not we should give it to you, but I think you need to read it." I put my hand on her hand and squeezed. "If you want, I can stay with you while you do."

"I can't," she whispered.

"Yes, you can," I said.

"What if he hates me?" she asked. "What if he tells me it was all my fault, what happened to Sabra?"

"Do you really think he'd say that? He wouldn't have written this letter if he wanted to hurt you," I said. I'd met him only once, but I felt like I could say for certain that Byrne Griffin cared about my sister, even if he couldn't bring himself to face her. I picked up the letter and placed it in her limp hands.

"Why do you want me to read this?" she demanded.

"It's not some magical cure-all, you know, no matter what it says. It's not going to make me instantly better."

"I know that," I said. "I just think it's the first step on a long road."

She hesitated, staring at the letter once again, probably contemplating her options. Finally, she gave a little sigh and slipped her fingernail underneath the flap of the envelope, prying it open carefully. Then she shook her head and shoved it back at me.

"What?" I asked.

"I can't read it," she said. "You do it."

"Aloud to you?"

"Yes," she said. "On one condition: if I say stop, you stop."

"Okay," I agreed. "Ready?"

She took a deep breath and nodded. "Ready."

The night before Hannah was supposed to leave for the rehab center, my parents went over to spend the evening with her. I wasn't allowed to go, because other than the science fair project, I hadn't exactly been doing any of my schoolwork since Hannah had entered the hospital. Madame in particular was spitting fire, waving her hands melodramatically and going on about how I was going to lose my A in French and my GPA would drop and *probably I would also die.* She called my parents, and

I was effectively grounded ("'Grounded' is such a harsh word," Mom said as she passed down the sentence. "I see it as a *very strong* suggestion.") until all my work was turned in.

So I was stuck at home, but I stubbornly refused to do my schoolwork. Instead, I wandered sort of aimlessly around the house, picking things up and turning them over in my hands, examining framed pictures so close my nose touched the glass, switching lights on and off in different rooms to watch the objects go from light to dark to light again. I tried to imagine what it must've been like for Hannah to walk through this house like a stranger; she'd lived here once, but long ago. The mere thought of leaving my home indefinitely broke my heart; how Hannah had managed to do it was completely beyond me, but maybe she was less attached than I was. Or maybe she really was running away, as much as she didn't like to admit it.

I was about to finally settle down at the kitchen table to write one of the many French essays I'd neglected to turn in over the past several weeks when the doorbell rang. I wasn't expecting anyone, and I was wearing a set of flannel pajamas with cupcakes on them.

I got up and went to the door to glance through the peephole. When I saw who it was, I whipped open the door so fast I didn't even have time to think about how I was, in fact, wearing cupcake flannel pajamas.

"Pawel," I breathed. I thought I'd gotten to a place where I could subdue my crush on him, but ever since the science fair, it had flared back up.

"Oh good, I was afraid you wouldn't be home," he said. "Sorry I didn't call first. I just went out for a drive and then . . . ended up here, I guess. I know that's weird."

"No, no, it's not weird at all," I insisted. "Do you want to come in?" It was freezing outside, and the wind coming through the door was turning my bare feet blue.

He nodded, shrugging off his coat as he stepped over the threshold. I took it and draped it over the knob at the end of the stair railing, and then we walked together into the family room, where we settled in on the couch.

"So," I said, hugging my knees to my chest. "How's Bubba?"

Pawel was perched on the very edge of the couch cushion, his hands folded in his lap. He looked tense and nervous, but in a good way, if that was possible. He grinned. "He's great. Although I'm afraid the others might have a little trouble accepting him."

"Why's that?" I asked.

"Because they know he's my favorite," Pawel said.

"And why's *that*?" I said, softer this time.

"Because you made him for me." He got this look in his eye like he was about to say something Very Freaking Important, but I was suddenly too afraid to hear it.

"Pawel—" I said, but he caught me off guard by

leaning over and kissing me. It was a long kiss, a long, wonderful kiss that transformed my entire body into a bag of rubber bands, and as soon as it broke, he came right back with another one. But true to form, my head was filled with a circus of confusion and doubt. The barker was screaming, *"What the hell is going on here?"* in my ear, the elephants were trumpeting warnings to be careful, and the acrobats were tumbling around so fast I couldn't get a read on their expressions.

I put my hand on his chest and pushed him back slightly. "Pawel, wait," I said, touching my fingers to my lips. "What're you doing?"

"I think that's obvious," he said, cupping the nape of my neck in his palm and pulling me gently toward him.

"Hold on," I said. A look of genuine bewilderment crossed his face.

"What's wrong?" he asked. "I thought you still . . . Oh, God, I'm sorry. I shouldn't have assumed."

"Oh, Pawel, slow down!" I took his hand and squeezed his fingers. "I just need a second to think."

"Okay," he said. "Take your time, then."

There was a long pause while I figured out what to say next. This is what I landed on: "I thought you said we were just friends."

"Yeah, I know," he said, reaching up and rubbing the back of his neck absently. "That was a mistake. I was freaked out by what happened with Hannah, and in front of your parents, and we hadn't known each other for very long and I just—I thought it would be easier. But I never stopped liking you, and when I showed you the machines, you didn't laugh, and then you *made* me one, I couldn't pretend we were only friends anymore. Because we're not, Caro, you know?"

"I know," I whispered.

"You have a ton on your mind, with Hannah and school and everything," Pawel said. "I don't want to make things harder for you. But I want you to know that if you have any feelings for me at all, I'm right here. I've never liked someone so much before."

"Me neither," I admitted.

He sighed. "That's a relief. I was half afraid that you were going to tell me you were back together with Derek."

"You were not," I said.

"Well, no, not really," Pawel said. "But, ugh, running into you guys at his party was my least favorite moment in recent memory. I just wanted to be sure. . . ."

I kissed him lightly. "You can be sure. Derek and I are—"

"Just friends?" Pawel supplied hesitantly.

"Less than," I assured him. "Reasonably polite acquaintances."

"I can live with that," he said, kissing me back. We kissed each other for a long time, giving in to the headiness of being able to touch each other without apologizing, or feeling awkward, or trying too hard to be casual. I loved the sensation of his skin under mine, the downy soft hairs on his arm standing up as I ran my fingers over it, causing a ripple of goose bumps. It was the best feeling in the world, the feeling of finally starting to understand what sharing pieces of yourself was all about.

"I promise," I said. "I'll never lie to you again."

"I know," he murmured, covering my mouth with another kiss.

31

Hannah left for Colorado the next morning. She called me for one last short chat before I went to school.

"I'm scared," she told me, a tremor rippling through her voice.

"Me too," I said. "But you're going to be okay. Everything's going to be okay."

☆ ☆ ☆

"Karolcia," he whispered in my ear. "Are you all right?"

"What?" We were in French class, but Madame was

out sick, so we had a sub who smelled like onion dip and spoke no French—therefore, it was silent work time. We were supposed to be writing our next essay, or reading Camus's *L'etranger,* or studying for our final, but I was too busy staring into space. After school, my parents were picking me up and we were going to the airport together to meet Hannah. She'd been at the rehab facility for three months, and my thoughts were consumed by what she might look like, what she might *be* like. I might have found out Hannah's secret, but I still didn't know her very well, and after ninety days' separation, I was starting to fear that I'd hallucinated any feeling of closeness I might've shared with her in those last weeks before she left.

Really, it'd been like she'd gone back to the convent. We only got occasional letters from her, since she was forbidden contact with us for the first month, and then allowed only sporadic correspondence and even rarer phone calls. The point was to separate her from all her "triggers," which I guess meant us, our house, our life, and any reminders of who she'd been or what she'd been through. I got clearance to send the Escher book I'd given Hannah for Christmas, though, which made me feel a little less helpless.

Pawel knew all this, of course. He'd even offered to come with me that afternoon, but I'd said no. It was a family thing. Part of me was looking at this as an opportunity to start fresh with my sister again; I'd been detached and disinterested at the train station nine months earlier, but this time I was going to be positive and upbeat and thrilled to see her. This I vowed.

Since Hannah had gone to the rehab facility, I'd stepped up my visits to Father Bob. I was going to see him at least once a week now, sometimes more. I'd always meet him at his office, but most of the time we walked two blocks to a Starbucks that'd just opened, and every once in a while on a Sunday, we'd have brunch at a diner just up the road after Mass. One time, I even went to Mass, but only because I knew Pawel was going. I sat with his family and we held hands and I thought of Hannah and Sabra and actually found it in me to pray for both of them, in my way—even though "my way" consisted of talking to God like I would talk to Reb on the phone.

I turned around now to see Pawel twirling a pencil between his fingers. I could tell from his expression that he was mildly concerned.

"I'm fine," I told him. He raised his eyebrows. "I *am*. I'm just thinking about Hannah. I'm worried."

"I can tell," he said. "It's going to be okay, though. Everything's going to be okay."

Those were practically the exact words I'd said before Hannah had left, and for some reason that made me feel calmer. Sometimes, Pawel would say things that made me think that the universe was speaking through him or something, but then I would realize that he was just *listening* to me, filing away the things that interested me or made me feel better, and then reminding me of them when I seemed uneasy. I couldn't imagine what the past three months would've been like without him. Reb and Erin were great friends to me, but I felt weird about putting all this Hannah stuff on them. But Pawel, he'd been there, had taken me to the hospital the night Hannah collapsed and had comforted me when I was scared, and it'd tied us together. It was such a great connection that I was terrified I was going to blow it, but so far, so good.

"What if she's still sick?" I asked him. The sub cleared her throat and threw us a nasty look, but I ignored her.

"You can't expect miracles," Pawel said. "There are going to be things she needs to work through long term. You've been saying that yourself for months."

"I know," I said. "I wish she had talked to Father Bob before she left."

"Maybe she will one day," Pawel said. "The cool thing about not knowing who's going to walk off that plane is that there's a pretty good possibility it's going to be a healthier, happier Hannah than the one who got on it, Father Bob or no Father Bob."

"Yeah," I said. "You're right."

"No, *you're* right," he said, smiling. "These are all things you've said before. Just try not to forget them when you're wigging out in the car later."

"I'm not going to wig out," I protested.

"Definitely, you definitely are," he said, lifting a piece of hair out of my eyes with the eraser end of his pencil. "And when you do, just text me, and I'll remind you. Deal?" He stuck out his hand.

"Deal," I said, taking it and giving it a nice, firm shake.

I ended up ducking out of my last class early. I just couldn't sit there any longer, being lectured at about Pearl Harbor ad nauseam. I found World War II to be an exhausting topic, even on days when I wasn't nervous about something. I wasn't paying attention on my way through the main corridor, and I ran smack into this girl I vaguely knew from some swim team parties Reb had invited me to. Her name was Paris, or Perrier, or something.

"Sorry," I said. I looked to my right and saw that we were standing directly beneath *Waste,* the hideous painting Pawel and I had discussed when we'd first started getting to know each other. The memory of it made me smile.

"It's no problem," Paris or Perrier chirped. She bent down and I realized I'd made her drop whatever she'd been holding. The floor was covered with custom-printed postcards advertising some big end-of-the-year art show. I bent down to help her pick them up.

"You coming to the exhibition?" she asked.

"Oh, I, um—" I turned one of the cards over and saw what was on the front—Escher's *Waterfall*. Or, well, it was sort of Escher's *Waterfall*. It was the same image, but instead of a drawing, it was a photo of the lithograph built entirely of Lego.

Which, as you might imagine, is physically impossible.

"What's this?" I asked Perrie. (Seeing *Waterfall* had sent a jolt through my brain that had released her name from it like a marble in one of Pawel's Rube Goldberg machines.)

"Isn't it cool?" She grinned. "It's from this series called *Almost Impossible*. This guy brought all of these Escher drawings into 3-D using Legos and took pictures of them. Do you know M. C. Escher?"

"A little, yeah," I said. I really couldn't believe what I was seeing. I kept looking at the picture and it would seem perfectly normal, and then my mind would scream, *But it's impossible! It can't exist in real life!* "Is this Photoshopped?"

Perrie nodded. "I guess it would have to be, wouldn't it? I think that's why it's the pictures that are being displayed, not the sculptures. Some of them require very precise perspectives to work, or I guess Photoshop in this case."

"Makes sense," I said.

"Still," Perrie said. "It's pretty cool."

"Totally," I said.

"So . . . are you going to come to the show?" Perrie asked. She looked a little desperate, in the eyes. "I'm sort of the PR person, even though I don't have any pieces in the show. I hate to see the artists do all this work and then have nobody turn up to look at it, you know?"

"When is it?" I asked.

"Tomorrow night at seven," she told me, relaxing a little. She must've thought she had me on the hook.

"I think I'll be there," I said. I waved the postcard at her. "Can I keep this?"

"Yes! Take as many as you want," she said, shoving a small stack in my general direction. "I have tons."

"I'll take one more, then," I told her, smiling. "Good luck spreading the word."

"Thanks."

When Perrie was gone, I pulled out my cell phone, dialed the St. Robert's rectory, and asked for Father Bob.

"Hi, Caro," he said. "What's going on? Aren't you supposed to be in school?"

"Mom and Dad are picking me up to go get Hannah in a few minutes, so I cut out early," I told him. I knew he probably didn't approve of skiving off class, but he didn't lecture me.

"Is everything okay?" he asked.

"Everything's fine," I said. "Father Bob, do you believe in signs?"

"Be more specific."

"Like, signs. From You-Know-Who."

"You mean signs from God?" Father Bob sighed. He didn't like it when I talked about God like he was Lord Voldemort, which I guess is understandable.

"Yeah."

"Sure, why not?" Father Bob said. "I think that the universe"—he knew I was more receptive when he said "the universe" instead of the G word, but we had a tacit agreement that the terms were interchangeable, at least as far as our powwows went—"has many ways of speaking to us, and we need to be open to all of them. That said, don't go looking for signs as a way of avoiding having to make your own choices. That's just a cop-out."

"Noted," I said, slipping the postcards into my bag. Maybe, if she was up to it, Hannah would want to go with me to see *Almost Impossible*. She more than anyone else I knew would get a real thrill out of seeing such strange worlds brought into the real world—even if it was just in Lego, and even if there was some shady photo manipulation involved. I also had a feeling that Escher would approve. Several of his drawings were of art coming to life.

There's this Escher called *Reptiles* that I have always loved. In it is another drawing, a tessellation of alligators, and at the edge of the paper one of these creatures crawls out, becomes three-dimensional, and climbs over several random objects before settling down again into the flat mosaic. I hadn't known it then, but before Hannah, before Pawel, before Father Bob and Rube Goldberg machines and single-bubble sonoluminescence, my life had been like that tessellation—technically proficient, but flat and lifeless. I didn't think about my place in the world, I wasn't brave or creative, and I'm not sure, looking back, if I really believed in anything. I still wasn't sure *what,* exactly, I believed, but ever since Hannah's first night in the hospital, when I'd prayed for her and me and us all, I'd been feeling this stirring in my heart that told me that I wasn't alone, even when I was by myself. That something—*someone*—was there, if only to listen. And in return, I was trying my best to listen, too.

I saw Dad's car swing around the little roundabout where I was waiting. "Gotta go, Father Bob," I said.

"You take care," he said. "See you Sunday?"

"Wouldn't miss it," I told him.

I wasn't the only one with some anxiety about seeing Hannah for the first time in three months. Mom kept fiddling with the radio dial, apparently unhappy with all the possible choices of music. Finally, in a fit of annoyance, Dad just shut it off entirely, which I was grateful for. Although, the music was helping fill the otherwise complete silence.

When we got to O'Hare, we parked and walked to the terminal. Hannah's plane had just landed, and we were supposed to meet her by the baggage carousel. It was weird to think that when we'd dropped Hannah off, we'd all been bundled up in winter coats, but now we weren't wearing any at all. In fact, it'd been an atypically warm day, so I was wearing a thin T-shirt over a camisole and that was it. It was one of those moments when you thought something completely cliché—*strange, the way time passes*—and yet it seemed like the most significant, foreign, original thought in the entire world.

A whole flood of people emerged from the terminal and descended on baggage claim. I scanned them hopefully for Hannah's face, wondering again if I would recognize her, and when the crowd finally cleared and I saw her, my heart swung up into my throat. She looked *so good*. Like a healthy, whole person. I couldn't believe it, so I turned to the closest person—Dad—and read his expression: utter relief, and happiness. It was enough to send a calming rush of endorphins into my bloodstream, and I felt my shoulders relax.

Hannah raced toward us, and my parents folded her into their arms.

"Hiya, Goose," Dad said, beaming. We all knew intellectually that we couldn't take too much comfort in the way she looked, or the ear-to-ear grin she was wearing; what she had gone through, what she was still going through, was complex and difficult, and this wasn't a miracle that we were seeing before us. But it still felt like one. Hannah was radiant, and we were overjoyed to see her standing there.

I shooed Mom and Dad out of the way and replaced their arms with my own.

"It's so good to see you," I said softly.

"Same to you," she said, pulling away. She put her hand on my cheek. "I missed you."

"I missed you, too," I said, and I meant it, more than I'd ever meant anything. I couldn't believe my good fortune. I had my sister back, even though I'd tried my hardest, when I was young and stupid, to drive her away. That was the miracle, I decided. That I'd found a way to overcome my most childish, selfish impulses and make room for her in the cluttered chambers of my heart. So much space, it turned out, that it felt empty when she was gone. I had a sister. *We were sisters.* For the first time, it felt like more than a possibility—it felt like a sure thing.

ACKNOWLEDGMENTS

Many thanks to:

My parents, Jim and Barbara Jarzab, for loving me no matter what, and for being the best traveling companions a girl could have.

James and Alicia, for growing up with me (not that you had a choice), and for making me laugh. Ditto to the rest of my family, who are kind and gracious and wonderful to the last.

Joanna MacKenzie and Danielle Egan-Miller, for caring so deeply about this book, and Françoise Bui, for her keen editorial guidance and enthusiasm for Caro's story.

Eesha Pandit, for listening, and for always being on my side.

Mary Dubbs, for the dinosaurs, and for taking me seriously.

THE Cambria Rowland, THE Kim Stokely, and THE Jenny Symmons, for more than a decade of friendship and listening to me babble on about people who aren't real.

The authors and subjects of the following books: *How the Universe Got Its Spots: Diary of a Finite Time in a Finite Space* by Janna Levin; *Gödel, Escher, Bach: An Eternal Golden Braid* by Douglas R. Hofstadter; *Unveiled: The Hidden Lives of Nuns* by Cheryl L. Reed; *The God Theory: Universes, Zero-Point Fields, and What's Behind It All* by Bernard Haisch, PhD; and *Extraordinary Ordinary Lives: Vocation Stories of Minnesota Visitation Sisters* by

Elsa Thompson Hofmeister. Thanks especially go to Karen Armstrong, whose marvelous memoirs of the convent and afterward (*Through the Narrow Gate* and *The Spiral Staircase*) helped to inspire and shape this novel.

Everyone at Random House who works on and supports my books.

My friends at Penguin Young Readers Group, especially Emilie Bandy (work twin and keeper of my sanity), and the authors whose books I've had the pleasure of working on, for supporting me on the other side of all that we do together.

All the religious who have ever taught me anything.

Alex Bracken, without whom I probably would not have gotten through the past few years. It's very rare to meet someone who is willing to read every bad partial manuscript and half-baked idea and is still capable of telling me not to give up and meaning it.

And, finally, to the late Helena Bieniewski, whose devout faith, impeccable advice, and enduring love have served as some of the great inspirations of my life. How I wish she could have read this book.

ABOUT THE AUTHOR

ANNA JARZAB is the author of *All Unquiet Things*. She lives in New York City and works in children's book publishing. Visit her online at annajarzab.com.